Odd One Out

Odd One Out

LISSA EVANS

VIKING
an imprint of
PENGUIN BOOKS

VIKING

Published by the Penguin Group
Penguin Books Ltd, 80 Strand, London WC2R ORL, England
Penguin Group (USA) Inc., 375 Hudson Street, New York, New York 10014, USA
Penguin Books Australia Ltd, 250 Camberwell Road, Camberwell, Victoria 3124, Australia
Penguin Books Canada Ltd, 10 Alcorn Avenue, Toronto, Ontario, Canada M4V 3B2
Penguin Books India (P) Ltd, 11 Community Centre, Panchsheel Park, New Delhi – 110 017, India
Penguin Group (NZ), cnr Airborne and Rosedale Roads, Albany, Auckland 1310, New Zealand
Penguin Books (South Africa) (Pty) Ltd, 24 Sturdee Avenue, Rosebank 2196, South Africa

Penguin Books Ltd, Registered Offices: 80 Strand, London WC2R ORL, England

www.penguin.com

First published 2004
1

Copyright © Lissa Evans, 2004

Set in 12/14.75pt Monotype Dante
Typeset by Rowland Phototypesetting Ltd, Bury St Edmunds, Suffolk
Printed in Great Britain by Clays Ltd, St Ives plc

A CIP catalogue record for this book is available from the British Library

ISBN 0-670-91203-4

For my mum

Acknowledgements

With thanks to Anne Evans and Davina Ross-Anderson, for their professional insight, to James Connell and Dave Hastings (again), for listening patiently and offering supremely sensible and useful advice, to Juliet Annan and her team at Penguin, for all their thought and care and encouragement, to Georgia Garrett, for practically everything, to the London Library, for being just about the only place where I can concentrate, and to the Dulian School of Dance, who taught me how to step-ball-change.

August

I

There were only two bedrooms in the flat. They were almost identical, but one had a picture of a flock of sheep on the wall so Paul chose the other one. He looked briefly at the view from the window (sky, treetops, back of Tesco), admired the poster on the back of the door (a lion disembowelling a gazelle, with the words 'Meet Mr Gorman' handwritten underneath), bounced on the bed a couple of times, lay down, closed his eyes for a few seconds, and then sat up again, unable to keep still. A soda stream of nervous excitement was beginning to fizz through him and he felt as if he could bounce across the room like a moon-walker. He'd done it, he was *here*. For once in his life he was in the right place at the right time, fully qualified, kitted out, official, bona fide and poised to begin; the moment was real, and yet completely unbelievable. He wanted to pin it on a card and re-examine it at regular intervals; he wanted to wear it next to his skin, like a vest.

He began to unpack, feverishly, stacking his textbooks by the bed, draping his lucky tie around the dressing-table mirror and throwing his shoes into the bottom of the wardrobe. He had packed his white coats first, as a measure of their status, and they were therefore right at the bottom of the bag, crushed beneath his trainers. He shook them out, tried to scratch what looked like a smear of tar from one of the pockets and then hung them reverently on the rail. Finally he coiled his stetho-scope on the bedside table, placed the 'Good Luck' cards from his parents and his grandmother beside it and removed from his coat pocket the envelope that had arrived in the post a couple of mornings before, and which was now flaccid with handling. It contained his contract, a letter about accommodation and a rectangular white plastic name badge. He took out the badge and gazed at it: 'Dr Paul Gooding'.

Dr Gooding.

Paul.

Those, and only those, were to be his names from now on. Or Dr Paul, possibly – that had a friendly yet dignified ring to it. 'That Dr Paul, he's superb. Was he a high-flyer, do you know?' 'No, actually, he had to retake his first-year exams and repeat his entire third year and resit his . . .' He mentally revised the conversation. 'No, he was academically average.' 'Shows you can't tell, doesn't it? Because he's superb *now*.' 'That's right, but you often find the exam successes can't cut it when it comes to the everyday work of the wards.' 'And they tend to lack innate sympathy.' 'Yes. Whereas Dr Gooding –' 'Dr Paul, we always call him . . .'

He put the badge down next to the stethoscope and went back to the wardrobe. Selecting the least crumpled of the new white coats, he tried it on and stepped back to examine himself in the full-length mirror. He had done the same thing on a visit home, yesterday, at his mother's insistence, but since her verdict had consisted of a wordless clutching of his hand accompanied by simultaneous dabbing of the eyes, he felt that a cooler appraisal was needed. The shorter version of the coat, as worn by medical students, had not suited him. The back of the jacket had rested just on the shelf of his buttocks, making him look (as an ex-girlfriend had noted) as if he were wearing a bustle. He had hoped that the extra length would add a certain dignity, perhaps even shave off a pound or two. ('You wouldn't call Dr Paul overweight, would you?' 'No, he's more beefy, isn't he?' 'Or chunky.' 'Yes. Either way, it gives him a reassuring presence.') The result, now he was able to give himself a long, critical, private assessment, was unsatisfactory. The bustle effect had gone but instead he looked pear-shaped. He undid the buttons and let the sides swish loosely. Better. He viewed his side elevation, and was reminded of a milk bottle. He turned his back on the mirror and looked at himself over one shoulder, and decided to try to erase that particular image from his mind altogether. Perhaps there was a gym in Shadley Oak. Slightly disappointed, he returned the coat to the hanger and shoved the suitcase under the bed.

It took him about two minutes to explore the rest of the flat. It appeared to have been recently cleaned, and was neat, cheaply furnished and almost devoid of decoration or frippery. There was a video player but no videos, a magazine rack but no magazines, a kettle but no tea, coffee, squash or milk, and no food at all, apart from a single hamburger of indeterminable age, iced immovably into the bottom of the freezer. Paul made himself a mug of hot water, stirred in the contents of a sachet of tomato sauce that he'd found in a drawer and wandered across to the kitchen window, where a faded orange blind was obscuring most of the view. He gave the cord a gentle tug and the blind, instead of briskly snapping upwards, unrolled as far as the windowsill. He gave another, sharper tug and a further length of material bellied across the sink. He tried a slow pull and then a fast pull and then a series of delicate twitches, and ended up standing halfway across the kitchen with seven feet of canvas stretched between himself and the window frame.

In the end the simplest solution was to climb onto the draining board and remove the blind from its moorings altogether. The view, suddenly revealed, was vertiginous and Paul hesitated with one foot in the sink before carefully leaning forward to take a look.

The most noticeable feature was the chimney of the hospital

incinerator, directly ahead and so close to the window that the maintenance ladder looked almost within reach, but to the left was a bird's-eye view of the jumble of buildings that comprised the hospital, and to the right, across the perimeter fence, a street of picturesque houses, mainly converted into shops. He'd driven along it on the way to the hospital and had passed the market square and the Woolworths and the Ryman's and the – he caught his breath and then craned as far to the left as the kitchen cupboard would allow; just visible at the very edge of the window was a tall terraced building, the brickwork between the upper windows adorned with a large white cut-out of a leaping figure in a winged hat. He scrambled off the draining board and hurried through to the living room; from there the view was uncluttered and panoramic and the frontage of the *Shadley Oak Mercury* was clearly visible.

He had passed it earlier – he had slowed his car and gawped and imagined Marianne stepping through the door, camera around her neck, the fine strands of her pale hair soft-lifted by the breeze, her grey eyes rising to meet his, her cushioned lips curving into a – and then someone had sounded their horn and he'd had to concentrate on driving again. And now, in a fantastic and completely unexpected bonus, he'd been granted his very own, private view. He'd be able to watch Marianne going to work! Grinning, he slapped his chest in a brief, happy tattoo, and wondered what to do with the rest of the afternoon. Explore the town? Drive to Tesco and stock up? Have a wander round the hospital to orientate himself? Phone his parents? Read 'Essentials for House Officers'? Check the view from the other bedroom, just in case it was possible to see the *Mercury* office from there?

He checked the view from the other bedroom; the office was out of sight, hidden behind a row of evergreens. In front of these was the staff car park, across which an oddly dressed man was pushing a supermarket shopping trolley full of bottles. Somewhere a church clock struck four, and as the final stroke sounded there was a thunderous hammering on the door of the flat.

'Arrrrrrriba!' Before the door was half open he was knocked backwards by a friendly punch on the arm and a blast of beer-scented laughter. 'It *is* you! It is The Pudding! All hail to The Pudding. Hail!' Crispin Finnerty, bottle of Rolling Rock in one hand, fell to his knees and banged his forehead against the kitchen floor in a mock salaam. A stream of lager poured across the lino. 'Oh fuck – oh never mind, what are cleaners for anyway?' He lurched to his feet and planted an extravagant kiss on Paul's right ear, deafening him temporarily. 'Glad to see me?'

'No,' said Paul, meaning it. Crispin laughed hugely, like a pantomime villain. 'I saw your name on the rota, knew there couldn't be two of you. Pudddeeeeng!' He raised his arms and did a little hip-waggling dance around the kitchen. 'Mind your backs. Hey, Almond!'

'It's "Armand",' corrected a pencil-necked figure, appearing in the doorway.

'This is Almond. I bumped into him in the corridor – he's living with you, in a manner of speaking. Or maybe not – I've only just met him and you'll try anything once, wontcha Pud? Haaaaaaaah. Almond, meet Pudding, your fellow surgical house officer. Paul Gooding, Pudding. Geddit?' He raised his arm to drain the bottle and then stopped, assailed by a sudden thought. 'Are you French?' he asked, suspiciously.

'French Canadian,' said Armand.

'That's all right then.' He saluted with the bottle. 'Pass, friend.'

Armand wheeled an enormous suitcase into the kitchen.

'Hey, Pud,' said Crispin, throwing an arm round his neck. 'This has to be fate – you know this flat is always occupied by pissheads, I mean *always*, and when Beggsy left yesterday, that's the old medical SHO, he filled seven bin bags with empties – seven! It's a world record!'

'I'm sorry to interrupt, but what is this?' asked Armand, pointing to the length of orange cloth that bisected the kitchen.

'Oh sorry,' said Paul, 'it's the blind. I haven't mended it yet.'

'He's broken the blind!' shouted Crispin, joyfully. 'This man, Almond, this man is *wild*. This man, OK, this man – under the influence of alcohol, mind you, a very great deal of alcohol indeed – this man once smashed the door of a public lavatory and then danced *naked* in *broad daylight* in the fountain outside Birmingham art gallery!'

'That was five –'

'*Broad daylight!*'

'I was only –'

'And, Pudding, you know what –' Crispin brought his face within an inch of Paul's and lowered his voice conspiratorially '– I've still got the photo.'

'Oh God, have you?'

Armand stood watching them, frowning slightly.

'It was when I was student,' said Paul, as much to himself as to Armand. 'Pre-med. Ages ago. What happened was –'

'Which is my room?' asked Armand, as if Paul hadn't spoken.

'I'll show you.' Paul disentangled himself from Crispin and led his flatmate down the corridor. 'You know,' he said matily, when they were out of earshot, 'he's talking about a really long time ago. I was a bit of a prat in those days but I . . . you know what it's like, I've had to hit the books for the last couple of years. I've changed a lot.' He glanced at Armand, hoping for an understanding nod, but Armand was looking around the bedroom with a jerky little series of head movements, like a meerkat checking for predators. There was disbelief on his face.

'What's the matter?'

'There's no hand-basin.'

'Oh.' Paul looked around vaguely. 'No, you're right. There's one in the bathroom though.'

'Is there a hand-basin in *your* room?' His tone was suspicious.

'Er . . .' Paul made a mental inventory. 'I don't think so.'

'I have to have a hand-basin.'

'Well, why don't we check – I don't mind swapping.' Armand followed so closely behind him that he trod on Paul's heels.

'Nope. No hand-basin in here.'

'Well . . .' Armand's neck flushed patchily, and he plucked at the skin over his Adam's apple. 'I have to have a hand-basin.'

'Okaaay,' said Paul, a little uneasily. 'Maybe one of the other flats on this floor has got . . . we could ask Crispin, he might know.'

'Ask me what?' Crispin loomed round the door; he was wearing the roller blind like a sari, one end looped over his head. 'Mother Teresa,' he said, by way of explanation.

'Armand needs –'

'Hang on just a moment –' Crispin held up one hand like a traffic policeman, opened his mouth widely, paused for a second and then belched. '*Now* you can ask.'

'Armand wants a hand-basin in his room.'

'Does he? Shame.' He pulled a section of blind in front of his mouth. 'Yashmak. How many camels would you pay for me, Pud?' He took a coquettish step forward, staggered slightly and sat heavily on the bed. 'You know,' he added, unnecessarily, 'I am *well* oiled.'

'You mean there are *no* individual basins in the rooms?'

Armand had gone rather white, throwing into relief a dappling of pimples around his mouth.

'Why do you need one?' asked Paul.

'I need one for reasons of hygiene. I am a diabetic and therefore have to take particular care . . .'

'OK,' said Crispin, supine now, 'I'm calling for silence – Silence!' he added as Armand tried to speak. 'Exam time, your starter for ten. You'll need to know this, right, it's important. What is the only pre-fourteenth-century building in the whole of Shadley Oak? You've got five seconds, tickatickatickaticka-tickaticka. Almond?'

'Excuse me?'

'Ding! Failed. It's the Malthouse in the market square. Next question – Pud.'

'What?'

'When was the Eddery Building built?'

'The what?'

'The Eddery Building.'

'I've never heard of it.'

'You're *in* it, you twat. It's the main hospital block with all the wards in, and this flat's on the fifth floor.'

'Oh right.'

'So when was it built?'

'I've got no idea.'

'1963. Memorize it.'

'Why?'

'Oh my child, my innocent child,' said Crispin, his voice wavering in sudden mock-decrepitude, 'let King Crispy the Wise instruct you in the ways of schmoozing consultants and you will thank me in later years for my wise words of wisdom. Your new boss, Mr Gorman, is totally obsessed by –'

'Excuse me for interrupting,' said Armand, sounding determined and a little desperate, 'but could you tell me where

I can find the administrative department in this hospital? I shall have to see someone immediately about the hand-basin situation.'

'It's Sunday,' said Paul.

'Nevertheless I think something should be –'

'You know, you guys,' said Crispin loudly, 'this flat is always *the* party flat. I've got rat-arsed more times in this flat in the last six months than you would believe *possible*.'

'Why don't you wait till tomorrow –'

'I simply can't be expected to –'

'PARTY FLAAAAAAT!' Crispin flung his arms wide and knocked over the bedside table. Armand left the room abruptly.

'Get her.' Crispin crooked an effeminate wrist towards the door, then heaved himself upright and started to pick up Paul's scattered possessions. 'Loonman,' he added. He examined Paul's name badge closely and then scraped at it with a fingernail.

Paul felt rattled, literally rattled, as if someone had given him a good shaking. The happy fizz of ten minutes before had dissipated, leaving only the undercurrent of nervousness.

'So what are you doing here, then?' he asked Crispin. 'I thought you were working in Stoke.'

'Stoke for house jobs, Moseley for SHO and now, my fine Pudding, I am a surgical registrar.' He lifted his hands to acknowledge an imaginary admiring crowd.

'Oh,' said Paul, the back of his neck suddenly cold. 'Which means –'

'Which means that from nine a.m. tomorrow morning, you – my fine Pudding – are my house officer. Reunion of the "A" team. Hey look!' He made a final adjustment with his thumbnail, and then turned the name badge round so that Paul could see it. Some of the black lettering had been picked off. It now read 'Dr P ooding'.

2

'I know why you're going to Shadley Oak,' said Kelly, twisting and untwisting a tube of lipstick so that the pink tip flickered like a tongue.

'So do I,' said Netta. 'I'm going to help my brother and my mother move house.'

'No. There's another reason.'

'Is there? Kelly, please stop fiddling with that, you'll break it.'

'It's too neutral for you anyway. I told you loads of times you should wear something in the red-brown range.' Netta's stepdaughter dropped the lipstick and picked up a mascara instead. 'You want to know my theory about your real reason?'

'What, my real, deep, subconscious reason?'

'Yeah actually,' said Kelly, who had just passed a Higher in psychology and had thus become Sigmund Freud. 'There's no need to take the piss.'

'Sorry. Go ahead.'

'You're going because you've run out of people to worry about. Dad's off to the States, I'm leaving home and there'll be no one around for you to organize. It's like when hens sit on china eggs when there aren't any real eggs to sit on.'

'Right.' Netta finished untangling a pair of tights that had emerged from the washing machine in a knot. 'Do I really remind you of a hen?'

'No, that's a metaphor,' said Kelly, impatiently. 'I mean a simile.'

'Big bust, short legs.'

'*No*. Anyway, your bust's not that big; Eleanor Kerr in my class is a double-D and she just shoves them into people's faces, she thinks they're fantastic. And if you've got short legs, then mine must be like a tiny dwarf's or something.'

'You've got lovely legs.'

'Look, you haven't said about my theory.'

'Oh, um . . . no, that's not why I'm going.'

Kelly shrugged. 'If it's subconscious, you wouldn't know anyway. Dad, tell her what I said was right.'

'What?' Mick, lying on the bed next to Netta's half-packed suitcase, opened his eyes.

'Tell Mum she's only going so she can boss them around.'

'All right. Netta –'

'Yes, Mick?'

'You're a wonderful woman.'

'Thank you, Mick.'

Kelly groaned. 'What about me, then?'

'You're wonderful too,' said Mick.

'What about Shona?'

'She's wonderful.'

'Clare?'

'Wonderful.'

'Jeanette?'

'Wonderful. You're all wonderful. I'm surrounded by wonderful women.' He closed his eyes again and clasped his hands across his stomach. 'I'm a very lucky man.'

Kelly looked at him pityingly. 'You're so pathetic, Dad. You think just because you put women on a pedestal they'll do anything for you. What about Auntie Vi?'

'Wonderful.'

'Yeah, *right*.'

'If that really was my subconscious reason,' said Netta, 'wouldn't I be looking forward to going?'

Kelly looked at her. 'Aren't you, then?'

Netta snorted and shook her head, and carried on sorting socks; some things were just too complex to explain, even to herself.

It was odd to be travelling south on a Sunday; as Netta worked her way through the newspaper she kept catching herself thinking that the scenery should be moving in a different direction, that hills should be bulking the horizon and the prospect of home and Mick and a nice glass of wine in front of the telly moving ever closer. Instead, by the time she had reached the arid pages of 'Your Money and You' the countryside had flattened into a series of hedgeless fields, all stubble and seagulls, and the accents of those boarding the train were beginning to acquire the clanging 'g's that still infected her own speech.

'It's all very well leaving us lists,' her mother had said on the phone, after one of Netta's recent visits, 'but Glenn and I are busy people.'

'I know, Mum. That's why I left the list. I thought it might simplify things for you – furniture you want to hang on to, furniture you don't want but that you could sell and furniture for dumping. All you have to do is show it to a clearance firm and they can give you a quote. And I left you a list of clearance firms. With numbers.'

'Yes, now I'm not at all sure what you did with that particular piece of paper.'

'I left it on the sideboard in the living room. It had "Clearance Firms" written on the top of it. As a sort of clue.'

'Was the back of it blank, though?'

'I don't know. Probably.'

'You see, the telephone's on the sideboard and if I need to take a very important message and I'm looking around for something to write on, then I might just use the nearest . . . in any case I'm not at all sure the small maroon sofa should go.'

'But I thought you said that – '

'And Glenn's decided he wants to keep his desk.'

'But I talked to him about – '

'Coral's just arrived, dear. I'll phone you during the week, oh, did I tell you that we decided against the Lilley Road bungalow?'

'What? You did what?'

'I went back there with Glenn and do you know – I walked into that dark front hall and I had a frisson. I suddenly thought, no – no, this is not for me. Bungalows are for *old* people.'

'But . . . but, hang on, the whole reason you're moving in the first place is that you can't manage the stairs any longer, and you won't get a stairlift. What are you going to do? Buy a tent?'

'There's really no need to be sarcastic, Brianetta.'

'But you told me you liked that bungalow.'

'The proportions were all wrong, I felt stifled. And before you say anything, Glenn completely agreed with me, and as well as that he was worried he wouldn't be able to get his trolley in through the side gate.'

'But you were supposed to *exchange* next Monday.'

'Don't shout, dear. Wasn't it lucky I had the urge to look round one more time? It would never have suited us.'

It was at this point that Netta (who had measured both gate and trolley and yes, it would have fitted, with room to spare) had realized that traipsing from Glasgow to Birmingham every third weekend was not only ruinously expensive but also completely pointless, since there were all those unmonitored days in between during which everything could slide out of control again.

'Mum still doesn't get it,' she'd said to Mick. 'After all these years she still doesn't understand how much Glenn prefers order and predictability, and . . . and *decisions*.'

And she'd made a decision of her own: if she wanted her brother's first move in more than three decades to be as trauma-free as possible, then she would actually have to *be* there, ensconced in Shadley Oak over the crucial period, observing, nudging, guiding . . .

Outside the train, fields had given way to warehouses and concrete stanchions and odd sections of wasteground, splashed purple with buddleia, and people in the carriage were beginning to assemble their luggage. Netta collected up the unread bits of the paper and put them into the bag that Mick had thrust into her hand just before seeing her off at Glasgow. It contained a box of Black Magic, which he considered to be her all-time favourite confectionery, since he had bought her some on their first date seventeen years ago and she had praised his choice lavishly, as she had also praised the bunch of carnations and the, frankly, dreadful Italian restaurant to which he'd taken her; he was so pleased to have nailed her taste that she'd never had the heart to tell him that she really preferred milk chocolates.

There was no fast train to Shadley Oak. After she'd wheeled her suitcase the length of New Street Station, and bumped it down a steep flight of stairs, and waited the expected twenty minutes for the arrival of the 3.05, and then a further, entirely unexplained, sixteen minutes, two little carriages eased their way shyly up the platform and, after a long pause, opened their doors with a hiss. 'Arriving at Platform 4 is the 3.05 to Shadley Oak,' said the announcer, mendaciously, as everyone surged forward and Netta, using her suitcase as a wedge, attempted to get a seat, 'stopping at Fretley Hall, Adstone,

Calls Cottage, Salley Bridge, Opley, Cherton, Stagg Street, Hoddles Green, Spittles Green, Shotton, King's Heath, Clay Hill, Sprent and Shadley Oak.' She was within feet of success when a crocodile of narrow-hipped teenagers shimmied past her and settled in triumph in the last remaining free spaces.

'Brilliant,' said one of them. He looked up, caught Netta's eye, flinched at her expression and looked away again. She rested one buttock on her suitcase and braced herself as the train moved off.

She could have recited the list of stations in her sleep. The quaint names, which should, by rights, have belonged to a chain of half-timbered villages jingling with morris dancers, were merely the labels on a series of identical suburbs oozing outward from the city. All that could be seen from the train were steep embankments, topped with fences and sheds and sticky-leaved trees. Netta tried to read the sports supplement and then gave up and stared out of the window. She could feel the familiar itchy sense of claustrophobia creeping across her, the prefiguration of Shadley Oak, a place so horribly small that you could see the edges from the middle.

'When you come back from there,' Kelly had said recently, 'you know, after you've been for a weekend on your own, without Dad, when you come back you're always really crabby and smart-arsy.'

'Says Queen Crabby of Smart-arse.'

'Yeah, that's the sort of thing. That's exactly the sort of thing you say. And if anyone says anything back you give one of your death stares.'

'Do I?'

'Yeah. And you're really sarcastic. *Much* worse than usual.'

It had been a chastening conversation; if that's what a weekend could do, what kind of monster would she turn into over a longer stay? She was going to have to watch herself. She was going to have to practise patience and good humour. She made a creditable start by not swearing when the carriage lurched just outside Stagg Street and she fell off her suitcase and all the teenagers laughed. She dusted herself off and graciously accepted the offer of a corner seat from a man in a suit, and almost instantly fell asleep, her head drumming gently against the window.

She awoke with a jerk, and the awareness that she was dribbling. Wiping her mouth discreetly, she glanced around; the teenagers opposite were all asleep, keeled over like a row of toppled dominoes. The carriage was half empty, and outside – she saw with a slump of the heart – was the last vestige of the green belt, the sweep of farmland that separated Shadley Oak from Sprent. Ahead she could see all the familiar land-marks: the cluster of trees on a tump just outside the town, the tower of the fire station, the spike of the abbey spire, and reaching across the fields, further on every visit, the mud roads and neat brick outlines of the new estate.

It was easy to spot her brother among the small crowd waiting on the platform. He had a bright-red Puffa jacket, an A3 clipboard and a shopping trolley filled with old bottles. Netta waved as he slid past the window but he failed to see her, his attention fixed on something a few feet above the roof of the train. There seemed, she noted, something indefinably wrong about the shape of his shoulders, a kind of lumpy asymmetry reminiscent of Richard the Third.

She stood for a moment in the aisle, trying to prise the telescopic handle from the top of the suitcase. 'Hey,' said one of the teenagers, newly awake, a girl with fluffed blonde hair like duck down and eyes made small by fiercely applied eyeliner. She was staring at something further along the plat-form. 'Hey Jamie – hey, look who's come to meet us.' Her mouth split into a laugh, and Netta stiffened, mid-task. The girl's neighbour unglued his eyes and blinked towards the window. 'Oh yeah.' He smiled; not a cruel smile, but a sleepily derisive one. 'Yeah. It's the Rubbish Man.'

Glenn was still looking skywards as she approached him, and she followed the angle of his gaze. On the parapet of the footbridge that crossed to the other platform was a three-quarters empty bottle of Grolsch. There was a tension about his body as he looked at it, a sense of a gundog straining at the leash.

'Hi Glenn.'

He swung round, rather unwillingly.

'Oh, hello.'

'Thanks for coming to meet me.'

He nodded a couple of times, one eye still on the bottle.

'Glenn, what's happened to your jacket?' She'd been right about the shoulders; the coat, which he'd chosen for his last birthday, had lost its smooth, inflated profile and now looked as if an enterprising designer had tacked a piece of red nylon across a relief map of the Pennines.

'I washed it,' said Glenn.

Netta gently fingered, and then squeezed, one of cuffs; the stuffing had the consistency of a cardboard eggbox.

'What did you wash it *in?*'

There was no answer and he moved his arm away, uncomfortable with being touched for too long. 'It's quite rare for me to find one of those bottles. They have a unique ceramic swing-top, patented in 1898.'

'Do you want to get it? I'll keep an eye on the trolley.'

He was off before she could finish the sentence and she watched him walk towards the staircase with the strange arrhythmic gait that made him look as if he had a stone in each shoe. He overtook a couple of pensioners and took the steps two at a time, clipboard swinging erratically.

Sunday was bottle day; she'd forgotten. Monday was plastic and polystyrene, Wednesday cans and if she'd been unwise enough to book her ticket for Friday, then Glenn would have turned up at the station with the haul he classified as 'miscellaneous', and she might therefore have been greeted by an old gas burner and a roll of mouldy lino.

On the footbridge he picked up the bottle, looked at it carefully and then continued across and disappeared down the steps on the far side. Netta nudged the trolley a little way up the platform, towards the exit. After a moment she was overtaken by the teenagers, already deep in conversation ('Froggy's a twat.' '*She's* a twat.' 'No, you're a twat.'); they looked at her in passing, snorted and shambled off through the mock-Pugin archway. After a moment they reappeared, and one of the boys sprinted up the platform and – before she could say anything – lobbed a half-empty 7-up can into the trolley, spraying her with an arc of droplets.

'There you go.'

'It's bottle day,' she said coldly, picking it out again.

'You his new assistant?'

'Bugger off.'

'Don't you fucking swear at me,' he said, with sudden aggression. He lingered, staring hard at her, until one of his friends called him away.

'Fuck you, Mrs,' he said, venomously, over his shoulder.

She took the can to the nearest bin, her heart beating uncomfortably fast, aware that she had mishandled the situation. Something similar probably happened to her brother almost every week but without the same consequences, his very impassivity seeming to act as a shield, whereas she'd gone off like a landmine at the first provocation. It was her old Glenn-defence button, still touch-sensitive after all these years. She rubbed a streak of 7-up from her chin and looked around for him; the train was pulling away, revealing an empty platform opposite and a picture-postcard view of Shadley Oak.

The town looked lovely from up here; she'd give it that much. It lay in a shallow valley, the abbey and its green grounds at the centre, the gunmetal curve of the old moat separating church land from the medieval streets; even Mick, not renowned for noticing anything that wasn't either edible or on fire, had admired it on his first visit. The residential edges had thickened and spread over recent years and the skyline was pocked with bad planning decisions, but the abbey was still the dominant building – lichened, buttressed, its image reproduced on a million tea towels, together with those of its famous swans. Netta could see three of them now – flakes of white on the dark water. Between the ages of eleven and fourteen Glenn had been phobic about swans, necessitating a long detour on the way to school. The phobia had disappeared overnight, to be replaced by a fear of spoons. He still hated spoons, though nowadays he didn't mind being in the same room as one.

Where *was* he? There now seemed to be no one on the entire station, apart from herself. There were no buildings on the other side of the tracks, only a long spiked fence and a gateway that opened onto a steep path down to the car park, the latter invisible from where she stood.

'Glenn!'

In the silence that followed her shout she could hear the abbey bell strike four. She parked the trolley by the exit, left her suitcase beside it, crossed the footbridge and spotted him immediately. He was coming across the car park, walking fast, his head thrust forward with excitement.

'I've worked out exactly what happened,' he said when he was still yards away, his words emerging in a pauseless, monotone rush, 'you see until last year there was a bottle bank at the end of the car park and some people aren't aware that it's been moved which is why they've all been left.'

'Glenn,' she said gently, 'I don't know what you're talking about. I haven't seen whatever it is that you've seen.'

'I'll show you, there was a similar example last month –' he turned around mid-syllable and Netta followed him down the path and across the tarmac ' – only it was to a lesser extent which is why I decided to check the area on a regular basis although because of the amount left here today it was obvious to me from the top of the footbridge that there was going to be work needed, look –' He thrust out a hand. Piled in a corner, heaped against the chain-link fence, were hundreds upon hundreds of bottles – some in bags, some loose and lying in pools of their own contents, some crusty and ancient, some in pieces. 'I may find when I've checked my figures that this is definitely a record,' said Glenn; he smiled, showing an endearing line of gum above his top teeth.

'That's certainly a lot of bottles,' said Netta, fatuously.

Her brother leaned over and plucked at one of the carrier bags. It split as he raised it and the contents rolled across the tarmac. 'I shall definitely need my trolley,' he said. 'It may well take two loads, I may well be working late into the night.'

'Can't you do one load now and one tomorrow?'

'Tomorrow's plastic and –'

'Polystyrene. Sorry, I wasn't thinking.' This last remark was to herself; Glenn was already halfway across the car park. She followed him. 'Glenn, I think I'll phone for a cab and let you get on with it.'

'Yes, all right.'

'Shall I tell Mum to keep tea for you?'

'Yes, all right.' He was sprinting up the path to the station, focused utterly on the task ahead.

'Glenn, you will be careful with that broken glass, won't you? Do you have any glov–' She stopped as her eyeline reached the level of the platforms. Apart from Glenn's trolley, they were completely bare. Her suitcase had gone.

'Camera?'

'No.'

'Walkman?'

'No.'

'Wallet?'

'No, everything like that's in here.' She patted her handbag.

'So it's just the clothes then. And toiletries and things.'

Netta sat back and rolled her shoulders. She simply couldn't get Constable Whittaker to comprehend the seriousness of what had happened. He was a sweet-faced, rather nervous young man, who hadn't yet bulked out to match the breadth of his shoulders. She couldn't imagine him chasing villains over walls; indeed, filling in the boxes on a sheet of paper seemed to be testing his strength to the limit, necessitating frequent pauses and effortful sighs at the challenge of the task.

'Right. So, anyway . . .' He ran his finger down the form. 'So what is the, um, the work that you do, Mrs . . . Etter–'

'Mrs Lee,' she said, for about the tenth time. 'Brianetta Lee, except that everyone calls me Netta. I'm a dietitian.'

'Right. That's like, er, Weight Watch–'

'No,' she said. 'I work in a hospital. I've taken a six-week locum job at the General.'

'Right.' He nodded a couple of times. 'But with fat people.'

'No, more usually I'm helping people to put on weight, rather than the other way round. People with chronic illnesses and –' Why am I explaining this, she wondered, what is this, a careers talk? 'Dietitian,' she said with finality, pointing at the form.

'Right.' She saw his pen hesitate after writing the first two letters of the word.

'I could fill it in myself,' she suggested, tactfully, 'if you found it helpful.'

'No, we have to do it. It's er . . . security.' He paused a little longer and then, with sudden decision, wrote a flurry of letters, all crammed unreadably together. It looked, from where she sat, as if there might be an 's' and an 'h' in there somewhere.

'Right,' he said again, leaning back with the air of a job well done. 'Well, we'll contact you if we hear anything, Mrs Etterly.'

'Lee. If I was Mrs Etterly, that would make my first name Brian, wouldn't it?'

He nodded, absently. 'So when you get people who need to put *on* weight, how do you do it?'

'Can I – before I answer that – can I ask you if anything's going to happen?'

'Sorry?'

'Is anyone going to look for this suitcase?'

'Oh yeah. Definitely. We'll issue a description.'

'Because there's nothing particularly saleable in there, and I'm sure it was those teenagers and they just did it out of spite, because I had that . . . because I swore at them. So I'd imagine it'll end up simply being dumped. In a front garden or, I don't know, a piece of wasteground or something. And it's labelled,' she remembered suddenly, 'there's one of those built-in bits to write on, just under the handle, under a flap; I filled it in when we went to France last year – it says "B. Lee", I think, to match my passport.'

'I'll make a note,' he said, not making a note. 'So when you get people who –'

'Look, Constable . . .' He straightened slightly, the title acting like a hook on the back of his jacket.

'Yes Mrs – madam.'

'I know it's just a suitcase and it's just some clothes, but the thing is – the thing is, I would rather have lost my Walkman *and* my camera *and* my wallet, because they'd be much easier to replace.' Her work outfits, she could hardly bear the thought that her work outfits had gone – those long-jacketed suits that made her feel streamlined and professional and even sexy in a managerial sort of way. It had taken the fashion industry years – decades – to get round to a style that suited her, and she'd plenished her wardrobe against the long dry season of buttock-length skirts and wispy tops that was bound to follow. And her bras, her lovely bras from Grey's of Glasgow – all the support and none of the whalebone – big bras that didn't look as if they'd been lashed together by a team of scaffolders, big bras that masqueraded as tiny, chic, lacy . . . she shook her head involuntarily, as if listening to an exquisite piece of music.

'You all right?'

'Yes, I'm fine,' she said, with a slight, shameful, husk to her voice.

'Only I've got . . .' Looking a little panicked, he fumbled in one of the desk drawers. 'I've got something for you . . . it's here somewhere. I saw it this morning.'

'I'm all right, really.' Crying over a bra. That was what ninety minutes in Shadley Oak had done to her.

'It might be in the other drawer. Hold on, hold on –' He held out a warning finger, as if she were poised to cast herself, weeping, over his desktop. 'Yeah, I've got it, I've got it. Here it is.' With an air of triumph he pulled out a small orange leaflet and handed it to her. She turned it over and read the title: 'Dog Fouling and the Law'.

'Oh.' He took it back again and looked at it. 'I thought it was the victim-support one.'

'It doesn't matter.'

'There's a pile of them on the main desk.'

'Thanks. I really ought to go now.' She should get to her mother's, phone home, arrange for the remains of her wardrobe – tracksuit bottoms, faded beach dresses, underwear of fraying antiquity – to be packed up and sent express delivery. 'Please, *please*, call me if you find anything – you can get me at the General during the day. Or at my mother's in the evening.'

'No problem.' He glanced down at the form again. 'Monk's Way?'

'Yes.'

'Is that that road where there's no numbers, just names?'

'That's the one,' she said.

The nine-house cul-de-sac had been built by her father's firm and the keynote had been individuality: 'No one here's just a number,' he'd say as the postman randomly distributed letters and the neighbours convened in the middle of the road to swap envelopes, 'we gave every house a touch of character.' He'd liked the concept so much that he'd kept the central plot and greatest characterization for himself. Netta, feeling like a day-tripper without the ballast of her suitcase, walked up from the main road past Glebe Cottage (curved drive edged with green brick), Abbey View (wrought-iron balcony above the garage), Moatside (eyebrow window in the roof) and The Leas (Victorian lamp-post beside the front door) before turning along the familiar pink and yellow path. None of the other houses had both a lamp-post *and* a carriage lamp. None of the other houses had a green bottle cemented onto the wall beside the garage, angled so that it appeared to be pouring champagne into the pewter-lidded tankard cemented just below it. As a child Netta had been proud of these eccentricities, as a teenager she had been ashamed; now they simply seemed symbols of a bygone age, as remote as wattle and daub. The name of the house was obscured by the 'SOLD' sign stuck in the terracotta wheelbarrow beside the front step, and as she waited for her mother to answer the door Netta tilted the board to get a glimpse of the varnished oval with its poker-work italics. She wondered what the next owners would make of the single word it bore: 'Briglennia'.

3

Her father had converted the cupboard under the stairs into a soundproof telephone booth, with a neat little padded seat and a door inset with multi-coloured stained glass. As she waited for someone to answer Netta found herself closing one eye and moving her head very slightly from side to side, so that the hue of the hall shifted from amber to rose and then back again; an old habit, forgotten and then rediscovered on every visit. She moved a little along the seat and altered the view to a steady green.

'Yes?' Kelly's voice was brisk, impatient.

'It's Mum.'

'Oh, hi. I'm just on my way out, I've literally not got one second to talk.'

'Can I speak to Dad, then?'

'He's at Shona's. They're going for a pizza or something.'

'Oh. I'd left a casserole for him. Labelled.'

'He's put it in the freezer. Look, I've got to go, I haven't dried my hair and I've got to iron my blue . . .' The last few words drifted from audibility as Kelly turned away from the phone, presumably to examine herself in the mirror.

'No, hang on – listen Kelly, I've had my suitcase stolen. All my clothes have gone.'

There was an audible gasp. '*What*? They've *what*?' Netta could almost feel the sudden suck of interest, the switch of attention from enlarged pores to the stark horror of a world without clothes.

'Someone took my suitcase off the platform. I need you to –'

'*All* your clothes?'

'Yes. Well, everything I usually –'

'Oh my God, that's *terrible*. I'd kill myself if that was me, I'd –'

'Kelly, I need you to send –'

'Was your navy suit in there?'

'Yes.'

'Not your *shoes* as well?'

'Yes, but Kelly, I –'

'Not those grey *suede* ones?'

'Kelly, I –'

'God, if I lost my shoes . . .'

Netta had just about reached the parcel post versus Red Star delivery stage of the conversation when an emerald version of her mother entered the hall, moved inexorably towards the booth, opened the door and announced, 'Coral's your size!'

'Mum,' said Netta, holding up the receiver as evidence, 'I'm in the middle of a phone call.' She could hear Kelly squawking at the other end.

'I'm sorry,' said her mother, 'it was just one of those sudden ideas. You carry on.'

She let the door swing shut, stood for a moment with a hand at her throat, apparently wounded by Netta's lack of interest, and then limped back down the hall again.

Netta lifted the phone to her ear again. 'Right, I –'

'I've got to go,' said Kelly. 'Dezza's just got here. I'll send the stuff, OK?'

'There's just one more –'

'I've gotta –' There was a sudden, delighted scream, and a smothered giggle.

'Hey Mrs Lee,' shouted Dezza, 'your Kelly's got her hand down my kecks and she's –'

Netta replaced the receiver.

'Coral,' said her mother, unpeeling a wet slice of ham from a packet and arranging it on the plate with as much delicacy as if it were a shaving of cured lark's tongue, 'is very nearly your size.' She lifted the top of a cheese dish to reveal a rectangle of something orange and shiny.

'Really?' asked Netta, wondering where this was leading. Coral, her mother's business partner, was built along the lines of a roll of carpet, with no perceptible change of width between shoulders and knees. 'We're completely different shapes though, aren't we? I've got a waist, for a start.' She was still brooding slightly about the casserole, Mick's favourite chicken chasseur, cooked lovingly to his narrow tastes (no garlic, no herbs) and then, apparently, shoved among the frozen peas in favour of something more coronary inducing.

'So I've just called her,' continued her mother, 'and she's sorting out one or two items.'

'Sorry?'

Her mother paused, grater in one hand, chunk of processed Gouda in the other. 'Coral's going to lend you an outfit,' she said, as if imparting delightful news.

Netta laughed incredulously.

'What's the matter?'

'Oh come on, Mum, I can't wear what Coral wears.'

'I don't see why not. She's a fully trained dressmaker, all her clothes are beautifully finished. *Beautifully*.'

'Yes but they're – they wouldn't suit me. She's nearly thirty years older than me and she puts braid on everything. She wears boleros.'

'Well, perhaps they're not quite as conventional as your clothes,' said her mother, repressively, 'but I think you could look very smart in them.'

'I wouldn't look smart, I'd look like a complete . . .' A complete what? Weirdo? Loony? She took a breath; in this house, back in this world, there was no possible way to end that sentence. 'I can't, Mum. Sorry.'

'So what are you going to wear tomorrow?'

Netta glanced down at her blouse and jeans. 'This, I suppose. What I'm wearing already.'

'*Jeans*? For your first day in a new job? What kind of impression would that make?'

Netta shrugged. 'I don't have any choice.'

'Which was what I was trying to give you. Never mind.'

'I –'

'It was just a teeny suggestion, no need for us to fall out, I'll ring Coral and tell her. She won't be hurt.' She picked up a slotted spoon. 'One egg or two?'

'One please.'

'I've cooked you two.'

'You could put one in the fridge.'

'Yes, but they're not quite as nice the day after, though, are they?' She tapped the shell against a cup and started to peel it with nails that were today painted a purplish-slate colour, matching perfectly her shoes, her belt and the collar of her dress. 'Did Glenn say if he was hungry?'

'No,' said Netta, 'but then he never does, does he?'

'Well . . .' said her mother, doubtfully, as if it were a point for discussion rather than a statement of the purest fact, a Glenn-defining characteristic. 'He might work up an appetite clearing those bottles, and of course he was up at six with his little wheel.'

'With his what?'

'It's his new special project.'

'What is?'

'Oh it's . . . something technical. Distances, I think he said.' She waved the egg in vague illustration. 'Now, did I tell that it's all signed?'

'What is?'

'The paperwork on the Mellis Hall flat. I went to the solicitor's on Friday.'

'Good,' said Netta, firmly, determined to be upbeat about her mother's final, *final* choice of relocation. 'That's good, isn't it? It's convenient and light and the rooms are a nice size, and there's lots of storage, and it's . . . it's just right for you both, isn't it?'

'Yes.' There seemed just a trace of hesitation in her mother's reply. 'Yes.'

'You're not having second thoughts, are you, Mum?'

'No, no. No. Absolutely not. The builder says we can have a look round next weekend, as long as we don't touch the walls.'

'Wonderful. That's great, Mum.'

'Yes . . .' There was a pause that was indefinably uneasy, and then the last bit of shell tinkled into the bowl and her mother placed the egg on Netta's plate. 'Supper's ready.'

It was a Monk's Way protein special; Netta paused, fork in hand, and tried to summon up some anticipatory saliva. The Gouda, now transformed into a pyramid of day-glo waxen curls, sat in the middle of the plate, flanked at the major compass points by the two boiled eggs, a flaccid slice of ham, rolled and impaled with a cocktail stick, and a tiny heap of tinned coleslaw. Two stuffed olives filled the gaps at south-east and north-west. Her mother's cuisine had always smacked of summer picnics, but what had seemed to Netta a daily treat at eight years old had palled with age. She speared an egg.

'How are the girls?' asked her mother, painfully hoisting herself onto one of the tall stools beside the breakfast bar. The sides of the counter were flush with the top, and all meals taken there had to be eaten with legs swivelled to one side and torso to the other, something that Netta was sure had contributed to her mother's back problems.

'They're fine, as far as I know, Jeanette and Clare are somewhere between Melbourne and Adelaide and they're on a promise of bar work, though Clare can't add up so I don't know how long they'll last at that, and Shona's still teaching, and Kelly's off to college in two weeks. She's decided on Huddersfield.'

'And what will she be studying?'

'Drama,' said Netta, her voice a bell of doom.

'Oh – how exciting.' Her mother grasped the edge of the counter, as if almost faint with anticipation. 'Don't you think that's exciting, Brianetta?'

'Well . . . no. Not really.' She was not in the mood to fake enthusiasm.

'Why not?'

'Because I think she's only doing it because she's too lazy to do an academic course, and I'm worried she'll end up being unemployed and poverty-stricken, just like every other actor I've ever met. Like Ted, for a start.'

Her mother ignored the reference. 'Well, *I* think she has talent.'

'Do you? But you haven't ever seen her act, have you?'

'Her face is very expressive. And she moves so well, she has a certain . . .' Her mother drifted an arm through an elegant arc.

Netta slid off the stool. 'You should hear her coming in at

33

three in the morning, it's like a Panzer division smashing through the front door. Is there any mustard?'

'In the provisions carousel. Oh, while you're on your feet could you bring over that envelope? There's some photos I want to show you.'

Inevitably they were of Natalia. Her mother dealt them out in rows across the breakfast bar, like a hand of patience, and then looked at Netta expectantly.

'What do you think? She's looking well, isn't she?'

'Mmm.' Netta popped one of the olives into her mouth and inspected the pictures of her sister. They showed her posing on a beach of travel-brochure perfection, the sand white, the sea almost turquoise, her tan golden, her teeny bikini emerald green. 'She does look good, yes.'

'Lester surprised her with the tickets. Apparently they only let a limited number of people on the island at one time – it's very exclusive. Look at this one.' Lester was holding his wife upside-down, his arms locked around her waist. Natalia's hair hung like a swatch of silk, just brushing the sand.

'Lovely,' said Netta. 'So Lester's in the money again, is he?'

'Yes, he's just done very well in . . . oh, Natalia did tell me . . . something to do with business.' She tapped her lips with a finger, trying to remember.

'Insider dealing?' suggested Netta.

'Yes, that might have been it.' Her tone was so innocent that Netta felt a surge of guilt. She had nothing against Lester; she'd only met him once and he'd been perfectly charming, albeit in a 'so these are your quaint English relatives, thank God I don't have to live anywhere near them' kind of way. 'Where's little Lester, then?' she asked, scanning the pictures for a photo of her nephew.

'With big Lester's mother, in Perth. When he arrived there he said to her, "My mummy and my daddy are going on a second moneymoon."'

'Did he?' Netta thought of the kind of gesture that the girls made when a conversation turned sentimental, a forward heave with a finger pointing towards the back of the throat.

'And when they came back he said, "My mummy looks like a princess now so does that mean I'm a prince?"'

Pure invention, thought Netta. It bore all the classic hall-marks of a Natalia anecdote – solipsism, cuteness and basic improbability. Like the time an Arab businessman had suppos-edly been so struck by the sight of her teetering around some cabaret stage with a pile of fruit on her head that he'd offered her a pedigree white foal for a single kiss. Even true incidents, incidents that Netta had herself witnessed, were often adjusted in the retelling, the mundane embellished, the focus nudged so that everything became a drama starring Natalia.

'Apparently little Lester's just been moved up a class,' continued her mother. 'The teacher said to Natalia that he's exceptionally gifted in almost every subject. She says she's never come across a pupil like him.'

'Really.'

'And she says he shows a quite extraordinary level of maturity. Isn't that a wonderful comment?'

'Certainly is. So do they have any plans to come over here?'

Her mother started gathering up the photos, tweaking the upside-down shot out of Netta's hands with unnecessary briskness.

'What's the matter, Mum?'

'You *know* that I have an open invitation to go to Sydney, all expenses paid.'

'I do know that, but I also know that you have a bad back

and it's a twenty-hour flight. It would be much easier if they came to you.'

'Lester has a business to run.'

'And Natalia doesn't work at all. There's nothing to stop her from jumping on a plane but then she never does anything unless –' She hauled herself up, mid-sentence, causing her vocal cords to creak in protest; her mother's face had begun to tighten, as if a thread were being pulled from the inside, pursing her features and turning the delicate lines into deep seams. For a moment she looked her age, and weary. She slotted the photos back in the envelope and snapped an elastic band around it.

'Natalia never criticizes *you*,' she said.

That's because she very rarely thinks about anybody but herself, thought Netta, leaving the words unspoken; Natalia came to England only when she could ensure that she'd be the centre of attention – by the possession of a colossal engagement ring, for instance, or a brand-new husband or a baby son. Simply turning up because her mother might want to see her obviously fell outside this category.

There was a silence, that stretched. Netta ate both her eggs and searched for another topic of conversation. She was aware that had Kelly been present over the last half hour the word 'crabby' might have been used more than once.

'Mum –' she began.

'I have another suggestion about what you could wear to work,' said her mother. 'Would you like to hear it, or will you get cross again?'

'I won't get cross,' said Netta. 'I'm sorry, Mum, I haven't been good company this evening. I'm sorry I said that about Natalia, it was . . . petty.'

'That's quite all right, dear.' She reached across and patted Netta's hand. 'Do you know what's just occurred to me?'

'What?'

'It could be your age. One of my aunts went through the menopause at forty.'

'I am not going through the menopause!'

'Don't shout, dear, it was only a passing thought. Now, do you want to hear my suggestion?'

'Go on then.'

'Coral was here yesterday and she's been doing some scavenging for the autumn show. There's a very plain charcoal jacket from Oxfam that she's going to adapt for Gemma Lacey from Stage Seniors to wear as Mary Poppins. We're having "A Spoonful of Sugar" as the Act 1 finale.'

'And this very plain charcoal jacket might do for me?'

'Yes, I think it might.'

'All right, I shall go and have a look. Where is it?'

'In your room. Somewhere in that large blue holdall.'

'Very plain' turned out to mean 'possessing gigantic built-in shoulder pads'; Netta took off the jacket – too tight under the arms in any case – and folded it again. She'd half emptied the holdall in her search and the contents were heaped on the bed, a multi-hued taster of the forthcoming show: a brace of silver raincapes, heralding (she'd guess) a futuristic-type robot number, a fun-fur hat and muff, redolent of the steppes, a pile of gingham dresses just waiting for a posse of six-year-old cowgirls, a violet sk–

Netta twitched aside a fold of raincape and stared at the knee-length violet skirt with diagonal zip pockets.

'It's not actually your old school skirt,' said her mother. 'It's from a clearance sale in the uniform section at DH Evans in Wolverhampton. I believe that Coral bought twelve.'

'Are you doing St Trinian's?'

'I'm sorry?'

'Are you doing a St Trinian's dance in the autumn show?'

'Oh no, that would be terribly old-fashioned,' said her mother, scathingly, 'none of our girls will have seen those films. No, we're doing a World War Two medley with the seniors. We'll dye the skirts saxe blue and they can be WAAF uniforms. Do you know, I think that colour suits you.'

'You're kidding.' Netta turned to the hall mirror and held the skirt up against herself. Objectivity was impossible; granted the colour, *as* a colour, was not completely repellent but the associations made her want to screw it into a ball and find the nearest furnace. 'You see,' said her mother, edging in beside her, 'it's complimentary to your skin tones. And that length's very good for you too, why don't you try it on?'

'I'd rather stick needles in my eyes.'

'Oh *really*, Brianetta.'

They crossed gazes in the mirror, and her mother gave a little huff of exasperation. She still stood like a dancer – the Bluebell Look, as she always termed it, with feet in third position and head pulled back so that her neck tendons stood out like guy ropes. Her hair was smoothly coiled into a chignon, her features neat and sharp, her parting on a level with Netta's chin; she looked just as Natalia would look in thirty-five years' time. Netta, recipient of her father's genes (curly hair, sloppy posture, fondness for carbohydrates), started to fold the skirt.

'Oh, there's Glenn,' said her mother, hearing the key in the lock. 'Starving?' she asked as he appeared round the front door, clipboard in hand.

'I think so,' said Glenn, employing the answer he used to circumvent difficult questions.

'I thought you would be. Supper's in the fridge.' She patted her bun and moved towards the kitchen.

'So, did you shift the whole pile, then?' asked Netta.

'Yes I did, and I phoned the police to warn them about the broken-glass hazard for both cars and pedestrians.' He looked at his clipboard. 'I may be collating for most of the evening.'

'Hey Glenn –' she held up the skirt '– recognize this?'

'Yes I do. Legg Hill Comprehensive, the Purpular Choice.'

'Christ! The Purpular Choice!' The phrase left her almost bereft of breath. 'I haven't thought of that in, my God . . . twenty years? What were the others? There was . . .'

'Top of the Purps,' said Glenn, taking off his jacket.

'That's right. God . . .' The purple puns: she'd invented the concept one morning as they walked to school together, she in her violet skirt, he in his violet tie, and it had evolved over months into their own private lexicon. 'Purp goes the weasel.'

'Purpulation control,' said Glenn, who never laughed at jokes but who seemed to savour the structure of puns, to appreciate the fact that they could be dismantled, explained and then reassembled. 'Snap, Crackle and Purp.'

'Squash or Coke?' called their mother.

'Purping the question,' said Glenn; Netta laughed and he nodded, apparently gratified.

4

Paul, hurrying through Ward 2 in search of a patient called Mrs Dimoglou, was feeling a little less than crisp. He'd meant, on his very first morning as a house officer, to arrive on the ward at half past eight and thus give himself a leisurely half hour for orientation before the start of the round; instead, after hitting the snooze button at least four times, waking with a shout of panic and getting dressed in forty-five seconds, he had turned up, panting slightly, at ten to nine. At which point Sister Blake, visibly annoyed, had issued him with an operation consent form for the first patient on the morning list and had told him to go and get it signed, *now*.

What was worrying was that he had fully intended to have a quiet night in. He had said to Crispin, calmly and firmly, 'I am not going out for a drink,' and Crispin had replied, 'Christ, Pud, don't be such a pathetic dildo,' and ten minutes later he'd somehow found himself in the snug of the Ball and Crown with a glass in his hand. And when he'd arrived back at the flat, six pints to the bad and ravenous, there'd been nothing to eat apart from the contents of a cupboard labelled 'HANDS OFF! EVERYTHING IN HERE BELONGS TO ARMAND'. Paul had wrestled with his conscience and won, and had turned instead to the only other edible object in the entire kitchen: the Jurassic-era hamburger at the back of the freezer. The strange thing was that even as he had chipped away at the ice with a butter knife, even as he had watched his meal dwindle under the grill to the diameter and thickness of a beer mat, even as he had raised the flabby grey disc to his mouth, he had known to the core of his being that it was a bad idea.

It was a familiar sensation, this occasional compulsion that impelled him not only to start doing the wrong thing but to carry it through with masochistic thoroughness. It was the same impulse that had persuaded him, in the third year, to scale the rusting access ladder that led onto the roof of the medical school. Everybody else had *thought* it was a great idea, but only Paul had actually got to the top, placed a wavering foot on the parapet and then found himself dropping twenty feet into a flower bed, thereby breaking only his leg and not, as the Dean had acidly put it, his miserable spine. He had spent six weeks in hospital, failed his exams and had to repeat the entire year; nevertheless, he had still heard the incident referred to as the funniest thing that had ever happened at Birmingham Medical School. By Crispin, in fact, now he came to think of it.

He found Mrs Dimoglou standing between her bed and the window, slowly taking family photos out of a plastic bag and arranging them on the top of her locker. She looked to be, at a rough first estimate, about three hundred years old – a tiny woman, her face meshed with wrinkles, a white plait hanging halfway down the back of her quilted dressing gown.

'Hello, I'm Doctor Gooding,' said Paul, smiling and nodding and speaking rather loudly in the way that he found hard to avoid when talking to extremely old people. 'I've come to consent you for your operation this morning – to make sure you know what it's all about and what's going to happen and everything.'

'Thank you,' she said placidly, angling a photo frame so that it could be seen from the bed, 'you're very kind. You know, when I first had operations in this country, no one ever tells me nothing about them. I come in, they cut me open.

And then when I come in three years ago for my knee operation there's a lovely lady doctor call Ann and she draws a
picture and tells me so clear about what they're going to do,
and tells me to ask anything I want, and when I wake up and
there's no kneecap on the middle of my leg I don't get a
sudden shock. And now you're coming to explain like that,
are you?'

'Yes.'

'You're a good boy.'

'Thank you.'

'Because when I see Mr Gorman the surgeon, it's always
too quick to ask things I want to ask. What is the "P"?' She
pointed to his mutilated name badge.

'Paul.'

'Paul is one of my favourite names. My cousin was called
Paul, what was in the navy during the war. We used to call
him Paulie. Does your mother call you Paulie?'

'No. No, she doesn't. OK, so shall we have a –'

'This picture,' she said, gently rubbing one of the frames
with her thumb, 'this is my youngest son, Trevor, he was born
in England so we give him an English name but for a joke my
husband always call him Trevios, like a Greek name.' She
smiled at the middle-aged multi-chinned porker in the photo
and then looked at Paul. 'You look a little tiny bit like my
Trevios,' she added, encouragingly.

'Oh,' said Paul. 'Thank you.'

'On Wednesday it's his birthday. Today I was going to
make him a special honey cake what has to stand for two days
but then the hospital ring me and say to come in for the
operation, so it's a shame he won't get no special cake, isn't it?'

'Yes,' said Paul, holding up the consent form and waggling
it slightly as a reminder of what they were supposed to be
talking about. 'So, if you've had operations before, then –'

42

'Twenty-two operations,' she said. 'Not counting having my babies. Twenty-two, and I remember every operation like it's yesterday. The biggest is in 1968, I have my heart valve replace because I keep falling in a faint and my own doctor hears a noise in my chest and sent me to hospital and the surgeon, he's call Mr Crabbe, come in and make me take off my top in front of six doctors, writes a big mark on my chest with a pen and say, "See you tomorrow, Mrs Dimoglou," and I only knew what happened inside my heart when a nurse tells me afterwards. I have a scar from *here* to *here*,' she added, drawing a sweeping crescent across her breast. 'And two years after that there is a gland in my neck that keeps working too much and a different surgeon, Mr Slater, he say, "Don't you worry, Mrs Dimo–"'

'Sorry,' said Paul, 'sorry to interrupt.' Out of the corner of his eye he could see Crispin heading for the ward office, the designated start of the round. 'It's just that I need to get this signed before the ward round starts.'

'Of course, of course,' said Mrs Dimoglou, lowering herself onto the edge of the bed. 'You are very busy – it's very important, your job.' She lifted a large green handbag onto her lap and took a pen from the inside pocket. 'So, you explain to me and then I sign.' She looked at him expectantly; a few yards behind her Armand hurried into view, caught Paul's eye and tapped his watch.

'OK,' said Paul. Precision, he thought – precision, clarity, speed. 'OK. Well, what you're having done today is an elective cholecystectomy, which means a non-urgent operation to take your gall bladder out because it's got stones in and it keeps getting inflamed, and it's safer to have the operation than to keep getting the inflammation.'

'Paulie?'

'Yes?'

'You speak a little bit fast.'

'Sorry. OK, what you're having done today is . . .' He repeated the explanation rather more slowly and tried not to think about the imminent arrival of Mr Gorman.

'And I don't need my gall bladder?' asked Mrs Dimoglou, tentatively.

'No.'

'Why not?'

'Because the gall bladder's just a storage organ for bile, which helps you digest food – it's just a bag, really.' Her expression remained doubtful. 'Like a handbag,' he added, inspired by the one on Mrs Dimoglou's lap. 'Which is why it can be cut out, you see. Because although it's useful, it's not essential.'

'No, it is essential,' she corrected, stroking the bag protectively. 'If someone cut out my handbag, I never find another as good.'

'But what I meant was, you don't really need it, do you?'

'Yes I do.'

'No, I mean, what you need are the things that are in it, not the bag itself.'

'I need this bag,' she said, with a tiny edge of steel in her voice.

'Yes, but what I meant –' Paul could see one end of the notes trolley nosing out of the office '– what I meant was that if, say, you needed your wallet in a shop –'

'Purse, I have a purse.'

'– OK. If you needed your purse in a shop, it wouldn't make any difference if you had a handbag or not, because you could take your wallet –'

'Purse.'

'– I mean purse – you could take your purse into town whether you had a handbag or whether you *didn't* have a handbag. It wouldn't make any difference.'

She took a moment to absorb this. 'What about my house keys?'

'It's the same thing. Look, if you think of your gall bladder as the handbag, and your purse – or your keys – as the bile, and the . . . the . . .' He stopped; the whole simile, he realized, was sliding inexorably out of control. What, for instance, could possibly represent Mrs Dimoglou's liver? Her house? Her sideboard? Her purse manufacturer? She was still looking at him, mouth puckered with faint puzzlement. 'Let's start again,' he said. 'What you're having is an elective cholecystectomy. "Elective" means it's not an emergency, so it can be done at a convenient time rather than –'

'A convenient time?' She looked suddenly hopeful.

'Yes. But –'

'Because today was not really convenient for me, I want to be at home to make the honey cake but they phone me yesterday to say someone else can't come in for an operation and can I come instead.'

'Well, by "convenient" what I really meant was –'

'Ready, Dr Gooding?'

Mr Gorman, Crispin, Armand and a cluster of medical students were standing at the end of the row of beds, Mr Gorman wearing an expression of dangerous politeness. 'Nearly,' said Paul, realizing immediately that this was not an answer that would win him many points.

'Nearly,' repeated the consultant, as if the word were unfamiliar to him. 'Well, perhaps in future we can all remember that the ward round commences at *precisely* nine a.m. rather than *nearly* five minutes later. And perhaps,' he continued, apparently gratified by the chorus of student titters, 'you'd care to join us when you've *absolutely* finished?'

'Yes,' said Paul, stolidly.

'He's very, very good,' said Mrs Dimoglou, patting Paul's

hand as the group started to move away. 'He's explaining things to me. About my handbag.'

He's explaining things to me about my handbag. Paul watched Mr Gorman lead his little audience up the ward, and knew that each of them would have marked, learned and inwardly digested that particular phrase, and that it would be resurrected on every possible occasion for the rest of his time at Shadley Oak unless the memory of it was superseded by something even more embarrassing. He sighed.

'You go,' said Mrs Dimoglou, giving his hand another pat. 'Don't be late.'

'But I need to finish talking to you.'

'You go. Look, I write my name down now –' she carefully appended her signature to the consent form ' – and then when it's convenient it's all ready. Isn't it?'

'Yes,' he said uncertainly.

'So, go then.'

The others had already gathered round a bed at the end of the ward. 'Ah, a belated welcome to our fashion advisor,' said Mr Gorman as Paul eased into the back row, 'we were just discussing the differential diagnosis of right iliac fossa pain in a young woman. Would you care to name five potential causes that might result, rightly or wrongly, in surgical intervention?'

'Er . . .' Paul looked at the occupant of the bed, a comatose teenager on an antibiotic drip. 'Appendicitis, mesenteric adenitis, endometriosis, ruptured ovarian cyst, ectopic pregnancy.' The teenager's eyes opened very suddenly. 'Which this isn't,' added Paul, hopefully.

Mr Gorman looked faintly disappointed. 'All right,' he said and Paul wanted to punch the air and roar with victory; all that revision had paid off after all. He waited, with something approaching confidence, for the next question.

'So could you also tell me,' said Mr Gorman, meditatively,

'could you also tell me . . . what *that* is?' He pointed suddenly towards the window, and Paul turned and gazed in the direction of the finger and saw nothing remotely medical, only sky and a church spire.

'What?' he asked, stupidly.

'No,' said Mr Gorman, 'I'm afraid that's not quite the answer I was looking for. Dr Roux? Do you know?'

Armand looked at the view and then back at Mr Gorman, his mouth slightly open.

'Dr Finnerty?'

'It's the spire of Shadley Oak Abbey, the finest example of English perpendicular architecture in the West Midlands,' said Crispin, warmly, 'begun in the 1380s but not finished until 1465.'

Mr Gorman nodded. 'Extensively damaged in the Civil War, of course, the dates of which were . . . ?' He looked at Armand and Paul again and absorbed the silence for a moment. 'Well, I'm sure you'll know next time,' he said, genially.

'I'm Canadian,' said Armand as they followed the notes trolley towards the ward office at the end of the round. 'I . . . I simply can't be expected to know these things.' He looked shocked, as if some international law had been violated.

'I had a teacher like him once,' said Paul. 'He was called Mr Lever and he always had to find something you couldn't answer, in fact one day he asked a question about –'

'Have you two decided who's on call?' Crispin was waiting for them in the door of the office. He was different this morning; not just sober but somehow detached. It was as if he'd taken a pace back or grown a couple of inches in the night, so that the angle of his gaze had changed subtly; he no longer felt like a contemporary, and the effect was dislocating.

'I'm taking the bleep,' said Paul. 'We tossed for it yesterday.

47

I've told switchboard.' His pulse had danced a little samba when the coin landed tails up.

'In that case you'd better get on with your routine admissions before the GPs start bleating on the phone.' He held up a sheaf of folders. 'Three hernias each and a couple of circumcisions. Take your prick.'

'Listen Crispin,' said Paul, accepting a random handful, 'I think I might accidentally have confused Mrs Dimog–' There was a sudden burst of electronic pips from Paul's chest pocket and he clutched it self-consciously.

'There she blows,' said Crispin. 'Typical Monday. Phone zero and give your bleep number and remember we're *acute* surgical. No time wasters. That means virtually any admission from the Ferris Road surgery.'

'Right, I –'

'And always check we've got a bed before you start sending out invites.'

'OK, so –'

'And do up your coat, you look like a butcher's assistant. Though that's what you are, I suppose. Ha.' The pips began again. 'You'd better answer it, hadn't you?'

Fumbling with a coat button, Paul moved towards the office and as he did so the noise stopped momentarily, and then resumed as a deafening, continuous warble, like a pelican crossing at volume eleven. He spun around. 'Does that mean a cardiac –'

Crispin shushed him violently; under the noise a disembodied voice said something with the word 'arrest' and the word 'unit' in it.

'Go,' said Crispin. 'I'll deal with the GP.'

Paul ran a few paces up the corridor, and then turned and ran back again. 'Where did it say?'

'The Pickering Unit.'

'Where's that?'

'Downstairs, out the back, next to Obstetrics, get going, *get going.*'

Two visitors pressed themselves against the wall of the corridor as Paul tore past, and he caught their look of alarm; all over the hospital, he realized, the scene was being repeated as on-call staff hurled themselves towards the Pickering Unit and he felt a rush of exhilaration, an awareness that he was living the cliché of the TV doctor, sprinting to save a life. For a moment he wished his mum could see him.

Spurning the bank of lifts he pushed straight through the swing doors to the stairwell and galloped down the four flights, biros rattling in his pockets. He could feel his shirt pulling free from his trousers and he hastily retucked it before bursting into the foyer. The seating area was half empty, but a long queue wound from the reception desk, and a row of heads watched as he jogged past, scanning for the rear entrance. There didn't seem to be one, specifically, but he spotted a fire exit, and wrenched it open and emerged into a dank passage between two prefabs that led in turn to a yard full of giant bins; he squeezed between two of them, skirted a hillock of green plastic bags, tore past the back of the mortuary and found himself, unexpectedly, at the edge of the staff car park, only yards from his own Peugeot. He looked around, disorientated; there appeared to be no logic to the layout of the hospital – the components were scattered as if someone had upended a bucket of buildings and cemented them where they fell. The Pickering Unit might be the nearby high-tech structure with the glass porch, but then again it might be that distant thing that looked like a Nissen hut or even the yellow plastic igloo with the laundry lorry outside.

In any case it seemed imperative to keep running and he maintained a sort of sideways canter as he looked around for help. A bosomy woman in jeans was walking up the internal road towards him and he shouted a query.

'It's my first day,' she said. 'Sorry. Why don't you –'

'It's OK, I've just seen something . . .' and he was already past her, accelerating towards the green sign revealed by the departure of the laundry lorry, straining as he did so to spot the vital three words. He picked them out while still yards away and executed a teetering ninety-degree turn in order to follow the new direction of the arrow; the Nissen hut, the Pickering Unit had to be the Nissen hut. He stretched his stride and swallowed a mouthful of vile-tasting saliva. It was a long time since he'd run this far and this fast and from all over his body little protests were being raised – random twangs in his muscles, sudden sharp pains in his joints, an uneasy slopping of his viscera.

He was within ten yards of the entrance when the door of the Pickering Unit opened and a doctor came out, immediately followed by another. Paul flailed to a halt just in front of them.

'Crash call?' he managed to ask, and then had to lean forward with his hands on his knees.

'Balls-up,' said one of them, a gingery girl with glasses. 'A man with dementia who was supposed to be Do Not Resuscitate but no one looked at his notes till we'd been pounding away at his chest for five minutes, and he died anyway. All a bit depressing, really.'

'Did you get lost?' asked the other, brightly. She was a small Chinese woman with a coat that came almost to her ankles. He nodded and she broke into delighted giggles. 'He got lost!'

'So are you all right?' asked the ginger girl.

Paul nodded again, tried to smile and made do with an insouciant wave.

'See you later then.' They ambled away across a stretch of grass, back towards the Eddery Building, and Paul dropped his head and got on with some serious breathing. What was beginning to worry him even more than his general level of fitness was the growing awareness that yesterday's hamburger was hanging around, still very much . . . *undigested*.

After a while he straightened up and began to follow his colleagues across the balding lawn, maintaining a careful, even, elderly pace. Twenty yards ahead the two other doctors entered the Eddery Building, and as they did so Paul's bleep sounded again with the imperious trill that signalled yet another cardiac arrest, and a tinny voice summoned him to Ward 2, his own ward. Running was now impossible, but he began to glide a little faster, like someone doing an impression of a cross-country skier. He swung onto the path, overtook a man on crutches and pushed aside the flabby polythene doors to the foyer, and it was then, as he inhaled the mingled aroma of Jeyes fluid and boiled vegetables, that his stomach gave a rolling heave and a wave of nausea reared up his throat and lapped at the base of his tongue. He halted just beside the queue for reception and stood very, very still. He could feel a rime of sweat on his forehead and his face tautened with concentration, as if sheer will could hold back the tide. People in the queue began to look at him. He stared hard at a spot on the far wall.

'Are you ill, love?' asked a woman, placing a gentle hand on his arm.

'No,' he said, through stiffened lips. 'Just need a . . .' He tried to look around, and found the movement challenging. 'Is there a toilet near here?'

'He wants a toilet,' said someone in the queue.

'There's one by the shop.'

'It's just on the other side of the desk, by the seats.'

'Shall I show you?' asked the woman.

'No I . . .' Before she could actually take his hand and lead him there he started walking very slowly, keeping his torso as level as possible, moving his legs only from the knee downwards.

'Wrong way,' said someone. 'It's more to your left.'

He shifted direction gradually, like a dinghy heeling to the wind.

'Left,' called someone, with some urgency. 'More to your left.' Paul raised his eyes from the point on the floor on which they'd been fixed and saw that he was heading for the ladies. He adjusted his angle of approach.

'That's the way.'

'He's got it now.'

'In you go.'

As the door swung to, he just caught a little burst of applause.

He wasn't actually sick but it was fifteen minutes before the nausea subsided – fifteen minutes of sitting in a locked cubicle with his eyes closed and his head resting on the soft cushion of the toilet roll while in his pocket the bleep chirruped monotonously and in his mind the scene on Ward 2 played to its tragic conclusion. ('Damn. She's gone. We could have saved her with just one more pair of hands.') Though there were always too many doctors at an arrest, he reminded himself, too many thrill-seekers, getting in the nurses' way and clashing hips round the bed. He dried his forehead with a piece of toilet paper, checked his pulse and when the bleep called him for the tenth time he was ready; he rose gingerly and, relieved to feel no more than fragile, left the cubicle.

He tried to be diffident in his jumping of the reception queue; he apologized and said 'excuse me' and held out the bleep like a talisman, but the old man at the front with the bizarrely trendy flat-top haircut and a face like a clenched fist was having none of it. He half rose from his wheelchair and spread his arms along the desk, claiming the entire expanse.

'I've been waiting ten minutes. *Ten minutes.*' His voice was a half-vocalized roar, as if there was still plenty of volume held in reserve.

'I just need to use the phone,' said Paul.

'*No*, no, you'll just have to get in line.'

'Dad . . .' said the man behind him, wearily.

The receptionist, a small, pale youth, wordlessly passed the phone to Paul.

'Oh, that's right,' said Fistface, 'let him jump the queue – I'll just lie down here and die on the floor.'

'Dad, he's a *doctor* . . .'

'Hello?' said Paul when switchboard answered. 'Dr Gooding.'

'Oh there you are,' said an irritated voice. 'I thought you'd run away. Let's see . . .' There was a rustle of paper. 'The first time I bleeped you was to say that the arrest call on Ward 2 was a false alarm. The next three times were admissions, which I ended up telling that French doctor about, and the last five were Ward 2 wanting to know where the bloody hell you are. So call them on 6868 and tell them where the bloody hell you are.'

Paul dialled. It was engaged.

'Of course, I'm here against my will,' said the old man, leaning further across the desk. 'The GP's arranged these tests behind my back.'

'I'm just reading your letter, Mr Riceman,' said the receptionist in a monotone.

'You needn't, because I can tell you what's in it – he says he doesn't like my blood pressure.'

'Dad, just let him read the letter.'

'My GP thinks I shouldn't be working fifty-five-hour weeks.'

'Dad . . .'

'And my son thinks so too but then he would, wouldn't he?'

'Dad, for God's . . .'

Paul redialled with the same result; it would be quicker, he realized, just to return to the ward.

'And if either of them thinks I'm going to stay in when I've got an entire central-heating system to install by a week Monday, then . . .'

The doors on the lift were just closing as Paul approached, and he hurried forward and hit the button. For five seconds or so nothing happened, and then with a clunk they reopened, revealing a row of irritated faces. 'Sorry,' he said, easing his way between the passengers. He pressed 'Floor 4', the only number not already illuminated, and a series of sighs rustled round the interior. Another long pause ensued. Paul stared at the wall and listened to the buzz of voices drifting round the corner from reception; as the doors at last began to close one voice, louder than the rest, became detached from the background rumble.

'I'm not staying in. I've got a sink to collect. Two sinks, and one of them's a reconditioned –'

Paul just caught a glimpse of the wheelchair before the doors slid together. He saw the whole of it five seconds later when they reopened. There was a collective groan, and then a shuffling rearrangement to allow room for the chair.

'Sorry . . . sorry,' said the son, blushing miserably as he adjusted the brakes. He was middle-aged, shoulders drooping like a bent coat hanger. Mr Riceman looked around irritably.

'Why aren't we moving? "Floor 2", someone press "Floor 2".'

Paul looked at his watch and wondered if he could have

made it up the stairs by now. The doors closed for the third time, and with a little preliminary shudder the lift suddenly descended. There was a chorus of 'oh for Christ's sake' and Paul placed a hand on his stomach; the unexpected direction had been bad for it.

'We're going *down*,' said Mr Riceman, outraged. 'Why are we going down? What's down here?'

His last question was answered when the doors opened onto a dim and empty corridor, heavy with heat, ringing with the unmistakable din of the kitchens; as the occupants shifted impatiently a little electric car trundled by, driven by a man wearing a white hairnet and towing a train of metal trolleys, each stacked with plates. Accompanying the train was a warm blanket of air, laden with breakfast smells: bacon fat and kippers and tinned tomatoes and fried bread and scrambled eggs and kippers and baked beans and overcooked sausages and kippers. It drifted into the lift and curled chummily around the occupants, and as the doors closed Paul's stomach finally and irrevocably rebelled.

It was Mr Riceman who, when the doors opened at ground level, headed the stampede into the foyer, fleeing for the exit while his son, still pushing the chair, pleaded behind him.

'Dad, come back –'

'No.' There was a certain triumph in his tone.

'Dad, the GP said that your blood pressure was –'

'NO!' The roar, at full volume, snapped all heads towards him. 'I DID NOT COME HERE TO BE VOMITED ON BY A DOCTOR.' Paul, cringing in the horrible interior, pressed the 'Call' button and wished for instant death.

Back in the quiet flat he dozed for an hour or so, and then lay staring at the rectangle of clear blue sky visible between the half-open curtains. He felt limp, toneless, as if someone had scooped out his intestines and filled the cavity with damp kapok. He couldn't imagine any circumstance in which he would ever want to eat again.

'I shall not prescribe you anything,' Mr Gorman had said after being summoned to the scene, 'because that would be shutting the stable door after the horse has caused extensive decorative damage to the entire area. Dr Roux?'

'Yes, Mr Gorman?'

'Which famous pop record of the 1960s does Paul's face currently remind us of?'

'Excuse me? I –'

'Dr Finnerty?'

'"A Whiter Shade of Pale".'

'Very good, Dr Finnerty. And now, Paul, just before you go away and lie down, perhaps you could explain precisely what it was that you said to the elective cholecystectomy patient that caused her to get dressed, inform reception that she would return on a more convenient date and leave the hospital, thus missing her operation . . .'

A tiny plane dawdled across the cloudless blue, followed by a herring gull, followed, after a minute or two, by a cormorant. Paul had heard that, geographically, Shadley Oak was at the dead centre of England, equidistant from both the Bristol Channel and the North Sea, but it seemed that no one had told the birds and a second cormorant trailed the first. Sticks with wings, thought Paul; a photo taken of a cormorant in midflight barely gave a clue as to which direction it was travelling in – only on closer examination could you spot the slightly greater thickness at the head end. This was the type of information he had learned to keep to himself. No one was interested in birds – he wasn't so very interested in them himself any longer, but a country upbringing of supreme and solitary dullness had left him with a bedrock of ornithological wisdom. He knew about birds the way he knew about types of biscuit or the cast of *Neighbours*: he didn't have to delve for the knowledge, it was just *there*. Nothing since had stuck as firmly.

The only noise in the bedroom was the tick of the alarm clock, and he rolled his head and looked at the dial. Half past eleven; the ward round would long be over and Armand would be clerking the routine admissions by now, struggling to finish them single-handed before the emergencies started coming in.

In daydreams Paul had pictured a different sort of first day ('Well done, Dr Gooding, I've never heard of a house officer correctly diagnosing a phaeochromocytoma before.') but he was not really surprised by the outcome; nothing in his entire life had ever turned out the way he'd imagined – some stumbling carelessness or other had meant that he'd always missed the obvious path from A to B and ended up wading through an unmapped swamp. Maybe, he thought drearily, if he tried to confine his imagination to the mundane and the competent ('Well done, Dr Gooding, you've managed to take a blood sample without fatally injuring the patient.'), he might hit the mark a little more often.

He closed his eyes again, and when he awoke it was nearly two o'clock. He glanced at the window and saw a swan, startlingly near; it crossed the gap in two giant wing beats and seemed to leave the sky thrumming in its wake. Mute swans were the heaviest flighted birds in the world. In the *world*. As a ten-year-old that fact had delighted him, and even now it brought him a tiny tweak of pleasure. He stretched, and his body felt almost normal, intestines restored to their usual position; he might just possibly be able to manage a cup of tea, and maybe some toast. If there were any tea in the flat. Or milk. Or bread.

*

Armand's sugar-free pop tarts came in three flavours: cherry, apricot and toffee, and Paul chose the latter. He could buy another packet this afternoon, he thought, and substitute it without Armand ever knowing. And while he was out shopping he could happen to drive past the newspaper office. And when he got back, if he still felt well, he could return to the ward and humbly offer his services; there was time yet for redemption. He ate the whole of the pop tart in three bites, burning his lip in the process, and then started to wonder whether a simple glass of boiled water, sipped slowly, mightn't have been a better idea.

5

'When something's funny I go, "Ha Ha Ha,"' said the small boy, leaning against Netta's desk. 'Don't I, Mummy, I go, "Ha Ha Ha." This is what I go like –' He tipped his head back and reduced his eyes to tiny slits, 'I go, "Ha Ha Ha Ha HAAAAAAAAA."'

'James,' said his mother, her voice brittle with forced gaiety, 'Mrs Lee and I have really got to have a proper chat, because she's going to be doing my job for a while, so would you like to do some drawing? I brought your colouring book and some . . . some –' she groped about in the bottom of her bag '– some of those lovely felt-tips you got from –' She lifted out a brown eyebrow pencil and looked at it for a long moment. 'Oh God,' she said, in sudden self-disgust, 'I didn't even bring the pens. I didn't bring the pens, I didn't bring the *diary*, I forgot the *appointments* book, I . . . I . . . and there's yoghurt all over my sleeve, look, I've just noticed that. Look!' She held out her cuff towards Netta and pointed a shaking finger at the strawberry blotch. 'How did I miss that? How could anyone miss that? You must look at me and think: "She's useless. That woman sitting over there with yoghurt all over her shirt is a completely useless human being."'

'No, no –' began Netta, wondering how to nudge the conversation forward; it had been stuck on self-flagellation for several minutes now, and her own interjections were sounding less and less believable.

'"HA HA HA." I go like this, look, Mummy, I go –' James lowered himself onto the carpet, placed his hands on his stomach and rolled carefully from side to side. 'I go like this,' he said, his voice slightly muffled. 'When it's funny I roll around, look, Mummy, I roll around. Look, Mummy, *look.*'

There was a bleating noise from the buggy in the corner of the room and Jenny threw Netta a look of wintry despair. 'I am so very, very sorry,' she said throatily, as if to a bereaved relative.

'Look! Look! Look at me!' shouted James, hammering his feet against the leg of the desk.

Netta took the hole punch from her drawer, inserted a few pages of A4 between its jaws and pressed down very hard. There was a satisfying crunch.

'What's that noise?' asked James, springing to his feet.

'Oh, it's my special hole-maker,' said Netta, casually. She moved the pages slightly and made another set of perforations. 'I need a lot of holes made in this paper. It's a very important job.'

'I'll do it.'

'It's quite difficult.'

'Let me. Let me do it.'

'Brilliant,' muttered Jenny, shoving the buggy back and forth with a vigour that seemed to shock the baby into silence.

'You'll need to concentrate very hard,' said Netta, 'because you can't talk *and* make holes.' She snapped the pages together with a bulldog clip and handed them over the side of the desk. 'I think you should do it on the floor over there. No, even further away, right in the corner where it's extra flat. That's perfect.'

'I'd actually made arrangements,' said Jenny. 'Looking at me I know you'll find it hard to believe but I actually had it all organized. He was supposed to be at nursery, but it's been closed because one of the children there's got spots and then

I couldn't get anyone to . . . Oh God, I'm being boring, I can hear myself being boring . . .'

'No, no . . .'

'I'm boring, I know I'm boring, my children are bored by me, I even bore myself. I am a boring, boring person who has no conversation and looks like a bag person, and I'm going to tell you something that will completely amaze you, Netta: I used to be popular. I did! I had more boyfriends at college than anyone else and there was one term when I went out *every single night.*' Experimentally, she stopped rocking the buggy. There was silence apart from James's stertorous breathing as he leaned over the hole punch. 'Where were we?' she asked.

'Tuesday morning,' said Netta, pen poised.

'Tuesday morning, so –' she drummed her fingers against her upper lip '– at ten, no, wait a moment, no, they changed it, er . . . at ten-thirty, I think, or . . . no, that's right, they changed it back, so . . . at *ten*, there's the nutritional-support round on Ward 2. That's the general surgical ward. It's on the fourth floor of the Eddery Building – do you know it? It's that hideous block by the car park.'

'Oh, I know the Eddery Building,' said Netta.

'And there's something else on Tuesday, there's a menu discussion with the – no, hang on, that's Wednesday, no . . . no, hang on, I think it's . . .' She screwed up her eyes. 'You know, I can *see* the diary, I can actually visualize it, it's on top of the washing machine. I knew when I left the house that I'd forgotten something, I knew it, but then Becky started crying and of course like the fool that I am . . .'

'It's broken,' shouted James, holding up the bulldog clip that had become detached from the paper.

'Oh dear, let Mummy –'

'It's OK, Jenny. Just squeeze it like this,' said Netta, miming to James. 'It's like a crocodile opening its mouth and then you put the paper in. You have to be very, very strong and clever to do it. Try using both hands.'

'I can do it.' He crouched over the paper again.

'You are *fantastic*,' said Jenny. 'Do you have children? Please tell me you have children, because I can't bear it if you're this good with them and you haven't even . . .'

'Four girls.'

'*Four?*'

'They're stepdaughters. My husband was a widower.'

'So how old were they when you . . . took over?'

'Eleven, eight, five and two.'

'Oh my God. God.' Jenny put a hand to her mouth and goggled at her. 'God. How on earth did you manage?'

'I –' Netta paused to try to frame a reply; she sometimes wondered the same thing herself. It had often been hellish, the oldest girls unremittingly hostile, the youngest desperately competing for her exclusive attention, but there had been something exhilarating about being needed so much. 'I'm not –'

There was a loud metallic snap from the corner of the office and a scream so sudden and piercing that Netta's heart seemed to curl in her chest and then she and Jenny were on their feet and James had turned towards them with his face crimson and his hands waving a horrified semaphore and the bulldog clip dangling from his upper lip like a monstrous moustache. 'Let Mummy, let Mummy –' said Jenny, rocketing across the carpet with arms outstretched, but the screaming rose in pitch as she reached for the clip and he slapped her away, twisting under her grasp and diving for the door. It was half closed and he missed the gap and smacked his forehead against the handle. The door slammed shut and James sat down abruptly and lifted a hand to the blue egg already expanding on his temple.

His eyes met Netta's and his mouth opened and a vast accusatory roar of pain and outrage filled the air.

There was a good turnout to watch James being carried along the corridor by his mother; heads popped out of every office, and once the outer door had closed on the one-child Wall of Sound they swung round to look at Netta. She was, she realized, still standing with her hands clasped in front of her in an unconscious tableau of contrition. 'Is he all right?' asked a girl, and Netta said, 'I hope so, she's just going to get him checked out in Casualty,' and then, from the room behind her, came a tiny whimper that turned into a wavering cry.

Mrs Bossy strikes again, thought Netta, unclipping the buckles on the buggy with fingers that were still clumsy with shock. She'd simply been unable to resist showing hopeless Jenny how to manage her own child ('Pray silence for the world expert on everything,' as Kelly was wont to announce if Netta ever tried to give her advice), and now nemesis had neatly landed her with a baby, the one age group about which she knew nothing. She teased the straps out from under Becky's padded bottom. 'There we go,' she said, in the chirpy voice that babies seemed to require. Becky stared back at her, mouth half open, expression confused; after a moment she gave another, cautious wail.

'Do you want to come out?'

Children who answered back, loudly and often, that was Netta's forte. Becky continued to stare.

'Come on then.' She hefted the little bundle with its weighty head and settled her in the crook of her arm. 'What shall we have a look at? Shall we look out of the window?' There was nothing to see but a row of colossal bins, and even Becky seemed to find them dull. She flexed impatiently against Netta's shoulder.

'All right, let's find something else.' They checked out a print of *The Haywain*, and another of two little girls chasing butterflies, and then, as Becky began a half-hearted grizzle, moved across to the window in the corridor. 'That block over there,' said Netta, cautiously jiggling, keen not to injure another of Jenny's children, 'is the Eddery Building. My dad built that.' She eyed it appraisingly. It was, she had long realized, sensationally ugly, a real sixties stump, tuberous with textured concrete – winner, in fact, of the Ugliest Structure in the West Midlands Award run by the *Birmingham Evening Post* a few years back; but it was also the biggest commission her father's firm had ever received, and he had been so proud of the result that he had kept a photo of it in his wallet, to be cooed over by fellow builders.

'You see that blue frieze around the second storey?' asked Netta, lifting Becky a little higher and angling her in the right direction. 'It's made of premoulded polythene and I chose the colour. I was only eight. My dad showed me four different shades and I picked the one called "cerulean" and that's the colour they went with. It made me feel terribly important. What do you think of it?' Becky arched her back and mouthed briefly at a passing fist before beginning to cry in earnest. 'All right,' said Netta, 'I get it. Message understood.'

There was a feeding bottle in the cloth bag that Jenny had left on the desk, and Netta settled the baby on her lap and watched the frantic suction of the first few mouthfuls, and felt the gradual soft slump of infant contentment against her arm. Becky's gaze began to rove dreamily, and she curled a hand around one of Netta's fingers and started to beat a sleepy rhythm with a foot. The skin of her hand was so fine that there was no friction from her touch; Netta rubbed a thumb across the knuckles and it was like stroking air.

*

The knock on the door was perfunctory and the man was halfway to the desk by the time she'd looked up. 'It's Mrs Lee, isn't it?' he said, extending a hand. 'Craig Gebbard, hotel services manager. Oh, you can't shake hands,' he added, spotting Netta's grip on the bottle. 'Lovely baby.'

Craig Gebbard. Netta felt as if the building had just dropped half a foot, throwing her chair askew, jolting her angle of vision. *Craig Gebbard*. She'd last seen him nearly a quarter of a century before but the wide white face was the same, and the thick-lidded eyes and the wiry hair and the slightly dispro-portionate build – long legs, short body – that had always made his waistband appear too high. And the gust of anger that swept through her at the sight of him was the same as well. He seemed, she realized, to be waiting for something; Netta retrieved his last remark and unglued her lips.

'Yes, she is lovely, isn't she? She's not mine.'

'She's Jenny Haddon's?'

'That's right. I'm Jenny's locum.'

'For her extended maternity leave?'

'Yes. That's right.'

He nodded, briskly, small talk out of the way. 'Now, have you got a moment?'

'Er . . . yes, I suppose so.'

'Mind if I . . . ?'

Netta shook her head and watched him arrange a folder on the desk and carefully hitch up the knees of his trousers before sitting; Craig Gebbard, classroom wag, who'd thought it so hilarious to imitate Glenn's walk, to deride his speech, to steal his sandwiches, Craig 'Plateface' Gebbard, whose snickering adolescent wit had shaped Glenn's time at school and, in-directly, her own. She had, long ago, in the margins of note-books, imagined a variety of post-educational encounters with this man, but they had involved pieces of wood with nails in and paid heavies threatening to do him and his family over. They had featured him breaking rocks in a quarry or labouring as chief turd-sweeper at Cruft's, not sitting opposite her in a moderately expensive suit and a silk tie.

'Now,' he said formally, opening the folder to an annotated list of names and taking a pen from his pocket, 'I'm here to apologize on behalf of the hospital for any inconvenience or . . . staining . . . you may have suffered in the lift this morning.'

'Oh, right. That.' She wrenched her mind back to the opening incident of the day, the quick trip to Personnel that had turned into such a prolonged and messy saga. 'I was lucky really,' she said. 'I was right at the back. How is he, that doctor?'

'Better I think. We will, of course, cover any dry-cleaning bills incurred –'

'No, he only got my shoes. I just had to wipe them off.'

'– and I've been instructed to offer you compensatory vouchers for redemption in the hospital shop to the value of twelve pounds.'

'I really don't need anything.'

'Are you sure?' She nodded, and he made a note and offered her a brief, professional smile; he'd had his teeth whitened, she noticed. 'Thank you for being so understanding. If you have any enquiries –' he took out a card and placed it on the desk '– just phone me.' He started to get up.

'Craig,' she said, and there must have been an odd intensity to her voice because he sat down again.

'Yes, Mrs Lee?'

She paused, unsure of what to say. There was no hint of recognition in his eyes; if she wanted to cross-examine him on his past behaviour, then she'd have to first of all explain who she was and then remind him of a few choice memories. And in any case how, precisely, was she intending to punish this colourless, unobjectionable adult for his past crimes? Report him to teacher? Chuck his briefcase in the moat? Pin him against the wall and give him a wedgie? He was still waiting for her to speak.

'We went to the same school,' she said flatly. 'Legg Hill Comprehensive.'

'Did we?' He pulled a face. 'God – to be honest, I hated school. I try not to think about it. It seems about a thousand years ago, doesn't it? Anyway –' he pointed at the card, clearly keen to change the subject '– accommodation, catering, cleaning services. Anything else I can help you with, just let me know.'

'Yes. Thank you.' Feeling somehow cheated, she watched him gather up his folder and escape unscathed, and she must have shifted or tensed because Becky, who had been drowsing with the teat in her mouth, awoke with a start and began to cry; she was still crying five minutes later when Jenny and James returned. James was sporting a Power Rangers plaster and an iced lolly stuffed with E-numbers. 'I hate you,' he said to Netta, as clearly as his swollen upper lip allowed.

'Oh now, James, you don't mean that,' said his mother, looking – perhaps – ever so slightly pleased, and winding Becky on her shoulder. 'And *there* it comes,' she said, announcing the burp.

'I do mean it,' said James. 'I hate that horrible lady.'

'I think the only thing I can do is take this very tired, cross little boy home and get my hands on that blessed diary and then –' the phone on the desk began to ring '– and then I'll call you,' she mouthed. 'Come on James.'

'I hate that horrible, smelly bum lady.'

'Well she still likes you, and she's very sorry about your lip,' called Netta as he disappeared round the door. She picked up the phone.

'I'd like to speak to Mrs . . .' There was a long pause. 'This is Constable Ryan Whittaker. From the Crime Desk, Shadley Oak Police Station.'

'Oh!' The room seemed suddenly to flood with colour and light. 'Have you found it?'

'Sorry?' There was a rattle of paper at the other end.

'My suitcase. Has it turned up?'

'Oh. No, it hasn't, I don't think. I could check. If you want.'

Some of the colour leached out again. 'You mean you're not phoning about the suitcase?'

'Er, no. No, I wasn't.'

'Right.' The room resumed its former utilitarian beigeness. 'So why are you phoning?'

'Oh. Well, you know you're a dietitian?'

'Yes,' she said patiently.

'You said about helping people put on weight?'

'Yes.'

'Well I've seen this . . . this thing in a magazine about putting on, er –' she heard another burst of page rattling '– muscle bulk, and it says about eating protein and meat and eggs and things. But I don't like meat, except chicken, and I saw this programme that said if you eat eggs you'll die of a heart attack. Is that true?'

'Um . . . not entirely.' Netta glanced at the half page of notes she'd taken from Jenny that morning. Her first official appointment – *Midday, bi-weekly menu discussion with catering manager, tall Asian man, surname begins with S, in his office next to the canteen OR it might have been changed to Meeting Room 3???* – was not for another half hour. 'OK, Ryan,' she said. 'Let's have a little chat about the definition of a balanced diet.'

As it turned out, the bi-weekly meeting with Raj Subramani was indeed in Meeting Room 3 but as it actually took place at eleven, rather than twelve, Netta arrived nearly an hour late. This nicely set the tone for the rest of her day, and as she trailed from one missed appointment to another, peering at inadequate signage, sliding into half-completed meetings, apologizing, always apologizing for her tardiness, her unreadiness, her jeans, she wanted to buttonhole each dissatisfied contact and sit them down and inform them in tremendous detail about her daily life in Glasgow, where tasks interleaved with oiled professionalism, where she was a byword for reliability, where she even *looked* efficient.

Back in the office, she did her best to organize herself for the rest of the week and then sat for a while looking out into the shadows of bin alley, tapping her pen on the desk in a pensive rhythm. All at once she felt a flush of homesickness so intense that her hand seemed to reach for the phone of its own accord. Mick answered, and she knew from the startled clarity of his 'hello' that she'd woken him; he always leapt into instant consciousness, the legacy of a million night calls.

'I've got to go,' he said, almost as soon as she'd spoken her name. On cue, she heard the frantic pips of the alarm clock and then their sudden cessation.

'Where are you off to?'

'Night shift. I was just getting some kip first.'

'You're not on nights till Thursday.'

'Swapped with Neville. His son's in a play.'

'You're such a soft touch.'

'That's me. How's it going?'

'Bloody awful. I hate it here, Mick, I want to come home.'

'Just say the word,' he said, deadpan. 'I'll bring the ladder engine and I'll ring the bell the whole way.'

She felt her face relax for what felt like the first time in hours. 'Did Kelly pack my clothes?'

'Yes, she did and she said to tell you . . . hang on, there's a note somewhere . . . hang on . . .' She smiled then, hearing the sounds of a search, imagining him wandering round the room in his boxers; for some reason he disapproved of getting into bed with his trousers on, even for a ten-minute catnap.

'Here, I've found it. "Tell Mum I've sent everything in her wardrobe but she's not to wear the green-and-yellow sundress to work because it makes her look pregnant." She's cheeky isn't she?' There was a pause. 'I like you in that dress,' he said.

'Do you? I bet it's because it reminds you of holidays. Oh, now – remember to check about the visa.'

'Oh yeah,' he said. 'Yeah, I'd forgotten that.'

'And the insurance.'

'Done that one. Ticked it off. And I've picked up my travellers' cheques *and* my dollars,' he added triumphantly. 'So how's your mother?'

'Driving me mad.'

He tutted in mild reproof. 'You know, Netta, she's a wonderful w–'

'– woman. Yes, thanks, Mick. I do need that little reminder every now and again.'

'Yes you do,' he said, with gravity. 'And how's Glenn?'

'Carrying out some enormous project about distances. I haven't quite fathomed it yet; he's bought an Ordnance Survey map and a measuring wheel and –' There was another burst of pips from the other end.

'That's me again,' said Mick, 'I've gotta go.'

'I'm going to go too. Have you eaten?'

'I'll have something at the station.'

'*Not* chips. Please, Mick.'

'You want me to eat some green stuff?'

'Go on. Just for me.'

'Well . . . tell you what, I might have a couple of peas. Maybe three.'

*

As she passed the Eddery Building on the way to the main gate Netta found herself pausing to check out the cerulean frieze. Time had not been kind. The edges of the polythene had bleached and crinkled, whole sections were beginning to curl away from the wall like half-planed wood shavings and the original rich colour had weathered to the shade of an old lady's blue rinse. She craned upwards; it was barely possible, any longer, to make out the expressions on the faces of the dancing daisies.

'So he was in the middle of a ileo-caecal resection, patient open on the table, when he had to take a leak,' said an immensely loud voice, approaching at speed from behind her, 'so he went off and had a slash, *completely* forgot what he was doing –' Netta staggered slightly as a shoulder clipped her own, and a phalanx of white coats swept past led by the speaker, a floridly handsome boy in his twenties, stethoscope draped round his neck like a scarf '– sorry – so anyway, *completely* forgot what he was doing, gave himself a shake, got dressed and drove home. When theatre finally tracked him down he was sitting in front of *Baywatch* with a double vodka.' There was a burst of sniggering from his acolytes; all looked freshly hatched, their short coats cracking with starch, their stethoscopes poking from their pockets like new toys. The speaker glanced back over his shoulder. 'Come *on* Pud,' he shouted at someone behind Netta. She looked round.

Coming across the car park, and looking less pallid than when she'd last seen him although almost as preoccupied, was the doctor who'd been sick in the lift. He was a large young man with a round-shouldered gait and short, stiff brown hair, and he was searching his pockets for something, patting and rootling in an unfocused way – he looked, Netta thought, rather like a domesticated bear who'd lost his door key. He came to a halt a few yards from her and spent another few seconds carrying out a final and obviously pointless check before looking up at his summoner. 'I've left my notebook somewhere,' he called, his voice hoarse and rather earnest. 'I better go back. I'll catch you up.'

Whatever the florid boy replied was inaudible to all but his followers, but there was a burst of derisive laughter before they headed for the foyer and Netta looked back at the bear-doctor to gauge his reaction; he appeared not to have noticed and was absently patting his pockets again, his eyes scanning some mental map of where he might have dropped or mis-placed or accidentally eaten or inadvertently shredded his notebook. She wanted to tap him on the shoulder and say, 'Look, just buy a new one.' She wanted to take the leaky biro out of his breast pocket and pull the loose thread from the bottom of his coat and adjust the tie that looked as if it had been knotted by a circus strongman. She wanted to run after that plum-faced, plum-voiced shouter and take him to one side and give him a stiff lecture on not subjecting colleagues to public humiliation. Instead she turned and walked away through the stream of incoming visitors, and tried to recall the menu for Monday nights at Monk's Way. Cheese straws, she thought. Cheese straws, turkey roll, Angel Delight.

6

'Red hot,' said Crispin, with relish, easing the inflamed appendix to the mouth of the wound. 'Red hot and ready to pop. You ever seen one that hot before, Pud?'

'No,' said Paul. He had just swapped the retractor from his right hand to his left and was already contemplating swapping back again; the patient was an aerobics instructor with stomach muscles like sheet metal and Crispin had made the incision so small that it was taking all of Paul's arm strength to keep it open. He flexed his fingers.

'Don't move,' said Crispin, dramatically, clamping the base of the appendix and picking up a scalpel. 'One slip now and it's peritonitis city.' The theatre nurse rolled her eyes.

The tip of the appendix was an incandescent red and so swollen as to be almost spherical. As it rested on the oozing line of the incision, framed by a patch of sallow skin, Paul inexplicably found himself thinking about cakes. About iced cakes. About iced cakes of the sort that his mother made for bake sales, with raspberry filling and a large crimson glacé cherry on . . . revolted, he pushed the image aside and tried to concentrate on Crispin's demonstration of a purse-string suture. That was the trouble with being so tired: he couldn't control his thoughts, they wandered all over the place like a flock of sheep without a sheepdog, falling into gullies, floundering in streams, mistaking green crisp packets for patches of grass . . .

'Hey, Pud, the next one's yours,' said Crispin, snipping off the end of the catgut and using his gloved thumbs to push the bulging pink cushion of the caecum back into the cavity.

'Sorry, the next what?'

'Retractor out. The next on-call appendix, you pillock. You can do it and I'll assist.'

'Oh. Good.' Paul clanged the instrument onto a tray and tried to inject a little enthusiasm into his voice. 'Great.' It was extraordinary what surgeons seemed to regard as a treat at four o'clock on a Saturday morning.

'Or do you wanna close this one?' Crispin offered him the curved needle, his eyebrows interrogative above the mask.

'No, I think I'll just, er, wait for one of my own.' In his present state of consciousness he felt capable of sewing his glove and part of his gown into the wound.

'Okey dokey. So –' Crispin's needle nipped a pleat of muscle fibre '– what were we talking about, before?'

'Pud's party,' said the theatre nurse.

'Pud's *party*,' repeated Crispin, with enthusiasm.

'No,' said Paul, hurriedly, 'I just wanted to know –'

'– where to go for a birthday drink . . .'

'No, I said –'

'And we all know that the best place for a birthday drink is the Party Flat.'

'No, a meal. I just wanted to know where to take someone for a meal.'

'Le Chien Gris,' said the theatre nurse. 'It's just opened, it's very good. I went there with my boyfriend last week and we had duck.'

'Meal,' said Crispin, derisively, carefully aligning the cut edges of muscle. 'Wasted opportunity. We had a vicars-and-tarts party last year and by midnight the Pope was hanging out of the window by his ankles. It was *fantastic*. When's your birthday?'

'I just wanted to know about a good restaurant,' said Paul, doggedly. 'For a special occasion.'

'Parrdy for the birthday boy!' said Crispin, trimming the thread and looking admiringly at his handiwork. 'I bet I only need four skin clips. Practically keyhole.' A muffled chirping came from the scrub room. 'That your bleep, Pud?'

'Yes. You don't need me here any more, do you?'

'Nope, off you go and answer it. It's probably an admission.'

Struggling was pointless, thought Paul, peeling off his gloves and dusting the talc from his hands. Conversations with Crispin always took on their own momentum; it was like trying to steer an encounter with a door-to-door salesman – whatever topic you began with you always ended up buying three grand's worth of unwanted steam-cleaning equipment.

'What about a toga party?' Crispin was saying.

'A bit eighties,' said the nurse. 'What about heroes?'

'Heroes? *Yeah.*'

As he emerged into the long, cold corridor outside the operating suite Paul saw the porters before they saw him; one of them was wheeling a commode and they were deep in serious conversation. Seizing the moment he darted into the darkened anaesthetic room and watched through the crack in the door until they were safely past, and then he quietly re-entered the corridor and headed for the stairwell. Such manoeuvres had become necessary. On the day after the incident in the lift every single porter in the building had acquired a can of air freshener and Paul had progressed through the hospital in a fug of Norwegian Pine. Along the way he had been offered buckets labelled 'Aim Here', and packets of Kwells and fistfuls of Wet Wipes, and most of the time he had managed to grin. It had been less funny the next day, and by the day after that he had started taking evasive action.

It wasn't the constant iteration of the joke that he found hardest to cope with, it was the instant fame. Since his plunge from the roof of the medical school he had reassumed his natural place at the back of the crowd, half a step and a couple of beers behind everyone else. It was where he felt most comfortable, and it was unnerving to be regurgitated into the limelight, to possess both a name and a reputation when most of the other new doctors were interchangeable blurs. Unfairly, they were being allowed to inch quietly into their roles whereas Paul felt as if his every move was preceded by a couple of drummers and a bloke with a trumpet.

The one positive aspect of the whole bloody experience was that he was getting fitter. His avoidance of lifts (after all, there was no need to actually get down on his knees and *beg* for trouble) meant that he could now walk from the ground to the fifth floor without once having to lean against the wall and pant. The two flights from the operating suite to the admissions ward were a mere bagatelle and he was no more than slightly pink-cheeked as he pushed through the swing doors from the stairwell, banging someone on the shoulder as he did so.

'Oh, sorry.'

It was the gingery doctor he'd met on the first day, and she turned vaguely towards him as if waking from a trance. 'Do you know where the coronary care unit is?'

'Yes,' he said, with triumph; he had been working hard on the subject of hospital geography. 'First floor, turn left out of the stairwell and it's second on your right. It's between Pathology and the orthopaedic ward,' he added, in an unnecessary flourish.

'Only . . .' she looked at the long strip of paper she was

holding, 'I'm going there to check this with the nurses, but are you any good at ECGs? I'm almost certain it's within normal range. I'm almost certain the patient's just got indigestion and this is an incidental finding but frankly –' she gave a sudden, wild gesture '– with my record it's a risk I can't take.'

'Erm . . .' He scanned a section of the printout; the inky spikes seemed to be bounding across the page in their usual fashion. 'Looks all right, doesn't it?'

'But don't you think the p–q interval's a bit long? It could be Type One heart block.'

He looked again. 'No, I think it's all right.'

'Do you? Do you really?'

'Yes.' He nodded with rather more confidence than he felt. 'Yes. But maybe you better check it with the nurses.'

'That's what I thought, that's what I'm going to do. God,' she adjusted her glasses and tucked some stray hairs behind her ears, 'this isn't what I expected. Not in the *least*.'

'What isn't?'

She stared up at him, her left eye blurred by a smear on the lens. 'Being a house officer. I had this mad idea that I'd really get to know my patients, really be able to help them. Well, ha ha ha. Ha!' she added for good measure. 'They all keep dying on me. One on the first day, three on the first night, another tonight; they just seem to wait for me to arrive. I get out my stethoscope – they die. I say, "Hello, I'm Carrie, I'm your doctor" – they die. Sometimes I don't get as far as my name, sometimes I just open the curtains and they're dead already. My registrar calls me The Terminator.' She sucked in a deep breath. 'And I can't say anything to Wai because she just giggles the whole time. She says –' she tilted her head brightly to one side '– "Carrie, it's so *fun*!!" Do you think it's fun?' she asked, with sudden intensity.

'No,' said Paul. 'Fun's the wrong word.'

'And do your patients die?'

'No, they discharge themselves. They see me coming and they run away as fast as they can.'

'Really?'

'Well, almost. Two in an hour on the first day.'

'And what happened to them?'

'One of them's right back at the bottom of the waiting list for a cholecystectomy and I don't know about the other; emigrated, probably. Opened a plumbing firm in Tonga.' He shrugged, and then a bleep went off and they both dipped their heads towards their breast pockets in automatic obeisance. 'Me,' said Carrie. 'Me again, always me.' She forced a smile. 'I better go. So little time, so many patients to kill.' Paul watched as she pattered off towards the lift.

'*There* you are,' said a voice behind him. A few yards along the corridor a shaven-headed nurse was peering round the door of the admissions ward.

'Sorry,' said Paul, breaking into a trot. 'Has the patient arrived?'

'No, not yet.' The nurse took a moment to inspect him, a quick head-to-foot survey. 'No, we've just been desperate to meet you.' He extended a hand. 'Gwyn Parry.'

'Hello,' said Paul, awkwardly.

'Come on in, tea's on.' His voice dropped to a stage whisper as they entered the darkened ward. 'We never meet anyone on night shift, see, and you're a bit of a celeb in hospital terms, and we've been gagging for a chat. *Gagging.*' Slightly thrown, Paul followed him into the spill of light issuing from the open door of the office. 'Honestly, Dr Gooding, Lexie's having palpitations at the prospect.'

'Is she?' For a moment Paul thought confusedly of cardiac symptoms and lignocaine dosage and then he registered another person sitting in the corner, a small student nurse with chopped dark hair and blood-red lips and an expression of such intense interest, such open-mouthed expectancy, that he missed his stride and walked straight into a chair. The mouth opened further and emitted a loud cawing noise, and he realized that Lexie was laughing at him

'Sorry,' he muttered, sitting down hurriedly. 'I didn't mean to, um . . .'

'Can't blame you for looking,' said Gwyn, putting a hand on his arm, 'she's absolutely *gorgeous* isn't she, 100 per cent goddess if she grew her hair a bit and kept her mouth shut. Spoken for though, aren't you, Lexie?'

'I'm not, you twat,' said Lexie, in an unexpectedly deep voice. 'Not since Tuesday.'

'Oh, that's permanent, is it?' said Gwyn, with a quickening of interest. 'I thought that was just a tiff.'

'No.'

'So you'll not be seeing him again?'

'I'd rather shag a dog.'

'So, you're in with a chance there, Dr Gooding, and she goes for men who put a smile on her face. So to speak. Sugar?'

'No. Yes. Half a spoonful.'

'Ginger biscuit? Good for nausea, of course.' There was a machine-gun laugh from Lexie's corner.

'No thanks.' Paul tried to clear his head; repartee was clearly called for, but at this time in the morning he was capable of producing only rough-cut lumps of speech, truthful but dull. 'I'll have a Jaffa Cake.'

'Now,' said Gwyn expectantly, hands on knees. 'We've been working on a little list of pertinent questions, haven't we, Lexie, but first things first – it's Paul, isn't it?'

'Yes.'

'Or do you prefer Pud?'

'Paul.'

'Yes, much more dignified. And how old are you?'

'Twenty-three,' said Paul, reluctantly. 'Nearly twenty-four.'

'And where are you from?'

'Shropshire.'

'Halfway to Wales, better than nothing. Town? Country?'

'I grew up on a farm.'

'Oh, son of the soil. Hands rough but firm, shoulders broad with manly labour. Control yourself, Lexie. And what made you decide on a job in Shadley Oak? Because, let's be honest, it is a little bit of a –'

'Shithole.'

'Thank you, Lexie. Backwater, I was going to say. Paul?'

'Well, I . . .' He flogged his neurones, trying to come up with a plausible lie. 'I heard it was nice.' Oh well done, he thought, wanting to smack his forehead repeatedly against a hard surface. Plausibility factor zero.

A tiny frown briefly creased Gwyn's brow. 'So, have you seen anything of the town yet? Fed the swans? Been to the abbey teashop? Visited the cinema? Oh no, sorry, there isn't one.'

'No, tomorrow's my first day off. I mean today.' He checked his watch. Another four hours and he'd get his first chance to –

'And what's your star sign?'

'Er, Taurus, I think.'

'Yes, I can see that. I knew you'd be an earth sign. Reliable – deep but steady. And are you married? Oh no, no ring. So are you taken?'

Paul was beginning to feel punch-drunk. 'I'm not, no. No, I'm not. No.'

There was a pause.

'So I'll take that as a no then,' said Gwyn. 'Anyone in mind, though? Apart from Lexie, that is?'

'Fuck off, Gwyn,' said Lexie.

'Manners. Anyone hovering in the wings? So to speak?'

Unbidden, Marianne's image drifted through his mind and he felt his heart rate climb as quickly as if someone had turned a dial. 'Maybe,' he said, looking at his hands.

'Maybe!' repeated Gwyn, savouring the word. 'I like that, that's a little bit enigmatic. And what do you do for fun?'

'What do I . . . ?'

'*Lexie.*'

Above the braying, Paul heard the fabulously welcome noise of a trolley coming through a set of swing doors and he almost leaped to his feet, tipping his cup in the process and sending a puddle of cold tea across the desk.

'Sorry. I . . . sorry, I'll . . .'

'Lexie,' said Gwyn, snapping in an instant from prurience to efficiency, 'get a cloth for Dr Gooding and I'll go and sort out his patient. Give me two minutes, Paul, and then he's all yours.'

'Thanks.'

He was left for a moment with Lexie. She stared at him with unnerving directness, her beautiful mouth curved in an anticipatory smile, as if awaiting a punchline.

'I'll get the cloth,' he said, righting the cup and sprinting for the kitchen.

'Then there was –' Paul flicked back through his notebook '– Mr Ritchie, a twenty-eight-year-old who came in with an infected pilonidal cyst at five a.m. I explained the procedure to him and he said if anyone went near him with a needle, he'd get out of bed and go home so I had to get Crispin to come over and he told Mr Ritchie that if he wanted the boil on his arse to get into *The Guinness Book of Records*, then he was going the right way about it, and Mr Ritchie signed the consent form in about two seconds flat and went straight down to theatre . . .' he glanced up at Armand, who was sitting with his back to the office window; the morning sun had turned him into a gilded silhouette and it was hard to gauge his expression, but he seemed to be watching Paul rather than listening to him. 'And he's all right this morning, he's having his breakfast and he's just complained to me about the bacon, and I was bleeped about three minutes ago by Ward 4 who want a patient written up for anti-fungal mouthwash or something, and I said I was almost off shift and they said it could wait for you, if that's OK?' There was no response. 'And we've only got two emergency beds left unless Gorman discharges someone this morning, and Crispin's gone to bed and said if anyone wakes him before midday he'll cut their balls off.' He clapped the notebook shut and yawned hugely. The short nap that he'd managed between six and seven seemed, paradoxically, to have made him more tired than before and there was a peculiar qualitative difference to the tiredness. He'd once read that the ancient Egyptians, after removing the brains of a mummy by dragging them through the nostrils with a hook, had packed the resulting cavity with hot sand, and something along the same lines seemed to have happened inside his own skull. 'Hey Armand,' he said, mid-yawn, 'do you think it's better to have one hour's sleep or none at all?'

'Before we discuss that, I need to have a word with you,' said Armand.

'Yes?' Paul shifted his chair slightly so that his flatmate's face came into view. Its expression blended severity with nervousness.

'Mr Parry,' said Armand, 'could you please excuse us?'

Paul looked round and saw the charge nurse poised before the admissions board, felt pen in hand. 'You what?' said Gwyn.

'I need a brief private discussion with Dr Gooding.'

'And I need to get on with my work I'm afraid, Dr Roux, so tough titties as we say in Pontypridd. I can hum if you want, drown you out.' He began a busy little tune, overlaid with the squeaks of the marker pen.

Armand swallowed, and drew himself upright in the chair. 'I'm sorry to have to bring this up now, Paul, but I think these things should be dealt with as soon as they arise.'

'What things?'

'Usually,' said Armand, brooking no interruption, 'I have my breakfast in the canteen but this morning I decided I would eat in the flat. Imagine my feelings, then, when I discovered that the packet of pop tarts I bought last week had been removed and substituted with an entirely different packet of pop tarts.'

Paul heard a nervous cackle and realized that it came from himself.

'Can I ask,' said Armand, 'if it was you who substituted those pop tarts?'

'Yes it was. Sorry.'

'I see,' said Armand, gravely.

'I made sure they were sugar-free but I couldn't get exactly the same flavours. I should have said something really, but I didn't think you'd notice. And I didn't think it was very important. Is it? Important, I mean.'

'I think *honesty* is important. I think reading notices that people have left on cupboards in the interests of privacy is important.'

'Yes, but . . . you know, it was just some –' his face cracked in a yawn again '– pop tarts.'

'Paul, I'm not talking about pop tarts. I'm talking about principle.'

'But . . . I mean . . . if we're going to start . . .' Irritation suddenly flooded him. 'You never get out of the bathroom.'

Armand drew his head back as if Paul had jabbed a fist in his direction. 'I'm sorry?'

'I was going to wait until a better time, but since you've brought up this thing of getting stuff out in the open I wanted to say that I'm really tired of standing around waiting for you to get out of the bathroom. Yesterday morning you were in there from half past seven to a quarter to nine and I knocked four times – in the end I only had time to clean my teeth before we started the ward round. I couldn't even shave. And also, while we're on the subject of you hogging things, it's not just the bathroom, it's the washing machine as well. I haven't been able to do any laundry because it's always full of your socks.'

There was a bursting noise behind them, and he looked round to see Gwyn industriously dabbing a series of random dots beside the words 'Side Room 2'.

'Let's talk about this another time,' he said. 'Perhaps we need a rota or something.' The word brought back memories of dust-caked student houses and chippy arguments about washing-up and pasta purchase. 'Half past eight till twenty to nine. How about that? That would do me, I'm really quick.'

'Wait, no, I need time to think,' said Armand, flustered. 'You've sprung this on me. I can't . . . I can't be expected to make a decision this fast. You've turned this whole discussion around, you've distorted my argument.'

'Look, it's quite straightforward,' said Paul, wearily. 'I won't eat your pop tarts if you let me use the bathroom occasionally. Just let me know when.' He rubbed his eyes. 'I'm going to go now. I've got something planned.'

As he stumped up the corridor he was left with an after-image of Armand's face, the features elongated with outrage, the mouth trembling with unvoiced objections.

*   *   *

There was a fair amount to look at in the front window of the *Mercury* office but not enough to justify the fact that Paul had been standing on the pavement staring at it for almost twenty-five minutes. He had read the front page of the current edition ('MAN ATTACKED BY MOAT SWAN', 'ZEBRA CROSSING ARGUMENT RUMBLES ON') and the front page of the edition from twenty-five years ago ('NEW ZEBRA CROSSING FOR MARSH LANE', 'BOWLING GREEN "A DISGRACE" SAYS COUNCILLOR'). He had studied the blown-up photos of junior football teams and people planting trees and he had tried to avoid meeting the eye of the teenage girl on reception, whose initial heavy-lidded lack of interest had sharpened into obvious curiosity tinged with suspicion. She kept shifting her chair along the desk so as to keep him in view between the items in the window and he wondered if she had a panic button somewhere; if he hung around for much longer he might find himself wrestled to the ground by armed police.

The trouble was that his remark to Armand that he had 'something planned' for the morning was not so much an overstatement as a complete invention; what he actually had wasn't a plan but a piece of mental theatre, honed over several weeks into a satisfying, if improbable, playlet: *Enjoying his first free weekend, the young doctor takes a morning stroll around the town centre and chances upon the offices of the local newspaper. He pauses to look in the window and glimpses, amidst the bustle of the newsroom, someone that he recognizes – Marianne Cray, an acquaintance from university. He knocks on the window and she looks up, exclaims and hurries out to meet him. 'Hello Paul! What on earth are you doing in Shadley Oak?' she asks, smiling.*

'I'm working at the General. How about you?'

'I'm working here. As a photographer.'

'No! That's an incredible coincidence. I didn't think I'd know anyone in this town.'

'Neither did I!' Laughter, coffee, a promise to meet again later in the week. Her flat. Mutual lunge. Big cooked breakfast.

He had previewed this little scene so many times in his imagination that when it transpired that there was no bustling newsroom to be glimpsed through the window, only a foyer furnished with two hard chairs, a desk and a coffee machine, he'd felt utterly disorientated and had drifted into an unrehearsed 'Plan B': *Enjoying his first free weekend, the young doctor goes to the town centre and stands around on the pavement like a complete tit on the vague off-chance that a girl he's spoken to twice in his entire life, and whose job plans he happened to overhear in a bar in the student union, will wander into view. In her continued absence he reads the newspapers in the window for a second time, and idly watches as a bearded man enters the foyer from a side room and tries to persuade the coffee machine to accept a fistful of small change.*

'Can I help you?'

Paul looked round, startled; the receptionist was standing in the doorway with her arms folded, one stilettoed foot on the pavement.

'Can I help you?' she asked again, her inflection implying that she'd rather drink bleach.

'No, it's OK,' he said casually, using his cuff to wipe away the nose-smudge he'd left on the window.

'Only you've been standing there for three-quarters of an hour. Staring at me.'

'I wasn't staring at you,' he said. 'I was reading the papers in the window.'

'What, for three-quarters of an hour?'

'Yes.'

She said nothing, but cinched her lips in disbelief.

'I was waiting for someone,' he offered, as a palliative.

'No you weren't.'

'Sorry?'

'If you were waiting for someone, you'd have looked up and down the street for them, wouldn't you? You didn't do that once the whole time you were there, you just looked in the window. Or if you'd been waiting for someone who works in the newspaper, you'd have come in and sat down and waited for them indoors instead of hanging around outside for three-quarters of an hour. Wouldn't you?'

'Well, I –'

'Unless you hadn't arranged to meet them at all and you were hoping they'd just happen to come into reception and then you could pretend you were only passing and you'd seen them by accident. Is that what you were doing?'

'No,' said Paul, feebly.

'Wasn't it?'

'No, it wasn't.'

'Because if it was, there's hardly anyone here on a Saturday anyway so it'd just be a waste of your time. There's only me, and Ally, and Addison. Did you want to see Ally or Addison?'

'*No*,' said Paul, with acerbity. He was beginning to feel as if he'd spent the previous twelve hours under continuous interrogation, first Crispin seizing the thumbscrews, then Gwyn and Lexie, then Armand and now this seventeen-year-old with the deductive skills of Inspector Morse and scary little steel-chip eyes that seemed to be memorizing his appearance for a future photofit. 'Look,' he said, trying to sound bluff and self-assured, 'I'm sorry if I bothered you, but I was just glancing at the papers and now I've got stuff to do.' He started to walk away.

'And Marianne's coming in later,' added the receptionist. Paul's involuntary lurch was as good as a signed confession and when he turned back her expression was triumphant. 'At least I *think* she's coming in,' she amended, looking back into the foyer. 'Hey, Addison –'

'Yup?' replied the man with the beard, still feeding pennies into the coffee machine.

'Is Marianne coming in? Only there's a bloke out here who's desperate to see her.'

'No,' said Paul, cringing, 'No, I'm just . . . er . . .'

'Hang on,' said Beardy. He pressed one of the beverage choices and wandered over to the door. 'She's taking photos at the dog show,' he said, eyeing Paul coolly, 'but she'll be in soon to look at some contacts. Want us to give her a message?'

'No, that's all right, I can come back, there's nothing urgent, it's not a problem.'

'Well it seems a real shame,' said the receptionist, with sugared malice, 'after you've been standing here for so long.'

'No, it's fine.'

'You could leave a note,' said Beardy.

'Yes,' said Paul. 'I'll do that. I'll go away, I'll write a note and then I'll come back.'

'Okey doke,' said Beardy, sticking his hands in his pockets. 'See you later then.'

'See you later,' echoed the receptionist, waving her talons.

He could feel the pair of them watching him all the way down the street.

Dear Marianne,
Hi Marianne!
Dear Marianne,

This is such a small world. Yesterday I was talking on the phone to a mutual friend, acquaintance, friend, neighbour in Argyle Road, friend in Argyle Road, fellow Argyle-Roader –

Paul wiped the sweat from his biro hand with a paper

napkin and took a slug of cappuccino. The hammering sense of urgency that he was currently feeling was not helping his writing style. He was, as far as he could see, involved in a straight race: either Marianne's first intimation of his presence in Shadley Oak would be a carefully worded letter from him or it would be a verbal report from two of her colleagues that she was being stalked by a demented fat bloke. He picked up the pen again and turned to a fresh page of the hastily bought pad.

Dear Marianne,

I was speaking to a mutual friend and he mentioned (to my amazement) that you had taken a job in Shadley Oak. Because by coincidence so have I. He hesitated. By this point she would be looking to see who the signatory was and just 'Paul' wouldn't be good enough; there had been loads of other Pauls around and he doubted whether she'd ever heard his surname. *We were near-neighbours at university (I lived at number 91 with Gez and Penny) and we quite often said hello in the bus queue, and we once had a bit of a conversation at Suzanne Moffatt's party on 17 June where you ended up saying how much you liked men with a bit of meat on them, although I think you were fairly drunk at the –*

Dear Marianne,

Until two months ago we were almost neighbours in Argyle Road (I was at number 91, the house with the stone-cladding), and now, by coincidence, we're almost neighbours again!

He nodded, spurring himself on.

I'm currently doing a surgical house job at Shadley Oak District General, and I happened to hear that you're working at the newspaper. As we're both 'strangers in town' I wondered if you'd like to meet up one –

He was jarred by a blow to the back of his seat and he

turned to see a small, podgy girl sitting at the next table. As he watched she extended a foot and quite deliberately kicked his chair again.

'Stop it,' he said.

In reply she flattened her nose with one finger, dragged down the corners of her eyes and lolled her tongue wetly against her chin.

'Stop it Melanie, *now*,' called a bulky woman queuing at the counter.

Melanie rearranged her face and then, as the woman turned aside to pick up a tray, she leaned across and wiped her fingers on the back of Paul's chair. 'I hope you die,' she said, pleasantly. Paul stuck out his tongue half-heartedly and resumed work.

– evening and go for a drink or a meal? I can be contacted on 3485 8855 extension 2431, which is the hospital flat I'm living in. Hope to see you soon, Paul (Gooding). He reread the letter and felt dissatisfied; it all seemed so factual, lacking any indication that he was the sort of person with whom it might be enjoyable to spend an evening. It needed something that showed his lighter side. He turned to another page and tapped the pen against his teeth.

'Mum, I've got a sore throat,' said Melanie, loudly. There was no reply.

'And I've got a sore neck.'

Paul tried to concentrate.

PS Shadley Oak's a lot smaller than Birmingham, isn't it?! He winced and crossed it out again.

'And I've got a sore foot.'

'Drink up your orange.'

'I don't want to go.'

'I've paid for the whole term. You're going.'

'But I've *really* got a sore neck.'

PS I'd suggest going to a film, but there's no cinema! It would have to do, he thought, though he couldn't see Marianne wiping away tears of mirth. He turned back to the letter and appended the line. As he wrote the last word there was a tremendous blow to the back of his chair and his pen jerked and sliced a line across the page. He swung round irritably.

'Sorry dear.' Rather than the daughter's foot it had been the mother's backside, and he was forced to nod an ill-tempered acknowledgement as the pair left, Melanie pausing at the door to give a demonstration of how far back she could roll her eyes, the whites fluttering sightlessly at him.

'Come *on*.' The little girl was pulled from view, and in the instant the doorway was clear Marianne walked past. He saw her for only half a second but the effect was as if he had been dropped into a vat of iced water, breath huffing from his lungs as his chest muscles spasmed, his heart actually seeming to stop for a moment or two before bounding on with extra impetus. The force of it shocked him; he hadn't seen her for, what, six weeks, but in that time his involuntary response to an accidental sighting – what he thought of as his Mariametric reaction – seemed to have gone off the scale. At this rate he'd actually die the next time he spotted her. He fumbled for the letter, trying to keep his eyes on the door as if there were still a few of her molecules hanging around, like scent lingering in a room. Folding the sheet in half, he scribbled her name on the outside and hurried out of the café.

7

'Polly, remember you're a horse,' called Netta's mother above the drum roll of steel-capped shoes. 'You should be tossing your mane. Look at how beautifully Roxanne's tossing her mane. Toss those lovely silky manes and listen to the music and two and three and *down* goes the flag and off you all go!' The line of little girls shuffle-ball-changed thunderously along the length of the old scout hut and Netta felt the floorboards flex as it passed her chair. At the piano Ted was smiling benignly as he swung through a jazzed-up version of 'The Camptown Races', the lowest notes buzzing at a frequency that rattled the cluster of mugs on the table beside Netta.

'And paw the ground, paw those hooves. Look at me, Abbie, not at your watch and listen to the beat –' she began to clap her hands in a springy flamenco style, palms cupped and fingers splayed '– and-a *bet*-a my-a *money* on the *bob*-a tail-a *nag* and *two* and *three* and – listen to the music, Eleanor, you're not listening to the music, you're talking to Nicole – and gallopy-gallopy-gallopy and *hop* and *hop* and –'

Out of the corner of her eye Netta saw one of the mugs suddenly disappear off the edge of the table and she lunged forward, far too late to do anything but swipe at empty air. The mug survived the impact, spun a yard or two across the floorboards and was sent cannoning into the wall by a flying hoof. Shards of china ricocheted the length of the room, there was an excited scream and then the line broke into giggling fragments; like the pianist in a saloon gunfight, Ted played on.

'Girls.' Netta's mother stood with her hands clasped before

her, her expression severe. '*Girls!*' The giggling ceased and 'The Camptown Races' slowed to a trot, ending prematurely with a plinked staccato chord. 'Girls, you've shocked me.' There was some shuffling, some sneaked and chastened looks along the line and a couple of half-suppressed snorts. 'Do you know why I'm shocked?' The question was clearly rhetorical, the pause only long enough to allow her mother to glance, purse-lipped, along the line. 'Not by the breakage, Melanie, I know that was an accident so there's no need for you to look so worried.' Melanie, already plump and pink, became pinker. 'No, I'm shocked by the fact that, as a group of *performers* –' the emphasis was reverent ' – who in just a very few weeks will be showing this routine to a paying audience, a *paying* audience remember, you didn't . . . you didn't what?' This time it was clear that a response was demanded, and several hands went up. Netta was tempted to raise her own; she certainly knew the answer, just as she had recognized every step of the routine.

'Sarah?'

'We didn't carry on, Mrs Devon.'

'That's right. You Didn't. Carry. On. And the first rule of performing is that you carry on. *Whatever* happens. I'll give you an example.'

Anecdote time, thought Netta. She enjoyed these glimpses of her mother's glory days, the roll call of pantos and obscure television shows and summer seasons through which she had high-kicked her twenties and half of her thirties, permanently wrecking her lower vertebrae before being carried off to provincial wifehood by Brian Devon. The stories were only ever aired for their improving content, never for their pure entertainment value – 'I don't dwell on the past,' as her mother would say, grandly, if pressed – nevertheless Netta could think of half a dozen that could illustrate this particular professional virtue: there was the collapsing set during *Aladdin* at the Oldham Alhambra, or the time that Desirée Parks sparkled through a seven-minute version of 'It Ain't What You Do' with the Barry Lethbridge Dancers in *Follies of 1953*, and then staggered off the stage of the Palladium with fulminating peritonitis, or the story of Torchy Watts and the wrong tap shoes in –

'Who has seen *The Sound of Music*?' asked her mother unexpectedly. Every hand rose. 'Then you'll know there's a scene in that film where the eldest girl sings "I am Fifteen Going on Sixteen" while performing a number of grands jetés – that means "bounding jumps" in ballet language – around the seats of a summer house. Do you remember that scene?'

'Yes, Mrs Devon.'

'That young actress – yes, what is it, Abbie?'

'It's sixteen going on seventeen, Mrs Devon. The song is.'

'Thank you, Abbie, and try not to interrupt when I'm telling you something important. That young dancer had sprained her ankle just before the scene was filmed. Just imagine that for a moment. Close your eyes and try to imagine the pain she must have suffered performing that scene.'

Eyes were obediently closed and Netta saw small fat Melanie, apparently under the illusion that she was now invisible, give her bottom a good scratch. In the silence Coral's anxious voice became audible through the partition wall, entreating the ballet juniors to '*Please* concentrate and Ashley, you can show your new bracelet to Cassie after the –'

'And now open your eyes. Did you imagine that, girls?'

'Yes, Mrs Devon.' The answer was a little perfunctory; there was a certain restlessness beginning to creep into the class, an awareness that the hour was almost up and that their own mothers were starting to congregate in the cloakroom.

'Now that young dancer, in spite of the pain, performed the

scene perfectly and when she had finished everybody on the film set applauded. She was very brave, wasn't she?'

'Yes, Mrs Devon.'

'So do you think if she'd had an accident with a mug halfway through the take – that means the time when the camera's rolling – she would have stopped dancing and giggled in a silly way?'

'No, Mrs Devon.'

'No, that's right. Because she was what we call a *trouper*.'

And now, thought Netta, she's probably in what we call a *wheelchair*.

'I want you all to remember that word. Trouper. And now, before you go home, Mr Shepherd's going to play some music while everyone picks up every single little bit of broken china and puts it in the bin. Straight backs, remember, kneel gracefully. Imagine you're curtseying to Princess Diana. Mr Shepherd?' She nodded to Ted and he performed a series of scampering arpeggios while the girls clattered round the room.

'New anecdote, Mum?' The effort of standing up for a whole hour had intensified her mother's limp, and as her class headed for the cloakroom she lowered herself carefully onto the chair beside Netta's.

'Yes, I think it's always very important to use contemporary references in teaching. Ted showed me an article in the *Radio Times* on the making of the film.' She raised her voice slightly. 'You showed me an interesting article, didn't you, Ted? In the *Radio Times*.'

'That's right,' said her accompanist, locking the piano; Netta judged him to be slightly too far away to have actually heard the question, but twenty years of working with her mother seemed to have furnished him with telepathic powers.

'Hi Ted.' Netta stood to give him a kiss, catching a whiff of Murray Mints as she did so. 'How are you?'

'Very well, thank you.' He smiled diffidently, exposing the long yellow teeth that gave him the look of a kindly camel. 'You're looking as lovely as ever, Netta,' he added, with apparent sincerity.

'Oh Ted . . .' She looked down at today's back-of-the-wardrobe scrapings: a pair of shapeless cords and a jumper with a poorly darned elbow. 'It's very nice of you but I know I look a complete frump. Kelly informed me I wasn't allowed to leave the house in these trousers.'

'Brianetta has never understood that one should always take a compliment with grace,' said her mother. 'One should say –' she lifted a hand to her throat '– thank you. Thank you so very, very much.' She bowed her head, as if ducking a flying bouquet.

'And how is your family?' asked Ted.

'They're fine, thanks. Mick's just on his way to –' she checked her watch '– Mick's just *arrived* in San Francisco. His brigade's twinned with one on the West Coast, and last year we had Kevin Smith from Berkeley staying at our house for a month doing a job swap, so now it's Mick's turn and he's been trying to pretend that he's not wildly excited, but he is really. And the girls are –'

'You know, it's just occurred to me,' said her mother, rising to join the conversation, 'that in a very similar way, when something's *complimentary* one should accept it without questioning the pri–'

'Mrs Devon?' said a voice at her elbow.

'Yes Melanie, what is it?'

'Mrs Devon, I wanted to ask –' Melanie paused to sniff a runnel of snot back into one nostril '– I wanted to ask, am I expelled?'

'No, of course not, dear, it was an accident. And you're doing quite nicely this term, as long as you remember to tie your hair back. We always need to see a dancer's neck, don't we?'

'So I'm not expelled?'

'No.'

'Oh.' Visibly disappointed, Melanie turned away.

'And don't forget to bring a hankie to class next week. And what do we do when we walk?'

'We walk tall,' said Melanie, dolefully.

'We walk tall and we look the world right in the eye. We don't shuffle along peering at the cracks between the floorboards. I wish,' she said, lowering her voice as the metallic footsteps receded, 'that you'd have a word with that child's mother about her weight.'

'I can't, Mum. Be reasonable.'

'Why can't you?'

'Because she's not my patient and I've never met her before.'

'But isn't that just like a doctor ignoring a road accident?'

'No, Mum, it's absolutely nothing like that.'

'I think I'll just go and check that I definitely locked the piano,' said Ted, drifting away.

'You know, Brianetta, you're always telling me that a poor diet can lead to disease –'

'I may occasionally have said that, yes, but I can't go round –'

'– and then when you're given the opportunity to help someone who *doesn't* understand that you shy away. It seems very odd to me.'

'Mum, my qualifications do not give me licence to start shouting at fat people in the street.'

Her mother seemed to brood on this remark for a second or two before drawing breath for an apparent rejoinder. 'I'm thinking of calling it "Roses and Champagne",' she said.

'What? Calling what?'

'This year's autumn show. I wanted a celebratory theme – Senior Tap and Stage are doing "We are the Champions" and Coral's working on a pas de deux to "The Girl that I Marry".'

'Oh, I see. So how will "The Camptown Races" fit in with that?'

'All races have a *winner*, don't they?' She rose stiffly, having somehow triumphed in that particular round, and Netta thought of the 'Communication in the Workplace' day-course that she and her colleagues had groaned through a few months previously. Conversation, they had been told, was like passing a ball, each participant catching it securely, holding it briefly and then swiftly moving it along; her mother's technique, on the other hand, seemed to consist of doing away with the ball altogether and replacing it with a random object of her own choosing – a frozen chicken, a hat, a piece of wood – thereby forcing the other participants into the role of speciality jugglers. Had she always been this bad? Was she getting worse?

The door at the end of the hall banged open and the junior ballet class began to exit, pink shoes pattering on the wooden floor, shining hair tied back with ribbons, a general air of being a cut above the proles of tap and stage. In the gaps between the self-important little bodies Netta caught a glimpse of Coral in earnest conversation with a parent. She was wearing one of her self-sewn, self-designed outfits, a matching beige bolero and skirt, the latter dotted with appliqué flowers in varying shades of blue. That, thought Netta, could've been me, on my first day of work at the General. She caught Coral's eye and gave a little wave, but received only a worried nod in return.

'Is Coral all right?' she asked quietly.

'Don't disturb her, she's talking to a *non-payer*,' said her mother, darkly.

'I thought it was you who did the strong-arm work.' Netta couldn't imagine Coral's gentle ineffectuality offering much of a threat; her current body language, hands clasped at breast level, nervous smile alternating with nervous frown, spoke more of supplicant than bailiff.

'I *normally* handle unpaid accounts, but Coral said that she thought I was already under quite enough strain from the move and that she'd deal with this one. Ashley, no jewellery in class, tell your mummy that's a very strict rule.'

Ashley, fingering her bracelet, hurried past.

'And are you, Mum?'

'Am I . . . ?

'Feeling under a lot of strain? Today in particular?' There did seem to be a peculiar jumpiness about her mother that she couldn't quite define.

'Well I . . .' For a moment her mother looked slightly flustered. 'Oh, thank you Ted.' She drew the proffered coat over her shoulders and removed a speck or two of invisible dust from the collar. 'Now we really should go. Ted's very kindly offered to give us a lift to the flat but I need to be back for the intermediate exam class at three.'

Netta followed her through the door of the scout hut. There was a short flight of steps to the pavement but her mother walked down the long, shallow wheelchair ramp instead. She had only recently started to make this minuscule concession to her lameness, but she still liked to pretend it was for sartorial reasons: 'This coat's a little long and it does tend to drag on the edges of the treads and, frankly, Netta, the hem is getting quite filthy . . .'

Glenn was waiting for them beside Ted's Mini, his long-handled measuring wheel held stiffly to one side, like a guardsman's rifle. Despite the mildness of the day he was wearing the distorted red Puffa jacket, zipped to the neck.

'I've recalibrated it,' he said as soon as he judged them

within earshot. 'It was underestimating total distance walked by slightly less than 0.2 of a centimetre per metre which –'

'In you get, dear,' said their mother, waiting beside the open car door. He complied without drawing breath.

' – works out at an underestimate of one metre per five hundred metres and as I'm working on a circuit of over seven kilometres then the discrepancy's quite considerable.'

'Yes, I can see that,' said Netta, wedging herself into the back beside him. The Puffa jacket seemed to take up about three-quarters of the available space and odd ripples of the rigid stuffing dug into her upper arm. The red fabric, she noticed, now that she was viewing it in extreme close-up, seemed to be stippled with tiny white dots; she scratched a section with a thumbnail, and created a micro-blizzard.

'Glenn, did you –' it seemed so unlikely that she hesitated ' – did you wash this in starch?'

'Yes I did,' said Glenn. He started to unfold an Ordnance Survey map of Shadley Oak. 'Fortunately I used a pencil to notate distances to the Wednesday route, because all the figures will have to be changed, but I've found that the nearest intersection point is in Conduit Street between Iceland and What She Wants.'

'Sorry Glenn, to interrupt, but why did you wash the jacket in starch?'

'I was looking for a squarer outcome. For the Sunday route I can cut through Quonian's Lane and join it just at the entrance to the B&Q car park.' Glenn unfolded the map to its fullest extent and angled it towards Netta. 'It's only eighty-five metres, after recalibration.'

'I wonder, Glenn, if you could lower that map very slightly,' said Ted, obviously struggling to see anything at all in the rear-view mirror. He regained a little glimpse of the road and moved smoothly into lane.

'I don't know what you mean by "squarer outcome",' said Netta. Glenn unfolded another section of map. 'I mean, are you pleased with how it looks now?'

'Yes.'

'Right. Because . . . you know, one shoulder's quite a lot higher than the other.'

'I had a coat with an asymmetrical collar once,' said their mother. 'It attracted a lot of attention at the time, it was considered quite outré for Weymouth.'

'But that was a fashion, Mum.'

'No, no, it was *ahead* of fashion. People used to point me out in the street.'

'Yes, but . . .' But Glenn already gets pointed out in the street, she wanted to say. Even without a free-form concrete jacket.

'The dressmaker said it was experimental. Of course, Brianetta, I know your tastes are rather more conservative.'

'But that's not what I . . . never mind. Glenn, would you like a new red Puffa for Christmas?'

'I've already got one.'

The direct distance from the scout hut to the new flat was only about half a mile, but in the narrow streets at the centre of town there was a set of traffic lights every few yards and a tourist coach blocking every side road. Ted had once let slip that he had worked briefly as a chauffeur after being demobbed and he handled the Mini as if it were a Rolls-Royce, avoiding the usual small-car neck-snapping decelerations and gliding up the gears as if there were a tray of eggs on the back seat. In some ways he was still working as a chauffeur, his 'very kind offer of a lift' being repeated on a daily, often hourly basis as he ferried his employer from home to class and then back again, but Netta had observed that he was thanked on each occasion as if the proposal had been both unexpected and unrepeatable – a sort of etiquette tango, performed each time with the same conviction and sincerity.

'Oh Ted,' said her mother, as the Mini inched past a group of teenage girls slouching outside a newsagent's, 'would you be kind enough to pull in for a moment?' She wound down the window as the car came to a halt, called out, 'Alice Stephens, remember, a dancer never forgets her posture!' and then wound it back up again. 'Thank you Ted,' she said, graciously. A lorry behind them hooted as the car pulled out again.

'Mum,' said Netta, struck by a thought, 'which removal company did you go for?'

'Sorry?' asked her mother, distantly.

'I made that list the last time I came down – I just wondered which one you'd decided on.' She had put in an afternoon of research, phoning local estate agents and contacting each of their recommendations with a set of questions gleaned from a newspaper article on the subject.

'Oh now, I'm not sure I can remember . . .' said her mother with careful vagueness; Netta was instantly suspicious.

'Well was it Brayman's? Or the Hartington Brothers? Or the Co-op?'

'No . . . ah, now . . .' She spoke as if the memory were just starting to trickle into her consciousness. 'Now that I think about it, it was one that a friend of Coral's recommended.'

'One that a friend of Coral's recommended.'

'Yes, that's right, the office is just round the corner from her in Clay Hill. Coral designed their uniforms.'

Netta nodded fatalistically. 'And of course you checked whether they're a member of the British Association of Removers, and if they have a comprehensive insurance policy for accidental damage.'

There was a long pause. 'Of course,' said her mother.

'So this uniform –' Netta could hear her own voice crisping

with sarcasm ' – are we talking fringed boleros here? Or a simple sequin-effect catsuit?'

'You're just being silly now.'

'Or perhaps Coral's managed to adapt those squirrel costumes from last year?'

Her mother lifted her chin and gazed, with feigned deafness, out of the window and Netta, feeling scratchily adolescent, did the same.

The gateway to Mellis Hall was fabulously imposing, a mighty arch topped with a couple of rampant lions, but it had been shifted from its old position a quarter of a mile from the house and now marked the entrance to a newly created drive that, despite a couple of laboured meanderings, failed to be more than thirty yards long. The rambling wooded grounds that Netta remembered trespassing in as a child had been reduced to half an acre, and around the edge, their upper windows peering over the perimeter fence, pressed the houses of the new estate.

Ted turned the car past the billboard ('EXCLUSIVE ARCHITECT-DESIGNED CLASSIC-STYLE TWO- AND THREE-BEDROOM APARTMENTS FOR SALE') and at Glenn's request halted just inside the gates. Netta climbed out with her brother and watched the Mini resume its short journey.

'I need to check an alternative parking point,' said Glenn, doing something with the digital display on the measuring wheel. 'The total distance depends on where I park the trolley.' He lowered the wheel to the ground between the gates, adjusted the starting position very slightly and then began to push it towards the house. It emitted a polite beep for every metre measured.

'The total distance from what?' asked Netta.

'From the alternative trolley parking point to the route intersection.'

'Which route?'

'It depends on the day.'

They beeped through a metre or two while Netta thought about this.

'You mean you're working out a new set of collecting routes?'

'No.' He sounded shocked at the suggestion.

'So . . . what are you doing?'

'I'm calculating the shortest distance between the alternative trolley parking point and the Sunday, Monday, Wednesday and Friday collecting routes.'

They rolled past the parked Mini from which Ted was gently extracting their mother, and along the length of the pretentious stucco façade that had been slapped over the original Edwardian brick box and round the thinly planted shrubbery that hid the residents' car park. Glenn crossed it diagonally, stopped in the far corner, noted down the figure on the digital display and unfolded his map.

'Glenn,' said Netta, 'I still don't understand what you're doing with all these measurements. Can you explain it again?'

Glenn never minded explaining anything again, and on the third try she got it. He wasn't changing his actual collecting routes – those circuits so immutable they could be used as chronometers: Rubbish Man + stack of discarded polystyrene cups + Marsh Lane = Wednesday, eleven a.m. – he was changing the point at which he joined them, and he had drawn a series of dotted lines on the map, radiating from the Hall, to show the optimum short cut to each one.

'Shall I explain it again?' he asked.

'No. No, I understand it now. Thanks. It's a good plan, Glenn.'

She leaned over the map and felt her face grow hot. She'd

been worrying for months about the fracture of her brother's daily pattern; she'd lain awake at night wondering if the move would fling him into crisis, if she'd find him camping outside the back door of Briglennia or pushing his trolley in an endless, nomadic circuit, and all the while he'd been preparing a sensible, entirely Glennish strategy that would result in minimal disruption to his routine. She'd done exactly what she always accused other people of doing: she'd underestimated him. 'It's a good plan,' she said again.

'I know.'

She studied the dotted lines. 'I wish you didn't have to cut through those garages behind the new estate though. There's always loads of teenagers hanging round and I worry they might . . . couldn't you take the main road instead?'

'No, that would be longer.' Glenn cast a glance over her shoulder and then began to refold the map. 'There's a man with binoculars,' he said.

'Sorry?' Thrown, she looked at him and then back at the previous direction of his gaze. It took her a moment to spot what he had noticed – a man in the upper window of one of the new houses peering through a set of binoculars, the lenses pressed flat against the pane. Netta stared back. 'I don't think he's looking at us,' she said, but there was nothing else he could be looking at, she realized, except the nose of Ted's Mini, just visible round the corner of the house.

'There you are,' said her mother. She was standing between the plaster pillars that framed the grandiose front door. Dressed, today, in eau-de-Nil with a touch of dark green at waist and neck, and carefully coordinated court shoes, she looked like a gracious hostess welcoming guests to her house party, ready to pass them on to the butler (Ted) who would take them to their suite in the west wing.

'It does suit you,' said Netta, reluctantly.

'What suits me, dear?'

'This house. It's your sort of house – it looks as if you were born here.'

'Oh.' Her mother laid a theatrical hand on her heart. 'Thank you, Brianetta.'

'You're welcome.' They smiled at each other, a little stiffly.

'So tell me,' said her mother, leading her between the pillars, 'what do you think of the colour of these walls? I must say I'm not taken . . .' Netta looked round the communal hall, still littered with painters' equipment.

'It's undercoat, isn't it? The decorators haven't finished yet.'

'What would you call this shade? Mink? Ted, what would you call this shade? Mink? Taupe? Oatmeal?'

'Mum, what are you doing?'

Her mother stopped, Chubb halfway into the door at the rear of the hall.

'I'm going into my flat.'

'That isn't your flat.' Netta swung round to look at the other doors. '*That's* your flat. Front right.' For a terrible moment she wondered if this was how Alzheimer's began – the little slip that preceded the dreadful fall.

Ted cleared his throat and wandered away, towards the foot of the stairs. Her mother turned the key and Netta could hear the smooth glide of the levers.

'Mum, what's going on?'

'There's nothing *going on*, dear. It's simply that just before I signed the contract – the pen was in my hand, you could almost say it was kismet – the person who was going to buy this flat rang to say he'd found somewhere else and the estate agent insisted I took a look at it and do you know, we thought it would suit us even better than the other one. Didn't we, Glenn?'

'I think so,' said Glenn, hovering just outside the front door.

Netta realized that her mouth was hanging open. 'You mean,' she said, rehinging it, 'you've bought an entirely different flat from the one I came down specially to see six weeks ago, the one you said was absolutely ideal for your purposes.'

'Yes dear. It was one of those unmissable opportunities.'

'Right.' She nodded, feeling strangely calm, punch-drunk perhaps. 'OK. So why didn't you tell me?'

'Because, Brianetta –' her mother's voice changed gear suddenly, becoming laden with reproof '– I thought you might make a fuss. I know you don't believe in spontaneity.'

'Mum, that's so un–'

'And there are one or two *minor* differences that I thought you might not approve of.' She opened the door to reveal a minute vestibule, parquet floored and reeking of varnish. 'The hall's a little smaller, as you can see. But the lounge is much larger than the other one, and it has Twin Alcoves.' That was the selling point, Netta could tell immediately. 'The lounge really is *exceptionally* large,' her mother repeated with a certain emphasis, 'and the bathroom has a separate shower and there's a utility area in the kitchen and a lovely fitted cupboard in Glenn's room for him to keep his hobbies in.'

'The first flat had all those,' said Netta. 'What was the other difference? You said one or *two* differences.'

'Well, it doesn't have that, er . . .' Her mother turned away slightly so that the rest of the answer was a little muffled, the words spoken quickly. 'It doesn't have that ridiculously tiny little third bedroom. Now come and look at the lounge and decide where you'd like your sofa bed to go.'

8

Carrie slid her tray along the rail and studied the puddings on offer in the staff canteen. 'Normally,' she said, 'I'd have had gooseberries and custard, but I've just been examining someone with a productive cough and I can't *quite* . . .'

'Yeah,' said Paul, hesitating briefly out of politeness before taking a large bowlful. 'I know what you mean.'

'On the other hand,' she said, 'the jam roll looks even worse.'

'Road-traffic accident?'

'Chainsaw, I was thinking.' She dithered for a few seconds. 'If you start really thinking about it, everything looks like something revolting, doesn't it? There's no end to it – I'll never eat again if I don't nip this in the bud now. I'll go for the worst one. I'll have *this*.' Shoulders braced, she took a dense, shining slab of chocolate mousse. 'Don't say anything,' she said, moving towards the till.

'You know what I was thinking?' asked Paul. 'It's OK, it's not horrible,' he added quickly, clocking her expression. 'I was thinking how this mashed potato I've got is the exact same colour as a woman's face I was seeing this morning. I wrote "pallor, probably anaemic" on her notes but really I should've put "face same colour as instant mash" and it would've given a much better picture.'

'I know what you mean, there's a sort of *greyish* look to instant mash that you get with really cytopenic patients.'

'In fact you could probably do a whole scale of anaemia based on canteen meals, you know, with full-fat milk at the –'

'Sorry to interrupt,' said Carrie, 'but shall we sit over there?' She nodded towards a half-empty table; at one end Armand was spooning soup into his mouth, arm curled protectively round the bowl.

'*No*,' said Paul, urgently, herding her away.

'Why? What's the matter?'

'I can't tell you. What about the one by the window?'

'Oh, please, *please* not next to Wai,' said Carrie. 'I spend enough time with her already.' She flinched as a giggle like the trill of an alarm clock cut through the chatter. 'All day. That's what I hear all day. And most evenings.'

'OK, well there must be somewhere –' As they stood back to back, surveying the room, there was a massed scraping of chairs and a group of student nurses began to drift towards the exit. Paul wove between them, keen to claim the empty table, and he had almost reached it when he felt a hand insinuate itself under his coat and give his right buttock a hard squeeze. 'All right, farmboy?' said a voice by his shoulder, and he crashed the tray onto the table top and looked round to see Lexie giving him a open-mouthed smile before following her colleagues.

'Bloody hell,' he said, gazing after her. 'I think I'm being sexually harassed.'

'Really?' said Carrie, following his eyeline. 'By the one with the mouth?'

'Yes.'

'God, she looks terrifying. Does it worry you?'

'I'm not sure. I think she might be doing it ironically.' He sat down carefully.

'Anyway, your anaemia scale . . .' said Carrie.

'Oh yeah, well I haven't really thought it through, but that cheesecake they do on Tuesdays would be right up there and the –'

Carrie's bleep went off and she jumped violently. 'I bet that's serious,' she said, getting up. 'I'm starting to get this *feeling*, I'm starting to know when it's going to be something trivial and when it's going to be another curtains-round-the-bed job and this feels bad, this feels like the lab ringing to tell me that Mrs Kingsley's white-cell count is in double figures.' Paul watched idly as she scuttled across the room towards the phone. Since their encounter in the midnight corridor they had shared a few lunches and he had found the intensity of her company strangely calming; it reminded him in a way of the single aeroplane journey he had taken with his grandmother, whose fear of flying had been so great that Paul's own jitters had faded to nothing. He had become, by comparison, a blasé globetrotter, carelessly dismissing every terrifying clunk and whine, shrugging off each inexplicable lurch. Travelling alone, of course, he was a sweaty wreck.

'No,' she said, returning. 'It's just a temazepam write-up. I can do it after –' Her bleep sounded again, and she turned silently and headed back towards the phone.

'So what's going on?' asked a throaty voice very close to Paul's ear.

It was Crispin at the next table, leaning so far back in his chair that his head was almost resting on Paul's shoulder.

'What do you mean?'

'You and Almond not speaking?'

'Of course we are.'

'So why did you just practically do the splits to avoid sitting by him?'

'I didn't. I . . .' as usual his imagination, so tropically fecund in the abstract, deserted him as soon as a direct lie was called for.

'Ooooh,' said Crispin, hurling himself upright. 'I smell beeeeg scandal. Tell Uncle Crispy.' He dragged his chair across to Paul's table and reached back for his bowl of crumble. 'Talk amongst yourselves,' he said, waving a dismissive hand at his former tablemates.

'There's nothing to tell,' said Paul, unconvincingly.

'The suspect denied any ill feeling,' said Crispin, *sotto voce*, into his spoon. 'And on the ward round, when Almond wouldn't stand within ten feet of you?'

'Look,' said Paul, trying to sound firm. 'It's nothing.' It would have taken bamboo splinters hammered under his nails to pry this particular secret out of him.

'Suspect once again – ' Crispin's bleep went off ' – interview interrupted 1.32 p.m. To be continued. *And* I've got something to tell you,' he added, laying down the spoon and getting up just as Carrie returned.

'Admission,' she said, reseating herself, 'but she's coming from Clay Hill, and Mrs Kingsley's fine, panic over, white count of five, though I have to say that there's just something about the look of her that I'm not happy with and . . .' She stopped, fork in hand. '*That's* the scale I need,' she said, with sudden conviction. 'I need a precise range of descriptions that cover degrees of not looking very well. Because it's really hard in the middle of the night, isn't it, when you're worried about a patient and you want to call up the registrar, and the only concrete thing you've got to report is that someone doesn't look too good and you know he'll just sneer at you? You should be able to say it – instinct should count for something.'

'Yeah,' said Paul, struck by the idea. 'You could have "really terrible" at the top of the scale; I'm always wanting to put that.' He opened an imaginary set of notes. 'On examination the patient looked really terrible. But during the course of the afternoon, she improved slightly until she was looking . . . er . . .'

'A bit under the weather?' suggested Carrie.

'Yeah. Or "fairly shitty", I was thinking.'

She snorted. 'But it does set the scene, doesn't it? It makes it all much more immediate, you can really picture the patient. You could have "on the seedy side" next.'

'Or "none too clever".'

'Or –'

'Interview recommenced at 1.37 p.m.', said Crispin, sliding into the next seat. 'PC Terminator has joined us in the interrogation room.'

Carrie reddened, started to say something and then shrugged and picked up her fork.

'The suspect maintains his right to silence,' said Paul, hoping that a little nod in the direction of Crispin's game might deflect further questioning.

'Oh does he? Well that's a bit of a bugger, because I was going to ask him all about Marianne Cray.'

Paul inhaled a chip, struggled briefly to avoid barking it across the width of the room, and managed to dispel it discreetly into a napkin. 'You what?' he said eventually.

'She phoned me up. Last night.' Crispin clasped his hands behind his head and raised his eyebrows. '*Long* talk.'

Paul could do nothing but wait dumbly; he felt as if he'd been turned to stone, a menhir with ears.

'There I was,' said Crispin, enjoying himself, 'lying in front of the telly, wondering why all the girls in British soap operas are such a bunch of lardy dogs – where are you off to, Carrie?'

'Somewhere else,' she said, tucking her chair in neatly.

'Okey dokey, don't kill anyone – when the phone rang and this voice asked if I was Paul.'

The menhir stirred. 'She asked for me?'

'Well, she asked for someone called Paul. And I said if she wanted the Mighty Pudding then she'd got the wrong extension.'

Paul closed his eyes briefly. So much, then, for the care with which he had worded the letter; so much for his sneaking pursuit of Marianne along the narrow streets of central Shadley Oak, for his sudden crouched dash behind a row of market stalls when the opportunity to overtake had presented itself, for the rapid dexterity with which he had tucked the folded paper behind the handle of the newspaper office door, making sure that her name was clearly visible before haring off round a convenient corner. For his stratagem had worked – from twenty yards away he had seen Marianne reach for the handle, catch sight of the letter and then hesitantly extract it, her forehead creased in a gentle frown of wonderment. (OK, that last bit was an extrapolation, based on the back of her head, but nevertheless her body language had pointed to a fair degree of confusion.) He had seen her unfold the page and start to read and then he had crept away, knowing that he had done his best. And now, it seemed, he might just as well have stood up in the café and shouted, 'Oi Blondie, fancy a shag?'

'You listening?' asked Crispin.

'Yes.' He opened his eyes again. 'But I wish you hadn't called me the Mighty Pudding. To her.'

'Listen, mate, it was lucky I did.'

'Why?'

'Because she said, "Oh *now* I remember who he is."'

'Oh fantastic.' There was no way of examining that statement and coming up with an optimistic interpretation: either his nickname had been common currency in Argyle Road or else it served as an instantly recognizable description of his appearance. 'We used to live in the same street.'

'I know, she told me.'

'She's just started a job here. At the newspaper.'

'She told me that as well. She likes a good old chat, doesn't she? I couldn't get her off the phone.'

Paul absorbed the blows and soldiered on. 'So how did she end up ringing you?'

'Well, you know your letter?'

He could only nod. What else had they discussed – his shirt size? His bowel habits?

'Well, Marianne said you'd put a line straight through the phone number; she had to guess the last digit and she guessed wrong.'

'But I didn't – Oh . . .' That horrible small girl. Or rather, he remembered, her mother, bashing against his chair and sending his pen skidding across the paper. 'So . . . did you give her my extension?'

'Goddd,' Crispin smacked his forehead. 'Knew there was something I should have done. But listen, I built you up, told her you were my trusty right-hand man.'

'But did you get her number?'

'Nope. But you'll see her anyway, she's coming to the party.'

Paul blinked a couple of times. 'She's not.'

'Yeah. She's well up for it, she doesn't know anyone here. Made a couple of suggestions for my costume.'

'How long were you talking for?' His anguished semi-shout turned a couple of heads at the next table.

'Now Pud,' said Crispin, seriously, 'you're a friend and I would never, ever move in on the girlfriend of a friend. It's what I call the Finnerty Rule and it's unbreakable.'

'She's not my girlfriend,' muttered Paul, more in the cause of superstition than honesty.

'Oh well, in that case, fair game. Is she blonde?'

Paul started gathering his crockery and banging it back onto the tray.

'Hey Pud, I'm only kidding, I won't go near her, I'll be a Bond-shaped smudge on the wall. What are you going as?'

'I haven't decided. I've got to go, Crispin, I've got a routine admission and a whole stack of bloods.'

'Have you done that potassium yet?'

'Yes. They're going to phone me with the result.'

'Mr Henderson's chest X-ray?'

'Yes, I'm waiting for the radiologist to ring me back, she's in clinic.'

'Consented the phlebectomy?'

'No, not yet.'

'Better get your skates on then,' said Crispin, back in professional mode, a gelid edge to his voice, 'he's second on this afternoon's list.'

In American TV series, Paul had noted, doctors would tend to unwind at the end of a shift by playing basketball, shedding their psychic trauma by shooting a few hoops before tooling off down the highway towards their lakeside condos. He, on the other hand, had only five flights of stairs in which to slough off the daily angst, and the plodded journey only ever seemed long enough to simply inflame the worst memories. The Marianne conversation aside, today had contained the usual collection of minimalistic satisfactions and major failures, the latter centring around his attempt to give a no-nonsense explanation of varicose-vein removal to a middle-aged farmer.

'They're . . . they're going to do *what* to them?' Mr Charlton had asked, blood draining from his face.

'Pull them out from a tiny cut at the top of your leg.'

'*Pull* them?'

'Yes. I know it sounds a bit odd but it's standard procedure. It's why they call it str–'

'Pull out my *veins*?'

'Yes. I mean I'll do you a diagram if you –'

'Actually *pull* them, I mean the surgeon actually stands there and *drags them out?*'

'Yes, but – look, I'll do you a diagram.'

'No, no, no, no, no. No.' Mr Charlton lay back, his face grey against the pillow. 'Oh my God, I never imagined how they'd actually do it, I just knew I needed it done, but *now . . .*' He closed his eyes and then quickly reopened them. 'Oh my God, I keep seeing the vet delivering a calf. Oh my good *God.*'

Mr Charlton had signed the consent form only after the promise of a huge slug of pre-op sedation, and Paul had slunk away, marvelling at his own seemingly limitless ability to strike the wrong note. It was tempting, sometimes, to emulate Crispin's approach to doctor–patient communication: 'We find the hole, we sew it up, bish bosh, couldn't be easier,' as Paul had heard him explain to the wife of a man with a perforated ulcer.

'Bish bosh,' muttered Paul, reaching the fifth floor, and taking only the briefest of pauses to get his breath back; what he needed this evening, he thought, was an unbroken three hours of horizontal TV-watching followed by a dreamless night, after which he might begin, tentatively, to think about his tactics for the party. What he would actually be getting was presaged by the smell of bleach, discernible in the stairwell, moderately strong in the corridor, and reaching an eye-watering climax as he opened the door of the flat.

'Do you think we should have a talk?' said Paul, checking under the grill. The pan of beans already reeked of Domestos and he had no great hopes for the toast. Armand continued wordlessly to scrub the sink. He had acquired a vicious-looking curly wire loop on a long handle and this, combined with large amounts of pink scouring powder, was producing a continuous gritty underscore abrasive to both nerves and stainless steel.

'You're just making scratches,' said Paul.

By way of answer, his flatmate poured another arc of powder into the sink. Paul scraped a little carbon off the toast and tried to think of another way of broaching the topic. In their two and a half weeks together they had developed no routines of friendship, acquired no ease of conversation. On the ward they were like passing ships, semaphoring the odd bit of positional information and chucking the occasional lifebelt when tasks were beginning to swamp the decks. In the flat, on the one evening in three on which neither was on call, Armand would spend much of his time in his room, on the phone, speaking in French, while Paul would lie on the sofa with the remote control, occasionally raising a languid hand to his mouth in order to insert food or beer. In a spirit of détente, he had, on one occasion, tried to have a matey chat in O-level French, but there had been no response beyond a look of faint alarm. Armand's habitual expression – he was wearing it now as he scoured the sink – resembled that of the unfancied foreigner two sets down at Wimbledon: lips compressed, forehead furrowed, eyes jumping at the unfairness of the crowd. Paul had never seen him smile.

The first mouthful of grilled bleach prompted Paul to action. He scraped the rest of the plateful into the bin with as much noise as possible, and then cleared his throat assertively. 'Armand, I apologized this morning when you walked in on me, and I'll apologize again now, but you have to understand that I didn't have much choice.'

Armand turned on the hot tap and Paul took a step nearer so that he could be heard over the drumming water. 'I knocked on the bathroom door five times between seven and half past. You must have heard me.' The amplitude of the scrubbing arm decreased slightly. 'I was absolutely desperate – you know, there's a story that a Chinese bloke in the emperor's court once died because he was too polite to ask to leave the room and eventually his bladder burst. That could have happened to me. And anyway, there couldn't possibly be any bacterial problems with the sink because you know as well as I do that urine's sterile. It's not as if I took a dump. This – this cleaning stuff isn't logical, it's just . . . weird.'

The scrubbing ceased abruptly and Armand dropped the scourer and turned to face Paul; in the split second since the last word had been spoken his face appeared to have length-ened and sagged, as if drooping from the bone. 'Don't call me weird,' he said, and Paul saw with shock that his eyes were welling. 'I'm not weird.' The water hammered against the sink bottom and without looking Armand reached out a hand and turned off the tap; a little wisp of steam curled across the kitchen. 'OK,' he continued, swallowing, steadying his voice, 'OK, I know I have a hygiene thing, but it's well compensated for, and it doesn't interfere in any way with my work in the hospital, in fact it probably makes me a better, more empathic doctor, as does my diabetes, which is, of course, related to the hygiene thing since it's especially important for me to avoid minor skin infections, which brings me onto my foot thing, which incidentally it was incredibly unpleasant of you to have mentioned in front of that nurse –'

'What foot thing?'

' – but frankly if you had more of a foot thing yourself then maybe the physical atmosphere in this flat would be a little more pleasant, and I know that I –'

'I wash my socks,' said Paul, indignantly, catching up.

' – and I know I don't always chime in with the light-hearted banter over meals but I think that you underestimate, firstly, the fact that I'm trying to deal not only with a demanding job but also, secondly, with an entirely different culture, and you know that I actually have no idea what you're talking about most of the time and it doesn't help at all when you start speaking to me in Welsh –'

'What? When?'

'– last Thursday evening in the flat –'

'That wasn't Welsh, that was *French*.'

'Oh.' There was a pause. Armand's eyes widened. 'Jeez.'

'I got a B,' said Paul, almost to himself . . .

'Well . . . anyway, I think in total I'm coping pretty well with a potentially disorienting situation and I don't think I deserve to have insults flung at me just because I have different and higher standards from my roommate. And I know that you think I also have a food thing but in fact I haven't, I just don't consider it polite to ignore carefully written notices and anyway the reason I became a little tense was because it was my mother who especially sent me that packet of sugar-free pop . . .' His voice quavered and with a visible effort he clamped his mouth into a manly straight line. 'Tarts,' he added, after a few seconds. He folded his arms, unfolded them again, and then, with an awkward attempt at looking casual, rested an elbow on the draining board. 'So I'm not weird,' he said, his voice firm.

Paul groped for an appropriate response. 'Do you want a cup of tea?'

'No thank you.'

'Right. Well . . . I think I'll have one.' He found himself whistling nervously as he filled the kettle and it took him a moment to identify the tune; it was the theme from *The Addams Family*. He stopped whistling, and instead leafed through a few mental questions. Did his own feet really smell? Had anything actually been resolved by this evening's cathartic explosion or would he be reduced to pissing in the sink again tomorrow morning? And did his own feet really smell? 'So, er . . .' he tried to inject a note of jocularity into his voice. 'What can we do about this, then? This . . . situation.'

Armand appeared to ponder for a moment. 'Well, I think if I put the plug into the sink and leave it filled with bleach overnight, then –'

'No, I mean are you going to let me in the bathroom occasionally?'

'Oh.' He shook his head dismissively. 'Sure. I know I tend to get . . . er . . . very intense in the mornings, very focused. I think you probably need to knock harder, I'm just not hearing you.'

Paul had a vision of a medieval battering ram smashing through the MDF panelling, revealing a naked Armand and a bathroom rank with foaming peroxide. 'OK,' he said, reluctantly; it was – he supposed – by Armand's standards a major concession. 'And if you, er, need any cultural translations, just ask away.'

'Seriously?' A look of startled eagerness appeared on his flatmate's face.

'Yes, of course.'

'Well . . . thanks.' With the look of someone about to plunge their arm into a vat of pig slurry, for charity, he held out a hand and Paul shook it firmly. 'Good,' said Armand, nodding pleasantly. 'Fine.' He stuck his hand in his pocket and edged towards the door. 'Excuse me a moment. I . . . uh . . . have to go to the bathroom.'

9

At some point in the distant past all the 'i's from the Scrabble set had disappeared, and Netta had spent a creative hour cutting and inking squares of polystyrene as substitutes. Apart from a tendency to blow off the board if someone slammed a door they worked quite well, but she found them sinfully easy to avoid when groping in the bag. Glenn, through a combination of bad luck and guilelessness, had accumulated four of them on his rack and was taking even longer than usual to decide where to go. They had been playing for thirty-five minutes, there were two words on the board and Netta had written nearly a page of airmail to Mick.

> .. . . it's not so much that the sofa bed's got a huge dip in the middle, it's more that, once we move, I won't have anywhere of my own to retreat to, unless you count the loo, although since I haven't eaten a single green vegetable since leaving Glasgow, I

'Ibid,' said Glenn. 'Is ibid a word? I think it may well be a word.'

'Hang on.' Netta leafed through the giant *Chambers' Dictionary* that adjudicated their games. 'Yes, it's in here, but it's an abbreviation of ibidem.'

'Oh.' He leaned his chin on his hands and stared at the letters.

'We could bend the rule on abbreviations, I don't mind.'

'No,' said Glenn. 'It would be the thin end of the wedge.' It was one of the few metaphors he ever used, and Netta could date it precisely to a brief period in his adolescence when he'd collected doorstops.

haven't been spending quite as much time in there as usual. I just think I'm more appreciative of Mum's qualities (and she's a wonderful woman, Mick – I don't know if you've ever realized that) when we get a little bit of time apart. At this very second she's in the lounge with Coral discussing the autumn show, and Coral's taking notes so fast there's practically smoke coming from her pencil and there's costumes piled all over the room. I think they're trying to work out an order for the programme and it's obviously an enormous logistical feat – lots of little girls dancing in lots of different numbers and dashing around backstage needing lots of different costume changes. It's the sort of thing that Glenn could probably do her a good diagram of, with arrows, but I promise you, Mick, there's nothing as concrete as that going on next door.

She could hear snatches of the conversation floating through the louvred saloon doors that separated kitchen from lounge, although 'conversation' was actually a misnomer, it was more a stream of consciousness with occasional interruptions. 'So Emily Lane . . .' her mother was saying, 'so Emily Lane and Emma-Jane Shockley are both in "Pink Toothbrush" but Emily's also a duckling, so before "Splish Splash" we need a seniors number; could Chantalle be ready for "Sugar Plum"? She'd only have "Pink Toothbrush" to change from –'

'Sorry Bel –' Coral's interjection was tentative '– but I think it's Emma-Jane who's the duckling.'

'Is it? No surely, she –'

'It was going to be Emily but then you decided to swap them, because –'

'Yes you're right, Emma-Jane's the duckling because there

was that incident with the umbrella and we had to move her to intermediates. Coral, did you remember to ask Ted about the opening bars of "'S Wonderful"?'

'Oh, er . . . oh, gosh, er . . .' There was an anxious giggle.

'I wonder if I should phone him,' said her mother, rather broodingly.

'I'll phone him, Bel, you've got enough to do. Remind me again what the new choreo–'

'There should be time for a chassé coupé, chassé coupé, chassé pas de bourée before Eleanor reaches centre stage.'

'Chassé coupé . . . chassé . . . pas de – I'll ring him after we . . .'

'Thank you, Coral. You know, it'll be *such* a shame if Eleanor's skin doesn't clear up before the show.'

'She's on antibiotics.'

'Is she? She's been very moody for the last fortnight. Don't you think she's been very moody?'

'Well . . . er . . .' Coral's voice took on the tremulous quality it always assumed when she was asked to criticize anything. 'I hadn't noticed, but I suppose . . . at her age . . .'

'I was beginning to wonder whether she might be on the pill.'

'Oh golly, Bel, er . . .'

'But if she's on antibiotics then of course I may be wrong. So –' Her mother cleared her throat as if about to make an announcement. '"Pink Toothbrush". So "Pink Toothbrush". And then . . .'

There was a long pause.

'"Sugar Plum"!' shouted Netta.

'Sorry dear?'

'"Sugar Plum",' she repeated, going over to the saloon doors. 'You said "Pink Toothbrush" then "Sugar Plum" then "Splish Splash".'

Bel and Coral looked at each other, and then at Netta.

'No,' said her mother, kindly but firmly. 'No, it can't have been. Chantalle wouldn't have time to change after "Rhythm of Life" – it's just before "Pink Toothbrush", you see.'

'That's right,' said Coral.

'OK,' said Netta, defeated. She sat down at the breakfast bar and picked up the pen again.

I was mentioning about the sofa bed at work, and one of the secretaries said I should phone hospital accommodation and see if they can put me up somewhere. I actually think it's quite a good idea – the hospital's only ten minutes' walk from Mellis Hall, so I could still spend evenings en famille and then just go there to sleep and unwind a bit. The only thing holding me back

'I think I've got one,' said Glenn. 'Debt. Thirteen. The "b" is on a triple letter score.'

'OK.' Netta watched him fit the consonants around an 'e' already on the board and then extract three new tiles from the bag. One of them was made of polystyrene and he arranged it on the rack beside the other four. She sensed a marathon in prospect, and decided to employ cunning.

'I think I might use this go to swap all my letters,' she said. 'They're really terrible.'

'All right.'

She tipped them back in the bag. 'Do you want to swap yours as well?'

'No.'

'Oh.' She placed a zero beside her own score and picked up the pen again.

is that the person in charge of all the hospital accommodation is someone I'd rather not beg for favours. Bit of history there – I'll tell

you about him when I see you (three weeks, three days and
counting). Anyway, I haven't quite made up my mind yet. The big
move's

'Coral's had an absolutely brilliant idea,' announced her
mother, over the top of the doors.

'Oh, well, er . . .' said Coral self-deprecatingly, as she followed Bel into the kitchen.

'Look!' Her mother held up a small sparkly top. ' "Rhythm
of Life", and now . . .' She covered it with a sweatshirt painted
to look like a Liquorice Allsort. ' "Kingdom of the Sweets"!
Problem solved; Chantalle can do both numbers one after the
other and we can move "Splish Splash" to just before the
interval. Brilliant. Glenn, don't you think Coral's brilliant?'

Glenn declined to comment. 'I spy Carmen Miranda,' said
their mother, looking over his shoulder at the letter rack. ' "I,
I, I, I, I like you verrrrrrrrry much!" You know, I've never
seen the *point* of Scrabble. Have you, Coral?'

'Well, I er . . .'

'I think before we make a final decision I'd like to check
this combination in the hall mirror. Just in case you can see a
little sparkle at the neckline.' The doors juddered shut behind
them.

in three days and packing's going as well as can be expected, I
suppose. After a lot of discussion, and my God, Mick, I mean a lot
of discussion, the UN's been on the phone begging for my services,
Glenn's decided to donate a few of his oldest collections to a
charity shop (as a form of recycling), which should free up some
much-needed

'Oh Glenn,' called their mother reproachfully from the hall,
'you're not getting rid of this lovely mug tree, are you?'

125

Netta was up and through the door before her mother had finished the sentence.

'Mum,' she hissed, '*please*. Do you know how long it took us to decide what to chuck out?'

'Yes, but look at the workmanship, Brianetta,' said her mother, holding it up; it was made of dowling, competently constructed and painted dark green. 'He was only twelve when he made it, wasn't he? It really is charming.'

'And so are the other nineteen,' said Netta, jerking open the top of a box in demonstration. 'Glenn won't just keep one, he's told me he wants them to stay together. Like a . . . a legacy to an art gallery. There isn't as much room in the new flat, something has to go or you won't be able to get in through the front door. He's decided to lose the mug trees, the extension leads and the wallpaper-sample books.'

'Oh yes,' said her mother, slightly subdued. 'The wallpaper-sample books.'

'There were nine boxes of them in the attic. Nine. We've only shifted three so far, they're incredibly heavy, and I don't want –'

'Well, of course I haven't seen the attic in years.' There was an edge of nostalgia in her voice, as if talking about a seaside resort of her youth.

'Trust me, Mum.'

'I do, dear.' She laid a hand on Netta's arm. 'It just seems a pity to be so very *firm* when –'

'Brianetta, I need you to check a word,' said Glenn, coming into the hall.

'Just the person,' said her mother, holding up the mug tree. 'Are you sure you don't want to keep this lovely thing?'

There was a slight pause. 'I think so,' said Glenn.

Their mother looked at Netta with a hint of supplication. 'It's only one box,' she said, 'and they'd be very useful for presents.'

'But it's . . . oh God . . . he'd made the *decision*, you'd made the decision, hadn't you, Glenn? You'd made the decision to let them go.' She could hear her voice cracking with angst and she folded her arms and swallowed hard as her brother gazed at the row of cartons that stretched from the front porch to the door of the living room, ready for taking to the jumble sale or to the dump. 'I think so,' he said again. He lifted the flaps on the nearest and revealed the vinyl surface of one of the sample books. 'Although I may have to look through these again tomorrow. I may have to check if I'll need them in the new flat.'

Inimic was not in the dictionary. 'You can have inimi*cal*,' said Netta.

'You're not allowed to give suggestions.'

'Sorry.'

He stared at the tiles, and Netta listened to the fizzing cascade of irresolution coming from the lounge and felt saturated with her own uselessness. In almost three weeks she had achieved nothing; her suggestions and hints had bounced off the Mum–Glenn juggernaut like so many loose chippings and she could only stand and watch as it swerved erratically into the distance. She picked up the pen and wrote *They manage to get along without me most of the time. Somehow I've never quite grasped that* on Mick's letter and then crossed it out again. She needed, very urgently, to do something concrete – to notch up an achievement, however minor.

'Glenn,' she said, 'while you're thinking I might carry on wrapping your pictures. I'll stick to your system.'

'All right.'

'Come and get me when you've had your go.'

One wall of Glenn's room had already been cleared, the rows of pictures removed and packed in strict order so that they could be rehung in the new flat in exactly the same sequence. The largest item still on display was a poster illustrating the stages in the life of a moulded glass bottle, from chemical works to supermarket. The second largest, also bottle-related, was a laminated full-page magazine advertisement for Coca-Cola, in which a grinning blond man in a red jacket, his shoulders like the continental shelf, was hefting an entire crate with one hand. All the other pictures, however, were home-framed photographs on a common theme: all of them – snapshots, newspaper clippings, passport duplicates, school portraits – featured Glenn.

Netta cut a sheet of bubble wrap and unhooked the next item, an enlarged shot from the *Shadley Oak Mercury*, taken about ten years before and showing her brother among a handful of people watching the Lady Mayoress plant an oak sapling in the local park. Everyone else was at least pretending to look at Mrs Hay's spadework; Glenn was staring straight at the camera, his expression severe. He had liked this particular photo so much that he had bought a print from the newspaper office.

'I think there's a just a little bit of the performer in Glenn,' was how their mother archly ascribed his fondness for appearing in front of the camera. Glenn himself, if pressed, would say, 'It's a hobby.'

'But what in particular do you like about this one?' Netta had once asked of the Lady Mayoress shot. 'Is it the way you look in it?' Silence. 'Or is there someone in the crowd you're interested in? Or is it the composition? Or . . . or do you just like the view of the park? Or . . . or . . .'

'I happen to think it's a very good photo,' Glenn had replied eventually, as if that explained everything.

In a way, Netta found the repetitive images reassuring. Her brother, who spent his days being avoided by people, had chosen to surround himself with views of a world in which he was at the centre of every event. If that was how he actually saw his life – and she doubted whether she'd ever really know – then she found it a comforting thought.

She finished wrapping Mrs Hay and the oak tree, and started on a faded shot of a school trip to the York Transport Museum. Amidst the crowd of posing, gurning teenagers, Glenn stood like a disapproving curator.

'Mimic,' he said, coming through the bedroom door. 'Sixteen points. I used a blank for one of the "m"'s. It's your go now.'

'OK, I'll just finish this one.' She picked at the end of the Sellotape.

'York,' he said, looking down at the print. '1970. There was a very unpleasant smell in the coach.'

'I'm not surprised, with that many teenage boys on board.'

'There was a breaking-wind contest on the return journey and I complained to Mrs Simms.'

'What did she say?'

' "Just try to ignore them, Glenn." '

'And did you?'

'Yes. I talked to the driver, who was a friend of mine; we had a shared interest in electrical flex.'

Poor old driver, thought Netta; she had witnessed the desperation in the eyes of those whom Glenn had classified as 'friends'. They were usually people who, because of their job, were unable to escape when he approached: lollipop ladies, road-diggers, disabled flag-sellers. With perfect politeness, and standing a good five feet away, Glenn would talk to them for as long as his schedule permitted. 'Oh, he's such a chatterer,' their mother would say, 'chitty chitty chat chat' – ignoring the fact that 'chat' was normally a two-way procedure.

'Hey Glenn,' she said, pointing to a big white head that

loomed like a full moon at the back of the group shot, 'do you remember him?'

'Yes, that's Craig Gebbard. He used to call me "Spack Man".'

'I know.'

'Which was inaccurate, because "spack" is an abbreviation of spastic so he meant that I have cerebral palsy, which I don't. He was a very ignorant person. He should have called me "Prob Man".'

'Why?'

'Because that would be short for "Probably falls within the autistic spectrum".'

Netta gaped for a moment and then started to laugh.

'Why are you laughing?' asked Glenn.

'Oh, because you're priceless sometimes,' she said, affectionately, 'as in "no one could possibly afford to buy you because you're worth too much".'

'That's not the case,' said Glenn. 'The average human body contains chemicals to the value of only eighty-five pence.'

'You know what? I actually met Craig at the hospital a couple of weeks ago. He still looks the same.'

'He could also have called me "Aut Man".'

'He could also have called you "Glenn",' she said hotly. For a fraction of a second her brother's eyes met hers and then slid away again.

'You called him "Plateface",' he said.

'I know,' she said, slightly embarrassed.

'And "Lardskin".'

'Really? I don't remember that.'

'And "Scrote Features", which is short for "Scrotum Features", which is also not an accurate term because the scrotum doesn't have any features. And also "Quasimodo" because you said his legs weren't in the correct proportion to his body. That was quite popular, a lot of people called him

"Quasimodo" after you did but they shortened it to "Quasi". And you called him "Trenchmouth" because his teeth were quite yellow. And "Brillohead" and "Frizzo". And you also said that he looked like a Neanderthal throwback and you photocopied a picture of an orang-utan from *Nuffield Science Volume One* and enlarged it and put it on the noticeboard of Hut 3 with a label with his name on. Your face is going red.'

Netta bent over the picture and began to wrap it hastily. She had somehow forgotten the degree to which she'd managed to even the score with Craig.

'It's your turn at Scrabble,' said Glenn.

'I know, I'll um . . .'

'That corner isn't fastened securely.'

'Sorry. I'll join you as soon as I've done it.'

The doorbell rang when Glenn was halfway down the stairs; answering it was one of his preferred household tasks and Netta cocked an ear for his idiosyncratic greeting, used to friends and strangers alike: 'Hello, who is it you wish to see?'

'Is Mrs Etterly in?'

'There is no one of that name in this household.'

'Just a minute, Glenn.' She was down the stairs in seconds. 'Hello. Have you found my suitcase?'

'Not yet, no, I just wanted to drop something by. And I wanted to ask you something.' Constable Whittaker jerked a thumb towards a police car parked at the bottom of the drive. 'We were on patrol in the area.'

'It's Mrs *Lee*, incidentally.'

'Sorry?' He was feeling about in his pocket. 'Here we go.' He handed her an orange leaflet. 'It's the victim-support one,' he said. 'I couldn't find it when you came into the station.'

'Thank you. So definitely no news of the suitcase?'

'No. But I've er . . .' he lowered his voice conspiratorially, 'put on just over half a kilo.'

'Very good.' He still looked about as hearty as a tent-pole, his shirt hanging slack against his chest.

'Yeah, I've started eating more fish. Mainly fingers.'

'Right.'

'And fruit.'

'Good. So what was it you wanted to ask me?'

'Oh yeah, it's about nutrition. Is it better to eat a banana before or after a meal?'

'I don't think it makes any difference.'

'But what about both?'

'Before *and* after?'

'Yeah. Is that too much?'

'No. I don't think it's possible to overdose on bananas.'

'And what about – I wanted to check, because I eat quite a lot of them – what about beans?'

'Beans?'

'Yeah,' said Ryan, seemingly undeterred by the lack of enthusiasm in her voice. 'Baked beans. I mean, are they good for you?'

She sighed. 'Well, I supposed it depends on what aspect of –'

'Which brand do you buy?' asked Glenn, listening in.

'Oh.' Ryan looked at her brother, clearly pleased to widen his audience. 'Crosse and Blackwell, I think. I'm not fussed really, I sometimes eat two tins a –'

'Crosse and Blackwell beans tins are actually manufactured in an identical way to Heinz beans tins,' said Glenn, 'in that they're both constructed of three separate pieces of tinplate, which is actually formed by the electrical deposition of tin onto a thin steel strip.'

'Oh,' said Ryan. His eyes flicked towards Netta and she smiled brightly.

'Tins of drink, on the other hand,' continued Glenn, 'don't contain the element tin at all since they're made of aluminium, together with trace amounts of magnesium, manganese, copper and silicon. It would be more correct to call them "aluminiums" of drink or even "amalgams" of drink, if you use the secondary definition of amalgam rather than the primary definition which means an alloy containing mercury. Unlike tinplate, which is wholly recyclable any number of times without any deterioration in quality, aluminium . . .'

'I'll leave you two chatting,' said Netta. 'Sorry to interrupt.'

Her mother was in the kitchen, arranging cheese curls on a plate. 'Coral and I have taken on board your criticism of the title,' she said.

'What criticism? What title?'

'Of the show. Don't you remember, you asked how "Camptown Races" fitted in with the title?'

'Oh yes. Vaguely.'

'Well, we're thinking of calling it "*Rosettes* and Champagne" instead of "Roses and Champagne", which I think is an improvement. Don't you?'

'Definitely,' said Netta, with enough conviction to forestall further discussion.

'And we may need you in a minute, to try on a headdress. You have the same sort of hair as Kerry Pritchett.'

'What, curly?'

'Yes, and rather coarse. Although your head's much wider than hers so we shall have to take that into account.' She picked up the plate and, still talking, began to move towards the lounge. 'Did I tell you that Chloe MacPherson's come down with something and her mother says she can't possibly allow her to attend rehearsals until she's discovered whether it's infectious and of course Chloe is lead rabbit –' the swing doors closed behind her '– in "Run Rabbit Run". Coral, I'm just telling Brianetta about Chloe . . .' Netta looked down at the leaflet she'd been given by Constable Whittaker. 'SOME-TIMES WE ALL NEED HELP,' it read, in white letters on orange. 'DON'T BE AFRAID TO ASK.' She thought of the possibility of a nice little hospital room, with its very own, fully locking, door, and she wondered where she might possibly have put Craig Gebbard's business card.

September

IO

In the week preceding the party Paul spent a great deal of time brooding on tactics. What he needed with Marianne, he felt, was a chance to make mellow conversation in relaxed surroundings – a little wine to take the edge off his nerves, a little background music to fill in any awkward gaps, a little spot of prolonged eye contact. Instead, thanks to Crispin, he would be wearing a stupid outfit, screaming above the biggest sound system that he had ever seen outside of a club and drinking cocktails made largely of blue curaçao, a two-litre bottle of which had been discovered in the back of a wardrobe at the nurses' home; there would be no margin of error between total sobriety and extreme drunkenness, no subtle gap between effortful small talk and sozzled blabber. And while it was true that most of Paul's previous relationships had begun with a booze-fuelled snog, it was also true that most of them had ended not all that long after both parties had sobered up.

It was time, he decided, for a more considered approach and the solution occurred to him one night as he was holding yet another retractor at yet another four a.m. appendectomy: he could be *on call*! It was perfect – he'd become an occasional visitor to the Bacchanalia, rueful yet dignified, a white-coated beacon of maturity who, while enjoying the antics of his friends, had yet a higher, finer, more *sober* purpose for the evening. ('I've hardly seen you all night, Paul.' 'I know, I'm sorry, but we had a cardiac arrest on Ward 4.' 'Did you – did you manage to save him?' 'Yes, but . . . you don't want to hear about serious stuff do you?' 'No, I do. Let's get away from here, let's find somewhere where we can really talk.')

All the plan needed was a minor rearrangement of the rota and a reason for the rearrangement that wouldn't attract Crispin's derision; a fictitious ear infection requiring antibiotics did the trick rather well ('Christ, Pud, you sad bastard, what a fucking *catastrophe* not to be able to drink at your own party!'), and the only crease in the plan was Armand's slight reluctance to swap shifts ('I don't see, Paul, why you can't attend this social get-together and simply stick to soda. Why is it necessary to drink alcohol at all?'), but Paul offered to spend their next shared free evening working on a flat-tidying rota and a deal was struck. Since the night of the sink Armand had thawed just a little and had become friendly in a slightly mechanical way, as if schooled through an earpiece. In return for the largesse of letting Paul use the shower for five minutes in the morning he had begun expecting a sort of simultaneous translation of British cultural mores, and would also jot down odd questions that occurred to him during the day.

'So, what is a clanger?'

'A clanger? Well, it means a big mistake. People say, "Oh I've dropped a clanger," when they've said something they shouldn't.'

'So when I overheard Gwyn Parry say that I sounded exactly like an outraged Clanger, that means . . . ?'

'Oh right, that sort of Clanger.' Sometimes the explanations were difficult; sometimes Paul lied.

His flatmate had been surprisingly accommodating about the party, and Paul wondered whether he had actually grasped the full extend of the squalor that might result. 'You know there'll be loads and loads of people here,' he'd said tentatively.

'Paul, I appreciate your concern, I can see how you might think it wouldn't be my kind of thing, but I enjoy social occasions and I'm more than able to deal with them as long as my own personal space is out of bounds. Which of course it will be.' The muscles around his jawline had flickered ominously.

'Right . . . and, er, who's your hero?'

'You mean, what costume am I going to wear?'

'Yup.'

'Well, I've had what I think is quite a clever idea. And amusing. You see, my personal hero is my maternal grandfather who emigrated from Caithness in 1927 when he was only fourteen and took a job in a bakery in Montreal, and I look a lot like him. Really a lot, I'll show you a photo. So I thought I could wear a name badge with *his* name. And maybe some sort of neckerchief, so that I look kind of dated.'

On the evening of the day before the party, therefore, it was Armand and not Paul who was on call when Mrs Dimoglou returned to hospital as an emergency with an inflamed and perforated gall bladder. She was taken straight to surgery, and from there to intensive care where – much to everyone's surprise – she survived the night and was transferred to a side room on the ward. 'Ah yes,' as Mr Gorman said acidly on the round the next morning, 'and now we come to a patient who should have had her gall bladder removed under controlled conditions three weeks ago, instead of as a desperate measure involving the midnight summoning of a senior surgeon who was hoping, for just once in his life, that the competence of his junior staff would enable him to have a full night's sleep. Dr Gooding, would you like to define the meaning of the word "elective" for the benefit of our medical students?'

After the round Paul returned furtively to the room and looked through the porthole window at the tiny figure in the bed. He was used to feeling inadequate in the face of patient suffering, but feeling directly responsible was a new and unpleasant sensation. There was no way around it: if Mrs Dimoglou had had her routine operation as planned, then she would not now be fighting peritonitis with the aid of four separate tubes and a heart monitor. Fat Trevios was sitting beside her, holding her hand; Paul watched impotently for a while and then slunk away.

Trevios stayed, but other relatives came and went throughout the day; Paul peered into the room whenever he was passing – and sometimes made a detour even when he wasn't – and witnessed across the hours a tiny and gradual improvement in Mrs Dimoglou's condition. By early evening her blood pressure and temperature checks were down from half-hourly to hourly, and she was beginning to take the odd sip of water.

'Still with us, is she?' asked Gwyn, coming on shift at seven and catching Paul on one of his sorties.

'Just about,' said Paul, subdued.

'Oh, don't give up on Mrs Dimoglou, she's tougher than she looks – stringy, you see, that's the build you need if you want to get old; all the ones who end up getting their telegrams are head-to-toe gristle.' He nodded encouragingly. 'Any admissions expected?'

'Not yet.'

'Well, thank God for that, you know how many staff I've got on with me this shift?'

'No.'

'One. Student. Guess how much ward experience she's had – go on, guess.'

'A week?'

'Two days.' He gave a mirthless bark of laughter. 'Bloody marvellous, isn't it, I'm surrounded by toddlers. No offence, Paul.' He took off his coat and yawned and then halted, mid-stretch. 'Hey now,' he said, 'I've just remembered something. It's your party tonight, isn't it – cocktails and hip-swivelling debauchery until the small hours?'

'Yup.'

'So why are you taking the bleep?'

'I can't drink – I'm on antibiotics for an ear infection.'

'Oh God, bad luck. Still, if it stays quiet you should be able to pop upstairs every now and again. You ought to make a point of viewing Lexie – she spent most of yesterday night making her costume. Mind you, that's about an hour per square inch of material so be prepared to shield your eyes from the glories of the flesh.'

'What's she going as?' asked Paul, stirred in spite of himself.

'Princess Leia in that scene where she's rolling round in front of the big slug – you know, the tin bikini. Doesn't do anything for me but I gather it sends you straight boys into a frenzy of lust. Or maybe you've got someone special of your own arriving? Little bit of a private consultation, maybe? Just step into my room, madam, and I'll demonstrate the use of my stethoscope?'

Paul shrugged with an attempt at nonchalance. 'You never know,' he said.

When, ten minutes later, he climbed the stairs from the ward to the accommodation floor he could feel the bass line pulsing through the soles of his feet, and he pushed open the door to the corridor expecting to be slapped back by a wall of music. Instead there was merely a slightly muffled version of the same beat, filtering up through the carpet tiles. Outside the open door of the flat Armand was sellotaping a row of bunting around the frame. He was wearing the neckerchief, together with a check shirt and a pair of jeans, both of which were covered in white dust.

'Flour,' he said, in answer to Paul's query. 'If you remember, my grandfather worked in a bakery. But I've actually used non-perfumed talcum powder.' His name badge, written in copperplate, read 'Archie McClaren'.

'Has anybody else arrived?'

'No, not yet. Oh, Crispin wanted a word with –'

'Pud! Is that you? Get in here.'

The sitting room had been cleared of most of its furniture and a bar constructed out of the kitchen table and a length of yellow crepe paper. A purloined whiteboard sported a list of available cocktails.

'What's a Shadley Oak Shafter?' asked Paul.

'Curaçao and Coke. I think the stereo's fucked.' Crispin gave the top an irritated smack. 'Know anything about them?'

'Not much.' Paul crouched beside it. 'What's an Abbey Arseholer?'

'Curaçao and Guinness. One of the speakers isn't working – listen.' He swivelled the volume dial, and Paul's entire body became one vast, thrumming bass note.

'See what I mean,' said Crispin, turning it down again. 'No treble.'

'That could be really dangerous, doing that,' said Paul. He felt as if his bowels were still sounding a low C. 'That's a biological weapon. I read about someone once who was killed by a low-frequency noise. At the post-mortem they found that his organs had disintegrated into a homogeneous jelly.'

'Curaçao and homogeneous jelly,' said Crispin. 'I could sell that. Here, Pud, you know I found a bunch of old party photos from our student days. How about I staple them to the front of the bar?'

'I'd prefer it if you didn't. Where did you get the stereo from?'

'Card in a shop window, dead cheap. So, can you mend it?'

'No,' said Paul, straightening up. 'At least, I can't see any loose wires and that's about my limit.'

'Bugger. I'll have to see what I can borrow – hey, while I'm gone can you stop that loon sticking labels on everything. Real atmosphere killer.' He caught sight of himself in the mirror over the gas fire and gave his bow tie a tweak before striking a brief pose, forefingers forming an upward-pointing gun. 'Mishter Bond,' he said, in a rough approximation of Sean Connery, 'you're looking sho fucking shexy.'

The notice outside the bathroom read 'Please leave this room as you found it', and just beside the toilet the cleaning materials had been corralled into one easy-to-find group labelled 'USE ME'. The kitchen sink had a slightly pointed 'Drinking Fluids Only Down Here' sticker, and on Armand's bedroom door was taped a sheet of A3 on which was written 'PRIVATE, THIS MEANS YOU!!' in large black letters. Paul rubbed the back of his neck thoughtfully and decided to leave any intervention to Crispin. He could hear Armand talking to someone outside the flat, and from the pink-knitted timbre of his voice he was feeling outraged again.

'Paul,' he said, when Paul had stuck his head round the door to see what was going on, 'did you know there's an empty apartment just up the corridor?'

'It's not empty any more,' said a woman standing nearby, a laden bin bag in her arms and a holdall over one shoulder. 'It's got me in it, for three weeks anyway.' She glanced at Paul and then did a distinct double take. 'Hello there.'

He looked at her blankly. She was, what – thirty-five, forty, more? He found it difficult to estimate women's ages once they stopped being obviously young. She had curly hair and very blue eyes and quite a big bust.

'You don't remember me?'

He shook his head, made slightly uneasy by the knowing slant of her mouth. Had she been a patient to whom he had done something especially incompetent? 'Sorry,' he added.

'That's OK,' she said, 'you were pretty busy when we met. You having a party?'

'Yes, we –'

'I'm sorry to butt in here,' said Armand, in a determined voice, 'but I just need to . . . to establish something. You are moving into a hospital apartment?'

'Yes, temporarily. It's one they save for married doctors, but there aren't any at the moment so it was offered to me . . .'

'You're a doctor?'

'No, I'm a dietitian.'

'So we're talking about a – a –' Armand seemed almost unable to articulate the next word, '*single*-bedroom apartment? A single-bedroom *doctor's* apartment with *bathroom*?'

'Yes,' said the woman. 'At least I think so, I haven't actually seen it yet.' She waggled a key at them. 'I'm just on my way in.'

'But I was very clearly informed by administration that there are *no* en suite doctor's rooms.'

'Well I doubt it's en suite,' said the woman, 'but as I say –'

'It's the *equivalent* of en suite.' He took a deep and quivering breath. 'I shall have to speak to someone in authority about this. Excuse me.'

'Can I ask,' said the woman, after Armand had darted back into the flat, 'why your friend's dressed as an extra from *Seven Brides for Seven Brothers*?'

'He's not. He's his own grandfather. It's a heroes party.'

She blinked a couple of times. 'And who are you dressed as?'

'I'm not. I mean, I'm working.'

'You could be Sir Alexander Fleming.'

'Yes, I suppose so.'

'Or Dr Strangelove.'

'Yes, maybe.'

'Or Dr Finlay. Or Dr Who. Or Dr No. Or –'

For once he was grateful for the interruption of the bleep; she looked capable of suggesting doctors all evening. 'I'd better answer that,' he said, patting his pocket.

'And I'd better unpack. Is your party going on late?'

'Er . . . probably.' It hadn't occurred to him to warn the neighbours. 'I mean, if you want to . . . you know . . .' The invitation died on his lips, strangled by insincerity.

'Thanks,' she said drily. 'That sounds lovely.'

As he criss-crossed the hospital over the next ninety minutes, listening to a chest here, taking a blood sugar there, pulled by his bleep from one task to another, he caught occasional glimpses of other party-goers on their way to flat 5K: Elvis holding the lift door open so that Superman and Superwoman could support an already rat-arsed Gandhi across the threshold; a pointy-titted Madonna and two Florence Nightingales, one of them male, sharing a joint in the staff car park; Mr Spock snogging Margaret Thatcher outside the coronary care unit. 'Hi Pud,' Margaret had said perkily just as he'd passed, and he'd been startled to see Wai's face under the blonde wig. Her giggle had followed him around the corner and as far as the stairwell, and it seemed to keep ringing in his head as he climbed, a feverish little refrain.

During his absence the flat had filled and then overflowed into the corridor, and he pushed his way to the door through a steamy press of bodies; the interior was a roaring crush, every mouth open in simultaneous yelled conversation, every hand clutching a bluish cocktail; the kitchen floor was sticky with spilled drink and plastic glasses cracked underfoot as he edged around the room, scanning the crowd for a glimpse of

Marianne. Over the din he could just hear Crispin bellowing, 'Wrong! Wrong!' and a woman's voice shouting something that was greeted with a scattering of applause.

'Hi Paul,' said a red-eyed girl wearing a sheet and a plastic Roman helmet. She looked vaguely familiar and he groped for a name.

'It's Carrie,' she said. 'I'm wearing contact lenses.'

'Oh sorry. And who are you dressed as? A ghost?'

'The goddess Minerva.' She pointed at the furry toy owl fastened to her shoulder.

'Oh.'

'I know, it's a bit esoteric, isn't it? Maybe I should have worn a name badge.' She blinked, rather painfully. 'And my lenses feel like dustbin lids. Still, it's nice not to wear glasses sometimes.'

'Yeah,' he said, momentarily distracted; he had just caught sight of Lexie sitting on the draining board. She was dressed in a tinfoil-covered bra and tiny tinfoil-covered knickers, and his balls seemed to wither at the sight. He realized after a moment that Carrie was telling him something.

'Sorry?'

'I said, Crispin's doing a Gorman quiz. He couldn't get the stereo to work properly so he's providing entertainment.'

'A what quiz?' Behind Carrie there was a sudden influx of guests into the kitchen.

'A Mr Gorman quiz. It seems to be a mixture of not very good puns and questions about the history of Shadley Oak. And if you get an answer right you have to drink a shot glass in one go. Who are you looking for?'

'Just er . . .' he dragged his eyes away from the group, 'a friend who said she might come. Actually I might go and see if she's in the living room, because she won't know anyone else here.'

'OK,' said Carrie, equably. 'Well I'm going to check if the loo's free. See you later.' Her helmet bobbed away through the crowd, and Paul revived long defunct scrummaging skills and forced his way in the opposite direction.

'I'm looking –' Crispin was shouting, standing on the windowsill with the lights of Shadley Oak behind him '– I'm looking for a two-word title here. A Surgical Snakebite awaits the correct answer.' On the floor next to him stood Armand, holding a tray of filled glasses; he was smiling in a fixed way but his eyes were desperate. 'I'm looking for a two-word title. Which pop song of the sixties, or maybe it was the seventies, answers on a postcard, anyway, which pop song – two-word title – did Gorman quote when our Canadian friend here accidentally tripped over a catheter stand? This is totally guessable even for those people not lucky enough to have been present at the aforementioned incident. Two words.'

'Sealed with a Piss,' shouted someone.

'Two words,' reiterated Crispin, over laughter, 'and neither of them are piss.' Paul stood on tiptoe and surveyed the room, his gaze darting between the few visible blonde heads; Marianne was not among them. His first feeling was of disappointment. His second, rapidly succeeding it and surprising him by its strength, was of relief – once again, he realized with a cowardly lift of the spirits, he could postpone the encounter, could keep it safely within the billowy realms of imagination; once again he could defer the need for witty aperçus and sophisticated charm. He was free, instead, to droop around the party feeling a bit sorry for himself – and also slightly unwell, now he came to think of it. The back of his neck was quite sore and he wondered if he might be getting a cold.

'Two words,' shouted Crispin again. 'Just imagine the scene, ladies and gentleman, our colonial pal here, a tube full of urine wrapped tightly around one ankle –'

'Yellow River,' answered Paul, to put Armand out of his misery.

'Correct.' There was a burst of applause, and Crispin lifted up a glass of violet liquid. 'And seeing as our mighty friend in the white coat is on the wagon this evening so as to keep his skills honed for the usual bunch of creaking timewasters –' Paul gave a modest wave of acknowledgment '– and also because he's got an earhole full of pus, I will drink this on his behalf. To Pud!' He threw the glassful neatly down his throat, turned scarlet and sat down rather suddenly, clutching at the bar as he did so and tearing off a section of photo-adorned crepe paper.

'Religion,' shouted Crispin, using one of Armand's shoulders as a crutch to haul himself upright. 'That's the next question. Your starter for ten. It's about what you can see from Ward 12. One of Gorman's harder questions. Religion. Quite hard. Starter for ten.'

'Get on with it,' shouted someone.

'OK. It's quite hard. Which *two* saints are the patron saints of Shadley Oak Abb–'

'St Joan and St Catherine,' said a loud, clear, female voice with a trace of the local accent.

'Very good,' said Crispin. 'Do I know you, or are you here with someone?'

'Neither,' said the woman. 'Do I get a drink?' As she reached forward for her prize Paul recognized her as the new neighbour. She took a delicate sip, grimaced and then took another.

'Right,' said Crispin. 'History. *When* – I'm looking for a year here and it's a geography question. I mean history. *When* – a year, remember, *when* was this building built? This building, I mean, here.' He waved an uncoordinated hand at the room.

'1964,' called the woman.

'No,' said Crispin. 'Close but no banana. Any advance on the lady?'

'It was 1964,' repeated the woman. 'I was there. My father was one of the builders. I can give you the exact date if you want.' She plucked another glass from Armand's tray. 'You are Kolly Kibber and I claim my five pounds. Cheers. I deserve this, I've had a hell of a day.'

Crispin swayed on the windowsill, temporarily at a loss for words. 'OK,' he said after a moment, 'I'll check that answer tomorrow. Almond, check that answer tomorrow.'

'Excuse me, everyone.' Armand cleared his throat, nervously. 'Excuse me. Could I just ask people to be careful about where they put their glasses, because I'm seeing a great many –'

'OK, next question, and you're banned,' said Crispin pugnaciously, pointing at the woman.

'Why?'

'Because there's an upper age limit.'

'Are you a bouncer?'

'I'm Bond,' said Crispin. 'James Bond.'

'With an IQ of double-oh-seven, apparently.'

Crispin flushed darkly. 'Who are you dressed as then?' he asked. 'Widow Twankey?'

There was a tiny moment of relative silence followed by a collective, excited 'Oooooh' from the audience and the woman looked slowly down at her faded green-and-yellow sundress and then back up at Crispin.

'Better Twankey than wanky,' she said.

Crispin looked at her, open-mouthed. 'Who *invited* you?'

'That doctor over there.' All heads turned towards Paul.

'She's a neighbour,' he said, feebly. 'In the next flat . . .'

'He goes for blondes normally,' shouted Crispin, 'don't you, Pud?'

With magnificent timing Paul's bleep went off. 'Gotta make a call,' he said, ducking away through the crowd. The phone in the kitchen was unreachable and he fought his way along the corridor towards his bedroom, hesitating a moment at the sight of the door, which was slightly ajar. You never knew what you might find in a bedroom at a party. He pushed it open quietly and saw Marianne and a man with a beard. He closed it again and went and leaned against a free patch of wall and began a frantic analysis of what he'd just witnessed.

Had they been actually doing anything? No, they'd been sitting next to each other on the far side of the bed, and Marianne had been talking. *Had any part of them been touching?* No, no part of their bodies had been touching because in the gap between them he could clearly remember seeing his own boxer shorts, hanging over the back of a chair. *Had they been smiling?* No, the impression had been one of serious conversation. *Had it actually been Marianne?* Well, he'd only seen the curve of her cheek, and the pale skin of her neck, and her blonde hair pushed carelessly – yes, yes, all right, it had definitely been Marianne, of course it had been Marianne and the trespassing bastard next to her had been that repulsive beardy git from the newspaper office. Well, he could just fight him for – Paul's bleep went off again and simultaneously Marianne and Beardy left the room, passing within feet of him. '. . . that's why it's so interesting to talk about it,' Marianne was saying. 'Yeah,' replied Beardy, 'do you know where we can get a drink?'

Paul slammed into the room and dialled switchboard and then Ward 12. 'Can you come over, Dr Gooding,' said a faltering voice. 'Nurse Parry's had to run down to Ward 6 to help with an emergency and I think Mrs Dimoglou might be having a stroke.'

★

The student nurse met him at the door of the ward. 'She says her arm's feeling all funny,' she said, huge-eyed. She was young enough to make Paul feel like an authority figure.

'What sort of funny?' he asked, walking alongside her.

'Just . . . funny really. She didn't say. But her pulse on that side feels . . .'

'What?'

'I don't know, really. A bit funny, I think. Not normal anyway.'

'And how's her speech?'

'Well it's . . .' There was a long, unhappy pause, 'it's always a bit, you know . . . funny.'

Trevios had gone and Mrs Dimoglou was alone in the room; she lifted one of her hands from the coverlet when she saw Paul, and caught his wrist with a grip so weak that it was almost imperceptible. She looked weightless, a figure of wire and parchment.

'Hello Mrs Dimoglou,' said Paul. 'How are you feeling?'

'My arm is bad,' she said in a sticky whisper, moving her head slightly towards her other hand. Paul studied the even set of her mouth and the symmetrical web of wrinkles across cheeks and forehead. It didn't *look* like a stroke. Gently he disengaged his wrist, and moved to the other side of the bed. Mrs Dimoglou's right arm seemed a little darker than the other.

'Is it numb?' he asked, carefully turning it palm upwards.

'It feels . . . squash. And my fingers are pins and needles.'

'And did it start suddenly or slowly?'

'Slowly.'

Paul took her pulse; it *did* feel funny, indefinably so, the blood butting against his fingertips with peculiar vigour. He asked her to hold his wrist and she did so with a grip no stronger or weaker than that of the other hand; he tested her reflexes on both sides and found them identical.

'What do you think it is?' asked the student nurse, and Paul shook his head. His mind was a frightening blank and he had the impression that the small, hot room was getting perceptibly smaller and hotter. Mrs Dimoglou's eyes were fixed upon his and he could feel the weight of her gaze.

'I'll just, er . . .' He tried to think of something, anything, that might aid diagnosis. 'I'll just do your blood pressure.'

'I did it fifteen minutes ago,' said the nurse as Paul pushed up the loose sleeve of Mrs Dimoglou's gown. 'It was a hundred and forty over ninety. I kept the . . .' Her voice wavered as Paul exposed the black cuff wrapped around Mrs Dimoglou's upper arm; it was still partially inflated, still tightly embracing the flesh above the elbow. He reached for the rubber bulb and twisted the little silver cog at its base. With a hiss the cuff released its air and Mrs Dimoglou's arm returned to its normal colour. She rubbed her fingers across the sheet.

'Oh,' she said softly. 'It's better. Thank you, it's wonderful.'

No residual neurological signs/symptoms wrote Paul in Mrs Dimoglou's notes, and then added a full stop before placing the biro on the desk. It was even hotter in the office than it had been in the side room, and he wiped his forehead with a sleeve and cautiously slid a hand across the back of his neck. There was a small, tender swelling on either side.

'Oh, tonight's just getting better and better,' said Gwyn, hurrying through the door with an empty box of tissues. 'She says she won't come out of the sluice until her eyes have gone down. I've tried to tell her there's far worse done every day in every hospital in the land, and it's my fault for not being here and that she's learned her lesson and there's no lasting damage to the patient, but she's in absolute floods. There *isn't* any lasting damage, is there?' he asked, suddenly anxious.

'No,' said Paul, 'and I'm going to put that in Mrs Dimoglou's notes.' He picked up a biro and wrote *No residual neurological signs/symptoms* and then noticed that he'd already written exactly the same thing on the line above. 'Oh,' he said blankly, and crossed it out again.

'Are you all right?' asked Gwyn, leaning over and peering at him.

'No, not really. I'm feeling a bit hot and I've got a couple of nodes up on the back of my neck.'

'Oh marvellous.'

'But I can't really remember what it signifies when you get occipital nodes. Can you?'

Gwyn shrugged. 'Is it something to do with the ear infection?'

'No,' said Paul, with certainty.

'Well, why don't you look it up?' Gwyn nodded at the books on the office windowsill. 'Look it up, take your temperature and then go to Casualty and get a couple of paracetamol. I've got to get on, sorry, I've got a million things to do.'

It took Paul a long time to find the right page. *Common aetiologies of occipital lymphadenopathy*, he read, running a finger beneath the line, *include tinea capitis, seborrhoeic dermatitis, insect bites, orbital cellulitis and pediculosis*. Pediculosis was nits, wasn't it? He scratched his head absently and thought about the mad stuff he'd said to Mrs Dimoglou when he'd first talked to her – wallets and purses and handbags – all rubbish, of course. He should have said, 'Bish bosh, couldn't be easier.' *Viral aetiologies include rubella, varicella and roseola infantum*. He'd never even heard of roseola infantum. Lucky it hadn't come up in finals, wasn't it? He closed *Radcliffe's Clinical Signs* and thought, with a sudden flush of indignation, about what an insensitive clod Beardy was. Marianne had obviously been trying to talk about something interesting and all Newspaper Man had wanted was a drink. What a hairy, booze-obsessed idiot. Paul should have knocked him to one side and called out, 'Marianne, tell *me* about the interesting thing.' He should have –

'You still here?' said Gwyn, appearing in the office door with an armful of sheets. 'What's your temperature, then?'

Paul removed the thermometer from his mouth and scrutinized it. 'Thirty-eight point five.'

'God almighty. Go to Casualty or go and *lie down*. I'll call you if I need you.'

The corridor outside the flat smelled as if someone had mistaken curaçao for carpet cleaner, and a scattering of pulverized tortilla chips formed a pathway to the door. Paul stepped over one of the Florence Nightingales and followed a dribble of chatter through the front door and into the kitchen. The few remaining guests were ranged around the walls, as if incapable of standing unsupported. 'Hey Pud,' said another Nightingale, noticing him very slowly, 'where d'you hide the drink?'; Paul shook his head and carried on towards the bedroom. He opened the door, gazed for a long moment at the bouncing blue jacket and pale chunky thighs of a knickerless Thatcher astride a trouserless Spock, and then closed it again. 'They're using my bed,' he said. 'Well they're not using my bathroom,' echoed Armand, throatily. He was seated on a chair that blocked the toilet door, and his arms were folded; he looked like John Wayne defending a pass against the Apaches.

'Armand, I'm feeling like shit, can I go and lie down in your room?'

'I'm sorry, Paul, but I'm expecting an urgent phone call. No,' he said, half rising as a stumbling party-goer approached. 'This portion of the flat is not for public use.' There was a new strength to his voice, as if he knew the cavalry was just over the horizon. Paul turned away and headed for the darkened living room.

'I love my husband,' said the woman from the next-door flat. She was seated on one end of the sofa, with her head hanging over the back, and it was hard to see who, if anyone, she was talking to. Paul, at the other end, closed his eyes. The thudding bass was quite soporific in a way, and Crispin's snore provided an hypnotic treble line. 'My husband's lovely. He's so strong and lovely, he can pick me up and put me over his shoulder. Look, you can see how lovely he is. Look.' There was a rattling noise directly in front of Paul's face and he opened his eyes to see a dangling keyring bearing a picture of a bald bloke. 'And he's gone away,' said the woman, with a lacrimose quaver to her voice. 'All the way to America.' There was a pause and then she started, very softly, to sing the words of the Joan Armatrading song; Paul shifted further along the sofa and sat on something that crackled. It was a piece of yellow crepe paper to which was stapled a trio of creased photos. One was a blurred group shot, all red faces and waving cans, one was of Crispin pretending to shag a statue of Queen Victoria and one was of himself.

'My dad built this building,' said the woman. 'I loved my dad. He asked *me* and I picked cerulean blue.'

The photo had been taken outside the Birmingham art gallery five years previously, and showed Paul in a John Travolta pose, in a fountain, in the nude. It had, presumably, been seen by most of the people at the party. His gaze slid away from the terrible image and drifted along the shallows of the wrecked room, taking in the jetsam of dropped glasses and trampled paper plates, and resting, finally, on the glinting knickers of Lexie who was curled like a seashell on the floor with her head on Crispin's stomach.

'I saw my dad today,' said the woman. 'I saw my dad for the first time in twenty-nine years. No, twenty-eight years, twenty-eight years and four –'

'Please,' said Paul, 'please, will you just *shut up.*'

II

It had taken a minimum of subterfuge to stay on alone in Briglennia for an hour. 'I'll give it all a final, proper clean,' Netta had said, before waving her mother and Ted off in the Mini and watching Glenn wheel his trolley down the drive for the last time. The removal van had departed a little earlier, every box, every chair, every picture bearing a sticker with details of the item's destined room and position within the new flat. The three-man team had been complimentary about the labelling system, and Netta had reciprocated by admiring their Coral-designed beige-embroidered blue waistcoats with as much sincerity as she could muster.

She finished the hoovering in ten minutes, and then retrieved the long, hooked pole from behind the bathroom door and opened the hatch to the loft. She had left the hatbox within reach of the top of the folding steps, and she lifted it carefully and carried it back downstairs.

Glenn had found it first, in the process of emptying the attic. He had changed his mind several times about what he was prepared to donate to the local Cancer Research shop, and had spent days moving boxes from his bedroom to the hall and then back again, but the green hatbox had remained stubbornly in the 'to go' pile, and one evening Netta had idly lifted the lid.

She had found Glenn in his room. 'Did you see what was in this?' she'd asked, breathlessly, incredulously.

'Yes.'

She'd waited a few moments, but Glenn had appeared to

feel that the exchange was at an end and had gone on packing his ring-pull collection, and Netta had taken the box and had put it back into the attic; she had known instantly that she wanted to view its contents alone, and uninterrupted.

She took the eight cans of film from the hatbox and lined them up on the breakfast bar; they were dated in grease pencil in her father's large, easy script. The earliest was from 1965, the summer before the move to Monk's Way, the latest from three years after that, just prior to his death. The cine-camera, ludicrously heavy by current standards, was packed in newspaper at the bottom of the box, and the projector was wedged alongside it. She took out the latter and plugged it in, and adjusted the oblong of light so that it fell centrally on the blank wall where the freezer had stood. Then, with the smell of burning dust filling the kitchen, she picked up the first tin and prised open the lid. The moment felt turgid with significance. Whatever the reel contained – and she had no memory of which social occasions or school triumphs or chastening family glimpses her father might have recorded – the footage dated from what she always thought of as 'before', an era that only ever seemed to exist in her own head, since her mother grandly declined to discuss the past and Glenn's memories tended towards the narrow and the specific. 'Before' was a time when there had been five in the family and not three; 'before' was when she'd felt normal at school and special at home, it was a time when life had been ordinary. 'Before' had been better. Netta wiped her hands, turned the reel over and looked at the label. It read 'MONK'S WAY SITE VISIT'.

There was no sound. The first shot was of a huge expanse of trampled mud, dotted with vehicles. Men in donkey jackets walked randomly across the frame and the odd spot of rain beaded the lens. The picture switched abruptly to a view of a hole filled with water, and then to a set of foundations. A man in a hard hat grinned at the camera. A dumper truck reversed all the way up a slope. Three blokes stood under an umbrella and looked at a plan, then put it away and looked at another plan. A large number of bricks were unloaded. More rain fell. A man climbed into a digging machine and then climbed out again. A sign containing the word 'Devon' was subjected to an interminable blurred close-up.

The second reel, 'MONK'S WAY SITE VISIT #2', at least had the virtue of being shot in sunny weather, and Netta sat through three minutes of static views of partially built chalet bungalows before cracking. Keeping half an eye on the screen, she began systematically opening the other containers. 'MONK'S WAY SITE VISIT #3' was followed by 'TOURIST OFFICE SITE VISIT', 'TOURIST OFFICE SITE VISIT #2' and 'TOURIST OFFICE SITE VISIT #3'. By the time she had read the label on reel number eight ('MOATSIDE SITE VISIT #2') she had conquered her sense of anticlimax and was feeling rather giggly. She would bring this little lot home to Glasgow, she thought, and arrange a showing for Mick and some friends, and offer popcorn and ice-cream and a running commentary on the male penchant for staring at earth-moving equipment.

The second reel ended with a slow zoom in to Briglennia's roofless second storey, and with ten minutes still to go before Ted was due to pick her up Netta threaded 'MONK'S WAY SITE VISIT #3' into the projector.

The very first shot was of her father. He was holding a huge pair of cardboard scissors and behind him was the Monk's Way road sign, over which someone had draped a red ribbon. He gave a thumbs-up to the camera and pretended to cut the ribbon, and then the picture changed to a panorama of the completed cul-de-sac and Netta realized that she'd spent the previous ten seconds saying, 'Bloody hell,' over and over and over again. 'Christ!' she said, by way of variation. He'd looked so young, so ludicrously alive! She hoisted herself onto the breakfast bar, beside the projector, and craned forward to watch the rest of the reel. The panorama was followed by a lingering close-up of every single house in the cul-de-sac and then by a peculiar high-angle view of the drive of Briglennia, presumably taken from the back of a lorry. After a few seconds the view tilted, sliding up the side of the house towards the roof, and then sliding back down again to reveal the drive now miraculously filled with workmen, all holding paper cups and mouthing 'Cheers'.

'Christ,' said Netta again. At the heart of the grinning group was her father and beside him – clearly uncomfortable at being wedged between so many bodies – was Glenn, aged about eight, dressed in the black and mustard of the prep school he'd attended before the money ran out and from which their father had sometimes collected him. As the celebration continued one of the men cheerfully grabbed her brother under the armpits and swung him up towards the camera, and Glenn instantly screamed and bucked, elbowing his captor in the face, knocking cups to the ground, kicking wildly and blindly and finally dropping to the floor where he lay curled with his hands over his eyes, oblivious to the tableau of shock and embarrassment that had formed behind him. Netta looked at her father's face and saw it crease with helpless shame, and then the reel ended in a flurry of random shots of tarmac and roof-top, and she turned off the projector and closed her eyes and listened to the tick and creak of cooling metal until Ted arrived to take her to Mellis Hall.

With the van only half unloaded, her mother was already ripping off stickers and reassigning chests of drawers to places where there was an unarguable reason that they shouldn't go.

'But I thought we'd agreed all this,' said Netta. 'I didn't write one single direction without checking it with you first.'

'But it's different when I can actually see the furniture in its place. You know, you can be very *rigid* sometimes.'

'How is it rigid to suggest that the sofa doesn't block two plug sockets and part of the door?'

'Oh, I meant to tell you, Glenn wasn't at all happy about where you'd decided his furniture should go. We had a little chat about it and I said that of course he should make up his own mind.'

Which was why Netta spent the remainder of the afternoon and half of the evening helping to shift her brother's bed from one side of the room to the other until the growing number of boxes confined him to a single positional option with which – fortunately – he appeared satisfied. They sat together on the duvet for a while, hemmed in by cardboard battlements, and Netta listened to Bel who was on the phone in the next room, giving a friend an account of the day's proceedings.

'. . . and, do you know, it feels almost as if I belong in this house. As if it . . . *welcomed* me. And Glenn's absolutely bubbling with excitement about his new room, it has the most marvellous high ceilings . . .'

Her mother's references to Glenn might not be recognizable, thought Netta, they might not even be entirely sane, but they were never, ever, tinged with shame or embarrassment. Her mother's Glenn was a chatty companion, a valued, if unusual, member of society. It was a benign madness.

'Oh there you are, Netta,' said Bel, peering around the door. 'Having a little rest? Only there are still *quite* a few of Glenn's boxes in the living room and I was wondering whether you'd worked out a place to put them.'

'No,' said Netta, 'I'm afraid I haven't.' She had a sudden

desire for solitude and a huge alcoholic drink. 'Would you mind if we called a halt tonight? I need to go and pick up my key for the hospital flat and I could come back first thing tomorrow. Say, seven-thirty? Mum?'

'Sorry, dear, I was just . . .' Frowning, their mother picked her way along an alley of tea chests towards the window and pressed her face to the glass. 'I thought so,' she said, after a moment, 'that man's there again, the one with the binoculars.'

Netta joined her and saw the figure silhouetted in the upstairs window of one of the new houses, his gaze swivelled towards the car park.

'What on earth's he looking at?' she said. 'There's no one there. There's nothing but cars.'

* * *

Because she found herself unable to fully open her eyes, it took Netta three attempts to lift the phone receiver off the hook, but it was worth it for the tiny, sweet moment of silence that followed. ''Lo,' she said, thickly. Her tongue felt flabby and alien, as if borrowed from a large dog.

'Brianetta?'

'Yes. Mum. Not feeling well.' There was a frosting of icy sweat around her torso and she could feel the pull of individual hairs in her scalp.

'Aren't you? You sound a little husky, I must say – did I tell you that five of Junior Tap and Stage were off with throat infections last week, and that large child, Melanie, has come down with –' Netta let her wrist slacken, so that the receiver dropped like a wounded paw and her mother's voice receded into unintelligibility. Time passed. At some point she registered the distant repetition of her own name and, as if hoisting a dumb-bell, lifted the phone to her ear again.

'Mum.'

'Yes, dear.'

'Got a bad headache.'

'Oh dear. Is it a migraine?'

'No, it's . . . I had a drink last night. When I got to the hospital. At a party.'

'Oh, you mean you have a *hangover*?'

'Yes.'

'I believe when you have a hangover you're supposed to lie down in a darkened room, in total silence.'

'Yes.'

'Have you tried it?'

'I will.' She swallowed, with difficulty, and tried to remember what was supposed to be happening today. 'So how's things?'

'Well, Glenn's just set out on his new bottle round. He said he'd help to clear the rest of his boxes out of the living room later, but I told him not to hurry because you'd be here first thing. Did you say you'd come at seven-thirty?'

'Yes. What time is it now?'

'Just after nine.'

'Oh.' The syllable emerged as a groan.

'So I've just started moving a few of the very light ones myself.'

'Oh, don't, Mum, please, you'll hurt your back, I'll be there in . . . in . . . soon. I'll be there soon.'

'Soon?'

'Soon.'

'Very well, dear.'

'Wait for me. Be there soon. Better lie down,' she said, her language contracting into telegraphese. 'Speak later.' The receiver missed the cradle and she sat, unable to move, on the edge of the bed, watching through slitted eyes as the numbers on the digital alarm changed silently from 9.06 to 9.07 to 9.08.

Her body felt steeped in poison, her brain blotted and wrung dry. 9.08 flickered dumbly into 9.09, and 9.09 emitted a hideous, octave-wide yodel that hurt her ears and most of her head and continued even after she had repeatedly pressed the 'stop' button. It wasn't until she had pulled out the plug and was suffering the dreadful visceral aftershocks of having bent over that she realized that the noise was coming from the phone. She edged the receiver back onto the cradle and it rang immediately.

'I hope this is a convenient time to speak to you,' said a transatlantic voice.

'No it isn't. Not really.'

'Could you suggest when I should call back, then? This is Armand Roux, we met yesterday evening.'

'Did we?'

'I was querying about the presence of an en suite bathroom in your accommodation?'

'Oh. Yes.'

'I've had great difficulty in speaking to someone in authority about this situation, in fact I waited all yesterday evening for a phone call, but it seems to me that, on reflection, we could come to some kind of mutual agreement independent of authority, and I wanted to confirm your statement that you'd only be in Shadley Oak for another three weeks. Is that right? Hello?'

'Can you call back a bit later?' asked Netta, realizing suddenly that he had stopped speaking, which meant that it was her turn.

'In an hour?'

'Two.'

She stared at herself in the cruel fluorescent light of the bathroom. She looked primordial, her eyes bleared slits, her skin the colour and texture of cement, her hair a cheap nylon wig recently used as an oven scourer and then discarded as a fire hazard. This was what excess alcohol did to women of forty: turned them into Peruvian mummies. Delicately, because her skin actually seemed to be tender, she splashed a little water on her face and then rested her forehead on the pleasantly cold edge of the basin and let out a low moan. Incidents from the party were beginning to surface in her consciousness. She could hazily remember trying to discuss her job with someone and failing repeatedly to enunciate the word dietitian. It had seemed quite amusing at the time. She had also – and she could only bear to recall this particular incident by the mental equivalent of peering between her fingers – recited the first verse of a poem she'd written in secondary school entitled 'Why I Hate Shadley Oak'. And at some stage of the evening she had fallen off the sofa. Christ, was there anything more tragic than a bladdered forty-year-old woman in a sunfrock? Yes, actually, there was: a bladdered forty-year-old woman in a sunfrock in a room full of twenty-year-olds.

Widow Twankey. She raised her heavy head and looked at herself again. Recently a shopkeeper had called her 'madam' for the first time; she had, she thought, been looking no different from usual and yet some subtle senile change had obviously taken place almost overnight, sliding her inexorably from one form of address to another. Now, thanks to yesterday evening, she was getting a sneak preview of her next shift in title – the moment when, in thirty years' time, someone would take one look at her, nod encouragingly and say, 'Yes dear,' in a nice loud voice.

Masochistically, she leaned in towards the bathroom mirror and examined – millimetre by millimetre – the surface of her face: the sags, the lines, the shadows, the monstrous pores, the blossoming veins, the whiteheads, the blackheads, the sleep-creases that she knew now were templates for future wrinkles, the freckles, the blotches, the flaky bits, the hairs, the hollows where there used to be plumpness, the ominous droop where once all had been firm. Thank God for make-up, she thought. Thank God for Mick, who never seemed to go in for this type of forensic appraisal. 'You look gorgeous,' was his invariable comment when asked for any kind of physical critique. Gorgeous. She closed her eyes.

Some time later she began, in slow motion, to run a bath, resting between the separate, tiny exertions that the process required. The phone rang just as she had placed one foot in the water, and she hesitated only for the briefest moment before lowering herself into the scented bubbles.

She was lying in cold water.

She was lying in cold water and the skin over her stomach and breasts was crawling unpleasantly and she had a crick in her neck and someone was softly but persistently knocking on the door of the flat. For a semi-conscious beat or two she hoped that Mick would answer it.

'Hello,' called someone. 'Excuse me.'

She groaned and then began to winch herself from the bath. The knocking continued.

'Wait. Just *wait*.' Her voice was bovine, hoarse, barely audible even to herself. She paddled around looking for her towel and found it lying in a pool of water, next to her nightshirt.

'Hello-oh,' called the voice.

'Oh, just . . .' She wrapped the bath mat around her waist and, clutching the damp shirt to her top half, shuffled to the front door of the flat. 'Yes?' she asked, opening it just a crack, far enough to be heard and not seen.

'My name's Armand Roux, we spoke earlier today.'

'I remember.' She scratched gently at the skin of her chest and her fingers encountered an odd, nubbly texture.

'I tried several times to phone you again.'

'Yes, I'm sorry, I was . . . busy . . .' Peering down, she saw a scattering of pinkish blebs dotted around her cleavage. She peeled away the nightshirt and stared at what lay beneath.

'I was wanting to discuss a potential switch of living arrangements in the interests of natural justice; however I now have an extremely urgent reason for wanting to move from my flat because my roommate appears to have contracted a severe case of –'

'Are you a doctor?'

'Excuse me?'

She replaced the nightshirt and opened the door a little further. Armand flinched and took a step backwards. 'Sorry. I said, are you a doctor?'

'I am, yes, and that's –'

'Do you know what this is?' She exposed a modest section of blistered torso and he emitted a whinnying sound and flattened himself against the opposite wall of the corridor, one arm across his nose and mouth.

'What?' she asked, suddenly terrified. 'What is it?'

He lowered his arm slightly, enough for her to glimpse an expression that was almost exultant. 'That,' he said, 'is chickenpox, and it's obviously at a *highly* contagious stage.'

12

Total concentration, thought Paul. If he watched television with total concentration, then all bodily stimuli would simply dwindle and fade. He would become a creature of pure mind, untouched by petty sensory demands. He took a deep, slow breath and fixed his gaze on the man in the quasi-medical white jacket. 'What's been happening, Leanne,' said the man, narrowing his eyes and holding up a card with lots of little brown squares on it, 'is that you've been using a foundation that's too beige for your complexion. You see you're very fair, and you have these lovely green eyes –'

'Yes, they really are *so* green,' chipped in the woman on the sofa.

' – but the problem is that your colouring's being swamped by –'

The problem, thought Paul, picking up the remote control and using one end to gently rub – not scratch – the crook of his elbow, was that Leanne actually looked like a bloke in a dress, and all the foundation in the world wasn't going reduce the width of her shoulders. He took another deep, slow breath and changed channels. BBC 2 was showing a black-and-white film in which an actual bloke in a dress and a woman wearing a uniform were standing in a queue to get onto a ship. Paul blew on a cluster of spots on the back of one hand and then shrugged several times, a technique he'd discovered that gave a momentary impression of light abrasion without actually causing any damage. He changed channels, caught the briefest glimpse of an advert for wood sealant, slapped the back of his neck as if squashing a mosquito, changed channels, watched the closing credits of a cartoon and then suddenly bunched his hands into claws and raked the air just above his torso in a mighty simulated scratching session. Then, sublimating his almost overwhelming desire for whole-body friction, he extended an evil finger and picked at a single scab, buried deep beneath his hairline. There was a moment of minimal pleasure, a tiny lacuna of cutaneous calm, and then, simultaneously, every pock resumed its crazed, insatiable plea for attrition. Paul leaned forward until he was an inch above the coffee table and then, quite deliberately, smacked his forehead against it several times. Feeling slightly dazed, he straightened up and switched channels again.

Netta looked up and down the empty corridor and wondered if she were going mad – she was sure she had heard a loud series of knocks. She closed the front door again, turned around carefully, as if reversing an invalid carriage, and wobbled back to the kitchen counter. It was the first time she'd been reliably vertical in forty-eight hours and she felt unnaturally light, her limbs like airy breadsticks, her head bobbing several yards above her body. She'd been looking for something to eat, something that would anchor her a little more firmly, but so far had found only the congealed remains of a Chinese meal and half a pizza with the cheese eaten off the top.

'Hello,' said Netta, appearing suddenly in the door of the living room. Paul realized that his right hand was under his pyjama top, doing a little freelance scratching, and he removed it hastily. 'Hello,' he said, awkwardly. They had had a surreal introduction a couple of evenings ago, a spotty handshake, a feverish nod of viral recognition as Netta had shifted her stuff into Armand's room. 'We are in a quarantine situation,' as

Armand had stated, unequivocally, 'which makes a relocation *imperative.*'

Since then Paul had seen her only as a shuffling figure in the hallway, a pink-eyed bundle in blankets, commuting between bathroom and bedroom. She was looking marginally more alive now but still dreadful, her hair in a sort of mad Afro, her eyelashes crusty, her face and neck blotched with calamine. She was wearing tracksuit bottoms and a jumper down to her knees.

'I'm sorry,' she said, 'but I can't remember your name.'

'Paul.'

She nodded. 'Hello again. I've just been looking for something to eat, and I can't find anything at all. Am I missing a cupboard?'

'Er . . . I don't think so. There's some stuff in the fridge.'

'You mean the takeaway?'

'Yes.' He had ordered a Lotus Banquet on the phone last night, leaving the money in a bowl outside the door, like a medieval plague victim; so far it had lasted him for three meals, including breakfast.

'So there's no bread.'

'No.'

'Or milk or eggs or marge or cereal or fruit or vegetables?'

'No,' he repeated, defensively. 'I haven't been able to get out, have I? And I usually eat in the canteen.' He tugged at his top, covering the triangle of spotted flab that his scratching session had left exposed. Great, he thought, sulkily, he couldn't even slob out in his own living room any more. Cleanliness King of the World had gone and now he'd got his mother. He very much wanted her to go away; instead she bent over with extreme slowness and picked up a biro that had been lying on the floor.

'I'm going to make a list,' she said, lowering herself into an armchair. 'I'll ask my brother to do a shop.'

'OK.' He changed channels. 'So, Angela,' a woman with a big chin was saying, 'is this silk . . . *or* is it a manmade fibre?'

'Can I use this?' Netta showed him the blank reverse of the Golden Dragon menu.

'Yes, if you want.' He flicked to BBC 2 again, where the actor in a dress had now reached a cabin.

'Oh, it's Cary Grant,' said Netta. 'This is *I was a Male War Bride*. It's really funny.' She started writing rapidly and Paul watched in silence a scene notable only for its extreme unfunniness. But then, he currently couldn't imagine laughing at anything at all, ever again; he felt as if that part of his brain had been cauterized. Over the months ahead the muscles that raised the corners of his mouth would gradually atrophy and he would become The Man That Never Smiled. ('Dr Paul . . . he's very serious, isn't he?' 'Yes, but when he looks at you, you feel that he understands. He understands suffering.')

'I've put down all the staples,' said Netta. 'Do you like jam?'

'Marmite.'

'Earl Grey?'

'Ordinary.'

'Potato?'

'What?'

'I was just making a joke – I say potato, you say potahto?'

He frowned. 'I don't know what you're talking about.'

'Never mind. *Christ*.' She clawed at her wrist.

'Don't scratch them,' said Paul, automatically. 'They scar.'

'I know.' She blew on the same area. 'They're just starting up again. I had a cool shower and that seemed to work for about ten minutes. How are yours?'

'Crap.' He switched channels and tried to concentrate on a

DIY demonstration. Netta fanned her wrist with the menu and gave him a surreptitious look. He had at least twice as many spots as her, and looked hot and cross and about six years old in his Christopher Robin dressing-gown (undoubtedly a maternal gift); it was almost impossible to believe that on a daily basis he was responsible for life and death and the painful bits between. Nevertheless . . .

'Can I ask you something,' she said, 'in your capacity as a doctor?'

'All right. But I won't know,' he added, with bitterness.

'I just wondered how long this goes on being infectious for.'

'Until all the lesions have dried up. Five to seven days.'

'You see, you did know,' she said, encouragingly, a tonal throwback to homework sessions with the girls.

'Only because someone got me a book.' Armand, wearing a surgical mask, had dropped off two litres of calamine lotion and a copy of *Viral Conditions in General Practice*, and Paul had avidly read the relevant section.

'So, a week,' said Netta, 'a week.' She caught a little glimpse of an army of ramifications marching towards her and quickly turned away from the vision; it was too much to take in when she'd only just resurfaced. 'And how long's the incubation period?'

'Ten days to three weeks.'

She counted backwards. 'And can you pass it on before the spots appear?'

'Yup. That's when you're most contagious.'

'I definitely know who I got it from then,' she said. 'A little girl in my mother's dance class.'

Paul looked at her. 'A fat little girl?'

'Yes.' She was startled. 'Fat-ish. Chubby, anyway. How do you know?'

'Because she coughed on me in a café.' That child had a lot

to answer for, he thought, remembering the unprovoked kick, the ruined letter, the misdirected phone call. She was like some evil dwarf, meddling with his life. To really complete the picture she'd have to be admitted with something rare that he'd misdiagnose, leading to a lawsuit and his permanent removal from the doctors' register. Then he could go and jump off a cliff and make everyone happy. In a burst of self-loathing he simultaneously scratched both sides of his neck.

'I'm going to put down baking soda,' said Netta. 'I heard once that it's good for itching, I think you can put it in your bath. Or gargle with it – I've even got spots inside my mouth, have you?'

He shrugged, desperate to avoid a comparison session. Yes, he had spots inside his mouth; he had spots in every crevice, fold and indentation, he had spots wherever skin lurked or mucous membrane glistened. He was one big spot and he would soon become one gigantic scab.

Netta read the silence correctly, wrote 'yoghurts' on the end of the list and then sat and watched the whole of an item on multiple-use shelving units before rousing herself with a jerk. 'I'll phone this through,' she said, rising unsteadily.

'What?'

It was a 'what?' of such irritability, such pubescent, 'what is it *now* you boring old cow?'-ness that Netta could feel herself shifting involuntarily into stepmother mode. 'Look,' she began, her voice on a basic firm-but-fair setting, 'there's really no need –' and then the phone rang and she answered it and held out the receiver for Paul. 'It's your mum,' she said.

He didn't want to go home. The realization shocked him a little as he heard himself prevaricating to his mother, inventing excuses, maximizing difficulties.

'Graham, he thinks his gearbox has gone,' he heard his mother shout, and though his father's reply was inaudible, Paul guessed the content.

'He says he'll come and get you,' said his mother. 'Or I could,' she offered bravely; he knew how much she hated driving on motorways. 'I want to give you a bit of home spoiling.'

'No, I think . . .' He could hear one of the dogs barking in the background, and the distant moan of ewes. He didn't want to go unless he could go in triumph. He wanted to amuse his parents by drawing up outside the house with a filched 'doctor on call' sign in the window; he wanted to be expansive yet modest about his experiences, humble yet enthusiastic about his new, independent status. He didn't want to be helped from the car, tucked up in bed, tiptoed round, cooed over or pitied. 'I'd prefer to come back when I'm feeling better,' he said, honestly.

'But I don't like to think there's no one looking after you.'

Involuntarily, his eyes wandered over to the kitchen door, through which Netta had disappeared. 'Mum,' he said, 'I don't need looking after.'

He had just settled back on the sofa, a process now as comfortable as climbing naked into a bag of chaff, when the phone rang again.

'Oh,' said a woman's voice, slightly affronted, when Paul answered. 'Who's that?'

'Paul.'

'Of course, you must be the young doctor; Netta mentioned that she'd moved in with a young doctor. She was supposed to be staying with me, of course, but she decided she'd be much too uncomfortable on the sofa bed.'

'Do you want to speak to her?'

'Are you a specialist?'

'No, I –'

'And you've caught chickenpox as well, of course?'

'Yes. Do you want to speak to her?'

'Yes, thank you,' said the woman, serenely.

There was no answer to Paul's shout, and he could hear the drum of water in the shower.

'She's in the bathroom,' he said, unwillingly resuming the dialogue. 'Do you want me to give her a message?'

'Yes, you can say that there's absolutely nothing for her to worry about, because she does tend to worry and she does like to think we can't manage without her.'

'Right. So that's the message?'

'Yes. And there's a very small problem with the washing machine. It's not draining properly but Ted has very kindly said he'll have a look at it so that's all under control, and I've pulled my back just a tiny bit lifting a box of wallpaper samples but I've taken two brufen. And we've –'

'Hang on a moment, I'd better get a pen.' He grabbed the biro from the table and returned to find her mid-sentence '– can't do the Tiller Girls routine with only three in the chorus line but it can't be helped. There's nothing urgent, she can call me back when she's got a moment.'

'Are you –' he took a punt '– her mother?'

'Yes, but you can call me Bel.'

Glenn was out collecting when Netta phoned, and her mother was having a little lie-down to rest her back, so it was Ted who answered (he had 'just popped by,' he said, to see how they were settling) and Ted who arrived with the shopping ninety minutes later, still managing to give his gallant bow despite bearing a Tesco's bag in each hand. For once, he didn't say, 'You're looking as lovely as ever, Netta,' which she found rather comforting, since it implied that he might be being sincere on all the other occasions.

He brought the bags into the kitchen and she began pawing through them immediately, her stomach roaring for sustenance, her lips burbling a demented running commentary. 'Ooh, you bought bananas. And honey. And tomato soup –' she was practically drooling, it was if normal sensation had broken down and she could taste each item through the wrapping ' – And *proper* tea, ooh, proper tea, I'll put the kettle on. You'll stay for a cup, won't you?' she added, remembering her deliverer. Ted had remained standing, his big-knuckled hands clasped in front of him.

'I won't, thank you,' he said. 'I promised your mother I'd look at the washing machine.'

'Well, let me give you the money. Oh . . .' The bank, she remembered: another place she now couldn't visit for the better part of a week. 'I'll have to owe you.'

'Do you need any cash?'

'No, really Ted – it's lovely of you but I've nothing to spend it on at the moment.' She reached out a spotty hand to squeeze one of his and then hesitated, mid-gesture. 'You have had chickenpox, haven't you?'

'Yes, when I was in the marines.'

She watched him walk along the corridor to the lifts; his gait had acquired a slight uncertainty with age, and from the loose hang of his beige mac she thought he might have shrunk a little. He'd already been white-haired when she'd first met him, two decades ago, after he'd answered her mother's advertisement for an accompanist, but he'd still had a certain vigour then, had still been a man in his prime. Now he was definably an old gentleman, the white curls reduced to a halo of wisps. The *marines*, she thought – that was a new one to tell Mick, another item for their list. Constructing Ted's Past was a sort of parlour game they played together, a facetious attempt to assemble a whole from a collection of snippets. The facts were sparse. He had once lived in Leamington Spa. He had taught himself to play the piano during the war. He had owned a cat called Fiddlesticks. He had 'done a little acting, mainly chorus line and character'. And now, apparently, he had crawled across shingle on his elbows, dodging gunfire. These hints were never elaborated; Ted's air of reserve deflected questions and if Netta's mother knew more than the bare facts, then she wasn't telling.

'I don't see why you have to *pry*,' she'd once said, when Netta had been speculating, in an entirely decorous way, about Ted's personal life.

'I'm not prying, I'm just interested. And you spend so much time together, you must know more about him than anyone else.'

'Ted and I are business associates.'

'Well I've never met a business associate who'd choose my cushion covers for me.'

'*Friendly* business associates.'

But viewed as a pair Netta always thought they looked far more like mistress and retainer, the old-fashioned, loyal sort of retainer who regarded his servitude as a vocation.

Ted turned at the lifts and raised his hand in farewell, and Netta blew him a kiss and closed the door once more on the outside world.

She ate her first yoghurt at speed, standing in the middle of the kitchen, watching only the trajectory of the spoon, slurping occasionally in her eagerness. She was attempting to eat the second a little more slowly when she heard Paul's bedroom door open, and a moment later he appeared in the room.

'You're dressed!' she said. He was in jeans and socks and a sloppy jumper, and he seemed to have brushed his hair, so that it was once again sticking up all over and not just at the back.

'Yeah, I'm er . . . feeling a bit better.' This was vastly untrue, denim and blisters being a bad combination, but he had felt peculiarly vulnerable, lolling around in pyjamas in front of a strange woman, and had wanted to regain a modicum of control.

'The food's arrived,' said Netta. 'Do help yourself.'

He opened the fridge, hesitated for a moment and then took out the remains of the chow mein. 'I'll just finish this,' he said, and Netta turned away towards the window so that she could roll her eyes in private.

The view, now she came to look at it, was tremendous. It was dominated by the chimney of the hospital incinerator, but beyond that she could see as far as the green southern edge of Shadley Oak and the doll's-house gables of the enormous B&Q that stood there. She started picking out landmarks: she could see the blue-roofed sports hall of her old school and the pale façade of Mellis Hall and the clapboard scout hut where her mother taught. She could see the green bins of the bottle bank and the statue of Charles the First in the market square. She could see – she pressed her forehead to the glass – she could see Glenn in his red jacket pushing the trolley along the road outside the hospital. 'Oh my God!' she said involuntarily.

'What?'

'I can see my brother from here.'

'Yeah?' Minimally interested, he drifted towards the window. 'Where?'

She hesitated and then, wondering who exactly she was protecting by her hesitation, tapped her finger on the glass. 'He's the man in the red jacket. With the shopping trolley.' Though he'd just parked it, in fact, and was standing on awkward tiptoe, pulling at a plastic bag that was snagged on the fence. It was an ordinary sort of action, but even from this distance his movements were utterly distinctive. It was if he'd been wired up by an electrician who normally did forklift trucks.

'That's your brother?'

'Yes. He's called Glenn.'

Paul groped for a response. He'd been expecting to see a bloke in a suit and he felt unfairly wrong-footed. What, precisely, did one say on finding out that someone was closely related to the local weirdo?

'Er . . .' He tried not to sound flustered. 'I've, um, I think I've seen him before. I mean, he's around Shadley Oak quite a lot, isn't he? Collecting stuff.'

'Yes,' she said, coolly. 'Yes, he has his set routes. He's into recycling.' They watched as Glenn rolled the bag into a tight sausage and wedged it among the other contents, before bending to pick up something large and yellow that was lying in the road.

'What's that thing?' asked Netta, squinting. 'Can you see?'

Paul peered forward. 'I think it might be one of those police No Parking cones.'

'Oh God, it's not, is it?' Glenn had been almost arrested once for taking away a Hazard Warning sign that had fallen over in the gutter, and which he'd therefore assumed came under his own jurisdiction. 'Are you sure? He might get into trouble if it is. Not that I'd be able to do anything about it.'

'Hang on.' Paul left the room, and returned a minute later with a large pair of binoculars. 'Yup,' he said, after a moment of careful focusing. 'It's a cone. But it's been run over, I think, it's split right in half.' Imperceptibly, he shifted the binoculars and looked at Netta's brother. He had seen Glenn around town a few times, had taken in the jacket and the walk and had carelessly filed him under the loose heading of 'a bit mad'.

Now, looking at him in close-up – really observing him for the first time – he felt a little as he'd used to in his birdwatching days when the greyish wader he thought was probably a dunlin turned out, on closer examination, to be something quite different. There was nothing mad about Glenn. He might currently be rearranging the rubbish in a purloined shopping trolley but he was doing it with logic and precision and utter concentration. He was doing it, in fact, as if it were a skilled job of which he was a leading practitioner. Paul lowered the binoculars. 'Is he . . . ?' He wondered how to phrase it. 'Has he . . . I mean, has your brother always been like this?'

'Yes.'

'So he's not . . . being treated for anything.'

'No. There was a hotshot new GP a few years ago who decided it's a form of autism, but when Glenn was growing up people just thought he was a bit of a loony.'

'Oh,' said Paul, chastened. 'Well, he looks very . . . well organized.'

'Mmmm.' She nodded, liking the description; it was both accurate and kind.

'Do you want a go of these?' he said, offering the binoculars.

'Thank you.' She watched a pin-sharp Glenn finish rearranging and continue his journey. For so many years, all the time she was growing up, she'd thought that he was unique, the sole exponent of Glenn's Syndrome, with herself as the leading interpreter; she'd found the GP's diagnosis strangely hard to digest. Glenn himself had seemed rather pleased with the label, but then, of course, classification was his forte. She lost him behind a belt of trees, and handed back the binoculars. 'They're incredibly powerful, aren't they?'

'I haven't used them for years,' said Paul quickly, before she could start wondering if he spent his free evenings scanning the horizon for women taking off their bras in front of uncurtained windows. 'I used to belong to the Young Ornithologists' Club when I was a, you know, geeky teenager. They're sort of a souvenir.'

'I'm all for geeks,' said Netta. 'Geek's the kindest word that most people ever use about Glenn. Do you want a cup of tea?'

'What? Oh . . .' He couldn't quite remember why he'd been so opposed to accepting her hospitality earlier. 'OK. Thanks. And can I have some chocolate?'

'Sure, have whatever you want. But don't scratch.'

'Was I scratching? God . . .' He opened the fridge door.

'You don't mind me reminding you, do you?'

'No.'

'Well in that case . . .'

'What?'

'You're still doing it.'

'*God!*' He held both arms away from his body, keeping them rigid as if separating two fighters. '*Fuck!* Sorry, but this is just . . . just . . . unbearable.'

'You don't have to apologize, I think you've got a much worse dose than me. And Melanie – the fat little girl? Apparently she only had about six spots.'

'Did she? Oh, well that's just typical, that is. That's just put the tin bloody lid on three bloody weeks of one bloody thing after another. I'm just *so* fucked off with it.'

'Yup. Yup, I'm with you there,' said Netta. 'I've had a pretty dire three weeks myself.'

'Not as bad as mine.'

'Oh, I don't know . . .'

'No,' he said, with brusque finality. 'No, mine have been the worst. No competition.'

The phone rang and Netta went to answer it.

'Good news,' said her mother. 'You won't believe what's happened.'

'Why? What is it?'

'Guess who's coming?'

'Coming where?'

'Coming to England.'

The answer took a moment to materialize, and then dropped into Netta's head like a lump of coal into a bucket. 'Oh, you're –'

'Natalia! I rang to tell her about the move and she said that it sounds like we certainly need a bit of help so she's dropped everything –'

'Oh, you're ki–'

'And she's bringing little Lester! Isn't that wonderful! So you needn't worry any more, you can just concentrate on getting better.'

Paul, carefully sucking the chocolate off a Kit Kat, looked up as Netta came back into the kitchen; under the calamine mask she was looking deeply pissed off.

'OK,' she said, 'we're neck and neck now. My sister's on her way.'

13

At half past five the stall holders in the market square were beginning to pack up. The woman who sold fruit looked like a teenager when out of focus, but at 7×42 she was revealed as startlingly ancient, with a fag welded to her upper lip and a sweatshirt that read 'DON'T SQUEEZE MY MELONS'. Paul shifted his gaze across to the newspaper office, where Beardy was still standing on the pavement, holding his bike and gabbing to a policewoman. He was wearing blue nylon cycle shorts, of the sort that displayed the genitals as fully as was legal. Was it really possible that women found that attractive? They never *acted* as if they found genitals attractive; a man with a magazine full of naked women was a solitary, furtive, largely silent creature whereas a woman with a magazine full of naked men got all her friends round and spent the entire perusal screaming with laughter. Maybe wearing shorts like those was a way of removing speculation; any woman bedding Beardy would know exactly what she was going to see when he took his pants down. Paul scanned the *Mercury* foyer for a glimpse of Marianne, saw nothing of interest and moved the binoculars on.

'Paul?'

'Hmm?' There were three swans on the moat, and two little flakes of black and white that were probably tufted ducks.

'I've found something and I don't know what it is.'

'Yeah?' He turned to see Netta holding out a pinkish pointed object.

'It was wedged under the living-room door.'

'Oh yeah.' He took it from her and turned it over, like an archaeologist examining a find. 'Yeah. That's one of Mr Spock's ears. From the party.'

'Thanks.'

He returned the object and raised the binoculars again, and Netta stood with the Vulcan ear in her hand and wondered what to do next. She had only picked it up in the first place because it had given her something to do; she had only asked Paul to identify it because it had given her something to say; and now, all too quickly, she'd come to the end of that particular chain of activity. In the world outside there were things to be done, and other people were doing them. Mick had forgotten to take his driver's licence to the USA and Shona had found and FedExed it. Kelly had suddenly, capriciously (and rather woundingly), decided to learn to cook before going to college and was having lessons from her boyfriend's mum. Glenn had moved all the boxes from the lounge into the bedroom and now couldn't reach his wardrobe or any of his drawers. The leg of a coffee table had apparently been knocked off on the day of the move and sneakily reattached with sticky tape; the removal firm was all injured innocence and clearly required a kick-arse face-to-face visit. The washing machine was dribbling suds all over the kitchen. And this evening, at great personal and financial cost, her sister Natalia would be arriving to take care of absolutely everything.

'Paul?'

'Yeah?'

'If I made chocolate cake, would you eat some of it?'

'Yeah.'

She had nothing, nothing, *nothing* to do. Before lunch she had written to Mick, phoned everyone in her address book who might be at home on a Thursday morning, defrosted the freezer and read most of an Agatha Christie she'd found stuffed down the back of the sofa. After lunch she'd had a nap and tried to finish the book and discovered, with a yell of frustration that had briefly brought Paul out from behind his binoculars, that the last three pages were missing.

He was clearly feeling better himself – the puffiness had gone from his face and he had stopped the continual, inadvertent scratching that had made him look like a distressed long-term zoo resident – nevertheless he had not become any more communicative, and she was beginning to feel as starved of conversation as of activity.

'Paul?'

'Yeah?'

'I've just realized we haven't got any cocoa. How about a lemon cake?'

'OK.'

Beardy, still in conversation, glanced sideways and looked suddenly furtive, leaning in towards the policewoman for a final few words, and then swinging a leg over the crossbar and weaving off between the tourist coaches along Marsh Lane. Paul moved the binoculars in the direction of his glance and saw Marianne walking out of the door of the newspaper office, pulling it shut with the sort of grace more usually seen on slo-mo dance videos, brushing a golden strand from her forehead and then walking straight past the policewoman and off down an alleyway beside the Swan of Shadley Oak souvenir shop, all unaware of the two-timing activities of Mr Lycra-Dick and his uniformed –

'Paul?'

'Any flavour,' he said, not moving his eyeballs, 'anything'll do.'

'It's not about cake.'

'What is it then?'

'Your friend's climbing the chimney.'

'My . . . ?' He lowered the binoculars and looked at Netta. 'Sorry, what did you say?' Silently, she pointed out of the window.

A small crowd had gathered beside the low brick frontage of the incinerator – a few medical students, a visitor or two, a couple of nurses, a gesticulating porter; all stood with upturned faces watching as Crispin confidently scaled the service ladder. Over one shoulder was slung a conical grey object that swayed as he shifted his weight from rung to rung.

'He's out of his mind,' said Netta, expecting, at any minute, the entire ladder to peel away from the chimney, catapulting him over the abbey. 'He's going to kill himself.' As if he had heard her, Crispin stopped and looked over his shoulder, scanning the front of the building in search of something. After a moment he locked one arm around the frame of the ladder and pulled at the conical object with the other hand, working it round to one side and then raising it to his lips. There was a repulsive tinny screech, and then the sound of Crispin's enormously amplified voice. 'DR PAUL GOODING. IS DR PAUL GOODING, AKA PUD, IN THE BUILDING?'

'Oh *God*,' said Paul. He raised a hand and waved it tentatively. Crispin continued to crane over his shoulder, swinging so far round that one of his feet dangled free of the ladder.

'The sun's behind him,' said Netta, hunched in vicarious terror, 'maybe he can only see reflections.' Paul waved more vigorously, brandishing a tea towel for added visibility.

The hideous feedback filled the air once again. 'PUD, WHERE ARE YOU? MAKE YOURSELF KNOWN. I HAVE NEWS FROM THE WORLD OUTSIDE.'

'Oh for –' With considerable, grunting effort, Paul hauled himself onto the draining board and reached for the narrow openable section at the top of the window. He stuck his tea-towel arm through the aperture and flapped manically.

'HELLO SPOTTY. I SEE YOU. HOW ARE YOU FEELING?'

'Bit better,' shouted Paul.

'CAN'T HEAR YOU. WAVE ONCE FOR YES, TWICE FOR NO. IS YOUR ENTIRE BODY STILL COVERED IN PUS-ENCRUSTED BUBOES?'

Suddenly aware of the upturned faces at ground level, Paul mendaciously flapped twice.

'EXCELLENT. AND HOW'S TWANKEY? TEMPER IMPROVED ANY?'

'Tell him just to let go,' said Netta. 'Tell him to aim for the ground.'

'What's your news from the outside world?' shouted Paul.

'WHAT?'

'*News?*'

'OH, OK. BUSINESS FIRST. GORMAN'S ISSUED INSTRUCTIONS. WE'VE GOTTA DO SOME PRESEN-TATIONS ON SURGICAL TOPICS – YOU KNOW, TALK AND SLIDES AND STUFF, HALF AN HOUR MAX. ALMOND'S DOING ONE NEXT WEDNESDAY AND YOU'RE DOING ONE THE WEDNESDAY AFTER.'

'What on?'

'I SAID YOU MIGHT DO FALL INJURIES, SEEING AS IT'S YOUR SPECIALITY.'

Paul flapped feebly in protest.

'YOU COULD SHOW THEM YOUR X-RAYS, FOR A START. NOW, WHAT ELSE? OH YEAH – I BUMPED INTO THE LOVELY MARIANNE IN THE QUEUE AT THRESHER'S. SHE'S A TIA MARIA GIRL, JUST IN CASE YOU DIDN'T KNOW.'

Paul switched focus and stared at the stains on the tea towel, dangling flat against the window.

'SHE SAID SHE ENJOYED THE PARTY AND SHE'S SORRY SHE HAD TO GO EARLY. I TOLD HER ABOUT YOUR POX PROBLEM AND SHE SAID SHE WISHES SHE COULD SOOTHE YOUR BROW AND RUB YOU VERY SLOWLY ALL OVER WITH COOLING LOTIONS, NO, I'M JUST HAVING YOU ON. PUD? HEY PUD, I'M JUST –'

'DR FINNERTY, YOU ARE TRESPASSING ON HOSPITAL PROPERTY AND UNLESS YOU COME DOWN IMMEDIATELY I WILL PHONE THE POLICE.'

'HELLO? ARE YOU TALKING TO ME?'

'DR FINNERTY, I AM BEING ENTIRELY SERIOUS.' Paul peered down and saw the Security Manager, a short but scary Scotsman with a voice that could etch glass, speaking into another megaphone.

'OK,' said Crispin, 'JUST DOING AN INFECTIVE FRIEND A FAVOUR. I'M ON MY WAY DOWN. PUD, LISTEN, DON'T GET JEALOUS, I PREFER THE QUIET TYPE – YOU KNOW, MOUTH OPEN BUT NOTHING COMING OUT IF YOU GET MY –'

'DR FINNERTY, I DON'T THINK YOU QUITE GRASP THE AMOUNT OF TROUBLE YOU ARE ABOUT TO GET INTO.'

'OK, OK.' He descended a few rungs before being struck by a final thought. 'HEY PUD, YOU KNOW THOSE FILMS WHERE SOME BLOKE GETS TRAPPED ON A DESERT ISLAND WITH A STRANGE WOMAN HE WOULDN'T NORMALLY LOOK TWICE AT AND THEY END UP SHAGGING EACH OTHER'S BRAINS OUT? I WAS JUST WONDERING –'

'DR FINNERTY.'

'COMING.'

Netta stood on tiptoe to see whether Crispin would slip

near the bottom and injure himself in some non-disabling but painful and humiliating way and it was with real disappointment that she watched him reach the ground safely.

'Is he a – would you call him a mate of yours?' she asked as Paul clambered down from the draining board.

'Well . . . I've known him ages, I mean he's –' He paused, cuffed by loyalty '– he's . . . he's a laugh.'

'Is he?'

There was a pause. 'He can be,' said Paul uncertainly.

It was extraordinary, thought Netta, returning to the task of grating a lemon with a blunt knife, what men would put up with in their friends. Mick had been to school with a prize ox called Macca who had, over the course of their friendship, borrowed nearly every item of electrical equipment the Lee family possessed and had failed to return what he hadn't broken; nevertheless, Mick still referred to Macca as 'one of the best'. And here was Paul – essentially amiable, apparently good-hearted, a bit on the dreamy side – loyally defending someone who possessed all the sympathetic qualities of a knuckle-duster. It was as if, once a friend-shaped space had been created in their universe, any subsequent lack of alignment could be ignored.

She gave up on the lemon after a while and started to hunt for a cake tin, and she was kneeling on the floor, digging around in the pan cupboard, when someone knocked at the door.

'Hello?' called Paul. 'Have you had chickenpox, whoever you are?

'When I was two,' said a small voice. He opened the door and Netta caught a glimpse of a doctor with a thick plait of tawny hair and a sprinkling of freckles.

'I've brought you something to cheer you up,' said Carrie, holding up a large Jiffy bag. 'A few convalescent videos and

'. . . er . . .' Her eyes darted past Paul and clocked another presence in the kitchen, 'something else.' She leaned towards him and mouthed an incomprehensible syllable. 'It's good for itching,' she added, in a whisper. 'I caught scabies when I was doing paediatrics and it was the only thing that worked.'

'What was?' asked Paul, with equal furtiveness.

She mouthed the same word again, and then raised two fingers to her lips and mimed a deep and satisfying inhalation.

'Oh right,' he said, getting it at last. 'Fantastic.'

'You won't believe me but it was a present from a patient, someone I didn't kill. He grows it himself for MS.'

'Great.'

'He says it's been proven over and over again in clinical trials that it gives good results in patients with demyelination symptoms, but that it's pressure from Interpol that prevents legalization.'

'Is it?' They were still whispering, practically nose to nose now, peering into the dark mouth of the bag.

'Apparently we have an intrinsic cannabinoid receptor system that works independently from the opioid receptor system.'

'Right.'

'And I chose the –' There was a huge crash and they both jumped violently, the bag dropping between them. A large and lumpy joint rolled indolently across the lino towards Netta.

'Sorry,' she said, 'greasy baking tray.' She picked up the joint and looked at it curiously.

'I'd better go,' said Carrie.

'You don't have a cake tin, do you?' asked Netta. 'Not *on* you, obviously.'

'No, sorry. Nice to meet you though.' Carrie flashed a

nervous smile and fled up the corridor. Paul closed the door and stood as if caught in the glare of police headlights.

'I'm shocked,' said Netta. She held up Exhibit A between finger and thumb. 'Really, I'm shocked. I mean, what do they teach you at college nowadays? This is much too loosely packed and it doesn't even have a roach. Doesn't anyone know how to roll a decent joint any more?'

Paul grinned sheepishly. 'We have to be a bit careful,' he said. 'We might get struck off.'

'I won't tell. Homegrown, is it?'

'Mmm.'

'Very nice.' She handed it back. 'Was that – can I ask, was that Marianne?'

He coloured as if slapped. 'No. Carrie. Her name's Carrie, she's just, you know, another doctor.'

'So is Marianne the one you've been watching out of the window?'

He opened and closed his mouth a couple of times.

'I'm prying,' she said. 'I'm very bored. I'm sorry, I don't know what to do with myself.'

'Well, there isn't anything *to* do,' he said. 'So why don't you just . . .' he shrugged, 'you know, relax? You never seem to just sit and do nothing.'

'Well I –' She clasped her elbows and scanned the room, as if searching for a reply. 'I'm not used to it. For me, relaxation is what I do when I've done everything else. *Then* I sit down. I sit down next to my husband and we watch television and drink whisky. Sometimes we eat cheese and biscuits.' She felt almost tearful at the sweet vision of domestic dullness.

'Well, give it a go,' he said, with a touch of asperity. 'Stop . . . you know, shuttling round. Please.'

'Am I driving you mad?'

'Yes.'

'Am I really?' She seemed alarmed.

'Yes.'

'Well . . .' She smiled a little painfully. 'I'd better sit down then. Before I turn into my mother.'

There were three videos in the Jiffy bag, and a brief note.

These are my favourite films to veg in front of when I'm under the weather. Hope they're not too girly.

'OK,' said Paul. 'Number One: *Dead Poets' Society*.'

'I've seen it,' said Netta, tearing a strip from the front cover of an ancient copy of *Reader's Digest*.

'So have I. What are you doing with that?'

'Making a roach.'

'Oh. Number Two: *Splash*. I haven't seen it.'

'I have, about . . .' she looked up at the ceiling and narrowed her eyes, 'oh, it's hard to be accurate, but it must be verging on two hundred times.'

'What? Why?'

'I've got four daughters and every girl under the age of twelve wants to be a mermaid.'

'OK, well . . . let's forget that one.'

'And every girl over the age of twelve wants to know how the mermaid and Tom Hanks are going to have sex at the end after she gets her tail back.'

Paul paused with his hand in the Jiffy bag. 'What's the answer?' he asked, in spite of himself.

'The *correct* answer is, "I don't know." Anything else just leads to disaster, they used to stand in a row and chant, "Netta's embarrassed, Netta's embarrassed." Here –' She held the joint out to him.

'You first,' he said, politely.

'Thank you.' He watched her light up inexpertly and take a tiny sip of smoke. 'I'm going to go very easy on this.'

'You know,' said Paul, 'I'd never call my mum by her first name. She'd probably faint.'

'They're stepdaughters,' said Netta. 'The oldest is only twelve years younger than me. Of course, now she's twenty-eight she thinks it's hilarious to call me Mum in front of strangers.'

'Why?'

'Because then people will think I'm at least fifty, won't they?' She peered at his blank expression. 'I know forty might sound ancient to you, but from my angle it's still quite young whereas fifty sounds frighteningly old.'

There was a pause. 'So,' said Paul, 'the other film's *Far from the Madding Crowd*. You seen it?'

'Yes, but not for a very long time. I don't mind seeing it again. Here, it's your turn, I've had enough for the time being.'

There was a slight wobble to the opening music, as if the orchestra was playing on a vibrating stage, and it worsened as the credits faded across a hill of hessian grass. Two collies tore across the width of the screen and then, at a shouted signal from a man with sideburns, wheeled around a pristine flock. 'Those,' said Paul, 'look like Leicester Longwools, also known as Bakewells. They go back about three hundred years. Fantastic fleece.'

'Sorry,' said Netta, 'but are you talking about *sheep*?'

'Yeah. My dad's a sheep farmer. I grew up on a sheep farm.'

'Did you? So do you know everything about sheep?'

He inhaled deeply, held his breath until he saw dancing specks in front of the screen and then let it out with a rush of words. 'I probably know more about sheep than I do about hernias. Or irritable bowel syndrome. Or Factor XIII deficiency. Or –' The list, he realized, scrolled limitless to the horizon. 'I know loads about them, yeah.' It was a pity, really, that Mrs Dimoglou wasn't suffering from foot rot, because he could have cleared that up, no problem, and then dipped her afterwards. *And* he wouldn't have had to explain to her what he was doing.

'So didn't you want to be a farmer?'

'No.'

'Why not?'

'Because I hate sheep,' he said. He had never uttered the sentence out loud before and had to fight the urge to check behind him, in case his father was lurking in the corner.

'Why?'

'*Why?*' He thought of those hundredweights of skittering idiocy, ricocheting round the farmyard like woolly pinballs, their eyes wide and barmy. 'Because . . . there's nothing to like about them.'

'So it wasn't some childhood trauma?'

'No. No, I think it was . . . you know . . . innate. I don't like celery either.' He thought about that last sentence for a while. 'Not that that's relevant,' he added.

'So if you're not taking over from your father, who is?' She had nailed the crucial question. He had spent his adolescence pretending to be thrilled at the prospect of becoming the seventh Gooding in a row to inherit sixty-four hectares of wet bracken, and all the while he had thrashed around for an escape route that wouldn't break his father's heart. And the answer had burst upon him like a biblical revelation during a social-studies lesson on 'community attitudes to the professions'; he could become something that his parents would unequivocally see as finer and better than sheep farming, as more noble, more lucrative, more *admirable*. And the idea had worked; he'd actually done it! He felt a retrospective burst of joy at the success of his plan.

'Paul?'

'Yeah?' Netta seemed to be waiting for something; on the screen the man with sideburns was eyeing up a woman with a horse. 'Oh . . . my cousin Gerry. He's a nice bloke.' And a bit dim, he thought privately, but willing. 'Here. Your go.'

She took another tiny drag. 'You've no siblings then?'

'No.'

'My mother was a dancer,' she said, '*is* a dancer, and I went to all the classes when I was little but I didn't have the . . . the knack and then once I hit adolescence, of course, it was a disaster.'

'Why?'

'You can't tap-dance with bosoms, it's too painful. I'm quite good at salsa,' she continued, 'because that's all jiggling and I can jiggle like a professional, but it's the vertical movement I can't handle.' Paul kept his eyes on the screen. 'Sorry,' she said. 'I didn't mean to embarrass you. I haven't been stoned since 1979.'

Paul did a slow calculation. 'I was six in 1979,' he said, with the air of a magician producing a particularly pleasing rabbit.

'Thank you. Thank you for pointing that out.'

'Sorry. So what happened in 1979 then?'

'I got married and my husband's a fireman and he's very anti-drugs; he says that people on drugs burn their houses down.'

'Don't drunk people burn their houses down too?'

'Yes. Yes, that's a good point. I don't tend to argue with him over fire-related matters, it's very much his field, but that's a good point. And then there's people who smoke.'

'And people with chip pans.'

'And people who make crème brûlée.'

'What's that?'

'Burnt cream. You sprinkle a thick layer of sugar over a creamy custard and then you whip it under the grill to melt the sugar and then you let it set and the top turns all crispy.'

'Could you make that now?' asked Paul, humbly.

'No, you need eggs,' she said, 'and I've used them all. I never did find that cake tin, did I? What a terrible waste of ingredients.'

'When I was small,' said Paul, 'I used to like raw cake mixture.'

He caught her eye.

'Just a little bowlful then,' said Netta. 'Although with raw eggs, it's a bit of a . . .' she stood up and took a moment to adjust her balance, 'it's a bit of a . . . I've lost the thread here.'

'Raw eggs.'

'Oh yes. Salmonella, it's a bit of a risk. You know, I was in the vicinity the last time you had food poisoning. If it was food poisoning.'

It took a moment for this to register. 'You what?'

'I was in the lift with you. On my first morning here.'

'Oh God, oh God, you weren't . . .'

'I'm afraid I was.' She wobbled off into the kitchen and he felt impelled to follow, apologizing all the way.

'It doesn't matter,' she said, handing a bowl to him, 'it's all vomit under the bridge now,' and this made Paul laugh so much that he had to lean against the fridge for a while.

'You know what's really weird?' he said.

'What?'

'That was *my* first morning too. Flukey, isn't it?'

'Or pukey.' This time he groaned. 'Sorry,' she said, 'I can never resist a pun. It's a family failing.'

'Yeah?' Her words triggered something, and he groped back

to a memory of the party. 'Did your dad really build this place?'

'Yup, he was one of the builders, and he also built the police station –'

'I don't know it, I don't think.'

'I'll bet you do. Purple brick with turrets.'

'I know it.'

'He built the tourist office –'

'The thing that looks like a washing machine?'

'That's the one. He built – well, just look round Shadley Oak and pick out all the eyesores, all the buildings that people make jokes about. In his defence, it was the 1960s.'

'Who was Eddery?'

She paused for a moment. 'Mrs Carina Eddery.'

'Who was she, then?'

'She was –' she forced the words out '– she was head of the local council planning committee.'

'Oh,' said Paul, sensing significance.

'Yes. There was a . . . a bit of a scandal about their relationship – a nasty small-town scandal.' She could hear her voice growing tight and she looked down at her bowl and tapped it gently with the spoon. 'He died of a heart attack when I was twelve, at the very beginning of the summer holidays. You know that row of townhouses opposite the moat – half of them are covered in ceramic tiles with a swan motif –'

'– and half of them aren't. Yeah, I've seen them.'

'Well, the tiled ones were finished before he died, and then it turned out he'd overstretched himself financially and the firm went bust and it was completed by another contractor who did it much more cheaply. Do you know the local nickname for them?'

'No.'

'Semi-Swan Mansions. Shall we go back in?'

*

Perhaps it was making him laugh that had tipped the balance, or perhaps it was just the dope; either way Netta realized that all of a sudden she was fully visible. She'd been noticing lately that to most boys of Paul's age (those she encountered non-professionally – in shops, for instance, or reading her meter or simply standing directly in front of a doorway that she wished to pass through) she seemed scarcely to register as female – was less a physical presence than a corneal smudge, a quasi-feminine blur, detectable, like a stealth bomber, only when engaged in actual combat. Now, for the first time, Paul was actually looking at her, seeing Netta rather than Twankey; his flatmate rather than someone's mum in a calamine-streaked mauve tracksuit.

'It's nice,' he said, judicially, his mouth full of cake mixture.

'Good.'

'Do you know what's going on?' He waved his spoon at the screen. 'Who's that man?'

'He's a rich farmer and he's in love with Julie Christie.'

'And who's the soldier who keeps turning up?'

'Sergeant Troy. He's in love with Julie Christie.'

'And who's the one with sideboards?'

'Faithful Gabriel Oak.'

'Is he –?'

'Yes, but she's ignoring him at the moment.'

'So who wins?'

'Faithful Gabriel Oak, but he has to wait years. Seven years, I think.'

'Oh.' The fact seemed to depress him. 'Why?'

'Because she has to grow up before she realizes what true love means.'

'Oh.'

The early soundtrack wobble had begun to worsen, imparting a phlegmy rattle to the dialogue. 'Clear your throat,' ordered Netta to a farmhand. 'Clear your throat before you speak.'

'It *is* Marianne I'm watching out of the window,' said Paul, the words leaving his mouth before he could catch them. 'She works at the local paper. I'm not spying on anything private, it's just I can see her when she arrives in the morning and when she leaves, and sometimes when she goes out during the day. And comes back. And when she uses the coffee machine in the foyer.'

'And . . .' she groped for a non-intrusive query, 'how well do you know her?'

She's done it again, thought Paul, she's gone straight for the million-dollar question. 'I don't really,' he said. 'She used to live in the same road as me when I was a student.'

'And you've – what? Admired her from afar?'

It sounded ridiculous; he nodded, unwillingly.

'Does she actually know that?'

'Well . . . I sent her a note once, but there was a fuck-up and she contacted Crispin instead.' How pathetic it sounded. Netta's expression was carefully neutral.

'You could phone her. Or you could send her another note – I'm sure she'd be flattered. There's nothing nicer than a letter; one of my daughters has kept the note a boy passed to her in class ten years ago, and all it says is "I like your hair".'

'Yeah?'

'Yes, honestly.'

'Yeah, well . . . I suppose I could,' he said, knowing that he wouldn't. He had shot his bolt and it was lost somewhere in the undergrowth.

'What's she like?' asked Netta. 'What sort of person is she?'

'She's –' He paused to inhale the last of the joint and found himself with a throatful of scalding smoke; half a minute later, wiping the tears from his cheeks and drinking from a glass of water fetched by Netta, he tried to disentangle the Marianne of a thousand imagined conversations from the tiny shreds of reality he'd actually witnessed. A good listener? Yes, in his head. Sympathetic? Same answer. Thoughtful? Interesting? Possessed of the ability to see past outward appearances and straight into his soul? Yup, she'd ticked every box in one daydream or another. He drank some more water while he thought about it.

'I fell for my husband from afar,' said Netta.

'Did you?'

'I was in the back row of a fire-safety lecture.'

'Yeah? So . . . next time you sat nearer the front, or what?'

'Oh no, there wasn't going to be a next time, it was a one-off – he'd been sent over from the local fire station. No, I went up afterwards and let him know he had a My Little Pony sticker attached to the back of his jacket. He was very grateful, no one else had told him. One of his daughters had done it.'

Paul looked at her in disbelief. 'And that was it?'

'More or less.' She smiled, remembering Mick's thanks: it was the first time in her life she'd ever been referred to as wonderful. 'His wife had died eighteen months before and his family was in chaos and he was just about to move back home to Scotland and he desperately needed someone to come and sort everything out. And there I was.'

'Bloody hell,' said Paul. 'God that's like – what's that Latin phrase they're always banging on about in *Dead Poets' Society*?'

'*Carpe diem.* Seize the day.'

'Seize the day, that's right. Seize the day.' It was something he never did, he realized. He edged around the day; he made vague waving motions at the day; he let the day shove him around a bit, grinned while it insulted him through a megaphone and lay back while it trampled him with big hobnailed

boots. 'I need to do more seizing,' he said. 'I need some . . .'
Was 'gumption' the word?

'Seizing powder,' suggested Netta.

'*Jesus*, that's terrible.'

'Sorry. Sorry, I seem to be in pun mode, I'll try to stop.'

'Seize the day . . .' repeated Paul, reflectively. On screen the
farmer was aiming a pistol at Terence Stamp. He could take
out Beardy's bike with a tripwire, he thought. He could throw
Marianne over his shoulder and run off with her. He watched
Terence Stamp exsanguinate in Julie Christie's arms and
cranked his own plans down a notch or two. He could find
the number of the *Mercury* through directory enquiries. He
could ask Crispin quite seriously and calmly not to call him
'Pud'. He could tell his mum that he no longer wore vests,
even in winter. He could say to Mr Gorman – the phone rang
and he groped around on the floor for the receiver.

'Hello?'

'Is that Auntie Brianetta?' It was the voice of a catarrhal
child, strangely accented.

'No it isn't,' said Paul, nettled.

'Oh. I'm supposed to speak to Auntie Brianetta.'

'I'll get her.'

He passed the receiver across.

'Hello?' said Netta, cautiously.

'Is that Auntie Brianetta?'

'Yes. Hello Lester.'

'I'm just phoning to tell you we've arrived safely and we're
delighted to be here in Shadley Oak with our English relatives.'

'Well, thank you, that's very nice of you.' Nice, but discon-
certing; the last time she'd heard him speak was about five
years ago when he'd said, 'I godda wed wabbit,' before dropping the receiver. He now sounded like a doleful, if high-
pitched adult. 'Where are you? In Granny's flat?'

'Yeh.' There was a pause. 'I've done it now, Mum,' she heard him say, and then Natalia took the phone.

'Hi Bri, international rescue here.'

'Good journey?'

'Yeh, little Lester was air sick but we got upgraded from supa-business to first, so swings and roundabouts.' Her voice was neat and clipped, her accent now almost entirely Australian, turning her speech into a succession of unanswerable questions. 'We've just popped in to see Mum but Lester's dropping on his feet so we're off to the hotel.' She lowered her voice. 'It's a total mess here, Bri, honestly, don't feel guilty or anything but it's a disaster. Mum practically fell on my neck she was so relieved to see me.'

'Really?'

'She was in pieces, Bri, pieces. I said, "Mum, stop worrying, because I'm here now," and she said, "Natalia, thank *God*." First thing tomorrow, Bri, I'm straight onto a storage company about Glenn's boxes, never mind the expense, and then it's over to the removal firm. So there's not a single thing for you to worry about, you just have to concentrate on your recovery. Are you using moisturizer?'

'Yes.'

'Beta-retinol-based moisturizer?'

'I'm not sure.'

'Because a friend of mine scarred so badly she needed a monthly peel for a year before she could even go out of the house without a scarf. Moisturizer, antioxidants and regular sunbed treatment. Do you have a sunbed place in Glasgow?'

As Netta listened, and chipped in the odd word, and listened again, she felt a strange, undoubtedly drug-induced sense of detachment; her usual automatic irritation with Natalia was entirely absent and she found herself riding the patronizing billows as if on a lilo. 'That's very generous of you,' she heard herself saying, with apparent sincerity. 'Thanks Natalia. Yes, it's lovely to speak to you too.' She was talking to her sister and she was smiling and nodding and reacting in the way that people who truly got on with their sisters reacted. This was what happened in normal families; people were happy to see each other. For a moment she didn't realize why the lights of Shadley Oak, visible through the undrawn blinds, had become a little blurred.

'You'll need a cossie,' said Natalia. 'I've got a spare but it's not elasticated and anyway you have to have those special reinforced cups, don't you? I'll try to pick something up at the market.'

'Thanks,' she heard herself saying. 'Thanks Natalia.'

Paul had paused the film during Netta's conversation, and by the time she replaced the receiver the frozen frame was juddering ominously. He pressed 'play' again and the picture fluttered and curled in on itself like a burning leaf; static filled the screen and there was an effortful whine from the video player, followed by silence.

'It's a happy ending,' said Netta. 'She marries him.'

Paul brushed a scab from his shirtsleeve. 'So how's your sister?'

'Just the way she usually is,' she said. 'But *I'm* feeling different. I've made a decision.'

'Yeah?'

'I'm going to lie back and let her take over and be grateful she's here. For the next two weeks I am going to become a passive observer.'

'Yeah?' he said, doubtfully.

'Yes. I've done enough seizing for a while. I've got to stop doing it, I've got to break the habit. It's like you said – if there's nothing I can do, then I should just do nothing.'

'Right.'

They both sat for a while and watched the dancing static.

'You'll like this,' said Paul. He cleared his throat. 'You know what you need?'

'No, what?'

'Some anti-seize.'

'That's very good,' she said, nodding appreciatively. '*Very* good.'

14

Lester drew up a chair beside Netta's sun-lounger, arranged the tape recorder on his lap, switched on the microphone and held it to his mouth. 'Testing for levels, one two three. Three. Three.' He paused to make a slight technical adjustment, his professional demeanour slightly undermined by the fact he was wearing an inflatable yellow life jacket. 'Three. Three. This is Lester Connell, Foreign Correspondent for the Woolleroo Primary School newspaper reporting on My Visit to the United Kingdom, Day Five. I am sitting here in the Health and Beauty Complex of the Sprent Spa Hotel, near Shadley Oak, England, with my Auntie Brianetta. Auntie Brianetta, can you tell us something about the Sprent Spa Hotel?' He moved the mike towards her.

'Not really, Lester, no. I've never been here before.' The face mask she was wearing had begun to tauten, and when she opened her mouth she could feel her lower eyelids being dragged down. A few flakes of greenish clay broke off and dropped into the cleavage of her brand-new swimming costume, a fully buttressed number in fuschia spandex. 'Nat, how long does this stuff stay on for?' Her sister, reclining with eyes closed on the next lounger, shrugged slightly and held up five fingers, the nails bloody with fresh varnish.

'Auntie Brianetta, can you tell us how this Health and Beauty Complex compares to other Health and Beauty Complexes you've been to?'

'Well, I've never been to one before, but I'm feeling very . . .' she groped for a word appropriate to someone who had had a massage, sauna, whole-body clay-bandage wrap, manicure, haircut and swim, '. . . clean.'

'And are you going to be using the fully e– What's that word there?' asked Lester, holding out the leaflet he was using as a crib sheet.

'Equipped.'

'And are you going to be using the fully equipped Act-i-fit Body-Shaper gym later on?'

'No, we're going for a great big meal instead at the hotel restaurant. I hope you're feeling hungry.' It was to be her sole financial contribution to the day, Natalia having insisted on putting the entire beauty package on her platinum express card.

'Do you get given broccoli in England?' asked Lester.

'Yes, but you don't have to eat it. You're on holiday.'

'I like broccoli. It's my favourite vegetable after Swiss chard. Now on to more – oh, wait a minute. Oh damn.' He peered at the tape recorder. 'Sorry for the bad language, Auntie Brianetta, but I think I might of leaned on "pause" by mistake in the middle, it's very easy to do by accident, my mum says it's a design flaw. We'll have to start all over again. Can you try to give the same answers, please?'

'OK.'

'Now,' he said, after rewinding the tape and decisively pressing the 'start' button, 'this is Lester Connell, Foreign Correspondent for the Woolleroo Primary School newspaper, reporting on My Visit to the United Kingdom, Day Five. I am sitting here in the Health and Beauty Complex of the Sprent Spa Hotel, near Shadley Oak, England, with my Auntie Brianetta. Auntie Brianetta, can you tell us something about the Sprent Spa Hotel?'

At eight years old Jeanette, her second stepdaughter, had been all bossiness and bustle, shiny hair and ribbons; Clare at eight had spent most of her time pretending to be a horse and Kelly had been a long-legged blur, sprinting from one scheme to the next: charming, capricious, histrionics never more than a single 'no' away. Lester, at eight, looked and sounded like a middle-aged man, his features fleshy and defined, his eyebrows heavy. He had the sort of hair – stiffly waved with a natural side parting – that was usually seen only on leading actors in black-and-white films of the 1950s and although he was dressed in predictably expensive kids' gear, he somehow gave the impression of wearing tweeds. It had been his own choice to don the life jacket though he had no intention of swimming ('I might slip and fall into the deep end when I'm walking by, and I've only got my Grade One Dolphin Certificate.') and his own choice to drink a prim cupful of milky coffee rather than anything with E-numbers. His expression, as Netta duplicated her replies, was sober and approving, like that of an accountant auditing a particularly well-managed set of books.

'Onto more personal matters,' he said, when she'd finished. 'I believe that you're related to my mother, Mrs Natalia Connell.'

'Yes, she's my sister. She's two years older than me.'

There was an immediate grunted denial from beside her.

'Sorry,' said Netta. 'She's fifteen months older than me.'

'So what was it like to have my mother as a big sister?' He pressed the 'pause' button, this time deliberately. 'You could tell a funny story here,' he said, 'it could be something that happened at school, maybe. My teacher says it's what reporters call "local colour".' He pressed 'start' again and nodded encouragingly.

Funny stories. School. It was like trying to couple a pair of railway carriages by hand. 'Well, let me see . . . er . . .' She cast about for something suitable and glanced at Natalia's face, serene under its pristine coating. It was a new experience to have her sister present yet effectively gagged. 'OK. In the summer holidays when I was twelve and your mother was thirteen she went for an audition and won a scholarship to a dance academy in Birmingham, but she decided she wanted to keep it a secret so she pretended to *our* mother that she'd already told me and that I didn't want to talk about it, and then she waited until the very first day of term, which was also our brother's very first day at my school, when we were both standing on the front doorstep all ready to go, and then she swanned out of the bathroom and informed us that she was never going to go to school in Shadley Oak ever again. And she didn't.'

Natalia's face under the mask was unreadable. There was a 'heh heh' noise from Lester and Netta realized that he was making a stab at polite, grown-up laughter, the type that would suit an amusing anecdote; his mini-accountant's face bore a fixed, slightly puzzled smile. 'I'm sorry, Lester,' she said, suddenly ashamed of herself. 'That wasn't funny at all. I promise to come up with a really good story for you, I'll just have to think for a while.'

'I can move onto my next question,' he said. 'Can you tell our listeners how you and my mother came to have such unusual first names? For our listeners' information, my mother's first name is Natalia and Auntie Brianetta's first name is Brianetta.'

'That's a really great question,' said Netta, 'and I think you'll enjoy the answer. When our –' She stopped as she heard the brisk click of heels that heralded the approach of their beauty-therapist-for-the-day, a teenager with gentle white hands and a rigid orange face. 'Time's up ladies,' called Emma, 'I need to whip those maskettes off and then work in some moisturizer while your pores are still *wide* open. Thirsty skin!'

'To be continued,' said Lester, into the microphone. 'Mum, can I stay here and interview the lifeguard for my careers project?'

They left him aiming questions at arm's length to a bemused man on a ladder and followed Emma back towards the Beauty Zone, passing the glass wall that separated the pool from the gym. Among the figures sweating at the machines, his pipe-cleaner physique nicely highlighted by a sleeveless black vest, was Constable Whittaker. For the last quarter of an hour Netta had watched him working on his pecs and had contemplated going up to the glass and writing, 'WHY AREN'T YOU OUT LOOKING FOR MY SUITCASE?' in back-to-front lipstick letters, but it would have contravened her new, laissez-faire stance, and in any case she was getting used to the daily sloppiness of her outfits, the ease of wearing a shirt because she liked the colour or because it reminded her of a weekend break in Lisbon four years ago rather than because it looked smart.

'I've told Lester all about Natalia Makarova,' said her sister, as soon as the mask was off. 'He likes to double-check his stories though. He said to me, "Mum, a reporter never relies on a single source." I'll have the Vitamin-E enriched,' she added, for the benefit of Emma who was holding up a choice of creams.

'Are you sure, Mrs Connell? The seaweed ultra-glow –'

'Not for my skin. You should have it though, Bri, it's good for texture.'

Netta stared at herself in the unnecessarily large and well-lit mirror. The last scab had fallen off the evening before but she had been left with a dusting of pale pink marks, like rosy freckles. 'They'll go, won't they?' she'd asked Paul, and he'd said, 'Oh don't ask me anything, I always get it wrong,' an answer that had failed to reassure her. His own skin was looking almost peachy, just in time for his date this evening.

'Natalia Makarova?' she said, spooling backwards to her sister's first remark. 'What about Natalia Makarova?'

'How Mum saw a newsreel of her dancing the Rose Adagio when she was expecting me, and I started kicking exactly in time to the music and she said to the woman next to her in the cinema, "I think I'm expecting another little dancer."'

Netta looked at her. 'Mum called you after her landlady's dog.'

'Excuse me?'

'When she was doing panto at Newhaven her landlady was given two puppies for Christmas, and they called one Noel and the other Natalia. As in "natal". And Mum always liked the name.'

'Who told you that?'

'I don't know . . . it's one of those family legends. Don't you remember, when anyone asked you how you got your name I used to bark.'

Her sister stared at her incredulously. 'Bri, that was just one of Dad's stupid stories.'

'No it wasn't. Glenn's middle name's Noel, isn't it?'

'That's after Dad's uncle.'

'Dad didn't have an uncle.'

'Yes he did, the one in the photo in the album, with the big moustache.'

'That was his father. Geoffrey.'

'Was it? Well, maybe . . .' Natalia's voice trailed away as she leaned into the mirror and examined the side of her nose. 'Did I tell you the outrageous thing that big Lester's boss said?'

'No.'

'He said, "Natalia, you have the most luminous skin of any woman over twenty I've ever met."' She tutted in well-simulated denigration. 'I mean, what an absolutely ridiculous remark . . .'

Netta closed her eyes as Emma approached with a cotton-wool pad; she'd have liked to have pursued the earlier conversation but it was always difficult to sustain Natalia's interest once the subject moved away from herself. Their father had been good at stories – streams of nonsense, spur of the moment fabrications that would spring from a single prosaic question: 'Who's that man?' 'He's a Russian spy come to steal our bricks.' 'Why?' 'Because they want to build an extension on the Kremlin . . .' – but she could have sworn that the tale of the twin dogs was true, that Natalia had been named after a Yorkshire terrier whereas she herself, looking so much like her father, had been named after him.

'Do you tone, Mrs Lee?'

She opened her eyes again. 'I'm sorry?'

'In your nightly beauty routine do you tone, as well as cleanse and moisturize?'

'Yes, when I remember. Sometimes.' Sometimes, if one of the girls had bought her toner as a present and was watching censoriously from the bathroom door.

'You should always tone, Mrs Lee.'

'Oh yes, Bri, you should always tone. I tone twice a day using an isotonic buf-pad combi.'

'Oh, those are *very* good,' said Emma approvingly. 'And have you tried the Clinique gentle gel programme, with the one-step daily strength increments?'

They hurried off along their own conversational track, and Netta stayed behind and watched her sister's face and wondered whether she had anything at all in common with Natalia beyond a set of genes and some roughly shared memories. She was struck by the bizarre thought that she knew more about the contents of Paul Gooding's head than she did about her sister's – had talked more with him over the past week than she had with Natalia in nearly thirty years. Once at dance school her sister had peeled away from her life in Shadley Oak, staying during the week with a family of another pupil and leaving home for good when she turned professional at sixteen, flashing her fishnets in the chorus of a London musical and working her way up the cabaret ladder via Paris to Las Vegas where – Netta suspected – she had flashed rather more before hooking big Lester. And then it had been birthday cards and Christmas phone calls, and now, it seemed, she and her sister were incapable of beginning a conversation that didn't end with either sniper fire or an inventory of beauty products.

'. . . he's inherited my skin,' Natalia was saying, 'that's why I couldn't risk my sister meeting him until the danger was completely past.'

'I'm sharing a flat with a doctor,' said Netta, 'and he went back to *work* before all his scabs had dropped off. So I think you were being overcautious.'

'Bri,' said her sister, seriously, 'one scar can mar. That's what the manager at the Crazy Horse once said to me when I told him I was considering going go-kart racing, he said, "Natalia, remember, one scar can mar." I don't want to risk limiting little Lester's career options, I want the world to be his oyster.' Her voice trembled slightly and she leaned into the mirror again and adjusted an eyelash.

'Is anything the matter?' asked Netta.

'No,' said her sister, brightly. 'You know, I've got a killer patch of rough skin just under my second toe. Do you have any citrus oil, Emma?'

What was galling, what *would* have been galling had Netta not been embedded in her new role as supine observer, was that

Natalia had solved almost all the problems caused by the move by simply opening her purse: she had arranged a private consultation with an osteopath for their mother, hired local storage space for Glenn's boxes, threatened the removal company with a lawyer if they didn't pay up for the table, and booked the scout hut for extra rehearsal time for the beleaguered 'Rosettes and Champagne'. She had not yet managed to persuade a plumber to schlep as far as Mellis Hall ('I mean, what is it with working men in this country, Bri, they just don't care, they've got no *morals*. Obviously, I'm not including Mick in that . . .') but she had achieved enough to establish her firmly as the heroine of the hour, and by the time Netta had emerged from quarantine there had been little left to do but thank her sister – a task that had left her jaw feeling stiff – and resume her old place as second-favourite daughter.

'Well . . .' said their mother as they walked into the hotel foyer, fresh from Emma's ministrations, 'Brianetta, I wouldn't have recognized you.' Netta, catching sight of herself in the bronze-tinted mirror behind the seating area, found the remark fully justified. Her features had disappeared behind a sheet of foundation, leaving her with two nose-holes and a pair of lips so glossed as to be reflective. 'Ted, don't you think Brianetta looks marvellous?'

'Even lovelier than usual,' said Ted, who was standing just behind his employer, holding her coat and bag.

'And where's my grandson?'

'He's finishing off an interview in the gym,' said Natalia. 'You know, he only got that tape recorder last week and the shop assistant said he'd never come across anyone who'd picked up the basics more quickly, and he asked me if Lester was gifted and I said, "It's not for a mother to say," and he said, "Surely you're not his mother, I'd have taken you for his older sister."'

'Oh isn't that marvellous. Ted, isn't that marvellous?'

'Yes, indeed.'

'But hang on,' said Netta. 'That would imply that you don't look more than about eighteen. I mean, admittedly, you look very, very good for your age, but that age is actually *forty-one*.' She found herself emphasizing the last two words to a degree that turned a couple of heads in the foyer.

'Ah, ah,' said Natalia, wagging a finger, 'a woman never admits to a minute more than thir–'

'–ty-two,' finished their mother, who had invented that particular rule and had repeated it at yearly intervals throughout their childhood.

'Why?'

'It's called mystique,' said her sister. She didn't add, 'you wouldn't understand,' but the implication hovered between them. 'Ah, here's my little laddie,' she said brightly as Lester rounded the corner by the reception desk, tape recorder in hand. His walk was rather ponderous, like that of a senior alderman after a good lunch, but catching sight of the family group awaiting him he injected a little skip into his step, an attempted joyous gambol that didn't quite come off. It was as if he had seen an instructional film on youthful behaviour and was having a stab at lesson one.

'Hello everybody,' he said. 'Hello Gran.'

'Do you know, Lester,' said his grandmother, 'I saw a film about the Russian royal family recently and they called their grandmother "Mamushka", which I thought was charming.'

'Was that before or after they were gunned down?' asked Netta.

'Before,' said her mother, blandly. 'Could you try that Lester? Mamushka?'

'Mamushka,' he said obediently.

'You see, you can speak Russian now,' said Natalia. 'That's something else to tell your pals in class, isn't it?'

'Now,' continued their mother, 'Ted very kindly gave me a lift here and we saw Glenn on the way. He's on his route home, he's had a very busy day and he's going to be a teensy bit late, and he said we should start without him, he's perfectly happy to go straight for a delicious main course.'

'Where was he?' asked Netta, addressing Ted in the hope of getting an accurate answer.

'Just cutting through the Maitland Estate.'

'Oh. Those awful garages. Well . . . we could have a drink first and wait for him.'

'Oh, let's start,' said Natalia. 'Glenn's never been bothered about food. Whereas little Lester's nearly . . .'

'It's my treat and I want it to be a family meal,' said Netta. 'And that means including Glenn.'

'But he just told Mum . . .'

'He didn't tell – oh, never mind.' She baulked at the impossibility of explaining to Natalia what the true exchange between Glenn and her mother must have been – the frothily discursive verbiage from one side and the phrase 'I think so' from the other. 'Why don't we all go to the bar for ten minutes? Lester, you'd like a Coke, wouldn't you?'

'No, I prefer bottled still water with just a dash of lime cordial.'

'And Ted, would you have time to join us?'

'Oh, that's very kind of you.' He tipped his wrist and carefully examined his watch. 'Yes, I believe I have ten minutes.'

'I could finish off my interview with Auntie Brianetta,' said Lester, holding up the microphone.

'Aren't you hungry, Lester?' asked Natalia sharply.

'Not really, Mum.'

'But you love your food, you're always hungry at mealtimes. Maybe you're overexcited.'

There was a pause as they all looked at Lester and he looked stolidly back. 'Yes . . .' said Natalia, uncertainly, 'that'll be the reason.'

They settled in a leatherette padded booth beside a wall lumpy with reproduction warming pans, and Lester resumed his role of junior reporter. 'They don't like letting kids go on holiday in term time,' Natalia had said, 'but I explained that the trip would be educational. He's got to write three features for the noticeboard and do a show-and-tell on the history of Shadley Oak. I bought him a reproduction monk yesterday as a starter item.'

'So,' said Lester, switching on the tape, 'this is Lester Connell, Foreign Correspondent for the Woolleroo Primary School newspaper, talking to my Auntie Brianetta again. Auntie Brianetta, you were telling me how you and my mother, Mrs Natalia Connell, got such unusual names.'

Netta caught her sister's eye. 'I think,' she said, 'that we should pass this question over to the expert. Mum?'

'Yes, dear?'

'What's the correct answer?'

'To what, dear? I wasn't listening, I was just thinking what a *strong* face Lester has – he looks rather like . . . what's the name of that actor in *From Here to Eternity*?'

'He doesn't look anything like Burt Lancaster,' said Natalia.

'No, no, the other one . . . oh, *who* is it? A fine, manly face. Not Montgomery Clift. Not Frank Sinatra . . .'

Ernest Borgnine, Netta realized suddenly, looking at her nephew's expectant face; unlucky Lester was the spit of Ernest Borgnine, eyebrows, jowls and all. Before her mother could arrive at the same conclusion, vocalize it and cause him lifelong psychological trauma she hurried in with a repeat of the question. 'Go on, Mum, you're the only person with the definitive answer.'

'To how you both got your names?'

'Yes.'

Her mother hesitated. 'It wasn't Ernest somebody, was it?'

'No, definitely not. Our names, Mum.'

'Names. Let me see if I can remember. As you know, I never dwell on the past . . .' With her usual flair for squeezing the moment, she drifted her eyes up past their watching faces and settled her gaze on the wood-effect panelled ceiling. 'As far as I can recall . . .' She paused and tapped a finger against her upper lip. 'As far as I can recall, I chose "Natalia" after I saw a film of Natalia Makarova dancing the Rose Adagio –' Natalia looked at Netta with what could only be described as smug triumphalism '– and your name, Brianetta, came from a make of leotard that I was ordering in bulk at the time for the junior class; you know how leotards always *sag* around the gusset? Well these were a new type with double stitching and I remember pausing when I saw what they were called and thinking, oh, now that's a distinctive name, and it's not only unusual and attractive but also, of course, given your father's name, rather approp–'

'I thought that Dad chose the name,' said Netta, the back of her neck suddenly cold, as if someone had opened a door behind her, 'because I looked like him. He thought about calling me Briany with an "a" and then when he was actually in the registrar's office he decided that Brianetta sounded more feminine.'

'No, dear, I'm sure that I put in the bulk order before you were –'

'Bri, that's just another one of Dad's stor–'

'Yes, but he –'

There was an ambiguous rumbling noise that translated,

after a moment or two, into Ted clearing his throat. 'Thank you so much for the drink,' he said, uncomfortably. 'I really should go.'

'Oh . . . sorry Ted.' Netta rose to let him exit. 'Sorry to embroil you in a family argument.'

'Not at all, in any case I have to . . . to . . .' He smiled rather fixedly, to cover his obvious lack of an excuse.

'Of course, today is Ted's day for paperwork and bills,' said Bel. 'Isn't it, Ted?'

He nodded, gratefully. 'That's right.'

'If you see Glenn on your way,' said Natalia, 'hurry him along, won't you?'

There was the briefest of pauses as they watched him leave and then the discussion resumed at its former pitch.

'Of course,' said their mother, her voice soaring above those of her daughters, 'as I say, I never like to dwell on the . . . yes, what is it, dear?' Lester had his hand up.

'Can I ask a thing?'

'Of course, dear.'

'He's got great intellectual curiosity, haven't you, Lester?' said Natalia. 'That's what it said on his report last term, it said, "Lester has great intellectual curiosity and likes to follow up subjects in depth." He was also class monitor for the whole of last year and the teacher said his sense of responsibility was almost adult.'

Lester's hand began to waver with fatigue.

'Go on,' said Netta, encouragingly. 'What do you want to ask?'

'I want to ask, what's a gusset?'

'Oh. Well, it's the bottom part of a leotard. Or of a pair of knickers. Or pants. It's the doubled-up bit of material that . . . that goes between your legs.'

Lester continued to stare at Netta for a moment or two

after she had finished speaking and then – apparently seeking confirmation – looked at his mother.

'That's right,' she said. 'What Auntie Bri says is right.'

'What, you mean it's part of a pair of . . . of . . .' The rest of the sentence disappeared into a messy splutter and then Lester tipped his head back and emitted a yell of laughter. All around the bar heads turned to look.

'Lester . . .' said Natalia in half-hearted admonition.

The noise transmuted into a series of yelps, and her son's heavy features flushed a deep pink and his eyes disappeared into twin creases. For the first time he looked like an eight-year-old. Natalia looked at her sister and gave a shamefaced smile.

'There you go,' said Netta, giving her nephew's earlobe an affectionate little tug. 'I promised you a funny story.'

15

Talking to your dinner companion:

i) *Straightforward compliment – e.g. 'you look lovely', delivered without looking down cleavage (if visible) or staring all round room as if at flitting bat.*

ii) *Simple, non-loaded starter topic of mutual interest – e.g. where did she eat out when she lived in Birmingham?/what's her accommodation like in Shadley Oak? (compare and contrast briefly to own).*

iii) *Suggest looking at menus. Don't close it after four seconds saying, 'I always have steak,' don't wait for her to choose and then say, 'I'll have the same as her,' to waiter. If she wants you to pick the wine, ask the waiter for suggestions. This is not a sign of ignorance/passivity.*

iv) *Try restarting conversation by asking about her job and then listening to the answer. Try to avoid talking about self unless asked, in which case talk away, but remember to leave gaps for her to speak. Ability to conduct a two-hour monologue is not one of the qualities women look for in a boyfriend.*

v) *The following are suggested light topics of mutual interest, which can be used to fill any gaps in the conversation (note each question has a follow-up question, to avoid the nightmare of one-word answers): What's the last film she saw and why did she like/hate it? Has she ever had chickenpox and what was it like/how did she avoid it? Is she keeping in touch with friends from university, and what are her best friends doing now? Where did she grow up and what's it like?*

vi) *If conversation completely grinds to a halt it is <u>fully acceptable</u> to smile at her and say, 'Sorry, I sometimes get a bit tongue-tied on special occasions.' She will find that flattering.*

vii) *Don't get drunk. This is an absolute.*

viii) *Be yourself. Dull advice, but valid.*

Paul refolded the list and put it back in his jacket pocket. Netta, at his request, had given him a crash course in date strategy and he'd been so impressed by her expertise that he'd ended up asking for written notes. 'It's having girls,' she'd said. 'You should hear them when they get home – "Oh my God, he talked to my tits all evening, he shouted 'garçon' at the waiter and thought he was being funny, he sank a bottle and a half of red by himself and then walked straight into the door on the way out." They don't want some show-off, they don't want a comedy act, they want someone who's interested in them and who's good company. And you are,' she'd added, and then – when he'd made some vague mumbling noises by way of reply – 'and if she pays you a compliment, say thank you.'

He peered in through the half-open blinds at the empty interior of Le Chien Gris; he had arrived ludicrously early and was beginning to get cold as well as nervous. The restaurant was on a side street not far from the abbey and it looked reassuringly classy, with a handwritten menu in the window and well-spaced tables. Also in the window was a framed copy of the 'new restaurant' column of the *Birmingham Evening Post*, which had given it two asterisks. 'The guinea fowl,' he read, 'was a little dry, but this was more than compensated for by the winy richness of the juniper-spiked reduction.' On the other side of the glass a bored waiter caught Paul's eye for the third time, and beckoned encouragingly. Faced with the choice of mouthing 'I've got a reservation and will come in shortly' or sitting at a table by himself for ten minutes, he took the third option and embarked on a brisk walk round the block.

After all the weeks of angst, arranging the date had been astonishingly straightforward. He had phoned Marianne at the newspaper and asked her if she would like to go out for a meal, and Marianne had said yes. Or, to be more precise, she had said, 'Oh that would be nice, Alex told me that that restaurant was lovely when he went there with –' and then Paul had been bleeped. He had decided, thinking about it afterwards, that the end of Marianne's sentence would definitely have been ' – with his wife,' and then he had battened down his imagination and refused to speculate further. While still scabbed-up on the fifth floor he had tacked a private addendum to his 'seize the day' plan; it was a vow to stop ruminating endlessly on every gesture and syllable that Marianne let fall. There was to be no more inference, no more extrapolation; from now on if he wanted to clarify anything about their relationship, he would simply ask.

The wind started to gust as he walked away from the restaurant and he could feel his hair shrugging off the hasty attempt he'd made at mousse-assisted styling. After a long and gruelling Gorman ward round ('Are we boring you, Dr Gooding? Or perhaps you've just been given a lovely new watch and you want to keep an eye on it.') he'd had only thirty minutes to wash and change; this had been reduced to seven and a half after Armand had called round with a typed manuscript.

'I've been working on the introduction to my lunchtime lecture tomorrow,' he'd said, 'but I would like to ensure that

I'm –' he'd paused slightly '– hitting the right note. If that's a correct use of the phrase.'

'Yes it is,' said Paul. 'I'm in the middle of drying my hair,' he'd added unnecessarily, the damp towel drooping round his neck.

'That's absolutely no problem, I'm more than happy to read it to you.' Armand had followed him back to the bedroom and positioned himself in the doorway. 'OK to start?'

'Armand, look, I'm getting ready to go out. I can't guarantee my full attention.'

'I don't need any type of detailed analysis, I'd simply like you to pick up on anything that's not *absolutely* clear to a British audience.'

'All right. What do you think of this blue shirt?'

'It has a small stain on the collar. Welcome,' he'd added, in declamatory style. 'I feel honoured to be the first speaker in this series of lunchtime lectures, and I've chosen as my theme Transatlantic Differences in the Approach to Clerking Non-emergency Surgical Cases.'

'Snappy title.'

'Excuse me?'

'Nothing, sorry.' That, he realized, had been a pure Netta remark; they'd obviously been cooped up together too long.

'Shall I continue?'

'Yup.'

'I shall begin by outlining the basic clerking procedure in St Luke's Hospital in Montreal, where I trained. As a Clanger I was often asked –'

'As a *what*?' asked Paul, pausing mid-aftershave.

'A Clanger. Am I not using it correctly? You told me that it was a colloquial old English term for an apprentice.'

'Oh God, did I?'

Sorting out that particular mess had taken far too long, and

Paul had been simultaneously speed-walking and buttoning his cuffs when Gwyn had pulled his Suzuki into the kerb just outside the hospital gates and offered him a lift. As a result he had arrived at the restaurant with fifteen minutes to spare, and with Gwyn's lucky rabbit's foot in his pocket. 'Though mind you,' Gwyn had said, 'our respective definitions of "getting lucky" might differ ever so slightly.'

The preprandial walk round the block took Paul past a row of souvenir shops and through an arch that led to the abbey moat. He had recently sent his grandmother a Sights of Shadley Oak tea towel for her birthday, but the swan-flecked, corn-flower-blue water of the illustration bore absolutely no resemblance to the present leaden surface, roughened by the wind and bobbing with flotsam. No swans were visible, and most of the ducks were crammed onto a chain of concrete hexagons that acted as nesting sites. The remainder – a group of shabby adolescent mallards – were jockeying for space on a length of blue plastic sticking out of the water near the bank. As Paul passed them a squabble broke out, a flurry of shoving and quacking and then a sudden, startling rattle of pinions, and he flinched as three drakes, beak to tail, shot over his head, so close that he felt the breeze of their wings on his hair and heard the wet splatter of shit rain all around. He halted, his right foot an inch from the nearest olivaceous smear. In an instant the towpath had changed colour and texture and he was now standing in the middle of a faecal Jackson Pollock. With icy fatalism he began to examine himself. He checked his hands, he ran his fingers across his scalp, he took off his jacket and inspected it from every angle, he peered at the back of his trousers, he gazed down at his pristine shirt front and unsullied cuffs. In growing disbelief, he patted the clean contours of his face. They had missed; the buggers had missed. He had stood beneath a guano monsoon and emerged untouched. It was almost a miracle. It had to mean something. It had to be a good omen.

There was a mutter of distant thunder and he checked his watch and set off again, this time at a brisker pace. He overtook an ambling couple and then a group of furtive teenagers hunched over a shared bottle of vodka, and then he turned back towards the town centre through a second arch and saw coming towards him a familiar figure in a craggy red jacket. It was the first time that Paul had seen Netta's brother without his shopping trolley and in its absence he was a fast if ungraceful walker, the swing of his arms slightly out of synch with the rhythm of his legs. He had the same curly hair and wide cheekbones as Netta, but he was currently looking agitated – a most un-Netta-like expression – and he seemed to be searching for something, his gaze flicking from side to side and his lips moving soundlessly; he passed Paul without making eye contact and continued along the path to the moat.

There was still no sign of Marianne when, with three minutes to spare, Paul arrived back at Le Chien Gris; he looked through the window, caught the waiter's eye yet again and turned his attention to the menu. Crème brûlée, he noticed immediately; well that was a bonus – eating one of those had become a minor ambition since the night of the joint. Moreover, he saw, the main courses included rack of Welsh lamb, so he could do his bit for sheep farming at the same time. He had just shifted his attention to the starters when he heard a diffident cough beside him, and turned to see the elderly man who had twice delivered groceries to the flat during the plague week.

'It's Paul, isn't it?' said the man

'Yes. Hello.' Paul shook the proffered hand with its delta of swollen veins and searched for the name. Ted. Fred. Ted. 'Is it Fred?'

'Ted.'

'Oh, sorry.'

'That's quite all right.' Ted gave a shy and toothy smile. 'I'm sorry to disturb you,' he added.

'No, I was just . . . you know, waiting for someone.'

'I was only wondering if, by any chance, you've seen Netta's brother this evening. Glenn.'

'Yes. A couple of minutes ago – he was heading for the path by the moat.'

'Oh splendid. Thank you so much.' Ted turned to go.

'Hang on though, he was walking quite fast. He might have gone a long way since then. He didn't have his trolley.'

'Really?' Ted looked troubled. 'Oh, I would have thought . . . he was supposed to be joining a family get-together once he'd finished his round, you see. I thought I'd find him nearly at the Hall, but I've worked backwards from there and not managed to catch him. I wonder . . .'

'I think he was looking for something,' said Paul. 'Or somebody.'

'Oh. Well, thank you for your help. I shall see if I can find him.'

Feeling vaguely guilty, Paul watched Ted walk away. There was another low grumble of thunder and, as if in reply, a volley of sarcastic quacks from the direction of the moat; no doubt 633 Squadron had returned, bomb bays reloaded. Ted disappeared around the corner of the side street, there was half a minute of emptiness and then Marianne rounded the same corner, beautiful in a blue jacket. She gave a little wave.

'Oh,' said Paul out loud, suddenly realizing something, suddenly visualizing the wire-ended blue plastic perch from which the ducks had launched themselves. 'Bloody *hell*.' He hurried towards Marianne. 'Hi, look, I've just got to catch up with someone and tell them something, I won't be a moment, I . . . I . . . You look lovely. Go on in, the table's booked and everything, I'll just be ten seconds, I'll just be . . .' it started to rain, 'ten seconds. Or less.' He jogged backwards for a few steps, smiling encouragingly at her startled face and then turned and legged it. Ted's beige mackintosh was visible a hundred yards away, and Paul caught up with him just before he reached the moat.

'I think,' he said, between gasps, 'I think I know what Glenn's looking for. I think his shopping trolley's in the moat, a couple of feet from the bank. I saw some ducks sitting on the handle but the water's so muddy you can't see the rest of it – it's sort of . . . halfway along.'

'Thank you so *very* much,' said Ted warmly.

'I'd offer to come and show you, but . . .'

'No, no. You mustn't miss your friend.'

'OK, but . . .'

'Glenn may well have already found it and taken it out,' said Ted. 'These incidents happen to him from time to time. I'll just go and check.'

'OK, if you're sure.'

'Thank you,' said Ted again; he patted Paul's arm. 'Most kind.'

'I'm really sorry about that,' said Paul, sitting down opposite Marianne. He brushed some droplets from his hair and wiped the back of his neck with a napkin; the window behind Marianne's head was beginning to blur with rain.

'That's all right,' she said, equably, 'I was late anyway.'

'Not by much.'

'Ten minutes, at least. Janice phoned literally as I was leaving the flat and she's going through a terrible time, I couldn't just leave.'

'No,' he agreed, wondering if he should know who Janice was. Perhaps she was the wife of the mysterious Alex, who had recommended the restaurant.

'She told me that Greg's threatening to leave if she doesn't stop seeing Evan.' No, not married to Alex then. Paul made a noise indicative of interest and Marianne continued speaking, and he looked at her lovely face, so animated, so friendly, so close to his own, and at the swatch of pale hair that swung around her jawline as she spoke. He had always liked that image; the first time he'd ever seen her she'd been at one end of a pub garden, chatting to another girl, and he had been at the other, nursing a sore head and a Sunday newspaper, and for a whole hour and a half he had sat and watched her talk, the light catching the curve of her hair. He was just about to ask, 'Who's Janice?' when he saw Glenn walk past the restaurant window, still at the same fast pace, still without his trolley, his dark hair flattened by the rain.

'Who's Janice?' asked Paul, determinedly ignoring the implications of what he'd just seen.

'She used to share with Leonie and Ann on Castle Lane.'

'Oh.' None the wiser he sat and looked at her again, and realized that he could skip item 2 on Netta's list, that their conversation was flowing like liquid honey and that he could therefore go straight for the menu. He offered the top copy to Marianne and, as he did so, he saw Glenn walking past the restaurant again, this time in the opposite direction.

'Oh God,' he said, with a plunge of the spirits.

'What? What's the matter?'

'Nothing, I mean . . . look, I've got to go and tell somebody something.' He got to his feet and she stared up at him, open-mouthed.

'Somebody's lost something, and I've got to go and tell them. Sorry, I know it sounds mad, it's a bit complicated, I'll explain when I get back. I won't be very long, I promise – you can go ahead and order if you want.' He caught the eye of the hovering waiter. 'I'll have the same as her.'

There was a large white shape on the water near the submerged trolley. In the half-light it took a moment or two for Paul to realize that he was looking at a sleeping swan, its neck a quiescent loop, its head tucked under its wing.

'Is it safe, d'you think?' asked Ted. 'I believe they can be very fierce when roused.'

'Well, hopefully it won't wake up,' said Paul. 'Hey, Glenn, if we both hold onto the railing with one hand and grab the handle with the other, I think we can haul it straight out.'

'I'm not keen,' said Glenn. He had not climbed over the low railing to join Paul on the narrow strip of grass beside the water and in fact had backed off a few feet. 'A swan can break a man's arm with its wing.'

'Yes, *I've* read that,' said Ted, unhelpfully.

Paul looked at his watch; Marianne had now been sitting alone at their table for nearly seven minutes. 'Look,' he said, 'I'll give it *one* go on my own and if it doesn't come out, I'll . . . I'll phone the council tomorrow. I'm sure they must have grappling equipment or something.'

'No,' said Glenn. 'I think it would be much safer to retrieve it tonight. Someone might borrow it again.'

'It's all right for you,' muttered Paul, eyeing the swan. He had always assumed that the wing + arm equation was a myth, but from this proximity it looked wholly believable, the twin muscular curves tense with latent power.

Glenn took a half step towards the water. 'Last February I left the trolley on the pavement because I had to buy a second-class stamp in a shop to write to the local council and two boys borrowed it and threw it into a skip and I had to replace the nearside wheel because the axle was bent. I couldn't use it for five days.'

'OK, OK. I'll give it a go.' Paul grasped the railing and felt the crackle of rust and old paint beneath his fingers. Netta's brother had greeted the sudden appearance of a complete stranger who knew both his name and the whereabouts of his trolley without visible surprise, but Paul's phrase, 'It's about halfway along,' had been dissected to such a degree ('Is that halfway between the outer wall of Woolworths' car park and the road bridge or halfway between the outer wall of Woolworths' car park and the end of the footpath, or is it halfway . . .') that he had ended up accompanying Glenn to the exact spot; they had found Ted standing guard nearby, taking what shelter he could beneath a canopy of dripping trees.

Paul reached out his other arm towards the handle. The swan, head still under its wing, suddenly hunched one shoulder and then relaxed again, the feathers fanning and closing like the blades of a Swiss army knife.

'I'd offer to help,' called Ted, 'but I have to admit that my balance is not quite what it was . . .'

'It's OK, I can manage.'

'Marvellous. You know, I think this rain's definitely easing off.'

Paul braced himself and began to pull. The trolley moved sluggishly towards him, and then jammed on something underwater. He shifted his grip, and started to haul upwards. It was much heavier than he would have thought, and he half squatted to increase the leverage. There was a moment of stasis, and then a moment when the trolley seemed to be rising, sweetly and easily, and then a moment during which he realized that the edge of the bank had just given way and that he was dropping/had dropped/was now standing waist-deep in freezing water, both hands clutching the trolley as if about to do a little sub-aqua browsing.

'Oh *dear*,' he heard Ted say. 'Are you all right?'

A mini tidal wave slopped against the raw edge of the bank and then surged back again, rocking the water so that the swan bobbed like a bath duck. It uncoiled its neck and – eye level now – drew back its head like a cobra and hissed at Paul. He found himself scrabbling at mud, grabbing onto the railings while his feet treadled for purchase, pawing at the broken bank while behind him the mighty white bone-snappers flexed and cracked.

'Be off with you,' shouted an authoritative voice, and there was a discrete splash, followed by two or three more. Paul twisted his head round and saw the swan apparently under fire, the water around it leaping from the impact of a series of small missiles. It pecked ineffectually at the nearest, attacked the next with the same result and then turned and in a great flurry of legs and wings began its bounding take-off run, an inelegant stamping charge that changed quickly and impercep- tibly into flight. It lifted away through the darkness and the furrow of white water settled into its former, rain-dimpled calm. Ted dropped the conkers he had been throwing and extended a hand over the railing.

'Trolley,' said Paul, in a voice he barely recognized as his own. 'I'm bloody getting this bloody trolley out now if it's the last bloody thing I do.'

In the absence of the swan Glenn helped assiduously, and within a couple of minutes both Paul and the trolley were back on the towpath.

'It doesn't appear to be damaged in any way,' said Glenn, looking pleased.

'Good,' said Paul, grimly, gazing down at himself. Below

the belt he was clean, if sodden; above the belt he was filthy, if dry. The effect might, objectively, have been quite amusing but neither Ted nor Glenn seemed to find it in the slightest bit funny, and for that Paul was grateful; it was nice, for once, not to be laughed at.

'My flat's just around the corner,' said Ted, 'and I could provide you with a change of clothing and then drive you home – Oh please,' he added, at Paul's half-hearted refusal, 'it would be the very least I could do. After your kindness.'

'I've got to go back to the restaurant first,' said Paul, looking at his watch. He had left Le Chien Gris seventeen minutes ago; Marianne would think he had simply abandoned her. 'I've got to go back and – and –' What, precisely? Wave at her through the window? Squelch between the tables and sit down as if nothing had happened? Attempt an explanation that didn't make him look like a third-rate clown? ('Anyway, once I'd fallen in the water the swan suddenly woke up . . .') Just the thought of the latter made him want to lie down and dissolve. 'There's probably no point,' he said, hopelessly. 'She's probably gone by now. That's *it*. I've had it.'

'We could look in on our way,' said Ted. 'If you'd like to accept my offer, that is.'

'Yeah, all right. Thanks.'

'And Glenn, are you off now?'

'I have to go for a meal,' said Netta's brother, rattling past at top trolley speed. 'I'm late.'

'Join the club,' said Paul.

She was still there – still there but no longer alone. She had joined a couple at another table and was chatting not only with them but also with the waiter, who instead of taking their orders was leaning against the wall with his arms folded and, it appeared, watching the play of light on Marianne's hair while admiring the equanimity with which she had changed her plans and the social ease with – Paul stamped on the brake and brought the Speculation Special to a violent halt. There was to be no more supposition; the waiter was leaning against the wall looking rather glazed.

'I can't go in,' said Paul, 'I look disgusting.'

Ted studied the group at the table. 'Is it the fair-haired young lady?'

'Yes. She's called Marianne.'

'Would you prefer it if I had a word with her?'

'Oh.' He looked at Ted. 'What, and tell her what happened?'

'I could give a précis.'

'Er . . .' It seemed the best offer currently available. 'OK,' he said, ungraciously, and Ted brushed the rain from the shoulders of his mac and entered Le Chien Gris.

Lurking beneath the awning, peering in through the gap between menu and newspaper clipping, Paul watched the mute explanation unfold. Ted began with a bow, and then spoke for some time, his hands gripping the back of an empty chair, his expression serious. Marianne said something in reply and then Ted bowed again, and as he walked away the heads of both women turned and looked wonderingly into the darkness.

'What did she say?' asked Paul as they set off along the street again.

'She was very concerned.'

'About what?'

'Your well-being.'

'What? Why?'

'Because you'd risked your life to help an innocent victim of crime,' said Ted, as if stating the obvious.

'Bloody hell! Is that what you told her?'

'Yes.'

'Bloody hell,' repeated Paul, reflectively this time. 'That is just brilliant.' He felt his mouth curve into an involuntary smile. *'Brilliant.'*

'No more than the truth,' said Ted, gravely. 'And she told me that she very much looks forward to hearing from you again.'

'Brilliant. You are brilliant. Listen, I didn't thank you for chucking those conkers. You've got fantastic aim.'

'I trained as a sniper during the war,' said Ted, stopping at a doorway beside a newsagent's and reaching into his pocket for a set of keys. 'And here we are.'

It occurred to Paul as he stood naked in Ted's tiny bathroom, drying himself with a lilac appliquéd guest towel, that his host might be gay, and his first, venial, instinct was to check the lock; he felt instantly ashamed of himself – what was he expecting, the sudden appearance of a lust-crazed Ted in a studded codpiece? ('Don't you realize your power, Paul, you're simply irresistible to gay men.') – and he tried, in pointless recompense, to dress slowly and carefully. Finally he stared at himself in the full-length mirror on the back of the door: brown lace-up shoes, brown twill trousers, only slightly too tight, white shirt with a faint brown check, blue jumper that stretched smoothly over his tummy. He was looking at his own father, dressed for an NFU social evening. 'Graham Gooding, Arrow Clough Farm,' he barked, extending a hand to his reflection.

'I've made a pot of coffee, Paul,' called Ted. 'How do you take it?'

'Milk and one sugar, please. I'm just coming.'

The flat was tiny and the kitchen no more than a screened-off corner of the living room. Paul sat in a winged armchair as Ted arranged biscuits on a plate and brought over a tray that bore, in addition to two mugs, a single balloon glass. 'Will you take a brandy?' asked Ted, holding up an impressively crusted bottle. 'I think it might be wise, medicinally, after your soaking – although, of course, you're the expert on these matters.'

'If only,' said Paul. 'Yes please. When.'

'Cheers,' Ted raised his mug. 'Happy days.'

'Cheers.'

The other armchair was so close that they sat with their knees practically touching, and a sudden, shy silence descended, broken only by the crunch of biscuits. Paul glanced around, searching for a topic of conversation; there was a piano on one side of the room, the top stacked with sheet music, and on the other, two shelf units, placed either side of the window. One was full of books, the other of knick-knacks – china and silver and odd miscellaneous items: there was a matchbox model of a Rolls-Royce Silver Cloud and another of a Bentley, a polished regimental cap badge mounted on a little shield and next to it a photo of what looked like the cast of a play about gangsters.

'*Guys and Dolls*, Leicester Haymarket, 1958,' said Ted, following Paul's gaze. He rose stiffly and reached over for the frame. 'I was Nicely-Nicely Johnson,' he said, pointing to the third gangster along. Paul studied the bulky figure with the unconvincingly vicious expression and the wooden machine gun. Only the teeth and the length of the face linked him to the old man in the opposite chair. 'I was the understudy,' said Ted, 'but there was an outbreak of pinkeye and I went on four times. Or five, I think.'

'So that's what you did – you were an actor?'

'Yes, for a while. Chorus, mainly. And character. But of course, it's not a . . . a *steady* living. Thank goodness for these,' he said, holding out his hands and miming an arpeggio. 'I can still sing for my supper, so to speak.'

Out of politeness, Paul looked at the photo a moment longer and then stood to replace it. Next to it on the shelf was a more recent shot of Ted, a colour print taken in what looked like a church hall. He was seated at a piano, hands resting on the keys, while beside him a timid-looking elderly woman was pretending to act as a page turner. A second elderly woman was standing in the foreground, occupying centre stage in a pose that suggested she'd just heard the voice of God and was considering her reply. Behind the three of them, against the far wall, a row of small girls in tutus stood holding hands and pointing their toes.

'It's a publicity shot for the Devon School of Dance,' said Ted. 'Have you met Netta's mother? The lady in the front?'

'No, but I've spoken to her.' He picked up the picture for a closer look. 'There's not a lot of resemblance, is there?'

'Not a great deal, no,' said Ted, 'though of course they're both very handsome women.' He took the photo gently from Paul and studied it for a while. 'So, are you going to see your young lady again?' he asked unexpectedly.

'She's not really my young lady,' said Paul. 'I've hardly ever spoken to her, I just . . . fell for her and then hung around like an idiot for ages and ages. This was going to be the first time we'd ever had a proper conversation.'

'How long ago?' asked Ted.

'How long ago what?'

'How long ago did you fall for her?'

'Oh . . . about five months.'

Ted smiled. 'That's not so very long, you know.'

'It seems long to me,' said Paul, 'seeing as I haven't made *one inch* of progress in the meantime.'

'I fell for someone twenty-two years ago.'

'Yeah?'

'And there's been not the slightest change in my feelings

towards them.' His tone was so light that it took a moment for Paul to register the import of the words.

'You mean, you never got anywhere in all that time?' he asked, incredulously.

'No, never.'

'You mean, you didn't even *tell* them how you felt?'

'Oh, I told them but they – this person – this lady –'

Oh, thought Paul, wrong again.

'– was somebody who had been ruled by her heart in the past and had made an unhappy choice and been badly wounded, and had decided not to . . .' he tailed off, his baggy features pursed in thought. Paul took a slug of brandy.

'As a matter of fact,' said Ted, 'I can remember her exact words, she said, "Ted, I never dwell on the past, but I do try to learn from it. From now on, my passion can only ever be for my work."'

'God,' said Paul, chastened as much by the eloquence as by the sentiment. 'And do you ever see her now?'

'Oh, I see her all the time,' said Ted matter-of-factly. 'I'm still very much part of her life, which of course has many compensations. "Sweet is true love, tho' given in vain", as Tennyson said. "Love is not love which alters" – Shakespeare.'

'"And after all, you're my wonderwall",' said Paul. 'Oasis. It's a song that came out last year, a really great song,' he added, at Ted's enquiring look.

'And after all, you're my wonderwall,' repeated Ted meditatively. 'I'm not sure if I quite . . . is there a *secondary* meaning to the word wonderwall?'

'I don't think so,' said Paul. 'I think it just rhymes with after all.'

'Ah, I see.' Ted looked at him kindly. 'Of course, context is everything with lyrics. I'm sure it would be quite different if I actually heard the song.' He took a final look at the photo and then placed it on the tea tray. 'Now, another brandy?'

16

It was difficult to walk out while being effusively thanked, and Netta tried not to think about the fact that she had promised to be at Mellis Hall by one o'clock at the absolute latest and instead sat nodding and smiling while Jenny Haddon explained how her entire life had been changed by a single phone call.

'You see, when you rang that afternoon I was almost out of my head; I had *literally* just burned half a can of baked beans because I'd left the pan on the stove when I went to investigate this awful crash in the living room which turned out to be James quite deliberately knocking over the CD stack – I mean, deliberately, he was brazenly laughing at me – and then the beans caught and the smoke alarm wouldn't stop beeping and I was jabbing at it with the end of a mop handle and, quite honestly, I was about to pack both children into the car and drive to my mother's and leave them there. I had turned into the kind of woman I despise – I was a *rag*, Netta, I was a feeble, bleating, puddle of *utter* self-pity and then the phone rang and it was you. And I thought – this woman, this dynamic woman who has coped with a career and four children that weren't even her own – this woman is in trouble, she's ill, she's letting people down badly, she can't do her job and she's asking for my help. And you know what – it seems a cliché but it gave me *backbone*. I suddenly thought: yes, I can do this, I can make arrangements for James and Becky, I can go back to work and help Netta out, I can make my children proud of their mother, I can become a fully rounded human being again. I mean, I know you've only been off for a week and a bit, but I feel as if I've turned a corner, I've become . . . *me* again.'

'That's wonderful,' said Netta, shooting a furtive look at her watch. It was twelve-forty-five; if she left now and walked fast, she could still make it.

'Anyway,' continued Jenny, delving into her bag, 'I've made complete and comprehensive notes of every single clinic and ward round, I've typed them up, I've printed them out, I've made a copy for myself, I've . . .' She froze, mid-sentence and stared at the sheaf of A4 in her hand and then, as if it had become suddenly too heavy to hold, laid it on the desk. The front page had been blacked out with felt marker pen. Slowly Jenny lifted it aside; the next page bore a large drawing of a blue man with orange legs on a red background, and the third was mostly brown. 'James,' said Jenny in a strangulated whisper, and began to leaf through more rapidly. Her son had been thorough in his work; every page had been rendered unreadable in a different way, and the final three or four had been glued together. For a few, delicate, fruitless seconds Jenny picked at the welded pages before giving up, ripping them down the centre and throwing the pieces onto the floor. 'Waste . . . of . . . time,' she said, between gritted teeth, 'my time, your time – all wasted.'

'You said you'd made a copy,' said Netta quickly, hoping to forestall a major incident.

'It's at home – no, no, don't try to say it doesn't matter, because it *matters*. It's my own fault for telling James where I was going, he still gets frightened whenever I mention your name, and I simply shouldn't have told him that I was bringing you a lovely present. It . . . upset him.' Jenny tossed the rest of her notes towards the bin and missed by a couple of feet; she closed her eyes briefly and then sat up and gave a wide,

239

rather frightening smile. 'I can remember almost everything,' she said. 'I'll take you through it.'

There was a vintage blue van parked in front of Mellis Hall and by the time Netta was halfway up the drive she could read the gold lettering on the side. It confirmed that the plumber ('A. Riceman Ltd, established 1952') had arrived before her, and would therefore probably be sitting in the front seat, busily doubling his bill. She was wrong; as she neared the van she saw that it was empty, and the glint of a dropped washer on the steps of the Hall seemed to indicate that somebody had already let him in.

'Oh, you're here,' called Natalia as Netta opened the door to the flat. 'We'd given up on you.'

'Sorry.' She edged into the kitchen. The washing machine had already been moved from its usual position and from behind it came a series of muffled clunks. Natalia dropped a lump of sugar into a mug, gave it a perfunctory stir and held it out to an unseen hand.

'How long did you let it stand?' asked an unnecessarily loud voice.

'Couple of minutes,' said Natalia.

'You have to let tea stand for at least four, if you don't let it stand for at least four then you might as well THROW IT AWAY. It takes four for the flavour to develop; I don't know why people don't know that, it's common knowledge.' The clunks resumed and Natalia, looking thin-lipped, fished a used tea bag out of the sink and dropped it back in the mug.

'Is Lester in the living room?' asked Netta.

'They've gone,' said her sister. 'Ten minutes ago. Mum and Ted have got a class at five so if they'd waited around any longer they'd never have got back for it. I'd said I'd stay to let er . . . Mr Plumber here in.'

'It's Riceman,' corrected the voice, at volume eleven.

'Yeah, OK.' Natalia flipped a hand in acknowledgement.

'You know, you were lucky to get me, I'm booked solid most of the time. My son says, "Dad, it's time for you to retire," and I say, "What, with my schedule, where would I fit it in?"' There was a tinkle of a dropped screw. 'I said it was the valve. Didn't I? Didn't I say it was the valve?'

Natalia rolled her eyes.

'Are you serious?' asked Netta. 'You've missed the trip because I was late?'

'Yup.'

'Oh God, sorry Nat. I just got stuck in the office – you know, first day back.'

Her sister shrugged listlessly. 'Forget it,' she said, 'I wasn't in the mood for a safari park anyway – you've seen one monkey's rear end, you've seen them all.' She picked at the varnish on one of her nails, inspected the result and then returned to the mug. 'Four minutes,' she said, apparently arbitrarily, removing the bag again.

'TANNIN,' shouted Mr Riceman. 'It's a preservative and that's what's preserved me. My GP says, "You have to slow down, Andy, or your pressure'll go right up again," and I say, "Save your speeches for those old chaps who can't pull their trousers up without a hoist, I've got work to do." Here –' His head, topped with a brutally trimmed mat of grey hair, rose above the machine and Netta at last placed the voice: he'd been in the lift with her and Paul that first morning at work – he and his son had been in front of her and had acted, in fact, as a useful shield.

'You see this valve?' he continued, holding a small object out towards Natalia.

'Yeah,' she said cautiously.

'It's buggered.' He dropped it and took a sip of tea. 'That's better,' he said grudgingly. 'I'll have another one after this. It's going to take me a good forty minutes to sort this mess out.'

As he disappeared again Natalia mouthed something and jabbed a finger in the direction of the living room.

'Jeeeeeeesus,' she said when Netta had closed the door behind them. 'Can't they force people to retire in this country? There must be some kind of law – I had to move the bloody washing machine for him; I pushed and he grunted.' She dropped onto the sofa and slumped back against the cushions. 'Jesus,' she muttered a second time, and started to rearrange the hair at the back of her neck, smoothing and then messing it again in a cycle of dissatisfaction.

'You all right?' asked Netta, taking a seat opposite.

'What?'

'You haven't given your usual critique of my outfit.'

'Oh . . .' Natalia cast a distracted eye over the green-and-yellow sundress. 'Yeah, it's terrible.'

'Thanks.'

'No, I mean, you should really take me up on my offer to buy you some new stuff. That suitcase is never going to turn up.'

'I'd rather buy it myself, if you don't mind. I'll wait till I get back to Glasgow.'

'Whatever,' said Natalia. She gave her hair a final, slightly vicious tug, and then laid her arm along the sofa back and sighed. 'I've got to ask you something, Bri.'

'OK.'

There was silence. Natalia shifted her position on the sofa and gave a cushion a flat-handed slap that sent a puff of dust into the air. 'I dunno,' she said, broodingly.

'Is it about Mum?'

'No.' There was another pause. There was no precedent, Netta realized, for the exchange of confidences between them, no easy mode for them to slip into. She tried to look receptive, and wondered whether it was something to do with her sister's marriage.

'The other day,' began Natalia suddenly, as if on an entirely new topic, 'when Glenn got his trolley back out of the water, he spent the whole of the next morning checking it over and servicing it or whatever – fiddling with the wheels and stuff – and little Lester interviewed him for the school magazine and then he sat and watched Glenn and asked questions about that *fucking* trolley until lunchtime. I practically had to drag him away and . . .' She stopped, the last sharp note of her voice seeming to ring in the air for a moment longer. 'Jesus,' she said, after a moment; her eyes were full of tears. 'You know what was on his last report? It said, "Lester's interests and general maturity sometimes get in the way of his interaction with other children, and this does lead to a certain amount of isolation in class. He should be encouraged to play more –"' Her voice broke on the last two words, and she gave the cushion another whack. 'Like I don't buy him toys. He's got a spacehopper in his bedroom that hasn't moved since the day we bought it. He said, "Mum, I don't like bouncing, I'd rather sit down on a nice chair." And when we took him to a rides park he wouldn't go on anything, he decided what he wanted to do was win a rubber-band dispenser and he just –'

'Lester is nothing like Glenn,' said Netta. 'He's not like Glenn now and he's not going to turn into Glenn.'

'You think? You sure?' Natalia looked pathetically eager. 'It's just that, you know, Glenn never had any friends either, did he, and he never looked like a kid and he never acted like a kid, and sometimes I just look at Lester and wonder where he came from, I mean –' She hesitated, and then said defiantly, 'I'm cute, all right? I've always been cute, I'm the cute one, and big Lester's got charisma, I mean, the man's a charisma factory, and it just seems *so unfair* that little Lester hasn't got the same – Shit! I don't like saying this about my son, I don't like it, I mean, I love him to death, you know I do.' She keeled over and hid her face in the sofa arm. 'I thought I could sort it out in my head,' she said, muffled. 'I brought him here to convince myself he's fine compared to Glenn and now I just don't know. I keep remembering how Glenn was quite sweet when he was little and then he kept getting bigger and weirder and I keep wondering about little Lester and thinking that maybe it's my fault, maybe it's my genes – everyone in big Lester's family's completely normal so it's got to be from my side.' She half rolled her head towards Netta. 'But you honestly think he's OK, yeah? I mean, you're the expert and everything.'

Instead of answering, Netta got up and went over to the window that overlooked the car park. Lined up on the tarmac were an MG, a nearly new Volvo, a mint-condition Saab and a shopping trolley with a recently realigned wheelbase; Glenn was just chaining it to the bar provided for bicycles.

'What's the matter?' asked Natalia, alarmed by the pause. 'You mean you *don't* think he's normal compared to Glenn?'

'Bloody hell,' said Netta. 'Is that why you came? To use Glenn as a yardstick? Is that his only relevance for you?'

'No, hang on, don't twist my words, don't get into some family . . . thing before telling me what you think about Lester. Please, Bri.' Her tone was humble. 'Please, it's just . . . I'm scared for him, all right? I'm being honest with you.'

'OK.' She turned to look at her sister. 'I think little Lester's absolutely fine. He's a bit of an eccentric but he's on the same planet as the rest of us, he understands the social rules and he has a good old go at sticking to them. Social rules are pretty much irrelevant for Glenn, they always were – he doesn't read expressions, he's not interested in what other people think of him, he can't tell white lies when they're called for. Nothing like that comes naturally to him. Someone has to – all right, in the end *I* had to, at school – I had to tell him the useful bits and he had to work at remembering them. Like not yelling when someone touches him, or turning to face the person who's talking to him – stuff that meant he could live with the rest of us without being punched all the time. Lester's not like that.'

'So you think he's normal?'

'Yes, for what it's worth, I think he's normal; as normal as you, or me or . . . or Mum. Granted, he might not be *average*.'

'But all the hobbies he does, he gets totally obsessed and – God, Bri, you should have seen him yesterday, he was thrilled by what Glenn was doing. He took a photo of the set of spanners for Christ's sake.'

'He's a boy,' said Netta. 'I gave Mick a power-washer for his birthday and I thought he was going to cry.'

'But it's all very well saying, "Oh he's an eccentric," as if that's a good thing, but what's going to happen when he gets older? Where's he going to fit in? Can you see him dating, or skateboarding or . . . you know, hanging out with the other kids? Being popular? I keep trying to picture him but I can't. Oh *don't*,' she added, fiercely.

'Don't what?'

'Don't do that sneery look of yours.'

'What sneery look?'

'That sort of "oh, Natalia's being silly and unintellectual as usual" look.'

'I don't know what you mean. I wasn't.'

'You were, Bri. You don't take anything I say seriously, you think I'm just some silly flibberty . . . thing, whatever that word is. You're doing it *now*.'

'No, I'm not.'

'You are. I'm the one who's looking at you, I can see you

doing it! There's nothing wrong with me wanting Lester to be popular, it's not a dirty word, there's no need for you to get all superior.'

'Oh for –' They both turned as the door opened and Glenn, wearing his Puffa jacket, entered the room. He walked straight towards the window, reached between them to pick up a Dixon's catalogue from the sill, said, 'There's that man with the binoculars,' and walked out again. There was a hiatus during which both sisters glanced outside at their observer, clearly visible in the upstairs window of his house, and then drew breath to resume. They were beaten to it by Mr Riceman. 'I ALWAYS STATE IN THE INITIAL CONVERSA-TION,' he began, shouting as he knocked as he entered, '"no heavy lifting". My doctor says, "Andy, if you consistently refuse hospital treatment, then the one thing I can beg you to do is to avoid heavy lifting," so if you want heavy lifting, you have to let me know and I put my son on the task; he's normally in the office, he doesn't have my range of skills but he can be quite useful. So if you wanted heavy lifting, then you should have said in advance. It's quite clear.'

'What?' asked Netta, groping her way through the storm of words.

'I think Mr Riceman wants me to move the washing machine again,' said Natalia. 'Can you just give us five minutes, please?'

'I can give you five minutes, but what do I say to the next appointment? Sorry Mrs Crawley, I gave the first five minutes of your central-heating check to Mrs Devon, so I'll miss out the upstairs radiators and just do the downstairs? You see it doesn't work like that, Mrs Devon; people simply don't understand how businesses are run.'

'We'll be there in a second,' said Netta.

'Sorry Mrs Crawley,' he said with fake contrition as he

closed the door, 'I gave the first second of your central-heating check to –'

'Jeeeesus.' The exclamation was simultaneous, and they looked at each other with a flicker of empathy before the door opened again and Glenn re-entered. 'The plumber says he wants someone to help with the heavy lifting,' he said. There was a pause.

'Can you do it?' asked Netta.

'No, I'm quite busy at the moment,' he said, shutting the door.

Netta rubbed her forehead wearily. 'Where were we?'

'God, I don't know,' said Natalia, plumping herself down on the sofa again. 'No hang on, I remember, I was telling you how worried I was and you were telling me how stupid I am.'

'Oh *come* on, Nat, I didn't say –'

'You implied. You're very good at implying.' She gathered up a cushion and hugged it, digging her chin into the fabric. 'You know, I just want people to *like* Lester. It doesn't seem a lot to ask, does it?'

'I like Lester,' said Netta, sitting down, 'and I won't be the only one. He'll find his own little set, I know he will.'

'You think?'

'Honestly I do.' She said the words and wondered to what degree she actually believed them, and then realized that there was no point in saying anything else. For Natalia – and, by default, for Lester – the best option was to travel hopefully.

'You know,' said Natalia, 'I can understand Mum's attitude a bit more now, the way she always pretended there's nothing wrong with Glenn, that he's –' she waved a hand '– artistic or whatever. Experimental. It used to drive me nuts when she said that, especially when he got older and he was obviously . . . you know . . .'

'Well, luckily for you, you weren't around very much so it

can't have been too painful.' The answer had come pat, dropping out of her mouth fully formed.

'Here we go,' said Natalia, 'I wondered when we'd get onto this. Thanks a bunch, incidentally, for telling that story about the scholarship in front of Lester; that was a really nice thing to do.'

Netta shrugged, shamefacedly. 'It was true, wasn't it?' she muttered.

'OK.' Her sister held up her hands in mock surrender. 'Crucify me, I was thirteen. I'd had enough of people making jokes about Dad and that woman, and I wanted out, and I knew it would make things worse for you so I didn't dare tell you till the last minute. Kill me for being a kid, why don't you?'

'You didn't stay a kid though, did you? You could have come back a bit more often, you could have got to know Glenn a bit better, you could have been more . . . sisterly.' She swallowed; she felt distended with old emotions. 'I needed a sister.'

Natalia's mouth had fallen open and she stretched it wider in a deliberate gape. 'I don't believe it,' she said. 'That is *rich*.'

'What is?'

'*Sisterly*? You've got a nerve.'

'What do you mean?'

'Listen, when I came home at weekends you were the world's biggest bitch to me. I couldn't say a single word without being sliced off at the knees, I would literally say hello and you'd be – ' she mimed a couple of vicious rapier thrusts ' – *at* me before I closed the door. You took the piss out of my dancing, which you *knew* was the only thing I was any good at, and you made fun that I was only doing CSEs instead of your high and mighty O levels, and you said clever-clever bitchy things about my friends and my clothes and my hair and my skin and my figure and the way I talked and the . . . the . . . Look!' she said, pointing savagely at her own face, which had become blotchy with passion, 'look, that's what you did to me and you're still doing it!' She blinked rapidly and fanned her eyes with her fingertips. 'Now I'll have to go and get another facial.'

Netta didn't say, 'Why not get two, one for each face,' or, 'Why stop at a facial when what you really need is surgery,' or even, 'Facial's an adjective in case you hadn't realized, which means it needs a noun. N. O. U. N. That means a person or an object – I'll have a CSE in English, please.' She didn't say anything at all but she felt aghast at the battery of adolescent ripostes that had leapt into her mind without any effort of will; it seemed that the arsenal was still loaded, still waiting on a hair-trigger for Natalia to offer a target. She looked at her sister's pink nose, at the wobbling tension around her mouth. 'Sorry,' she said quietly, after a moment.

'Yeah, well . . .' Natalia straightened her shoulders and fussed at a strand of hair. 'We've all passed a lot of water since then. And I *know* that's a joke,' she added quickly. 'I read it in a magazine.'

There was an awkward pause, during which Netta registered the silence in the flat. 'I wonder if Mr –' she began.

'You and Glenn,' said Natalia, her voice tight and determined, 'you were like a little . . . *unit*. You asked, why didn't I get to know him a bit better, and the answer is, well, a) because I didn't know what to talk to him about and I still don't, and b), secondarily, because you sort of guarded him, like he was your own personal property. It was like you were the only one who was allowed to love him, or something.'

'I hated him,' said Netta.

'*What?*'

'I hated him.' Saying the words was like dragging on an

anchor; she took a breath and hauled again. 'I'd quite liked secondary school before he got there – I never told you but there was a bit of cachet to being your sister, you were always Miss Popular, weren't you, and I got a bit of secondhand attention, and then . . . everything happened at once. Dad died and you left and Glenn started school and all of a sudden I was Spack Man's sister. That was my new role – that was *me*. All I wanted was for everything to be normal again and instead I was saddled with him and I couldn't bear it. I used to run off and leave him on the way to school, or I'd take the path by the moat because I knew he wouldn't go near the swans. And if I saw him in the corridor, I'd turn round and walk away, and when people took the piss out of him – which they did every single day, every *hour* – I'd pretend I hadn't heard.'

She'd tried not to see him but she'd always known he was there, just at the edge of her vision, a solitary figure who'd spent his lunch breaks wandering alone beside the chain-link fence that separated the school grounds from the town dump, eating his invariable ham sandwich, Kit Kat and apple whilst watching the loading of the skips, the tumble and smash of unwanted items.

'So what happened? How did it change?' Natalia was a little breathless, as if waiting for the end of a bedtime story.

'I – he asked me something. People had been passing round a notebook with Spack Man jokes in it and I added one. Out of spite. Anonymously. And Glenn –'

'What was the joke?' asked Natalia.

Netta hesitated. 'It's horrible,' she said. 'I came up with it during a maths lesson.'

'Go on.'

'OK. How does a moron count to eleven?'

'I don't know, how does a moron count to eleven?'

'One, two, three, four, five, six, Devon, eight, nine, Glenn.'

'That's clever,' said Natalia. 'Mean but clever.'

'Yes, well . . . it was a bit of a hit. Glenn overheard someone in his class repeating it and he asked me what it meant. He genuinely wanted to understand what it was that people found funny. I ended up having to explain my own insult to him.'

Defining the word pun for her brother had been a wretched, protracted task and the worst of it had been the pleasure with which he'd grasped the concept. He'd even, after several moments of thought, come up with one of his own:

Q. What's the top mark I can get in class?

A. Glenn out of Glenn.

'That's very good,' Netta had said, meaning it, and he'd given one of his infrequent smiles and she'd had been flattened by a sudden rush of love and guilt.

The next day she had walked all the way to school with him. The week after she had copped a detention for (accurately) calling one of his chief tormenters a rat-faced pea-brained wanker within earshot of a teacher. The week after *that* she had noticed her own best friends beginning to edge away from her, and gradually, inexorably, it had become Glenn and Netta against the world – or Netta, rather, Glenn having continued along his own unfrequented path while she acted as both trainer and viper-tongued bodyguard, replying to every shove, slight and insult with caustic speed.

'I went to the other extreme,' she said. 'I didn't let anyone get away with anything. I was vile to everyone, not just you. I ended up a lot more unpopular than Glenn.'

'Jesus,' said her sister. 'I didn't know.'

'I didn't tell you. I should have told you. I got myself into a pattern and I couldn't get out of it till . . . well, till I found someone else to look after, I suppose, and I've never lost the feeling that I'm Glenn's minder. Even though he's grown-up now. And every time I come back to Shadley Oak I find myself slipping into role again and being . . . you know . . .'

'Starchy and controlling and critical and bitchy, and a sort of all-round vinegar-faced cow.'

'Yes,' said Netta, with an effort.

'And negative and superior.'

'Yes.'

'And really, *really* irritable.'

Heroically, Netta managed a nod.

'You mean,' said her sister, wide-eyed, 'that you're not like that in Glasgow?'

'No I'm not,' said Netta, stung. 'I'm not Pollyanna there but I'm easier, I'm . . . I'm *happier*. Just ask Kelly – she's noticed how much I change when I come here.'

'OK, OK, I believe you.'

'Do you?'

'Yeh,' said Natalia, 'actually I do. I've seen how that big soppy bloke of yours looks at you.'

They stared at each other in silence for a few moments, and then Natalia slowly shook her head. 'God, Bri . . .' she said. 'You know . . .' she leaned forward and squeezed one of her sister's hands, 'I'm just so happy that you shared that with me.'

'Are you?'

'I am. I really am. We should share things more often, shouldn't we?' She paused, and seemed to make a decision. 'You know, I've been having an affair with my osteopath for the last three years.'

'Huh?'

'As we're spilling secrets. I went for a hip realignment and one thing led to another, his wife had just left him and big Lester was away on a business trip, but this guy's technique was so fantastic that it was like totally rediscovering my body, it was completely mind-blowing. I mean it's just a sex thing, I've got zero emotional involvement, I still love my husband with my whole heart. God –' she took a deep and delighted breath ' – you know, it feels *so* good to get that off my chest. I feel totally *released*, I can feel my intercostals relaxing – you know, it's easy to forget there's a strong physical side to psychological sort of . . . you know, things. Do I *look* different?' A door slammed somewhere in the flat.

'Not particularly,' said Netta, realizing that the warm moment of near-connection with Natalia was definitively over. 'I wonder if that was Mr Riceman walking out.'

'Oh God, I'd forgotten about Shoutee Man – we said we'd help him, didn't we?'

They rose, languidly; Netta felt like a squeezed wash-cloth. 'I was supposed to be back at work ten minutes ago,' she said. 'Perhaps I could –'

The door to the sitting room opened and Glenn inserted his head round the frame. 'I think the plumber's dead,' he said.

Netta phoned not only the ambulance but also Mr Riceman's office number, and his son, a slope-shouldered man with a pallid, pleasant face, spent some moments alone with his father in the kitchen before, with touching care, the body was loaded onto a stretcher and taken away. It was not possible to tell whether Mr Riceman had actually started to move the washing machine or whether it was the mere thought of having to do so that had raised his blood pressure for the final time, but the older of the two ambulance men had taken one look at the crooked, congested face and said, 'Stroke. Gone in an instant,' and Nigel Riceman had appeared to take comfort from that.

'I was waiting for this to happen,' he said in the living room, between gulps of tea. 'He just wouldn't stop working – I told him over and over again that he couldn't manage the physical labour any more, I told him to always make sure he got help if he needed to move anything heavy, but he wouldn't listen.' Netta and Natalia exchanged wincing glances. 'I think in his heart he wanted to die on the job. He hated illness. He hated doctors. He especially hated ill doctors.' He drained his tea. 'He wasn't an easy man.' He set the cup down and gave a sad little smile. 'To be honest he was a bit of a git.'

The three siblings walked him to his car. 'If you don't mind,' he said, turning the key in the ignition, 'I'll leave Dad's van here until tomorrow.'

'Oh God,' said Natalia, 'anytime, really – that's right, isn't it, Bri?'

'Absolutely. Don't give it a moment's thought.'

Glenn leaned in to the conversation. 'Do you need those sections of PTFE thread seal tape on the kitchen floor?'

'No,' said Nigel, looking slightly puzzled. 'They're offcuts I think.'

'Good.'

They watched the car follow the curves of the drive and pass between the curlicued gates, and then they stood for a moment longer, caught by the solemnity of the moment. 'There's that man with the binoculars,' said Glenn, 'except he's taking a photograph.'

Their observer was no longer in the upstairs window of his house; he had moved to the back garden and was standing on a ladder, pointing his lens over the perimeter fence. 'I'm going to have a word,' said Netta, feeling suddenly furious that old Mr Riceman's last exit had been monitored with such naked curiosity.

'I'm coming too,' said Natalia. 'Some things are sacral, aren't they, Bri? Coming, Glenn?'

'I think so.'

They crossed the grass and Netta shouted, 'Excuse me!'

She followed it up with, 'You on the ladder,' when there was no obvious response, and Natalia chipped in with, 'Hey, drongo, what are you doing?' The man shifted the angle of his viewfinder from the car park to his interrogators, and then slowly lowered the camera to reveal a square, impassive face, dominated by a pair of thick-lensed spectacles.

'Hello,' he said, 'my name is Anthony Andrews, which is the same name as a famous actor. Are you the owner of that 1957 Bedford Comma?'

'God Almighty,' said Natalia under her breath, 'it's another loon.'

17

Netta, Paul had noticed, seemed to have a knack for being in the loo whenever the phone rang. So far during their sojourn together – now heading into its third week since Armand had announced that nothing, *nothing*, would make him return to the horror of a shared bathroom – Paul had spoken to Netta's sister (Australian), Netta's mother (mad and – since Paul's altruistic dunk in the moat – seemingly under the illusion that he was now a member of her family) and Netta's husband (surprisingly normal), but this pert little Scottish voice was a new one on him. 'Am I speaking to Mr Trolley Rescue?'

'My name's Paul,' he said, with dignity.

'And I'm Kelly, pleased to meet you.'

He took a wild guess. 'Do you want to speak to your stepmother?'

'Not really, I'm going to ask her for some money and she's going to go completely off her head' – she launched into a moderately accurate impression of Netta's emphatic delivery: '"I only sent you a cheque two weeks ago; what did you do with it, eat it? You have *got* to learn to practise frugality; when I was a student we lived off cartons of sawdust and big leaves." You know the sort of thing. How's she doing?'

'OK,' he said, cautiously.

'Bossing you around?'

'No.'

'She's *not*?'

'No.'

'Oh my God, well, I think you should call in the army

because she's obviously been replaced with a robot clone. You seen *The Stepford Wives*? Did her bust get bigger overnight? Has she started agreeing with everything you say?'

'Er . . .' He was strangely reluctant to laugh; flatmate loyalty seemed to dictate that he was on Netta's side in this particular battle. 'I think she's in the bathroom, can I get her to call you back?'

'Yeah, in a minute. So, are you going to Grandma's concert?'

'I don't think so.'

'But she's given you a ticket, hasn't she? As a thank you for helping Uncle Glenn?'

'I know, but I'll most probably be working.' He was free, in fact, but was intending to save the evening for a possible Marianne date.

'Oh, you've got to go,' said Kelly. 'It'll be hysterical. It's all parents and video cameras and toddlers weeing on stage. I saw it a couple of years ago and it's 100 per cent kitsch-value, totally memorable. You should definitely go.'

'I don't think I can. Look, Kelly, I'll have to get off the phone, I'm a bit busy.'

'What kind of busy? Ironing?'

'Preparing a lecture for today.' Put like that, it sounded rather pompous. 'It's a talk, really. I'll get your stepmother for you.'

'God, you're no fun.'

Netta was just emerging from the bathroom, and she hurried to the phone.

'Hello chickie,' he heard her say, 'anything wrong?'

He returned to the kitchen table and the litter of notes from which he was trying to construct a coherent whole. Armand's lunchtime lecture had been long, thorough and crashingly dull, illustrated by a number of spidery diagrams shown on an overhead projector and ending mid-sentence with a cry of anguish and a frantic, fruitless search for the missing final page. 'And thank you to Dr Roux,' as Mr Gorman had put it, 'for the thrilling cliffhanger finale. I, for one, shall not sleep tonight.'

'What're you giving us, Pud?' Crispin had asked afterwards, as the audience dispersed.

Paul hedged. 'I haven't quite decided yet.'

'Go for something a bit juicier. I've got a slide of a bloke who fell into an industrial-size potato peeler – you could do Pin the Leg on the Torso and then compare it with what they ended up with after eight hours of surgery.'

'Mmm,' said Paul, judicially, as if weighing up a reasonable suggestion.

'Or surgical disasters – you know, "Oops, butterfingers, just removed the wrong head," that kind of thing. Make sure it's funny. You're the man for funnies, Pud – make 'em laugh and you'll have the audience in the crack of your arse. Almond's done himself *no* favours today. Did you hear that paeds SHO snoring?'

'Yes. What I was thinking –'

'Another idea, right – breast-reduction surgery, before and after pictures.'

'What I was thinking –'

'Or – now this is a fantastic idea – what about How Surgery Could've Saved Elvi– No, scrub that, I'm going to do that myself, I'm copyrighting it. I could do a whole series on hypothetical celebrity operations.'

'What I was thinking,' said Paul determinedly, knowing that there was marshy ground ahead but feeling that he should at least prod the surface, 'was that I might do something a bit more relevant . . . I mean relevant to me, because I don't want to be a surgeon. I was thinking that I might do something about explaining things to patients.'

There was a pause and then Crispin keeled over and began convulsing. A group of nurses skirted round him without breaking conversation and Paul sat down on a nearby chair and waited for the pseudo-fit to end.

'Whhuuuuuuuh!' shouted Crispin, sitting up suddenly. 'Sorry, Pud, I must have had a pre-ictal hallucination, I thought you said you were going to do something on explaining things to patients.'

'Yes, that's what I'm thinking of. I'm crap at it, you see, I never judge it right.'

'Pud,' said Crispin, reproachfully, clambering to his knees and slinging an arm around Paul's neck. 'Pud, Pud, Pud, Pud, Pud, Pud, Pud.' Each iteration of the name was accompanied by a little squeeze, serially cutting off Paul's blood supply. 'A word of advice. That's *sociology*, Pud. You're qualified now – you ticked off that bit of the course and now you don't have to do sociology any more. You start doing sociology, you end up like Almond, people throwing themselves out of the window every time you open your mouth – No offence,' he called amiably as Armand hurried out of the room, briefcase under one arm. 'You start doing sociology, you might as well –' he gave Paul's neck a little shake of admonishment '– have done a sociology degree. You might as well have just become a *teacher*. Trust me, Pud, what your audience wants is blood.' He patted Paul's face with his free hand and rose creakily to his feet. A few black spots danced in front of Paul's eyes, and he took a deep breath.

'Crispin.'

'What is it, me old Pud?'

'Can you stop calling me that?'

'What?'

'Pud.'

'Why? Oh, I forgot to tell you, Lexie's doing a three-line

whip of her mates for your talk so it better be good. Remember, if you sociologize, you'll have to apologize – God!' He looked awestruck. 'That just came out of nowhere! I am a *genius!'*

Paul lifted a page of notes that he'd copied out of a book and put it on top of a page of notes that he'd found in one of his old student folders. He spent a pointless moment or two making sure that their edges were aligned, and then he sighed. In a way – delving beneath the crassness – Crispin had a point; the audience was going to be comatose within seconds. 'Hey Net,' he called, hearing the phone replaced in the next room. 'Have you ever given a lecture?'

Netta slouched into the kitchen and leaned against the sink unit. 'Guess what my youngest wanted?'

'What?'

'Money.'

'Oh yeah, she said she was going to ask you. What's it for?'

'A toasted-sandwich maker. She's dying of malnutrition – apparently all she learned to cook from her boyfriend's mum was roast duck and she can't afford to make it. She says she'll pay me back. Pause for hollow laughter.'

'So you going to send her a cheque?'

Netta gave a guilty shrug. 'Yes, probably. Do you think I'm being soft?'

'Really soft. My mum didn't buy me a toasted-sandwich maker until the second term – Listen Netta, do you ever give lectures? At work, I mean.'

'As opposed to the ones I dole out to my stepdaughters? Yes, I give a basic nutrition course for student nurses.'

'Any tips?'

'A few. Keep it tight, give handouts of the bullet points to stop everyone from writing the entire time, use as many case histories and examples as possible, pick on specific people when you ask a question, don't use anything handwritten.'

'Oh bloody hell.' Moodily, he began to dog-ear all four corners of the top sheet of paper. 'I'm stuffed.'

'But nobody'll be expecting anything glossy. You're working ninety hours a week for God's sake.'

'I know, but the trouble is –' he creased the paper down the centre and started to make a plane '– that I've got this reputation for making people laugh and for doing daft things. So they're all expecting me to be hilarious and witty, but I'm not really like that. Stupid things happen to me; I don't *make* them happen, I just seem to attract stupidity. I'm a sort of . . . lightning conductor. Or a big dustbin, or a . . .' He reversed back up Metaphor Lane. 'All I'm trying to do is get on with things.'

'I know,' said Netta. 'You're quite serious really. And kind; you probably haven't realized but Glenn's added you to his official list of friends, you'll be getting one of his special festive recycling leaflets at Christmas.'

He grinned, embarrassed. 'You're the one who's good at witty,' he said.

'I spent a long time sharpening my tongue. It hasn't done me many favours.'

'Hasn't it?'

She shook her head. 'It's too easy to use as a weapon. Paul –'

'Yeah?'

She drew out a chair and sat down opposite him.

'Can I ask you something medical? Again.'

'Yes, of course.' He crimped a critical angle into the nose of the plane and launched it gently across the kitchen. It flew like a dream, curving past Netta's head, lifting as it hit the warm currents above the dishwasher and coming to an abrupt halt against a bag of sugar on the shelf above the kettle. The bag leaned a little under the impact, leaned further as its contents shifted and then fell heavily onto the unit beneath, landing on its side and discharging a cataract of demerara onto the lino. 'See,' he said.

Netta shook her head dismissively. 'Do you think –' she began, clasping her hands in front of her '– that if my sister and I hadn't been having our first proper talk for about a century and we'd gone into the kitchen and found Mr . . . found that plumber straight away, we could have done something for him – I mean, might he have survived?'

'If it was a massive stroke, no. He was probably dead before he hit the floor.'

'That's what the ambulance man said. And apparently he had a history of –' She stopped mid-sentence.

'What?'

'Never mind.'

He looked at her curiously and then carried on folding the second sheet of paper, this time with the aim of producing a flapping bird; Netta had been strangely cagey about the details of the case, avoiding the man's name and simply referring to him as 'the plumber'.

'I'd treat everything you tell me as confidential,' he said, 'you know that.'

'Yes, of course, of course . . .' She nodded earnestly but somehow unconvincingly. 'So we couldn't have done anything, even if we'd been there?'

'Probably not. And if he had survived he might have been really badly affected. How old was he?'

'Late seventies, at least.'

'Right . . . well . . . wham and straight over, it's not a terrible way to go, is it? It's most likely what he'd have wanted.'

'Mmm.' She looked at her hands. 'It's nice to think so, isn't it? The trouble with wham and straight over is what it does to the rest of the family. My dad was wham and straight over.'

'Yeah, I remember you said.'

'Wham and straight over in Carina Eddery's bed – or rather, on the desk in her office.'

'Oh. Oh God.'

'Uh huh.' She gave a small, grim smile. 'No second chances; no opportunity to apologize; no time for explanations. Out like a light and everyone else is left juggling the repercussions, which are almost endless because every question goes spinning off into midair with no one to catch it. If he'd got as far as hospital – if we'd all sat round the bed with him and held his hand and talked to each other, then it's possible . . . it's *possible* . . . that things might have turned out a bit differently.' She sighed. 'I'm sure Mr Riceman's son wouldn't have minded the chance of a few moments of reconciliation with the old . . .'

'Mr Riceman?' said Paul. 'Mr *Riceman*? That was the bloke in the lift. I killed your plumber.'

'No, no, no . . .' said Netta, trying to backpedal; she hadn't meant to give away the name.

'Yes. *Yes*. He had unstable hypertension and he went off without being treated, didn't he, because I was sick on him?'

Netta thought about lying, opened her mouth to give it a go and then looked at Paul and simply nodded.

'Oh God,' he said again. 'What a bloody prize-winning sort of a morning *that* was.'

'It wasn't your fault.'

'Half an hour into my first day and I technically kill someone? It's pretty good going. It means I even beat Carrie.' He rubbed his forehead with both hands, as if wiping out the memory. 'I wish I could start all over again,' he said. 'I wouldn't take the bleep. I wouldn't eat the hamburger. I wouldn't use the word "elective" to Mrs Dimoglou.'

'Who?'

'My first patient. I overslept and I ended up rushing an explanation and confusing her and she thought I'd given her permission to leave hospital so she went home and got incredibly ill as a result.'

'And is *she* dead?'

'No,' he said, startled. 'Not yet, anyway – she was actually getting better the last time I looked. You know what the weird thing is?'

'What?'

'She thinks I'm fantastic. She's been in hospital about a hundred times and she thinks I'm the best doctor she's ever seen, even though I've been *literally* worse than useless. Because of me, she ended up having a massive, serious operation instead of a ordinary, simple one. Because of me she thinks the gall bladder is a sort of fashion accessory.'

'Isn't it?'

'Ha ha.'

'Sorry. It's just . . .' she peered at him, 'I think you're being a bit hard on yourself. And a touch overdramatic. I'm sure Mr Riceman would probably have walked out anyway at some stage, and the fact that Mrs . . . Thingy likes you means you must be doing *something* right.'

'Maybe,' he said, moodily; he'd got used to his own special little extra-muddy patch in the soggiest stretch of the Bog of Despair.

'I think,' said Netta, continuing to briskly pave it over, 'that it's rather reassuring to have a fan, whatever the reason. It's a pity patients can't give references.'

'Yeah. Yeah, she'd do me a good one, she's a brilliant talker and she –' He paused; a small idea had occurred to him. He waited to see whether it would morph into anything useful.

'What?' asked Netta curiously.

'I just had a thought. Half a thought.' He checked his watch and got up from the table. 'Quarter of a thought. I'll tell you later.'

Room 6S was grandly referred to as the Conference Room but it was only a converted office on the admin floor, carpeted in tan nylon and furnished with Formica-topped tables and stacking chairs; the latter had been arranged in a few uneven rows and Mr Gorman cast a wintry eye over the occupants before beginning his introductory speech. 'Two announcements,' he said, 'before we unleash our instructor.' Paul, sitting at a table at the front, checked his watch for the fourteenth time. 'Firstly, I have been asked to inform you that a period of structural assessment work is commencing in the Eddery Building, which means, no doubt, that there will be theodolites littering the corridors and scaffolding and *ladders* liberally applied to the exterior. I am, of course, confident that these items will be left unmolested, my junior staff being far too mature, Dr Finnerty, to do anything as stupid as tamper with them. That *is* correct, isn't it?' Crispin nodded with the gravitas of a high court judge. 'Secondly, perhaps you all can spread the word among your missing colleagues that attendance at this Wednesday lunchtime talk is compulsory for medical staff below the level of registrar, their absence punishable –' there was a pause '– by my wrath. Ah, a late arrival. Come in Dr Roux.' Armand hurried to a seat in the front row and just had time to give Paul a gawky thumbs-up before his bleep sounded. He exited at a crouching run, clutching his pocket. 'And as the warm-up act departs,' said Mr Gorman, 'let us hope that the main event is waiting in the wings. Ready Dr Gooding?'

'I think it may just be another couple of minutes,' said Paul, beginning to sweat. 'I'm giving a case presentation, and the case . . . I mean, she wasn't quite ready when I checked. Any time now,' he added, reassuringly.

'I see,' said Mr Gorman. 'Intriguing. So we have five minutes at our disposal. Dr Leong, there is a large and famous statue in Shadley Oak Market Square. Can you tell me who it represents and – for a bonus point – the century in which he died?' There was a pause and then a prolonged giggle from Wai. 'No? Not a glimmer? I'll give you a tiny clue. It's a king called Charles.'

As Wai tackled the Stuarts Paul got up quietly and sidled along the edge of the room to the door. The corridor outside was empty. After a moment the paediatric SHO rounded the corner from the lifts, walked steadily towards Paul and then, his pace unfaltering, steadily straight past him.

'Eric,' hissed Paul. '*Eric*.'

Eric turned and refocused his eyes. 'Oh, hello Paul.'

'It's in here. The lunchtime thing's in here.'

'Oh sorry. Right. Twenty-seven minutes' sleep last night.' He managed a travesty of a smile before slightly misjudging the door frame and hitting his shoulder on the way in. Mr Gorman broke off his interrogation.

'Could we have an update on the possible starting time of your presentation, Dr Gooding?'

'Any minute now,' said Paul.

A wave of sniggering swept the back row, where Lexie and her claque had seated themselves. They had kicked off their shoes, as if at the cinema, and were surreptitiously sharing a bag of Maltesers; one hit him on the back of the neck as he turned to look down the corridor again, alerted by the sound of wheels on lino. Mrs Dimoglou was rounding the corner, being pushed at speed by Gwyn. 'All porters tied up in X-ray for the duration,' he said as he approached, 'and so muggins here gets to do the honours as well as trying to manage twenty-six patient lunches with one auxiliary and a student so dense he should be doubling as a table, *and* we've got five routines coming in this afternoon, I mean, why not just stick a broom up my arse and I'll sweep the floor – no, no, don't thank me, Paul, just try not to keep making my life more difficult than it already is. I tell you, I'm counting the individual minutes till I start on night shift again. All right, Mrs Dimoglou?'

'Oh yes,' said Mrs Dimoglou. Only her head and hands were visible, the rest of her buttressed by pillows, swathed in shawls and blankets.

'And are you absolutely *certain*,' continued Gwyn, aiming a look through the door, 'that you want to be subjected to a roomful of baby doctors most of whom ought to be tucked up in bed with a mug of hot milk and banned from using sharp objects?'

'I already explained really carefully to Mrs Dimoglou what's going to happen, and I'll make sure she doesn't get tired and that we're back downstairs in half an hour at the most,' said Paul, stung.

'Yes, but I just wanted to check that Mrs Dimoglou knew that it was *optional*. She might be thinking –'

'I'm very happy,' said Mrs Dimoglou. 'This is my lovely day.'

'Good,' said Paul, firmly.

'Well, best of luck to the lot of you,' said Gwyn. 'Oh, and can you tell Dr Finnerty,' he continued, raising his voice a decibel or three to ensure that he'd be heard by everyone in 6S, 'that he promised me two and a half hours ago he'd come and discharge Mr Clifford, since when the poor bloke's been sitting in the day room watching *Kilroy* and wondering if he'll ever see his home and family again.'

'Roger, wilco and out,' shouted Crispin.

Paul seized the handles of the wheelchair. 'Ready?' he asked.

'Ready,' said Mrs Dimoglou, clasping her hands as if in anticipation of a treat.

Paul arranged the two folders of notes side by side on the table in front of him, and then moved the one on the left so that it was slightly further away from him than the one on the right. After a moment he moved it back again.

'Any time this year would be splendid,' said Mr Gorman, brushing a speck of dust from the knee of his trousers.

'Sorry. OK.' He looked up and caught Carrie's eye; she was in the middle of eating an iced bun but managed an encouraging nod. Next to her, Eric was sitting with his eyes open but his brain on screen-save. 'OK,' repeated Paul, unfolding his crib sheet. 'I haven't really got too many specific notes for this talk, because I wanted it to be a sort of . . . question and answer session. Mrs Dimoglou, who has very kindly agreed to come along today, has a very long history of surgical admissions to this hospital and to . . . to other hospitals. And because Mrs Dimoglou is very articulate about her experiences I thought it would be instructive to talk through them chronologically, and to compare the changes over the years in the way that medical information has been . . .' he groped for an appropriately technical term, 'conveyed to patients by doctors. Or not conveyed.' He paused, impressed by his own eloquence; Crispin, in the third row, mimed a huge yawn.

'So,' continued Paul, 'Mrs Dimoglou is eighty-three years old, and is of Greek origin. She came to this country with her husband and two children in 1947, and she and her husband worked in the clothing industry in Birmingham before moving to Shadley Oak in 1952 to set up a shop.'

'Still there,' said Mrs Dimoglou, unable to restrain herself.

'In the arcade. My cousin's grandson runs it, changed its name to "Threads and Patches" but you look under the sign, you still see "Dimoglou's" what my husband painted. Sorry, I said I would only talk when you ask me a question.'

'That's all right,' said Paul.

'No, this is very special for you, I know, in front of all these important people, so I'll shut up like you said.'

'No, I . . . I don't think I quite said that. I think we just agreed to stick to the main topics, didn't we?'

'I keep my mouth closed till you ask a question,' she said again, meekly, as if Paul had wrenched the concession out of her after hours of beatings.

'Right, um . . .'

'He's a good boy,' said Mrs Dimoglou, apropos of nothing. 'He saved my arm.' Mr Gorman frowned.

'So . . . Mrs Dimoglou's first operation was in 1947. She'd been suffering from palpitations and her GP diagnosed an overactive thyroid gland. She was at first treated as an outpatient with radioactive iodine, and then it was decided that a partial thyroidectomy was required.'

He looked at Mrs Dimoglou and waited for her to say something, and there was an awkward silence before he realized that he'd forgotten the rules. 'That's right, isn't it?' he added.

She reached across for his hand. 'Paulie,' she said, tentatively. He heard stifled laughter from the audience.

'Yes?'

'You want me to answer your questions truthfully.'

'Yes. Yes, of course.' He tried, unsuccessfully, to disengage his fingers.

'OK. Well the truth is my first operation was in 1922, in Greece. I never told you about this because you didn't ask and it wasn't a doctor what did it anyway.'

'Oh.'

'You want me to tell everyone about it or will I shut up? I won't speak unless you say I can.'

'No, no, I mean . . .' Clearly he had to abandon his planned course or be for ever labelled a brutal abuser of teeny, fragile old ladies. 'I do want you to speak. Please, go ahead.'

'OK. Good boy.' She gave his fingers a squeeze. 'Now what happened was I had a big swelling under my arm. The pain was terrible, my God, it was terrible; I was only thirteen years old and I thought I was going to die. My family had no money for doctors, my father was only a small farmer, but there was a man in the village who knew some medical things; he was a blacksmith and he took people's teeth out and he had huge arms, like a fighter, but he knew about plants and medicine and sometimes he did operations. And so my father took me there and I said, "Where are we going?" and he said, "Don't be frightened," but I was – I was very, very frightened, and when we got to this man's house he made me lie down on the bed and put my hand up behind my head so he could see the swelling. It was like a hen's egg, but dark red.'

Mrs Dimoglou was still holding Paul's hand, swinging it occasionally as the story intensified, but there was no giggling from the back row, no restlessness, no fake yawns.

'So the blacksmith went away into the kitchen and he comes back with a big pan, and in the pan was a cooked parsnip. No, not a parsnip, what's that thing . . . oh –' she took away her hand and scooped a globular shape in the air '– you cook it in stews, with carrots, and it's white inside. Very big and heavy. Round. We eat it during the war all the time.'

'Turnip?' The suggestion came from one of Lexie's classmates.

'Yes! Turnip. OK, so he take the pan and he mash the turnip until it was no lumps at all, and then he take a big handful and he spread it over the swelling and he put a bandage round it, up over my shoulder, and make me put my arm down and keep it tight to my side, and the mash turnip was *so* hot and I wanted to scream but he said you must keep it there for six hours, so for six hours I walk round and round and round and round the village and first my mother walk with me and then my father and then my sisters, one by one, because it was less pain when I keep walking, and then after four hours I can feel that something changes under my arm –' Mrs Dimoglou paused to carefully wipe a fleck of spittle from her mouth ' – sorry for that, excuse me, but I keep walking and after six hours my father take me back to the blacksmith and he take off the bandage and the egg has burst and there is thick yellow . . . oh, *what* is it?'

'Pus,' said half a dozen voices.

'Pus, yes. And blood. And he take some water he's boiled before and he washes under the arm, and there's a big . . . hole under there, like a cave, my father tell me afterward it looks inside like raw meat, and the man takes a little piece of black charcoal – charcoal?' she repeated, looking at Paul for confirmation. He nodded quickly, not wanting to break the flow. 'And he crush it up so it's a powder and he put the powder on a little piece of paper and he say, "This looks dirty but it's clean because it was red hot," and then he say, "Lift up your arm," so I did, and he put the piece of paper just by the big cave and suddenly . . .' she left a superbly dramatic pause, and Paul sensed rather than saw the entire audience lean forward in anticipation, 'he blows! Blows very hard and the powder disappear from the paper into the hole and covers all the raw inside, and then he say, "It's all done." He put another bandage on and I go home, and my father say, "For such a brave girl there is sweets!"' She was breathless from the momentum of the story and a little flushed. 'In one week it was like it never was there, except for a little black curl under the skin, like a curly hair. And that was my first operation!'

It was Carrie who clapped first, but the applause spread rapidly and Crispin added a piercing, two-fingered whistle before shouting, 'More!' Paul opened his mouth to speak.

'My second operation,' began Mrs Dimoglou excitedly, 'was in Salonika in 1928 . . .'

Towards the end of the afternoon, Armand stuck his head round the door of the Ward 2 sluice.

'Paul?'

'Oh hello. Hey, look at this,' Paul held out the bottle of urine he'd been staring at and gave it a little shake. A minute speck of grit circled indolently before drifting again to the bottom. 'It's amazing, isn't it, this bloke was crawling up the walls – we had to give him thirty milligrams of morphine and this is all he ended up pissing.'

Armand nodded without surprise. 'Yes, if you remember there was a breakthrough paper published in the *New England Journal of Medicine* in 1992 confirming that there's no direct correlation between the diameter of kidney stones and the amount of analgesia required, and that it is in fact the crystal-line irregularity of the deposits that's the key factor in determining pain response.'

'Oh,' said Paul.

'I believe I have a copy of the article – it would be my pleasure to lend it to you.'

'Thanks.'

'Paul –' Armand squared his narrow shoulders ' – I stopped by to offer you my congratulations. I hear that your lunchtime talk was very, very interesting and enlightening and I'm truly sorry that I had to miss it. So . . . well done.' He stuck out his hand, and Paul shook it and realized that he was in the presence of true nobility.

'God, Armand,' he said, 'I didn't do anything. Your lecture was the real thing, it had diagrams, and proper research and . . . and . . .' he fished for another praiseworthy attribute, 'a title. It was really impressive, I learned a lot from it.'

'Did you really?' There was hope in Armand's voice.

'Yes. Yes, we all did,' said Paul, sounding to his own ears less convincing with every word. 'Definitely. Honestly. I mean, totally. Whereas mine was just a fluke – I just wound my patient up and let her go, I never realized she was going to hold the floor like that.' The Salonika anecdote had been brief but gory, and had been followed by a tangential show-stopper involving Mrs Dimoglou's uncle, a wheelbarrow and a twenty-three-pound cyst. 'Genuinely fascinating,' as Mr Gorman had remarked afterwards, 'albeit bearing not the slightest resemblance to the subject as introduced.'

Armand lingered in the sluice, apparently unaware that he was leaning against the bedpan-washing machine. 'Paul . . .'

'Yes?'

'What concerns me, currently, is the lack of respect in which I'm held by Crispin. Have you noticed that?'

'Well . . .' Prevarication seemed in order. 'To be honest, he's not really the respectful type.'

'No, I realize that, but I work extremely hard and I'm orderly and reliable and trustworthy, and it seems unfair that he should still mispronounce my name and make uncalled-for remarks about my nationality. Also, sometimes I feel that he's laughing at me behind my back. Do you think that's the case?'

It was possibly the most difficult question that Paul had ever been asked. He looked at Armand's anxious, pimply face. 'Crispin laughs at a lot of people behind their backs,' he said. 'Most of them don't deserve it. You certainly don't.'

'I see,' said Armand, gravely. 'And do you think I should discuss this with him? Man to man?'

The image was too cruel to contemplate. 'Tell you what,' said Paul, 'I'll have a word with him about it. I'll tell him to lay off.'

Armand's face uncreased a little. 'Really?'

'Yup, no problem.' He sounded more confident than he felt; he could almost see the expression of joyous incredulity with which Crispin would greet the idea.

'Well, thank you Paul.' For a moment it looked as if Armand might be going to smile, but he made do with a pleased lip-twitch and then turned to leave, noticing as he did so the proximity of the bedpan-washer and performing an impressive, involuntary standing jump that took him halfway across the sluice. 'Catch you later,' he added with attempted nonchalance, shaking the germs from his sleeve.

18

The noise level in the corridors of St Celia's Junior School was constant and shattering. 'White rabbits,' called Netta, forcing her voice above the babble. 'I'm still looking for two white rabbits who don't have their ears yet. Anyone here who doesn't have their rabbit ears?' She held up the two headbands with their fluffy attachments, and scanned the midget crowd – the crocodile of hula girls making their way from Hair to Make-up, the Liquorice Allsorts queuing outside the toilet, the single, wandering alien searching for another of her species, the gang of big girls in WAAF uniforms peering into hand mirrors as they slathered on extra eyeshadow, the pink tooth-brush posing while a blue toothbrush took her photo, the pair of earless bunny rabbits standing on a radiator and waving at someone in the car park . . . 'Got you!' said Netta, grabbing their paws and marching them back to the commandeered stockroom in which Coral was holding her surgery. They took their places meekly enough at the end of a row of chairs next to a cowgirl and a tin soldier and a duckling with a broken zip. Coral, her mouth full of pins as she sewed the nose onto a badger, nodded her thanks and Netta headed off to her next task.

'Me and Mum thought, Bri, that as hair and make-up isn't particularly your thing we could give you a sort of roving role this evening,' Natalia had said earlier, 'and you can go round doing whatever people need you to do. What's the word for that?'

'Peripatetic?'

'No, no, it's . . . er . . . I know, it's *gofer*. Is that OK with you?'

So Netta had swallowed her pride and made tea, and rushed out for last-minute hair-bobbles, and treated nervous stomachs, and carried chairs around and hunted for missing shoes, and it had been strange, and rather liberating, to not be the one in charge. And now, in the final fifteen minutes before curtain-up, she was hastily decorating the school gym for the after-show party, clambering up wall bars and tying yellow balloons into bunches with lengths of silver ribbon. Both items she recognized as leftovers from 'Silver and Gold', the previous year's show, which she had attended with Mick; he had fallen asleep some minutes after the interval and had jerked awake again in the middle of 'Money, Money, Money' (the finale) and said, 'Fingers,' very loudly, something that he'd been unable to account for afterwards. He'd been to quite a few autumn shows over the years – 'Bel's Big Night' was his nickname for them – and he always claimed that the best bit was his mother-in-law's introduction. 'When she comes on that stage it's like Wellington addressing the troops,' he'd said once.

'Can I have a balloon?'

Netta looked down to see a four-foot-high pink ovoid with legs and a face. 'They're for the party,' she said. 'But you can take one home with you afterwards. What are you supposed to be?'

'Soap. I wasn't tall enough to be a toothbrush and, anyway, Mrs Devon said I'd missed too much rehearsals to be something important. Like shampoo. I just do steps at the back of the others.' The soap leaned awkwardly against the wall and sighed, and Netta realized that she recognized the pudgy face and general air of disappointment.

'You're Melanie, aren't you?'

'Yeah.'

'Have all your spots gone?'

'What?'

'Your chickenpox spots. Have they gone?'

'Oh yeah,' she said, dismissively. 'Ages ago. I wish it'd been now.'

'Why?'

'Because I'm never important enough to be at the front. I'm no good at this *dancing*.' She said the word with vehemence and bumped the wall bars with a hip; a single balloon drifted down from its attachment and bounced a foot or two across the parquet.

'You can have that one if you want,' said Netta.

'Can I?' Melanie placed a foot on it and pressed down steadily and unflinchingly until it burst. 'Can I have another?' she asked immediately.

'Not till after the party.'

She nodded glumly and gave the wall bars another nudge, this time garnering only a dent in the side of her costume.

'I was no good at dancing either,' said Netta. 'I used to be in these shows.'

Melanie slid her a disbelieving look.

'I did, honestly. And it was worse for me, because my mother's Mrs Devon.'

'No she's not.'

'Yes she is. And one year I was playing a bumble-bee and I felt so stupid that I went and locked myself in the toilet and deliberately missed the whole thing.'

'No you didn't.'

'Yes I did.'

'What happened?'

'Nobody noticed.'

Melanie laughed uncertainly. 'Why didn't they?'

'Because I wasn't an important enough bee to really make a difference to the dance. There was a bit of a gap in the line but they just carried on without me.'

'They didn't look for you?'

'No.'

'Didn't they get the police?'

'No. I was disappointed too. Perhaps I should have locked all the other bees in the toilet with me.'

Melanie giggled.

'All bathroom accessories to Classroom 4D, Melanie,' said Netta's mother, appearing round the gym door with a list in her hand. 'You're not on until just before the interval but one of the mummies has organized pencil-and-paper games to keep you busy.'

'Hey Mum,' said Netta, 'do you remember the autumn show when I locked myself in the loo? I was a bee.'

'I don't think so, dear – oh now, wait just a moment,' she added, halting Melanie en route and running a finger over the dented costume. 'Oh that's a shame, isn't it? It ruins the contour. Go and visit Coral's little room for some repairs first, and then on to 4D. Hurry along dear, and remember, walk tall.'

'Soap doesn't walk *anyway*,' muttered Melanie, dragging herself away. Netta watched her go.

'You know, she's got a point,' she said. 'What sort of steps do you give a bar of soap?'

'Sliding ones, dear,' replied her mother, crushingly. 'Now I just came to tell you that your young man's in the audience.'

'What, *Mick*? But he's not flying back till tomor–'

'No, dear, I meant the doctor. Ted pointed him out to me.'

'Oh yes . . . Paul.' The surge of illogical joy dissipated, and Netta thought of Mick's nice, shiny bald head and greying pubes and smiled at her own absurdity. *Young man.* 'Yes, yes I know Paul's here. He wasn't going to come but his girlfr– his friend's a photographer for the *Mercury* and apparently she had to cover the concert.' It had seemed to Netta a bizarre idea for a second date, but he had appeared touchingly optimistic.

'Well, I'm delighted,' said her mother, 'and of course, Glenn's thrilled to bits to have *two* of his special friends here, and Anthony's been most helpful – such a splendid, clear voice. Now, before I go on, how do I look?' She arranged one forearm in a graceful diagonal across her chest, lifted her chin and fixed her eyes on a point a foot or two above Netta's head.

It wasn't Wellington, thought Netta – it was a more defiant, solitary image than that: Grace Darling battling through mighty seas, Boudicca galloping against the Romans. She thought suddenly of the first-ever autumn show, a few months after her father's death, when she herself, as the oldest, tallest, bustiest and last in a line of fairies, had waited in the wings while her mother took to the stage for the opening address. 'Welcome to one and all,' she had said, 'on behalf of the newly formed *Devon* School of Dance,' and Netta had been struck by the peculiar emphasis, the extreme clarity of the enunciation. It had been an act of reclamation, she supposed now, her mother's announcement to Shadley Oak that the word Devon was no longer shorthand for a local scandal but a new touchstone for grace and professionalism. Clumping on afterwards to 'The Rustle of Spring', she'd felt a poor advert for the venture.

Bel was still awaiting her verdict. 'You look wonderful,' said Netta, formally and truthfully.

'Thank you, dear.'

'Hey Mum,' she added as Bel turned to leave, 'what was the title of the very first autumn show?'

'Oh my goodness.' Her mother gave a little laugh. 'We're

talking about a *very* long time ago, aren't we? Why do you ask?'

'I was just thinking about it.'

'You know, Brianetta, I have noticed that for a relatively young woman you do tend to *dwell* on the past.'

'I don't dwell.'

'*Brood*, then.'

'I don't dwell or brood,' said Netta, crisply, 'but I do think about it sometimes. I don't see why I shouldn't.'

'Take heed and pass on,' said her mother, moving seamlessly into recital mode. 'Take heed and pass on, take a pebble not a rock, take a spark and not a lantern, take a key and not a lock. Take a message not a volume, take a needle not a thread – don't look behind, look ahead!' She accompanied the last line with a decorous hitch of her good leg, the ghost of a high kick.

'Where's that little gem from?'

'It was one of the numbers in *Follies of 1953* when I was with the Barry Lethbridge Dancers.' She threw one of her middle-distance gazes. 'That was the show I was in when I met your father. *No* tap shoes in the corridor!' she added as four girls in sparkly tops clattered along the passage outside.

'Sorry Mrs Devon.' The noise receded again.

'So how did you and Dad actually meet?' asked Netta quickly; it was so rare that Bel broke the seal on her marriage that she had learned to grab any chance of glimpsing the contents. 'Was he in the audience? Did he spot you from the stalls?'

'No, dear, it was at my engagement party to Barry Lethbridge, after the show,' said her mother, as if it were utterly unimportant. 'Now, I completely forgot, I have a message for you from Natalia. She asked if you could quickly sweep the stage while Ted's playing the overture.' She turned away and left Netta gaping after her. 'Thank you, dear,' she added, over her shoulder.

From his seat near the end of the front row Paul could serially tune into one of several voices, all talking simultaneously: there was the woman sitting directly behind him who was reading out the programme very slowly to someone with extremely poor hearing; there was the child standing at the edge of the stage – just visible in a chink between curtain and proscenium arch – reciting the lyrics to 'I'm a Pink Toothbrush' in an endless adenoidal loop; there was Glenn, over at a table beside the door, giving an unvarying ticket spiel to each member of the queue and, at another table, a man with thick glasses repeating, 'If you want a programme you can get a programme over here at the programme table,' at five-second intervals; and just beside Paul, in the very next seat, her thigh lightly brushing his own, was Marianne. 'They don't have a dress rehearsal,' she was saying. 'Most adult shows do, so I can get along there and take a few rolls and they'll stop and pose specially for me, but children's shows don't, so I have to come along and take what I can along the way. Of course the quality isn't as good but the only important thing is to get all the children's names right and that's not my job, that's Addison's job, isn't it, Addison?' She looked at Beardy for confirmation and Beardy nodded. 'So I'll have to keep leaving my seat during the show which might get a bit annoying, but you won't mind that, will you, Paul?' She looked at Paul and he shook his head. 'Great. Well, I might go and just check out my angles now; I won't be long and it'll save messing around later, is that OK?'

'Yes,' said Addison and Paul simultaneously, and Marianne got up and left them sitting on either side of her empty seat. As Paul watched her neat jean-clad bottom moving away between the row of chairs and the low stage he tried to remember the exact wording of the phone call that had led to this ménage à trois.

'Tuesday's no good,' she'd said when he'd proposed meeting for a drink, 'I'm taking photos at a dance-school concert.' 'What dance school?' he'd asked, and once they'd unravelled the coincidence it had occurred to Paul that accompanying her to 'Rosettes and Champagne' might be an amusing ice-breaker, a novelty second date that could end up as one of those cosy couple flashbacks: 'Hey, do you remember that evening when we . . .' 'God, yes, it was so funny when . . .' 'That was the first time I looked at you and thought . . .' 'Same here . . .' So he had suggested it and Marianne had said . . . had said what? He scraped around in his memory but could only recall doing some amiable noises of assent and a bit of pointless grinning and then putting down the phone with the thought that finding things to say to Marianne was not nearly the problem he had anticipated; it was finding gaps to say them in that was more of an issue.

'So,' said Beardy, 'Marianne says you're a doctor.'

'Yes,' said Paul. They both nodded for a while. 'And you're a reporter?'

'Yup. Technically, anyway. Most of the time I write up cake competitions, so it's not exactly Kate Adie.'

'Right.'

There appeared to be no more conversation in the world. Beardy shifted his gaze towards the side of the room where a small boy with a tape recorder was working his way around the audience, and Paul sat and wondered why he felt as if he had just begun to hear a very nasty rattling sound in a newly purchased car. 'Sugar plum,' said the woman behind him. '*Plum. Plum.* You know, like you have with custard. *Plum.*'

Over at the piano, Ted carefully arranged his music, shot his cuffs, straightened his jacket and eased into a mellow waltz version of 'We are the Champions'.

'I'm just off for a slash,' said Beardy, standing.

Paul watched him stalk off down the hall, and turned back to find a microphone directly in front of him. 'Good evening,' said the boy with the tape recorder. 'My name is Lester Connell, Foreign Correspondent for the Woolleroo Primary School newspaper, and I'm reporting on My Visit to the United Kingdom, Day Fourteen.' Stone me, thought Paul, Netta's right; Ernest Borgnine is alive, well, four foot tall and wearing a Gap tracksuit with a happy horse on the front.

'Can I ask you some questions for our listeners?' enquired Lester.

'OK.'

'Have you been to one of these concerts before?'

'No.'

'Oh. Did you ever go to any dancing classes when you were a child?'

'No.'

'And has anything exciting happened to you so far this evening?'

'No.'

In a gesture reminiscent of a tired businessman, Lester rubbed the back of his neck and sighed.

'Sorry,' said Paul, 'I haven't been a very interesting interviewee. Do you want to ask me something else?'

'No thank you very much. My teacher says that when you're trying to build up a picture of a big event, the best way is to keep using the same set of questions and then you can cut the answers together in a thing called a montage. Have you ever heard of that word or do you want me to explain it to you?'

'I've heard of it, thanks. And has anybody come up with anything exciting for you?'

'No.' Lester sighed again, and with a decisive gesture turned off the tape. 'I might have to think again.'

'You know, you spoke to me on the phone once. I share a flat with your Auntie Netta.'

'Do you?' Lester's squarish face reddened suddenly. 'Her real proper name's Brianetta,' he said, lowering his voice. 'Did you know that?'

'Yes I did.'

'Do you know what that's named after?'

'No.'

Lester went even redder; he half opened his mouth and then pinched it shut again.

'What?' asked Paul, curious now.

'I can't tell you,' said Lester, his voice buckling with suppressed laughter. 'My mum says I'm to regard it as our little secret, and that Auntie Brianetta doesn't find it at all funny because she's fixated with her father even though he was a cheating so-and-so who nearly ruined all their lives with his shenanigans.'

'Oh,' said Paul, wishing very much that he wasn't hearing this.

'But I'll give you a clue,' said Lester. 'It's got to do with . . .' he dropped his voice to a whisper, '*gussets*.'

There was a crashing chord from the piano followed by a twinkle of arpeggios that segued into 'The Teddy Bears' Picnic' played at three times normal speed; it had the effect – presumably intentional – of sending people scurrying to their seats, and Lester hefted his tape recorder and squeezed past a row of knees towards the exit. Eye level with Paul, in the inch or so between the curtains and the floor, a broom bumped along the boards in rhythm with the music.

'Here I am,' said Marianne, returning just ahead of Beardy. 'I'm all set. They've cleared a chair for me at the end of Row 3 and I can stand on the ticket table for wide shots. You know, I thought for a moment I'd lost my twenty-eight-millimetre lens but it was at the bottom of the camera bag – it's a bit of a problem with the inside of the bag being black, you see, you can lose all sorts of things in there. I once didn't find a film case for weeks . . . are you OK, Paul?' she asked, smiling.

'Fine,' said Paul. 'I'm fine.'

Rabbits were beginning to accumulate in the wings ready for the first number, and Netta's mother stood among them, eyes closed, expression serene, a dance-school Buddha revving up for a bit of wisdom-dispensation. Netta had changed the rhythm of her sweeping to match the slow climax of 'Chariots of Fire' and the chatter of the audience had receded to a low anticipatory buzz.

'Bri,' hissed Natalia from the other side of the stage. '*Bri!*'

Netta shunted a line of grit towards her sister. 'What's the problem?'

'You haven't seen two rabbits, have you?'

'Yes, I found them earlier, sent them back to Costume – they should be done by now. Hey Nat, did you know that Mum was engaged to Barry Lethbridge when she met Dad?'

'Yes. Can you go and get them?'

'You *knew*? How did you know?'

'She told me.'

'When? She never tells me anything.'

'Look Bri, we're in crisis here. I'm missing my two lead rabbits for the opener. Can you go and look for them?'

'All right, all right.' She took a step away and then turned back. 'Just tell me when you found out.'

'She told me just after Dad died, all right? The night after. Please, Bri.' She offered her hands in prayer and Netta parked the broom and walked offstage, and saw, as she hurried along the corridors, not the harlequin chaos of backstage but the image of her mother after the funeral, sitting in the kitchen of Briglennia, gracious and pale and upright, and not saying a word about their father, neither of criticism nor of praise. Not a word then, not a word later.

The door of the costume room was closed: 'Hello?' called a tremulous voice as Netta tried the handle.

'Coral, can you open the door? I'm looking for some rabbits.'

'I'm rather afraid it's locked.'

'Oh. Why?'

'I'm not altogether . . . there was a key in the door on my side, you see, I needed a room with a key because of all the scissors and needles, and then all of sudden it wasn't in the door any more and it was . . . no, don't cry Eleanor . . . it only happened a minute or two ago, and I can't . . .'

'Coral, who's in there with you?' asked Netta, already guessing the answer.

'There's quite a few of us, aren't there, girls? Unfortunately. There's Eleanor Price, who's being very brave, isn't she, every-body? And Emma-Jane Shockley – those are your two rabbits, Brianetta – and there's Alice Christie, Lauren and Claire Delaney, Melanie Judson, Chanta–'

'Coral, can I have a word with Melanie, please? As privately as you're able.'

'Of course, er . . .' There was a muffled conversation fol-lowed by dragging footsteps.

'What?' said Melanie, her voice gruff.

'I'm the lady you were talking to a little while ago,' said Netta, 'the one with the balloons.' There was a pause. 'Melanie?'

'What?'

'You've locked yourself in, haven't you?'

'Rosettes,' said Netta's mother, who appeared to be aiming much of her opening address directly at Paul, 'and *Champagne*. Rewards and Celebrations. Prizes and Congratulations. These are the themes of this year's Devon School of Dance autumn show, and could I just remind the audience that if you need to cough, then perhaps a more appropriate time would be during the applause at the end of each number.' She left a short silence, during which a man could be heard desperately trying to swallow a choking fit. 'This year infectious disease has greatly affected the smooth running of the rehearsal period, and it's only due to the gumption and the talent of our performers, and equally that of our behind-the-scenes team, that we are able to present a full-length show tonight. Let us thank them all, from Miss Anderton, in charge of ballet and costumes, to Mr Shepherd at the piano, from all the mummies and daddies who have coped with a great many changes in lesson and rehearsal schedules to Mrs Connell for her superb last-minute planning, from our special helpers on the night, Mrs Lee, Mr Devon and Mr Andrews over there by the ticket table –'

'My full name,' announced a loud voice, 'is Anthony Andrews, which is the same name as a famous actor.'

' – to St Celia's for once again allowing us to use the premises for such a nominal fee,' continued Netta's mother, magnificently ignoring the interruption, 'and to Brook and Son, Quality Printers, of 14a Hazel Grove, King's Heath, for their generosity in producing the programmes. Let us all admire the skills and dedication that have made this evening possible, let us enjoy the spectacle before us and, most vitally of all, let us say . . . on with the show!' There was a fusillade of coughs, partly buried under applause, and Netta's mother bowed and exited stage left. Ted struck up a toe-tapping introduction to 'Run, Rabbit, Run', a host of video cameras was raised to eye level, and with a swish and a rattle the curtains began to open. They continued opening until almost half the stage was visible and then they stopped opening and, after a few seconds' hiatus, began to close again. A badger ran across the diminishing gap and a childish voice shouted, 'No, you stupid bumhead, they can see you.' Paul snorted and, two seats away, Beardy emitted a bark of laughter and then covered his mouth with a hand. Ted, smiling fixedly, came to the end of the introduction of 'Run, Rabbit, Run' and began all over again, this time in a syncopated minor key. The curtains closed completely. And stayed closed.

'No one's going to tell you off,' said Netta, crouched by the stockroom door, 'no one's going to be cross. Just get it from wherever you've hidden it and that'll be the end of the matter. Melanie? Melanie?'

'God, *there* you are,' called Natalia rounding the corner, heels clacking like gunshots. 'What's going on? We're facing total *disaster* out front and Mum's practically collapsed in tears, I mean, what's –'

'Door locked, rabbits inside,' said Netta, succinctly. 'Also three WAAFs, two ducklings, a Rhythm of Lifer, the chief Allsort, the Sugar Plum Fairy and three cowgirls. And Coral.'

'Oh my God. Well, where's the key?'

Netta stood up and placed her mouth very close to her sister's ear. 'Melanie – the girl who's the bar of soap – has taken it but she won't admit it. She's just on the other side of that door. Before you say anything I have to tell you that it's partly my fault.'

'What?'

'I gave her the idea. Inadvertently.'

'Oh for –' Natalia stared at her in open-mouthed exasperation and then stepped over to the door. 'Melanie, give back that key this instant or there's going to be *such* trouble you wouldn't believe!'

'That is not going to help,' said Netta.

'Well, what's your plan, Einstein?'

'I've sent one of the mums round to the caretaker's house and another to find the name of an emergency locksmith.'

'But that could take – OK, *think* Natalia, *think*.' Her sister closed her eyes, pressed her fingertips against her forehead and vibrated them sharply.

'Helping, is it?' asked Netta, after a moment or two.

'Yes thank you, I've just come up with a solution – we can go straight to item four.'

'Is that tin soldiers?'

'Yes.'

'There's a tin soldier in there as well, I forgot. Sorry. Sorry, Nat, that wasn't deliberate.'

'Jeez.' Natalia turned on her heel and walked away.

'Where are you going?'

'I'm going to tell Ted to busk till we're ready and then I'm going to find a man with a great big screwdriver and then I'm going to come back and sort this out. Hi sweetheart, are you having loads and loads of fun?' she added, suddenly solicitous, as Lester rounded the corner.

'Yes thank you. I'm doing some wildtrack.'

'Well that's *fantastic*. Go and tell Auntie Bri all about it.'

'Auntie Bri.'

'Yes, Lester?'

'I'm doing some wildtrack.'

'Good.'

'That means I'm recording background noise.'

'That's fantastic.' They stood together outside the door, Lester holding the microphone. The only audible voice was that of Coral, gamely refereeing a round of I-Spy at the other end of the stockroom.

'Melanie?' said Netta. 'Melanie, are you still there?'

'Potato,' shouted someone on the other side of the door.

'*In* this room and beginning with *b*,' repeated Coral patiently.

'Melanie?' said Netta again.

There was no reply; having done the deed, Melanie seemed paralysed by her own bravado and Netta was nearing the end of her repertoire of child-persuasion techniques.

'Melanie? If you open this door I'll give you –' she lowered her voice ' – five pounds.'

'I'm not allowed to take money from strange people.'

'Me neither, Auntie Brianetta,' said Lester, censoriously. 'It's a bad thing to do.'

'I know,' said Netta, chastened. 'I'm sorry. You're both right.'

'I wonder what "a short delay" means,' said Beardy. 'I wonder if it means "long enough to go and get a quick pint down The Swan".'

'Oh no, it probably means five or ten minutes at the most, I expect,' said Marianne.

'Shame.' Beardy folded his arms and leaned his head on the back of the seat, and Marianne picked up the thread of the anecdote she'd been telling Paul, about a friend of hers called Alex and about Alex's camera, which was apparently a good camera, the type of camera that Paul should buy if Paul wanted to buy a camera, which he didn't really but which he was pretending that he did for the sake of the conversation. She had twisted around in her seat in order to talk to him but they were sitting so close together that eye contact was impossible, so Marianne was mainly looking towards the far side of the hall, where Ted was playing 'Everything's Coming up Roses' with tremendous dynamism, and Paul was mainly looking at an extreme close-up of Marianne's left cheek, where the skin was as smooth and as bloomy as a dawn-picked mushroom. And he was trying very hard to concentrate on this poetic, visual side of things because the aural side was beginning to worry him. '. . . and the man in the shop said the person who'd bought it had said something about collecting it later,' Marianne was saying, 'and they'd been trying to follow it up but he hadn't left the full code on his home phone number, and I think that kind of thing's quite annoying because it doesn't sound like the sort of reason that . . .'

'OK,' said Netta, 'what if I promise that if you get the key and open the door, you don't have to do your dance tonight. You can go and sit in the audience if you want.'

'But my mummy's come here specially to see me being the soap.' There was a watery sniff, and then another, as the lack of logic of her position began to sink in. 'Don't tell her,' she added.

'I won't have to if you come out right now.'

There was a pause. 'Can I be shampoo, then. If I come out?'

Netta winced at the impossibility of the demand. 'Probably not *this* year.'

'Oh.' Melanie took a sad and ragged breath, and then the sniffs resumed.

'A dog's not a mineral,' shouted someone in the background. 'You said it was a *mineral*.'

'Excuse me, Auntie Brianetta,' said Lester. 'I'm sorry to interrupt when you're thinking but can I ask you a question?'

'Go on.'

'Is this a hostage situation?'

'I suppose so. Yes, in a way.'

'So does that mean it's an exciting event?'

Netta sat back on her heels and sighed. 'It's probably the most exciting event that's going to happen this evening, Lester.'

'Is it?' He appeared pleased. 'Can I do a report on it?'

'Um . . .'

'Who's that person talking?' asked Melanie, suspiciously.

'My name is Lester Connell, Foreign Correspondent for the Woolleroo Primary School newspaper, and I'd like to conduct an interview with you.'

'What does that mean?'

'It means that you'd be in a newspaper,' said Lester.

'What . . . with a photo of me?' There was a raw note of hope in her voice.

'Yes,' said Netta instantly.

'With me standing behind all the others?'

'With *only* you,' said Netta. 'I promise.'

Paul was discovering that if he stared hard at Marianne's left ear and then let his eyes drift out of focus, it would suddenly appear as if she had two left ears, one growing neatly behind the other.

'. . . and then he told Alex about a docket that you pick up,' she was saying, 'except that he hadn't, he'd just left the lens. Anyway, we decided to go and . . .'

'Sorry to interrupt, Marianne,' said Beardy, not sounding sorry at all – sounding, in fact, as if it were a phrase that he had occasion to use quite often, 'but can anyone tell me what that badger we saw has got to do with the theme of the evening?'

'*I* was wondering that,' said Paul. 'I was thinking badgers

. . . bovine tuberculosis . . . mass culling – I couldn't get anywhere near the title.'

'Now that's interesting,' said Beardy, 'and it just goes to show how shallow I am, because I was thinking badgers . . . *Wind in the Willows* . . . jolly picnics in the sunshine . . .' He grinned at Paul and then switched his gaze. 'What were you thinking when you saw it, Mazza?'

'Oh, er . . . I don't know really.' She shrugged and smiled and then carried on explaining about Alex and his SLR, and Paul tried – and failed – to assimilate the incredible, appalling fact that although he was sitting right beside Marianne and could even smell the peachy scent of her hair and feel the cool rush of her breath on his cheek, he was nonetheless thinking of something else entirely; he was thinking of how pleasant it would be to get up, leave the hall and *go down The Swan for a pint with Beardy.*

'And then we bought some goats' cheese by mistake,' Marianne was saying, in a causal leap that he had failed to follow, 'and neither of us really liked it. I mean, Alex doesn't like the actual taste, which I don't mind, but I think it smells a bit strange and I don't like that funny mould stuff on the top, so anyway . . .'

Paul had a sudden sensation of sliding – of sliding down a bright wall of chatter, of leaving the sunny slopes and hurtling unchecked towards a bleak new world, a godless country where Marianne was just a girl who worked for the local paper and he was just a bloke who had once fancied her a bit. The tip of her nose moved up and down when she talked, he realized; he had never noticed that before.

'Excuse me.' It was Netta, standing at the end of the row, one hand resting on the business end of what looked like a giant pink suppository on legs. 'Could I have a word?'

'With me?' asked Paul.

'No, with your friend. I need someone to take a very important photo and I wondered if she could spare a moment.'

Paul watched Marianne follow Netta and her puce blob towards the exit, and realized that his heart rate was ambling along steadily, his breathing was deep and regular, his armpits dry. Either his Mariametric reaction was an unprecedented zero or the meter had finally, irrevocably broken.

'Hey Doc,' said Beardy, 'what's up?'

'Nothing,' said Paul. It felt an appropriate response.

Over at the piano, Ted lifted his head alertly, like a retired sheepdog hearing a whistle from its youth. 'Ladies and Gentlemen,' called Netta's mother, appearing between the curtains, 'Ladies and *Gentlemen* –' the rattle of conversation died away '– I am delighted to tell you that we are about to begin; a crisis has been averted and we can start anew. Mr Shepherd?' Ted nodded. *'Thank you.'*

The introduction to 'Run, Rabbit, Run' began for the fourth, or possibly fifth, time.

'You know,' said Beardy, 'I wouldn't want you to think that there's anything going on between me and Marianne. We're not an item, we're just workmates; I'm actually seeing this policewoman I met covering a court case. So if you . . .' he raised his eyebrows, 'you know, if you're keen, you go for it, mate.'

'Thanks,' said Paul, sadly.

'Marianne's a really nice girl.' Beardy nodded for emphasis, possibly too many times. 'Quite a talker, but *really* pretty and *really* nice.'

'Yes she is,' said Paul.

'And she's bright too.'

'Yes.'

'Knows a lot.'

'Yes.'

'Voluble.'

'That's the word.'

'Yup.'

They were both nodding by now.

'Hey,' hissed Beardy as the curtains began to open, 'if this evening ever ends, d'you fancy a pint?'

Glenn inspected his glass of Asti, holding it up to the light and tapping the side with a fingernail. 'The bubbles are composed of carbon dioxide from fermentation,' he said. 'They form at nucleation points which are tiny imperfections in the glass usually invisible to the naked eye.'

'Do you like the taste?' asked Netta.

He took a sip. 'No.'

'Has Anthony gone home?'

'Yes. He watches *Newsnight* at ten-thirty.'

'Did he enjoy the show?'

'I don't know.'

'So, when are you two seeing each other again?'

'Tomorrow morning at eight-fifteen a.m. at the end of his road which is called Mason Avenue. It's on my new linking route.'

'You're doing bottles tomorrow?'

'Yes.'

'And he's doing . . . ?'

'He wants to take photographs of a 1973 Saab that's parked in a drive on Fairfield Way, which is also on my new route. He asked permission from the owner last week.'

'That's nice,' said Netta, inadequately; it was comforting to think of Glenn and Anthony pursuing their parallel interests, walking the mean streets of Shadley Oak together. 'So you get on with him pretty well?'

'Yes, I think so. Although his interests are very boring.'

Netta choked on her drink. 'Sorry,' she said, wiping her chin.

'I've thought of a pun,' said Glenn.

'Go on.'

'Don't spew your Spumante.'

'That's very good. OK, OK my turn – how about this? If I do, I won't *wine* about it.' There was a pause. 'Asti Spumante's classified as a type of wine,' she added.

'Oh I see. That's very good.' He looked at his glass again. 'I don't want this, do you want it?'

'Yes please.'

'I've just remembered I need to ask Natalia something.' He took the shortest route across the gym, cutting straight through the middle of the mini disco, its blinking lights and dual turntable manned by the Sugar Plum Fairy's father. The stiff little blank-faced figures who'd earlier occupied the stage had transformed into grooving, hair-tossing, hip-thrusting divas, shaking their uninhibited thang in a selection of glittery tops; Melanie, her face as pink as a poppy, caught Netta's eye and waved.

Beyond the dance floor, over in the far corner of the room, Lester was conducting his own version of *Newsnight*, taping interviews with key players from the Siege of St Celia's in front of a small crowd that included his mother. Coral was currently in the hot seat, but the other hostages were clustered behind her chair, smiling fixedly at Lester, seemingly under the impression that they were on camera.

Netta drank from alternate glasses of Asti and watched her brother buttonhole Natalia. Her sister's initial pique at the interruption switched, after a few words, to focused attention and then both she and Glenn began to make a mystifying series of shoulder-high hand movements, brusque right-angled gestures that were accompanied by much serious nodding.

It was an intense, shared discussion, and apparently highly technical.

'That was "Agadoo" by Black Lace,' announced the Sugar Plum Fairy's father, lips clattering against the microphone. 'Keep those requests coming. This one's for Sarah-Jade and Katy Law from their proud Auntie Terri. It's Whigfield and it's . . . "Saturday Night". And hello sir,' he added as the introduction cut in and Ted approached the decks with his hand cupped round his mouth.

'Hey there, little sis,' said Natalia, approaching round the edge of the dance floor, 'how's it going?'

'Not too bad. I've been enjoying watching Lester.'

'Yeah, he's the man of the moment all right; they're *queuing* to talk to him. Hey, you'll never guess who I've just been having a chat with.'

'I was watching. What on earth were you talking about?'

'Removable shoulder pads.'

'Sorry?'

'Removable shoulder pads. *You* know – even you must have worn them in the eighties, Bri.'

'What about removable shoulder pads?'

'He wants to know where he can get some and how they stay in place. He saw me putting them in my grey silk coat before the show and he was totally fascinated; he'd never come across them before. We had a really good old chinwag.' She sounded almost thrilled and Netta felt an odd sensation, a pinch of the heart that she interpreted after a moment as fondness. For *Natalia*. 'What he wants,' continued her sister, 'is to put a pair of pads in that disgusting red jacket of his; he says he's looking for a "squarer outcome", whatever that means. He says there's a Coca-Cola crate he wants to lift.'

'Oh . . .' said Netta, light dawning at last. 'I get it . . . he wants to look like the man in the poster in his bedroom, that's why he starched his Puffa. He's got a picture of some all-American hunk with a red jacket and huge shoulders carrying a crate of bottles. I don't know why I didn't twig before.'

'Well there we are,' said Natalia, enjoying her moment. 'Case closed, just call me Sherlock.' She turned to go.

'Barry Lethbridge,' said Netta.

'Oh yeah. Barry Lethbridge.' Natalia clasped her elbows and looked back at Netta thoughtfully. 'What did Mum say?' she asked.

'That she met Dad at her own engagement party. Nothing else, and I think she only let that slip because she gets so hyped up on show nights.'

'Yeah, well, there's not a lot more to it. She was engaged to Barry Lethbridge and they were going to go on tour with his dancers to the Bahamas or the – those other islands beginning with "b" – and have the big glamorous life, and Dad was at the party because he was going out with someone else in the troupe and he saw Mum and he was charming and he had all these plans and he swept her off her feet. And then later on, when he started playing around, she sometimes wondered what life would've been like with Barry Lethbridge. So –' she shrugged. 'That's it, really.'

'And she told you –'

'In the kitchen after you'd gone to bed, the day after Dad died. She sat down with me because I was her big girl and she *carthed*, Bri.'

'She what?'

'Carthed. Catharthed. Oh, Jesus, you know what I mean – she let it all out in one go – and then afterwards she did her usual dramatic bit and she said tomorrow's another day and we'll draw a veil over the past and don't look back, look ahead, and if we can't say something nice about your father we won't say anything at all, especially not to Brianetta because she's Daddy's girl.'

Whigfield faded from the speakers and Netta heard the scrape of the guitar and the ordinary, melancholy voice that began a song she had heard a thousand times before, spilling from Kelly's room over the past year.

'Mum said all that?'

'Yeah. Why?'

'Oh . . . never mind.' Netta drained one of her glasses. 'I heard about Carina Eddery anyway. Kids at school gossip as much as adults. And I knew that it wasn't *just* Carina.'

'Well I never said anything.'

'I know. You never did. Not once.'

'Because I knew how much you loved him.'

'Didn't you, then?'

Natalia shrugged. 'He wasn't around that much, was he? Out at work, out with his mates, out with his ladies. And when he was around he never had time for anyone except you, because you were the brainy one, you looked like him, you were the chip.'

'The what?'

'The chip on the block,' said Natalia impatiently. 'He didn't exactly show Glenn off to his mates, did he? It was when Glenn started being . . . you know, really *Glennish* that Dad started drifting away. And he never asked me for my opinions, he never cared what *I* thought about anything.'

'I'm sure that's not –'

'Of course it is, Bri. Listen, I got reduced to two letters at the end of a bloody house name. It shouldn't have been Briglennia – *I* was the oldest, my name should have come first.' Her voice cracked at the ancient unfairness of it all. 'It should've been Natbriglenn, shouldn't it?'

'I never thought about it,' said Netta.

'Well I did. Or Natabrigle – that would've looked better. I used to write it in the back of my schoolbooks.' She fussed with a tendril of hair. 'I used to think about it a lot; I used to wonder what I'd done to come third. I suppose that's an advantage of having one kid. You don't have favourites.'

'I haven't got a favourite.'

'Oh gimme a break, Bri, do you know how many times Kelly gets a mention compared to the others?' Her eyes drifted from Netta's and fixed on a point over her sister's shoulder. 'Jesus God,' she said incredulously, after a moment. 'Look at that.'

The stately pace of 'Wonderwall' had cleared most of the under-twelves from the dance floor and instead three adult couples were revolving in the coloured light. Two were sets of parents locked in a standard smooch, but the third was gliding through a polished sequence of steps that formed a bizarre counterpoint to the music.

'They're doing the foxtrot,' said Natalia. Bel's expression was serene, her limp barely noticeable. Ted held her as if she were made of eggshell and his own face, as the light caught it, was beatific.

'I always think it's a pity Ted's gay,' said Natalia. 'I mean, he *is*, isn't he?'

'I don't know,' said Netta, her mind sliding elsewhere. 'I've always assumed so.'

She was thinking about how much she had longed for someone to mention her father at home, to say something kind, something nice, something complimentary about him. It hadn't occurred to her that – in a clumsy, well-meaning way – she was being protected.

'Mind you,' continued Natalia, judicially, 'Ted wouldn't ever have been Mum's type. She liked them handsome, didn't she? And a bit devilish.'

'Rogues and charmers.'

'Yup.'

'I wonder what ever happened to Barry Lethbridge.'

'Divorced, Mum said. Oh – and done for tax evasion.'

'And how about that!' said the Sugar Plum Fairy's father as the song dropped away. 'How about that! Round of applause called for there, I think.' Bel sank into a curtsey and Ted stood back modestly until she waved him forward, and then the first hideously jaunty notes of 'The Birdie Song' tweaked the air and the dance floor was invaded by eight-year-olds.

'You know this one, Bri?' asked Natalia.

'Yup,' said Netta, drily. 'I could run master classes.'

'Well, I might see if Lester wants a little go at it – it's a social skill, isn't it, dancing? Wanna join us?' she added, casually.

'OK,' said Netta. 'OK. Why not?'

19

The first sign of trouble as Paul entered the hospital grounds was the sight of Mr Gorman locking his Saab and then running – actually *running* – towards the accident and emergency department. He was – pleasingly – an unathletic mover, employing a rather girlie use of the elbows and a knock-kneed leg action that removed all drama from what was presumably a mercy sprint. He disappeared behind the scaffolding that obscured the entrance and Paul, who had stopped to watch, resumed his ruminative amble. He had rather hoped to be drunk by this stage in the evening but by the time he and Beardy had reached the pub, numb from a thousand hours of dancing moppets, there'd only been time for one round, and Paul had unwisely chosen to sample a local real ale. 'Abbot's Barrel' had tasted like sweetened Marmite diluted with bath water and three shuddering mouthfuls had left his mind clear and wincingly tender, shrinking – like a worm from a pin – from any coherent thoughts of Marianne. Instead, he found himself walking in rhythm to the mental refrain of 'Run, Rabbit, Run' and speculating on what might possibly be in the fridge when he got back, hoping that Netta had gone mad and whipped up a huge chicken pie with puff pastry, and a treacle pudding, and a walnut cake with butter icing and a – he glanced up sharply at the sound of more running footsteps; it was Crispin and Wai pounding along a distant semi-lit footpath, their white coats a dull khaki in the sodium glare, Wai clutching her stethoscope to her chest, Crispin holding his in one hand so that the tubing lashed back and forth with every stride. They vanished behind the concrete bulk of the X-ray department and the noise receded; the night was quiet again for a moment, and then from behind Paul came a fourth set of footsteps and he swung round to see Armand's long shadow loping towards him, closely followed by Armand.

'Hi there Paul,' he said, decelerating.

'What's going on?'

'Well there's been a . . .' Armand eased to a halt and caught his breath, 'the phrase actually used was "three-line whip", which I feel may have some kind of satirical sadomasochistic double meaning that I failed to understand but which nevertheless –'

'It's a term they use in parliament,' said Paul, 'for something you're not allowed to miss.'

'Oh really? Oh, that's not so bad then. OK. Well, there's been a train derailment in a place called Clay Hill and we're awaiting an unknown number of casualties, and we're all supposed to assemble in A and E, even people like myself who are on call and receiving admissions and who have yet to have a proper, sit-down evening meal.'

'Oh . . .' Paul felt a little stab of disappointment that he was not to be part of some great developing drama.

'I believe,' added Armand, 'that the . . . the *whip* also applies to relevant off-duty staff, if available.'

'Oh, does it?' Paul brightened. 'Do you think it matters that I've had about half a pint?'

'Half a pint of what?'

'Of beer.'

'Oh, I see. Beer.' Armand looked at him speculatively. 'Well, I think that taking into account your body–mass ratio, I'd estimate that ingesting less than two units of alcohol would be unlikely to affect your judgement adversely.'

'So you're saying you think it's safe to unleash Fatboy on patients?'

'Yes, I do.'

'Thank you.'

They assumed a fast walk, breaking into a jog as they neared the unit.

'Can I ask,' said Armand, 'if you were able to speak to Crispin about his attitude towards me?'

'No, not yet.' He had found no way of approaching the subject and had, in cowardly consequence, started to avoid Crispin altogether. 'I'm sorry.'

'That's OK, Paul.'

'I will though.'

'I know you will,' There was an alarming degree of faith in Armand's voice. 'I see you very much as a man of your word.'

For once there were more staff than patients in Casualty, and the air of expectation was almost palpable. Side rooms were being cleared and labelled, extra trolleys manoeuvred into the treatment area, and sterile packs piled in fives and tens on every clear surface. The night sister was dictating notes to a cluster of nurses including an uncharacteristically serious-looking Lexie, while in the waiting room Mr Gorman was advancing along the rows of seats, systematically questioning and then throwing out anyone not actually possessed of a fractured limb or personal pool of blood. Paul and Armand were handed sheets of paper headed 'Triage procedure – a summary' and hustled into a corner of the outpatients department, where half the junior medical staff were sitting in a row, all reading copies of their own.

'Hiya,' said Carrie, yawning. 'This is exciting, isn't it?'

'You've got a piece of hair sticking straight up from the top of your head,' said Paul, quietly.

'Oh . . .' She smoothed it down with a licked finger. 'Thanks. When they phoned to tell me I was asleep in front of the TV with a plate of cold lasagne on my chest and dribble all over the sofa cushion. Isn't that revolting? You look nice, been on a date?'

'No, it wasn't a date, it was just a sort of . . .' He tried, and failed, to think of a euphemism.

'What?' asked Carrie, bluntly.

'A sort of . . . of . . .' He decided to abandon the use of imagery, possibly for ever. 'A bit of a disaster,' he said. 'I realized I was bored listening to her and I don't think she's interested in me anyway.'

'Wow,' said Carrie. 'Double whammy.'

'Yeah. She's really nice though,' he added, in fairness, 'really nice and *really* pretty.'

Carrie nodded expressionlessly and looked down at her piece of paper. 'Have you read this?' she asked.

'No, I only just got it.'

'It's quite straightforward, it's all logical enough. I'm a bit nervous though – I mean, I've seen a lot of blood in my time, obviously. And a lot of dead people, of course, that being my speciality, but I haven't seen anyone who's . . .'

'Mangled?'

'That's right.' She looked at him soberly. 'Have you?'

'Only surgically.'

'I'm worried I might faint, or throw up.'

'No, that's *my* speciality,' said Paul.

'Excuse me,' Armand, in the row behind, leaned between them, 'but do either of you have change for a twenty-pound note?'

'Not me,' said Paul; Carrie shook her head.

'Or could I possibly ask for a short-term loan – say, fifty pence or even a pound? You see, if I'm not able to have a proper, sit-down meal then I really need to buy some kind of carbohydrate snack to keep my sugar levels from – '

'*If* I could have the attention of everybody in the room,' said Mr Gorman. The fizz of conversation died away. 'Thank you. We still have no clear idea of the number and severity of the injuries sustained in this accident. It occurred in an unlit cutting in a suburban area and access to the track by emergency services is apparently proving difficult. It was an express train with twelve carriages so we may be looking at a very large number of casualties indeed and we have agreed to split admissions with King's Heath General Hospital; they have a specialist burns unit, which we lack, whereas we have a greater number of orthopaedic beds, making allocation of injuries reasonably straightforward. We will be dividing all staff – nursing, medical, ancillary – into three teams; the red and blue teams will be treating Category 1 casualties, which I am defining as those with airway problems, uncontrolled haemorrhage, loss of consciousness or severe multiple trauma. The green team will be based in the outpatient area and will deal with Category 2 casualties – the definition is on your sheets – and, once these are stabilized to the satisfaction of your team leaders, Category 3 and 4 casualties. Initial triage will be carried out by Mrs Phillips, Mr Ray, Mr Levin and myself, and no, I repeat *no* changes of category are to be decided without referral to one of us. Is that clear?'

There was a hurried assent.

'Wards 2, 12 and 9 have orthopaedic beds available; Sister Claremont is in charge of all bed allocation. We are closing to all GP admissions; refer any calls to Shotton Wood Hospital.' He took a breath. 'The abrupt deceleration inherent in high-speed rail accidents can cause a wide range of injury but we must be prepared for severe spinal and head trauma, limb avulsion, massive blood loss, spleen and liver lacerations, and of course multiple and comminuted fractures. I am confident that you will all work calmly and cooperatively and prove a credit to your training and to this hospital. All relevant questions are to be referred to your team leaders.' Abruptly, he turned and left and there was a chilly pause, followed by an explosion of nervous chatter.

'I've never seen an avulsed limb,' said Carrie, 'except in films. I hope I'm not completely useless. I hope I can do some good.' She had gone rather pale, and Paul wondered whether he had too; certainly he could see duplicates of Carrie's wide pupils and chewed lower lip in the faces around him.

'Could I trouble you for some change?' said Armand, inserting his head between Paul and Carrie.

'Yeah, yeah, of course.' Paul reached for his wallet.

'Attention peoples!' shouted Crispin, hitting a metal treatment tray with a tendon hammer. 'Can I have your attention, please? Attention please!' He carried on with his makeshift gong for a while longer, clearly charmed by the noise.

'You've got our attention, you prat,' called Carrie.

'Okey dokey.' He rested the hammer. 'Thank you, Dr Death. Right – teams. I'll read out the names and pass round the stickers, and each of you take the correct coloured sticker and slap it on your coat. OK?' There was no response. 'OK, boys and girls?' he asked again, with another swing of the hammer.

'Shut up, Crispin,' said Eric, wearily, 'we're not idiots.' He was backed by a groundswell murmur over which Crispin noisily unfolded a sheet of paper.

'So, *Reds*. Team leaders: Mr Pencavel and Dr Matthews. Team: Ann-Marie, Ozzy, Deenan, Gerard, Eric, Carrie. *Blues*. Team leaders: Dr Jepson and Dr Perros. Team: Me, Pud, Wai, Richard, Almond, Mina. *Greens*. Team leaders: Dr Garrett and Miss Hirza. Team: Everyone else I haven't mentioned. OK?

Red and blue teams to assemble ASAP in the treatment area and green team to stay here in Outpatients. Any questions?'

Armand raised a hand.

'Fire away,' said Crispin. 'No, hang on, is it anything to do with the contrast between Canadian and British clerking procedures, because if it is, I'll get a chair.'

'No it isn't.'

'Excellent. Off you go then.'

There was a short silence. 'No,' said Armand, lowering his arm again. 'It doesn't matter.'

'Fantastic,' said Crispin. 'OK, so if there are no more top-notch clinical queries, then let's scramble!'

In the chaos of scraping chair legs and panicked small talk Armand continued to sit, staring into space.

'Here,' said Carrie, peeling off a blue sticker and affixing it to his coat. 'Don't mind *him*. What did you want to ask, anyway?'

'Oh . . . it was nothing.' He stirred. 'Paul, if I could trouble you for that small loan.'

'Yeah, yeah, of course.' Paul raked through the change section of his wallet. 'Here, have it all. It's mainly pennies, I'm afraid.'

'Thank you. Thank you very much.' Armand raised his eyes and Paul caught the defeated expression.

'I'll have a word with Crispin,' he said. 'Honestly. First thing tomorrow.'

There was no acknowledgement of the offer; instead Armand got up and went over to the vending machine, and Paul lingered guiltily for a moment or two before joining the exodus to the treatment room.

The swing doors had been wedged open and, like a row of oddly shaped superheroes, the four surgeons stood in readiness, facing the white light of the empty ambulance bay. Mr Gorman checked his watch, muttered something to Mrs Phillips and then resumed his watchful stance, hands clasped in the small of his back. Some distance behind him, at the rear of the blue team, Paul surreptitiously took his own pulse and found it to be hammering along at well over a hundred. He took a couple of deep breaths and comforted himself by glancing around at his companions; they formed a living tableau of tension, a foot-shifting, finger-clicking, throat-clearing testament to inexperience.

'How are you feeling?' he whispered to Wai.

'Crapping myself.' For once the answer wasn't followed by a giggle.

'All right, gang.' Ian Jepson, the senior registrar, with a face like a bun and gym-honed shoulders, swung round to the team. 'Let's have a quick Q and A about procedure, before we all start keeling over with stress. Anyone seen Dr Roux, incidentally?'

'He'll be through in a moment,' said Paul. 'I think.'

'OK. Dr Gooding, tell me the procedure in cases of suspected femoral fracture.'

'Establish a line and cross-match,' said Paul, 'before anything else.'

'Why?'

'Because it's possible to bleed out into the thigh muscle. Then stabilize and X-ray and . . . hand over to the orthopods.'

Ian nodded, and Paul felt a little steadier than before, as if the facts were ballast.

'Dr Leong,' said Ian, 'uncontrolled haemorrhaging – I'd like your IV fluids of choice in order, most to least desirable.'

'Cross-matched blood, O negative blood, colloid, normal saline, Hartman's – Oh shit.' Blue light flickered across Wai's face. 'They're here,' she said.

'Everyone ready?' shouted Mr Gorman and Paul could hear the deepening, hollow note of the engine as the first ambulance drove up between the high walls of the access road and emerged again just yards from the entrance, and in the spinning wash of blue he saw the driver jump out and walk with firm, unpanicked tread to the back door and open it and swing out the ramp and stand aside as the other ambulance man pushed a wheelchair down the incline and between the honour guard of consultants and into the main hall and towards the massed ranks of the assembled teams of the highly trained medical and nursing staff of Shadley Oak District General Hospital, at which point the wheelchair came to a halt and everyone stared at its occupant. It was a middle-aged man, fully dressed apart from one sockless foot, its big toe snugly wrapped in cotton wool. He looked back warily. 'I think,' he said, 'that I *might* have broken it.'

'If I had known,' said Mr Gorman, sitting on the desk in the casualty office with the phone to his ear, 'that the communications department of the West Midlands emergency services had just been replaced by a runner with a cleft stick, then I might have scaled down the – let me finish, please – no, I think you'll find that I can talk both louder and faster than you without any need to take it to formal arbitration, so if you'll just let me continue . . . thank you. No doubt it's petty of me but I feel the need to establish why I closed an entire hospital to admissions and mobilized thirty-eight members of staff in order to treat a man with a bruised terminal phalanx. No, I'm sure you don't, which is one of the many reasons why I'm a surgeon and you're a –' He caught sight of Paul and Carrie watching him through the open door, and swung out a casual foot and kicked it shut.

'Well,' said Carrie. 'I'm off to bed. Coming?' Her blush was instant and crimson. 'You know what I mean,' she added. 'Are you going to the lifts?'

'Yeah, I suppose so.' The sudden slump of adrenalin had left him feeling flat and tetchy. They passed the side room where Mr Henderson was recounting, yet again, the way that the entire train had seemed to leap a yard into the air before coming down on its wheels and bumping along the bottom of the cut for almost half a mile. He had been standing at the buffet at the time, and had dropped a newly purchased can of lager on his foot. 'And I never even got to drink it!' he added, a line that was becoming more jocularly rueful with every repetition.

'*There's* Armand,' said Paul. 'Hey, where have you been?'

'Like you care,' said Armand, swinging round the corner from Outpatients, a carton of Ribena in his hand. 'You lent me money that won't even go into the bloody machine because it won't take pennies, you . . . you . . . *fool*, so I had to give it a damn good kicking and this is all I got, and it doesn't even have a f– a f– a bloody straw!' He shouted the last remark over his shoulder and strode off towards the lifts.

'Christ,' said Paul, finally finding his voice.

'Is he . . .' Carrie peered after him, 'is he drunk?'

'He doesn't drink.'

'On drugs?'

'You're kidding, aren't you?'

'And another thing,' said Armand, turning in the doorway to the stairwell and hurling the remarks up the corridor, 'is that when I promise to bloody well do something I make sure I do it but you people, you . . . you . . . I'll tell you later!'

The door slapped shut but they could see through the porthole window Armand's long legs taking the stairs two at a time.

'He has to be drunk,' said Carrie, pressing the button for the lift. 'He's never like that normally.'

'No. No, it's me,' said Paul, badly shaken. 'It's me. I said I'd have a word with Crispin about what a git he is to Armand and I haven't done it, and even Armand's got an end to his tether. Apparently.' He glanced up at the illuminated 'G' above the lift and pressed the button again. 'This bloody lift,' he added. 'It's here but it won't open.'

'So . . .' Carrie gave him a tentative look, '*are* you going to say something to Crispin?'

'Oh yes. Yes, definitely. The time has come. I'll do it the next time I see him.' He pressed the button for the third time and with their usual reluctant scrape and clank the doors opened.

'Evening all,' said Crispin, beaming from the interior. 'Me and Twanks were hoping for a bit of company.'

'Hello you two,' said Netta, 'come on in.'

During the thirty seconds or so that they been alone together in the lift, waiting for it to commit to an upward journey, Crispin had enquired with his usual amiable gall about Netta's temper, her wardrobe and her insatiable desire for younger men and she, buffered by two glasses of Asti and a continuing mood of mild melancholy, had responded with a pleasant smile. Interestingly, this had seemed to rile him far more than if she had replied in kind, and she filed away the knowledge for future reference; it was a polite variation on the adolescent speciality of dumb insolence ('Shona, your father and I just need a yes or a no – you can even write it down if it's easier.') and clearly very nearly as annoying.

The sense of detachment stayed as Carrie and Paul joined them and the lift resumed its pre-move sulk, and Netta stood against the wall and watched rather than listened as they discussed a non-existent train disaster and its aftermath. Paul, she noticed, seemed oddly nervous, skittering between topics, his comments no more than perfunctory, while Carrie kept glancing between him and Crispin and making little involuntary urging movements with her head, as if Paul were a horse and Crispin Becher's Brook.

'And we're off,' said Crispin as the ascent began at last. 'Oh, spoke too soon.' With a ping they halted at the first floor. 'Hey, did anyone ever find out where Almond got to?'

'Um . . .' Paul's eyes flicked towards Carrie and then back again. 'Look, Crispin,' he began, with obvious determination, 'I want to –'

'Got to stop you there, Pud,' said Crispin, holding up a finger, 'because it sounded to me as if you were about to say something incredibly serious. Hang on a minute –' He tipped his head to one side and vigorously smacked the uppermost ear. 'OK,' he said, straightening up, 'try again.'

'What I wanted to say –' said Paul.

'I like it when Pud thinks he's looking stern,' said Crispin, conversationally.

'– what I wanted to say was that I think you – actually, hang on . . . hang on, the first thing I wanted to say was that I wanted to ask you to stop calling me Pud, and the second thing –'

'But I can't call you Pudding, it's so formal.'

'Paul,' said Paul, with the look of a man wading chest deep through a swamp, 'my name's Paul, so you can call me Paul. And the second thing is that I think it's time you stopped taking the piss out of Armand. It's not fair, he's a nice bloke underneath and he takes his job seriously and he tries very hard to fit in and it's not his fault that he comes across as a bit of a wee–' He stopped, open-mouthed, as a hand holding an unopened carton of Ribena was thrust through the earliest hint of a gap in the doors; it was followed by an arm, and then a shoulder and finally by the whole of Armand, who contemptuously shoved the rattling leaves apart and stalked to the back of the lift, where he leaned against the wall in a pose reminiscent of James Dean at his sneeriest. 'Floor five,' he said, and it was an order.

There was a pause, an exchange of incredulous looks.

'*Now!*' added Armand in a half scream and, mesmerized, Carrie jabbed the button.

'God almighty,' said Crispin, speaking for all of them. 'Been taking steroids, have we?'

'And you had better shut up,' said Armand, wagging a shaky finger at Crispin. 'Come to England, Armand, and learn about your UK roots and get some bloody . . . some bloody clinical experience, Armand, but they don't mention – they . . . they *fail* to mention in the prospectus for UK–Canadian Medical Link-up that everyone here has the manners of . . . of . . . of . . . I can't remember the word in English, and that people laugh at you and urinate in the sink and lend pennies that won't even go into the machine. No!' he added, turning suddenly to Paul. 'That was you, not him. Most of it's him but this is you, but most of it's *him!*' He whirled round again but overdid the spin and ended up facing Netta.

'Not me,' she said quietly. He seemed momentarily confused; his forehead was slick with sweat and he looked, she thought, close to violence or collapse, or both.

'Not me,' she repeated.

'No, not you,' he assented, grudgingly.

'He's drunk,' said Crispin. 'You drunk, Armand?'

'He doesn't drink,' said Paul.

'He's ill,' said Netta. Four doctors looked at her. 'Isn't he? Aren't you?'

Armand looked outraged. 'No I am *not*.'

314

'Oh my God.' Paul could have slapped himself. 'Why didn't I think – he's having a hypo, isn't he?'

'I didn't even know he was a diabetic,' said Carrie.

'I am not having a hypoglycaemic attack and that is simply libellous and I will sue the first person in this lift who . . . who . . .' Armand dived towards the lift button and pressed it again. 'What is going on? Why isn't this elevator moving? Why isn't this *elevator moving?*'

'Any second now,' said Netta, soothingly, and Armand tilted his body, flexed a leg and karate-kicked the centre of the door with surprising force; the lift, which had just begun to rise, stopped again with a nasty shudder. Somewhere within its mechanism a bell began to ring.

'Well that's fucking marvellous,' said Crispin. 'We're stuck now.'

'Armand . . .' Carrie placed a hand on his arm. 'Why don't you have some of your Ribena?'

'Because *there's no bloody straw, stupid!*' His voice was enormous in the confined space and Carrie recoiled against the wall. Paul stepped quickly in front of her.

'Come on, mate,' he said, with attempted cheeriness. 'Give me the carton and I'll open it for you.'

'You stay away from me.'

'I've got it,' said Crispin, grabbing it from Armand's hand. With a straight right, Armand punched him hard on the nose. Crispin slid slowly down the wall to the floor, his hands clamped to his face and blood running down the insides of both wrists. 'That's mine,' said Armand, picking up the carton from where it had fallen. He looked challengingly at the other three. 'Mine.'

For a moment no one spoke; the only sounds were the shrill of the alarm and the bubble and groan of Crispin's breathing. Armand wiped his forehead on his sleeve and yawned hugely.

'So Paul,' said Netta, barely moving her lips, 'he just has to have something sugary, does he?'

'Yes. I mean, he'll pass out eventually but he might have decked us all by then. Have you got anything?'

She shook her head.

'Nor me,' whispered Carrie, peering out from behind Paul. 'By doze is broken.'

'Pinch the soft bit,' said Netta.

'I *dow* how to fucking dreat myself, you dwat.'

'I was sick in this lift once,' said Paul, loudly and casually, as if making small talk at a noisy party, 'on the floor. I don't think it's ever really been cleaned properly since. I wouldn't be surprised if it's still caked in bacteria and er . . . prions and things. You're a dietitian, Netta, what do you think about . . . you know, picking stuff up off the floor?' His eyes did some desperate signalling and she remembered, suddenly, the painful cleanliness of Armand's bedroom when she had moved into the flat and the long line of disinfectants by the bath.

'Filthy,' she said, with conviction. 'Those waxed paper cartons have been proven over and over again to be totally ineffective germ barriers. That Ribena's probably seething with . . . with . . .'

'Campylobacter,' piped up Carrie. 'Pseudomonas. Staphylococcus.'

'Spirochaetes,' added Paul.

Armand's lips silently repeated the final word. He looked at the Ribena and then suddenly shook his hand, as if a wasp had landed on the knuckles. 'Why isn't this f– this f– this elevator moving?' he said, turning to the doors again and giving them a series of half-hearted kicks. Paul grabbed the carton from the floor and started to open it.

'By doze really hurts,' said a croaky little voice from the

corner and Netta looked down; Crispin was all white and red, a stripe of gore down his coat as far as the waist.

'It won't be long now,' said Netta. 'Soon be out.'

'What are you going to do?' hissed Carrie at Paul.

'I'm going to –' He glanced at Armand and got a baleful look in reply; the steady kicking continued. 'I'm going to . . . to . . .' He needed some kind of secret code, he thought. 'I'm going to *prendre son bras et quand si vous . . . vous . . .*'

'He's *French*,' said Carrie urgently.

'Oh yes. I'm going to . . .' He started to mime something and then, abandoning the idea, thrust the carton into Carrie's hand and grabbed Armand round the chest from behind, pinning his arms to his sides. 'Pour it in, pour it straight in!' he shouted and Carrie grabbed one of Armand's ears to steady herself and tipped some Ribena into his mouth. It was spat straight back out again and Armand dropped his chin, let out an incoherent roar and dragged Paul across the lift. Together they ricocheted off the wall and stumbled over one of Crispin's legs.

'Bind by doze,' said Crispin, desperately, trying to dig himself into the corner, 'please, *please*, eberybody, just bind by doze.'

'Try again,' shouted Paul, swinging Armand around to face Carrie, and another ribbon of blackcurrant arced across the lift, followed by another staggering charge.

'Oh please,' said Crispin, hardly audible. Netta crouched in the corner in front of him and braced her arms across the angle. 'It's OK,' she said, 'I'll stay here. They can't knock into you now.' Behind her the footsteps and yells and thuds and buffets continued, and there were squeaks from Carrie and a lot of coughing from Armand, and the bell kept ringing all the while and from outside the lift came another voice, shouting something unintelligible, and then there was a clang and a slither and then, quite rapidly, all noises stopped and there was only the sound of heavy breathing.

Netta turned around cautiously and saw a new and sticky world, inhabited by purple people.

'You OK, Armand?' said Paul, between gasps. 'You OK, mate? You had a hypo.'

'I had a hypo?' asked Armand

'Yes, you did.'

There was a pause. 'I had a hypo?' asked Armand.

'Here, finish this off,' said Carrie, handing over the carton; behind her there was a metallic screech and then the doors began to move apart in a series of jerks to reveal the top halves of two maintenance men. They gazed, open-mouthed, at the lurid interior.

'Fantastic,' said Paul, briskly, as if everything had gone exactly to plan. 'Good timing. Let's get out of here.'

Netta felt a hand grope towards one of her own, and she grasped it and hauled Crispin to his feet. 'Upsadaisy,' she said as he staggered a bit, 'keep holding my hand.' He didn't let go even when being helped from the lift, and when Netta had climbed down beside him he looked at her dumbly. 'Do you want me to come with you to Casualty?' she asked gently, and he nodded, and they walked away together down the corridor.

'Did I get abusive at all?' asked Armand, eating toast in the kitchen of the flat. 'That has happened very occasionally in the past.'

'Nothing to speak of,' said Paul.

'OK, well, that's a relief. Also, I may accidentally have hit someone, judging by the amount of tenderness over this whole metacarpal area.' He massaged the back of his right hand. 'Did that happen? I mean, if so, obviously I can't apologize enough.'

Paul looked at Carrie and she raised her eyebrows. One of

them was fair, he noticed, and the other was purple; the effect was both arresting and weirdly attractive.

'Er . . .' he began.

'You hit Crispin,' said Carrie.

'I hit Cr–' Armand took another bite of toast, chewed and swallowed. 'I hit *Crispin?*' he said.

Carrie nodded. 'Quite hard, actually. He'll need to get his nose X-rayed.'

'I hit Crispin,' repeated Armand softly, in wonderment. 'You know, usually I'm grateful for post-event amnesia but just this once . . .'

'Please,' said Carrie, 'let me describe it to you in endless detail. It would be my pleasure.'

20

Netta had made the custard with four egg yolks and a pint of double cream, so that it flowed like ivory silk, and then she had sprinkled a half-inch layer of demerara over the top and placed the dish under the hottest setting on the grill until the sugar had shivered and run. It had set, afterwards, into a sheet of toffee glass that would take a rap with a rolling pin to break. It was a sophisticated gift, she felt, a truly grown-up pudding that would remain so even after she had written 'GOODBYE PAUL' across the top with tiny blobs of clotted cream. She had got as far as the 'A' when the doorbell rang.

'There is a *very* peculiar smell in that lift,' said her mother, speaking as soon as the door was open, 'it's one that I can't quite put my finger on. Natalia, what would you say that smell was?'

'Blackcurrant air-freshener, I thought. You all ready, Bri? Your train's going in half an hour.'

'Yup, just give me two minutes. Where's Glenn?'

'Talking to one of the workmen outside. What's all that building stuff that's going on down there?'

'No idea.'

'Can I use your loo?'

'Second door off the hall.'

'It wasn't *just* air-freshener,' continued their mother. 'I'm sure I detected an undertone, a tiny *wisp* of something else. Lester?'

'Yes, Mamushka?'

'What did you think that lift smelled of?'

'Puke, Mamushka. Who's Pa?'

'Sorry?' said Netta, to whom the question had been addressed.

'On top of that dessert thing. Who's Pa? It says "Goodbye Pa".'

'When I put on a few more blobs of cream it'll say "Goodbye Paul", and he's the doctor who lives here. Do you want a lick?' She held out a spoon.

'No thank you,' said her nephew, visibly shocked. 'Cream gives you heart attacks. Can I have a go at those binoculars?'

'Of course you can. The view's even better in the living room – it's not blocked by the chimney.'

'Ah yes, now, the view,' said her mother, following Lester. 'That's what I've come to see.'

Netta finished the last two letters, and placed the Pyrex dish at the centre of the kitchen table. For a moment she wondered if she should leave a note as well but the usual farewell sentiments, the 'thanks for everything/give me a ring/see you again/drop by any time you're in Glasgow'-type epithets, seemed emptily verbose. She'd remember Paul every time she looked at the one remaining chickenpox scar on her forehead and he'd remember her whenever he ate crème brûlée, but she knew that they wouldn't stay in touch; the world simply didn't work like that. Although Paul would almost certainly receive a Christmas card and a selection of recycling literature from Glenn every year for the whole of the rest of his life.

'What are you grinning at?' asked Natalia, re-entering.

'Nothing much. I'm all set.' She picked up her luggage of three Tesco carriers and a handbag. 'You ready, Mum? Lester?'

'I had no idea that one could see quite so much detail from up here,' said her mother as they walked towards the lifts. 'I was looking at Market Square through the binoculars and I'm almost certain I saw Lucy Procter not only playing truant but *smoking*. I'll have to have words on Tuesday.'

'So, Bri, you totally desperate to get home?' asked Natalia.

'Yes,' said Netta; there was just a trace of reservation in her answer and her sister looked at her curiously.

'Is that a yes *but* I hear?'

'It is, actually. I mean, obviously, I can't wait to see Mick, but I won't have any of the girls at home. For the first time ever. I was just thinking about it today in the flat, making that pudding. Most people start as a couple and end up as a family, don't they? I did it the other way round, I'll have to learn what it's like when it's just the two of us. I hope we don't kill each other.'

'I think you'll find,' said her mother, 'that over the next year or two your mood swings will start to settle down and you'll become a lot less irritable.'

'Mum, I am *not* going through the menopause.'

'Christ, Mum,' said Natalia, outraged, 'I'm a year older than Bri and I'm nowhere near that stage – we're *young women*, we've got half our lives ahead of us, we could climb Mount Everest, we could –'

'What's a menopause?' asked Lester.

'Something that I'm clearly not allowed to mention,' said Bel, pressing the button to summon the lift. 'It was simply a tiny little passing comment,' she added. 'You don't object when I make tiny little passing comments, do you, Lester?'

'No, Mamushka.'

'So you won't mind if I just correct your pronunciation very slightly. It's Mamooooshka.'

He repeated it obediently, and Natalia caught Netta's eye and made a throttling gesture.

There was the usual ping and the lift doors opened to reveal first a neat little blonde girl in a short white coat and then Crispin in full braggadocio flow: '. . . and what they don't show you on the TV, of course, is that you have to actually lean your full body weight on the trocar to really *shove* it through the tissues and it makes an incredible sort of crunching sou–' At this point he noticed Netta, and it was as if a pin had been stuck into a puffer fish.

'Hello Crispin,' said Netta, kindly, 'how's the nose?'

'Bit better, thanks,' he said, almost inaudibly.

'Black eyes nearly gone, I see.'

'Yes.'

'And have the nosebleeds stopped?'

'Yes thank you, Netta.'

'Good. Well I'm off home now, so I'll say bye-bye.'

'Bye-bye.' Brief anguish flared in his eyes as the words emerged and he hurried off down the corridor, the girl giving him puzzled looks.

'What was *that*?' asked Natalia as they entered the lift.

'I'll tell you,' said Netta. 'But basically, it's about the unexpected satisfactions of being nice . . .'

Glenn was waiting for them outside the doors of the Eddery Building, a yellow flyer in his hand. 'There are four fundamental categories of listing in the West Midlands,' he said. 'There's Grade A, which are buildings of national importance including both outstanding grand buildings and the fine, little-altered examples of some important style or date, then there's Grade B+, which –'

'I'm so sorry to interrupt you,' said Bel, 'but isn't that your young doctor friend over there.' She raised a hand. 'Hello, dear. Hello! Or, rather, goodbye!'

Paul, a good fifty yards away, smiled and waved.

'– are buildings that might have merited A status but for relatively minor detracting features,' continued Glenn, reading from the flyer, 'such as impurities of design, or lower-quality additions or alterations. Also buildings that . . .'

Netta watched as Paul turned and continued along the path towards X-ray, Carrie by his side. He was looking, as usual, large and rather rumpled, but there was a definite sense of purpose about him; still a domesticated bear, she thought, but one who was at last beginning to remember where he'd left his door key.

'. . . and in view of its extraordinary adherence to the decade's vernacular we are issuing a tentative preliminary B2 categorization, which covers buildings of local importance or good examples of some period or style.' Glenn finished reading and looked up expectantly.

'You mean,' said Natalia, who had been listening rather more attentively than her sister, 'that they're wanting to preserve this heap of crap?' She pointed a disgusted finger at the scaffolding that surrounded the Eddery Building.

'It's just a tentative preliminary B2 listing,' said Glenn again. 'My friend's the structural engineer and he says it's dependent on the degree to which preservation is possible under current budgetary restraints.'

'They're listing it?' said Netta.

'As a tentative preliminary B2 listing.'

'A listed building,' said her mother, wonderingly. She looked up at the concrete and glass. 'My goodness. My *goodness*. Well, of course, your father was always very go-ahead.'

Netta stared at her, and then her sister jingled the keys of the hire car. 'It's time, guys,' she said, 'chop chop.' Bel took Natalia's arm.

'Auntie Brianetta,' said Lester as they followed on behind, 'what does "go-ahead" mean?'

'Er . . .' Netta gathered her thoughts. 'It's quite an old-fashioned term. It means being . . . full of ideas, and energetic and dashing.' She looked down at him and gave the back of his head a little rub. 'It's a compliment,' she said.

February

21

'Got a surprise for you in the front room,' said Mick, coming down the stairs as she hung up her coat. He was dressed for work but his face was still creased with sleep, and the kiss he gave her was a blast of pure toothpaste.

'What is it?'

He folded his arms and grinned. 'Go and see. It turned up just after you'd left this morning. You won't believe it.'

She actually shrieked when she saw the suitcase. It was as if the Tardis had materialized in the middle of the carpet.

'Happy?' said Mick.

'But I've gone and bought a whole new . . .' She peeled off the cellophane-wrapped envelope that was messily taped to the side. 'I mean, where has it *been*?'

The letter, headed with the logo of the West Midlands Police Force, was so encrusted with jargon that it was hard to discern the meaning behind the words. She skimmed it again – '. . . delighted to tell you . . . after intensive detection work . . . much improved crime rate . . . following a review of the automated filing system . . .' – and gave a little groan of comprehension.

'What?' asked Mick.

'OK,' she said. 'OK. Get this. They found it shoved under a car, just along from the station, about two hours after I reported it; however, as the label gave my surname as Lee, and the crime report was filed under "E" for Etterley, the connection was only made when they – stop laughing, Mick – now come on, this is serious, now come *on* . . .' She skimmed the envelope at him, and a square of shiny paper shot from the inside and fluttered to the floor. It had been snipped from a cheaply printed magazine and was a list of the prizewinners in a North-west Midlands local league bodybuilders' competition. The name of R. Whittaker (third reserve, 'Best Newcomer Category') had been heavily underlined.

There was nothing missing from the suitcase; all was exactly as she had packed it. The only jolt was the starkness of the contents – the dark suits, the sober shirts, the unexceptionable court shoes. Netta had got used to her makeshift, motley wardrobe and the replacements she had bought had been a little more – well, 'hippyish' had been the word that Kelly had used, home from college with the usual rucksack full of washing. 'Relaxed' had been Netta's alternative suggestion. 'Suits you, anyway,' Kelly had said.

Netta closed the lid.

'I'll take it upstairs for you,' said Mick.

'Thanks.'

'Most of it's not going to fit you for much longer anyway, is it?' He helped her to her feet and gave her a gentle squeeze. 'Felt all right today?'

'Yes, great.'

'Kept your breakfast down?'

'Yup.'

'Attagirl.' He lifted the case as if it were made of spun sugar, and headed for the stairs.